HARBOR LIGHTS

Also by James Lee Burke

Flags on the Bayou

Every Cloak Rolled in Blood

Another Kind of Eden

A Private Cathedral

The New Iberia Blues

Robicheaux

The Jealous Kind

House of the Rising Sun

Wayfaring Stranger

Light of the World

Creole Belle

Feast Day of Fools

The Glass Rainbow

Rain Gods

Swan Peak

The Tin Roof Blowdown

Jesus Out to Sea

Pegasus Descending

Crusader's Cross

In the Moon of Red Ponies

Last Car to Elysian Fields

Jolie Blon's Bounce

White Doves at Morning

Bitterroot

Purple Cane Road

Heartwood

Sunset Limited

Cimarron Rose

Cadillac Jukebox

Burning Angel

Dixie City Jam

In the Electric Mist with Confederate Dead

A Stained White Radiance

A Morning for Flamingos

Black Cherry Blues

Heaven's Prisoners

The Neon Rain

The Lost Get-Back Boogie

The Convict and Other Stories

Two for Texas

Lay Down My Sword and Shield

To the Bright and Shining Sun

Half of Paradise

JAMES LEE BURKE

HARBOR LIGHTS

STORIES

Atlantic Monthly Press
New York

The following stories first appeared in the *Southern Review*: "The Assault," "The Wild Side of Life," and "Going across Jordan."
"Deportees" was previously published in the *Strand Magazine*.
"Big Midnight Special" was previously published in *Delta Blues*.
"Harbor Lights" was previously published in *A Private Cathedral: Barnes & Noble Exclusive Signed Edition*.

FIRST EDITION

Published simultaneously in Canada
Printed in the United States of America

Text design by Norman E. Tuttle at Alpha Design & Composition
This book was set in 13 pt. Spectrum MT with Albertina MT
by Alpha Design & Composition of Pittsfield, NH.

First Grove Atlantic hardcover edition: January 2024

Library of Congress Cataloging-in-Publication data is available for this title.

ISBN 978-0-8021-6096-6
eISBN 978-0-8021-6097-3

Atlantic Monthly Press
an imprint of Grove Atlantic
154 West 14th Street
New York, NY 10011

Distributed by Publishers Group West

groveatlantic.com

24 25 26 27   10 9 8 7 6 5 4 3 2 1

Contents

HARBOR LIGHTS

I t was in late fall of '42, out on the Gulf of Mexico, just off the
Louisiana coast, the water green and cold and sliding across
sandbars in the sunset, when we saw the bodies bobbing in
a wave, all in life vests and floating belly-down, their arms out-
stretched, their fingers touching, like a group of swimmers studying
something on the floor of the Gulf.

My father was standing behind the wheel in the cabin. He wore
a fedora and a raincoat, the redness of the sun reflecting off the water,
flickering on his face, as though he were standing in front of a fire.

"Come here and hold the wheel for me, Aaron," he said.

"Are those dead people out there?"

"Yes, they are." There was no change in his expression. At age
eighteen he had been at Saint-Mihiel and the Somme, and had been
buried alive during an artillery barrage. He still had dreams about
the war, but denied their seriousness, even after my mother and
I had to shake him awake and put a cold towel on his face lest he
injure himself or others.

"They look burned, Daddy," I said.

"Just keep the boat steady. Don't look at these poor fellows."

He went out of the cabin and picked up a long-handled boat hook from the deck, then worked his way up on the bow and probed the figures floating in the waves. He was bent over, his raincoat flapping in the wind, peppered with spray from the waves bursting against the hull, his face sad, as if he knew these men, although I was sure he did not. He put down the hook and gazed at the horizon through a pair of binoculars, then came back into the cabin and picked up the microphone to our radio, his eyes empty. The sun had dipped out of view, leaving behind a sky that seemed filled with soot and curds of black smoke. A solitary piece of reddish-yellow flame wobbled on the horizon, so bright and intense my eyes watered when I looked at it.

"Mayday, Mayday," my father said into the microphone. "Tanker capsized and burning south of Terrebonne Bay. Four visible casualties, all dead."

He laid the microphone on the console and turned off the radio, then looked at the radio blankly.

"You didn't tell them who we are," I said.

He took over the wheel and reversed the engine, backing away from the bodies. "You mustn't tell anyone about this, Aaron."

"Why not? It's what happened."

He cut the gas and squatted down and wrapped me inside his raincoat and held me to his chest, the boat rising on a wave, dropping suddenly into a trough. I could feel the warmth of his breath on my neck and cheek. "There's a great evil at work in the world, son," he said. "All kinds. We mustn't bring it into our lives."

My father was a natural gas engineer, but like none of his colleagues. He hated the oil and gas industry. He scrubbed his hands up to his elbows when he came home from work and never discussed what he did on the job. Nor would he socialize with his fellow employees or even use their names in conversation. He had wanted to be a journalist or a historian and instead ended up a pipeliner during the Great Depression and hostage to both the job and my mother's hospital bills. Part of that job involved dredging channels through freshwater swamp and marshland, poisoning the root system with saline, and contributing to the erosion of the Edenic wetlands in which he had grown up.

We stayed at the Hotel Frederic in New Iberia, his birthplace, whenever his company sent him to Louisiana. The Frederic was a grand building, four stories high, made entirely of brick and stone and concrete, with a roofed gallery above the entrance and a ballroom and marble pillars and potted ferns and palms in the lobby and a birdcage elevator and wood-bladed ceiling fans and a saloon with batwing doors and a shoeshine stand where a man of color popped a rag in 4/4 time. I loved staying at the Frederic and riding up and down on the elevator and waking to the Angelus. I loved eating breakfast in the dining room with my father, just as I loved everything else we did together in New Iberia.

It was raining when we returned to the hotel. The sky was black, veined with electricity, the fog as soft and white as cotton rolling off Bayou Teche. We ate silently in the dining room. There was no one else in the room except a waiter and two men in suits eating in the corner with their hats on. My father looked casually at the two men, then ordered a bowl of ice cream for me and went into the saloon. When he came back I could smell whiskey and cherries on his breath. "Ready?" he said.

"Yes, sir," I said.

"Was that ice cream okay?"

"It was fine."

"You're a good boy, Aaron. Don't ever forget that. You're the best little boy I've ever known."

We rode up in the elevator, piloted by an elderly black man in a gray uniform and a white shirt and a black tie. "Mighty cold out there tonight," he said.

"Yes, it is," my father said.

The black man stopped on the third floor, the skeleton-like structure of the elevator rattling. "Mr. Broussard?"

"Yes?"

The black man's eyes were lowered. "These are dangerous times. That's when bad people tend to come around."

My father waited for him to go on, but he didn't. "Thank you, Clarence," he said.

After we were inside our room, he went to the window and looked down on the street, then pulled the shade and turned on the desk lamp and sat down. "I owe you an explanation, Aaron."

"About the dead men?"

"A German submarine was out there. I saw its conning tower and periscope go underwater."

"Why didn't you tell the people that on the radio?"

"The government always knows this. But they don't want to share their information."

"Why not?"

"Maybe they're afraid of panic. Maybe they wish to hide their incompetence."

"But they're supposed to tell the truth," I said.

"This is a different kind of situation, Aaron."

"The families of the burned men in the water won't know where they are."

He looked at the design in the rug. The fabric was worn, the colors softened with dust. "They knew what they were doing when they signed on. The world is for the living."

"This doesn't sound like you, Daddy," I said.

"The government is wrong to suppress the truth. If they question me, I'll tell them what we saw. But I'll also have to tell the newspapers. Not to do so would be dishonorable."

"I don't understand."

"The men who start wars never go to them," he said. "They kill people with a fountain pen and call themselves leaders. Never allow yourself to become their servant, Aaron."

That night I dreamed of a giant shark that had a human face. It broke the surface of the Gulf and crunched a toy ship in its jaws, a red cloud blossoming in the waves around its head, pieces of the ship and tiny men washing through the wetlands and into the streets of New Iberia and through the lobby of the Frederic Hotel and up the elevator shaft and into our room, drowning my father and me.

The next day was Saturday. My father took me across the street to Provost's Bar and Pool Room for lunch. That might seem strange in our current culture, but in that era in South Louisiana the pagan world and Christianity had formed a truce and got along well. The ceiling was plated with stamped tin that resembled pewter, and was hung with wood-bladed fans. There were domino and Bourré and pool tables in back, and a ticker tape under a glass hood below the blackboards, where gaming results of all kinds were posted. On Saturday afternoons the floor was littered with football betting cards.

There was no profanity in Provost's, no coarseness, no ill manners. When we went to Provost's we always sat at a corner table with a checkered tablecloth, and my father always bought me a po'boy fried-oyster sandwich and a side of dirty rice and a bottle of Dr. Nut, the best cold drink ever made. But as soon as I sat down I knew that today was different, that the world had changed, that the sinking of the tanker would not leave our lives. The two men who had been eating in the Frederic's dining room with their hats on came through the front door and walked past us and stood at the end of the bar. One looked like a boxer and had a scar across his nose. The other man was very big, and wore a vest, with a pocket watch and fob. They each ordered beer from the spigot and faced the bar mirror, one foot on the brass rail, while they sipped from their mugs.

I could see my father looking at them and knew he remembered them from the hotel dining room. My father was a handsome man, with soft, dark hair he combed straight back. His eyes were small and narrow, like those of his grandfather, who had been with Stonewall Jackson through the entirety of the Shenandoah campaign, and also at Gettysburg.

"Is there something wrong about those men, Daddy?" I said.

"Pay them no attention."

"Who are they?"

"I think they're police officers."

"How do you know?"

"A gentleman does not wear his hat in a building."

A black man put my sandwich and bottle of Dr. Nut in front of me, then came back with a bottle of Jax for my father.

"They're coming this way, Daddy," I whispered, my eyes on my plate.

"Don't speak to them or look at them. This is our home. Our family has lived on the bayou since 1836."

I didn't have any idea what he was talking about. The two men were now hovering over our table. The man with the scar on his nose was standing immediately behind me, his loins eye-level with me. "How y'all doin'?" he said.

My father wiped his mouth with a cloth napkin. "How can we help you?"

"We thought you might have been fishing out on Terrebonne Bay yesterday," the man in the vest said.

"Not us."

"The trout are running," the same man said. His eyes were like brown marbles that were too big for his face, his body too big for his suit and vest and starched white shirt. "I'd like to get me a mess of them."

"My name is James Eustace Broussard," my father said. "This is my son, Aaron. We live in Houston. I'm an engineer with an oil and natural gas company there, although I was born and raised in New Iberia."

"You know how to cut to it," said the man with the scarred nose.

"Sorry?" my father said.

"You keep your words neat and tidy," the same man said. "You don't clutter up the air."

"We were having lunch, gentlemen," my father said.

"Put your lunch on hold and take a walk," said the man in the vest. "I'm Agent Hamilton. This here is my partner, Agent Flint. We'll have you back in five minutes."

"I'm afraid I will not be going anywhere with you," my father said. "I'd also like to see your identification."

"I'll show it to you outside," Mr. Hamilton said. He pulled on his collar and rotated his neck.

"I know why you're here," my father said.

"Tell you what," Mr. Hamilton said. He pulled up a chair backward and spread his thighs across it. His teeth were as big as Chiclets.

"I'm going to do you a courtesy because of your war record. Yesterday you called in a Mayday on a fire that was put out by the Coast Guard. Right? End of story. You did your good deed and we take it from here?"

"How did you come by my name?" my father said.

"The people at the boat landing," Mr. Hamilton said. "We got us a deal?"

"A deal for my silence?"

Mr. Hamilton leaned forward in his chair. "Lower your voice, please."

"I will not," my father said.

The agent named Flint, the one who looked like a boxer, was still standing behind me, his fly inches from my face. He tugged gently on my earlobe. "You got you a right nice boy here," he said.

My father set his fork on his plate and rose from his chair, his fingers propped stiffly on the tablecloth. "Don't place your hand on my son's person again."

Mr. Flint screwed his finger into his ear, as though he were cleaning it. "Know a lady by the name of Florence Greenwald, Mr. Broussard?"

"I beg your pardon?" my father said.

"She's a looker," Mr. Hamilton said. "Enough to make a man turn his head."

"We're not knocking it," Mr. Flint said. "I've let my swizzle stick wander a few times myself."

"I think you're both evil men," my father said.

"Enjoy your lunch," Mr. Hamilton said. "We'll talk a little later." He winked at me. "See you, little fellow."

They walked out the door. My father sat back down, his eyes out of focus, his hands limp on each side of his plate, as though he had forgotten where he was or what he was doing.

*   *   *

I knew who she was. I also knew, without anyone telling me, that I was not supposed to mention her name. There was a great coldness in the relationship of my parents. In my entire life I never saw them kiss, hold hands, or even touch. Sometimes I would wake and hear them arguing in the bedroom, usually late at night after my father had come home from the icehouse, bumping against the doorway, scraping against the wall with one shoulder. Once I heard him say, "What am I supposed to do? Go in the kitchen and get a butcher knife?" It wasn't until puberty that I understood what he meant.

Miss Florence worked for the Red Cross and sometimes played bridge with my mother and her friends. For my birthday she gave me a book of stories and illustrations about King Arthur. Then she seemed to disappear from our lives. One evening in the kitchen I asked my father where she had gone. My mother was cleaning the stove, her back to us. She cleaned the house two times a day and washed her hands constantly.

"Miss Florence moved away," my father said.

"Why'd she move?" I said.

Mother scrubbed at a speck of grease next to the gas burner, then realized the burner was hot and grabbed her fingers, her mouth crimped, her eyes watering.

"I'm not sure, Aaron," my father said. "Why don't we go have a Grapette?"

Mother walked out of the room. Then I heard her slam the bathroom door.

But my real knowledge of my father's secret life did not come until weeks later, and to this day I cannot say with honesty that the evidence warranted my conviction. It was one of those moments you have as a child when you suddenly realize there is something terribly wrong with your family, and that the problem will not be corrected, and with a sinking of the heart you realize your life will never be the same.

On a Saturday afternoon, just before our trip to Terrebonne Bay, my father took me with him to the bowling alley. He had no interest in bowling, but the alley had an air-conditioned bar. Part of the *Houston Post* was folded back on the floor of his company car, the shoeprint of someone smaller than a man stamped on it. The crossword puzzle was exposed. The blank squares had been filled in with pencil. My father had less interest in crossword puzzles than he did in bowling.

That was when I knew he lived another life. I felt like I was on a swinging bridge above a canyon and the tether ropes had just been severed. I had seen Miss Florence working on a crossword puzzle in the reading room at the rental library in our neighborhood. She was from New Orleans and had been a nurse in France during the First World War. She read books my mother's regular bridge group did not. My father's loneliness hung on him like sackcloth and ashes. His colleagues in the oil and gas business had no inkling of his cultural frame of reference, one that included names like Malvern Hill and the Hornet's Nest, which were as real to him as the trench in which he had watched a sniper's round mortally wound his best friend on November 11, 1918.

The rain was blowing against the window of Provost's Bar and Pool Room. Men were cheering at the end of the bar. LSU had just scored a touchdown against Ole Miss.

"Aren't you going to finish your po'boy?" I said.

"I think I need another Jax and you need another Dr. Nut," my father said.

I knew he would be drunk by the end of the day, walking off-balance in the hotel lobby, an object of pity and shame. I felt as though a giant spider were feeding on my heart.

"Are you crying?" he said.

"No, sir."

"Then why are you looking like that?"

"Why were those men talking about Miss Florence?"

He watched the rain running down the window glass.

"Is she here, Daddy? Is this where Miss Florence lives?"

"Those men bear me ill will for political reasons, Aaron. I spoke up for a man who used to be a communist because I believed it was the right thing to do. These men are also angry because I don't believe the government has the right to control the news."

"What does that have to do with Miss Florence?"

"Nothing. They harm others because there is nothing else they do well."

The waiter saw my father's empty Jax and came to the table. Then my father surprised me. "We're through here," he said. "Give us a check, please."

"Where are we going, Daddy?"

"To the *Daily Iberian*."

"What for?"

"If a man ever tries to blackmail you, you dial up the newspaper and put the phone in the man's hand and tell him to do his worst. Are you my little podna?"

"Yes, sir," I replied.

I had never been inside a newspaper office. I sat with my father at the editor's desk, which was in a small office that gave onto the editorial room and the back shop, where the linotype machines and printing presses were. The air was warm and comfortable and had a clean, bright smell like freshly ironed clothes. The reporters wore ties and dress shirts, the copyreaders green visors. The society editor, a large woman in a deep-purple suit and frilly white blouse, had her own cubicle and a big smile for everyone who passed by. I felt as though I were in a special place, a fortress where virtue and truth would always be sacrosanct and would always prevail.

The managing editor was a round man, not fat, just a man who was round, like a series of sketched circles that had been hooked together. He also had thinning sandy-red hair and a soft, kind face. "You saw a submarine sink an oil tanker, Mr. Broussard?" he said, his eyes crinkling.

"I don't know that it was a tanker," my father said. "It burned with the intensity of one. But it could have been a freighter carrying something else."

The editor closed the door to the office and sat back down. He tried to smile. "The sunset can play tricks."

"I saw four bodies. I touched them with a boat hook."

The light went out of the editor's face. "I see."

"Will you run the story?"

The editor shifted in his chair. "These are unusual times."

"You don't think the shrimpers deserve to know there's a Nazi submarine operating a few miles from our shoreline?"

"Your father was an appointee of President Roosevelt," the editor said. "I would think you'd understand, Mr. Broussard."

"My father broke with President Roosevelt when he tried to pack the Supreme Court."

The editor nodded his head but didn't reply.

"Can I buy space for an ad?" my father said.

"An ad?"

"If you won't write the story, I will. I will also pay for the space."

"You're serious?"

"I was just threatened in Provost's by two men who claim to be law enforcement officers."

"The FBI?"

"If the FBI hires thugs."

The editor wiped his mouth and tapped his thigh repeatedly. "They actually threatened you?"

"With blackmail."

"About what?"

"Ask them."

The editor leaned back in his chair, pressing his fingertips to his forehead as though he were trying to flatten the wrinkles on it. "We don't run news stories as ads, Mr. Broussard. But I have the feeling you already know that."

"It crossed my mind."

The editor took a notepad and a fountain pen from his desk drawer. "I wish I had the flu. I wish I had stayed home today. In fact, right now I would welcome an asteroid through our roof. Okay, Mr. Broussard, let's start over."

The story ran two days later. It was on a back page and only four paragraphs in length. The story stated that no calls to the Coast Guard or the FBI were returned. That evening we ate in the hotel dining room. My father joked with people he knew from his childhood. No one made mention of his statement in the *Daily Iberian*. We walked down East Main inside a tunnel of oaks, past the plantation house known as the Shadows, built in 1832, and past other antebellum homes and Victorian ones, also; one resembled a beached paddle wheeler and glowed like a candlelit wedding cake in the gloom.

We stopped at the two-story, ivy-covered brick house where my father had grown up. His father had been one of the most admired

attorneys in the history of Louisiana, and also the state superinten-
dent of education and the president of the state senate and one of
the few men who had had the courage to testify against Huey Long
during Long's impeachment hearing. One year ago he had died a
pauper in this same house, and now the house belonged to others,
people from New York City.

The sky was as orange as a pumpkin, striped with purple
clouds. Tree frogs were singing on the bayou, and geese honking
overhead. My father stared silently at the house, his fedora slanted
over his brow. I put my hand in his. "Are you all right, Daddy?"

"*Pa'ti avec le vent*," he replied.

"What's that mean?"

"Gone with the wind."

"We have a house in Houston."

"Yes, we do," he replied. He stared at his birthplace and at the
rolling green lawn that tapered down to the bayou, where the moor-
ing chains of Jean Lafitte's slave ship still hung from the trunk of a
huge oak tree. "Let's get us some ice cream at Veazey's."

The evening seemed perfect, as though indeed God was in His
heaven and all was right with the world. How was I to know I was
about to witness one of the cruelest acts I would ever see one man
do to another?

Veazey's was on Burke Street, right by the drawbridge that spanned
Bayou Teche. I was sitting at the counter with my father, eating an
ice cream cone, when a two-door automobile splashed with mud
pulled into the parking lot. The bayou was high and yellow and fast-
running and chained with rain rings. The agent named Flint, the
one who looked like a boxer, entered the store, mist blowing inside
with him. He wiped the damp off his face, grinning. "Recognize
somebody out there, Mr. Broussard?"

14

Miss Florence was in the back seat of the two-door car. She was wearing a blue jacket and a dove-colored felt hat, sitting stiffly in the seat, as though she wanted to touch as little of her surroundings as possible. She turned her head and looked right at us. My father's face jerked.

"What has she done?" he said to Mr. Flint.

"She's done it to herself," Mr. Flint said.

"Answer my question, please."

"She applied for a job with Navy intelligence. She's a possible fifth columnist."

"Are you insane?" my father said.

"She wasn't in Spain in '36?"

"She was a nurse with the Lincoln Brigade."

"They weren't communists?"

"She's not."

"You're a goddamn liar."

I had never heard anyone speak to my father in that way. Everyone in the ice cream store had gone silent. I wanted my father to get up and hit Mr. Flint in the mouth.

"Daddy?" I said.

But he did nothing. My face felt hot and small and tight.

"I got to run, Mr. Broussard," Mr. Flint said. "Just so you know, we rented space at the women's camp in Angola for your lady friend."

"You can't do that," my father said.

"Tell that to the Japs in those internment camps out West. By the way, we're going to be talking with your wife in Houston. Hope you don't mind."

"Don't you dare go near her, you vile man," my father said.

Mr. Flint stuck a cigarette in his mouth but didn't light it. He looked down at me, then back at my father. "You paid your girlfriend's rent for a week at the motel at the end of town. You take your little boy with you when you're slipping around and judge me?"

I didn't know what some of Mr. Flint's references meant, but I knew he had said something awful to my father. His right hand was trembling on top of the counter as Mr. Flint walked out the door.

"What's going to happen to Miss Florence, Daddy?" I said.

"I don't know," he said, lowering his head to the heel of his hand. "I truly don't."

This was not like my father. But I was too young to understand that when good people stray into dark water, their lack of experience with human frailty can become like a millstone around their necks. He paid the waitress, then took me by the hand and walked me to the car. The rain had quit and the electric lights on the bridge had gone on, and a tugboat was working its way up the bayou. Through a break in the clouds I could see a trail of stars that was like crushed ice winding into eternity. I wanted to believe I was looking at heaven and that no force on earth could harm my father and me.

I should have known better, even at my age. Scott Fitzgerald said no one can understand the United States unless he understands the graves of Shiloh. The Broussard family took it a step further. They saw themselves as figures in a tragedy, one that involved the Lost Cause and the horns blowing along the road to Roncevaux, and in so doing condemned themselves to lives of morbidity and unhappiness.

My father hadn't gotten drunk on our trip to New Iberia, but I wished he had. I wished my defining memory of New Iberia would remain the gush of stars beyond the clouds, the red and green lights on the drawbridge, and the water dripping out of the trees on the bayou's surface. I wanted to hold that perfect moment, on the banks of Bayou Teche, as though my father and I had stepped into a dream inside the mind of God.

In the morning my father sat down with his address book and made several calls from the telephone in our hotel room. First he confirmed that Miss Florence was being held at the women's camp in Angola. Then he tried to get permission to see her. That's when the person on the other end of the line hung up. My father was sitting in a stuffed chair by the window, a slice of yellow sunlight across his face, dividing him in half as though he were two people.

"What is it, Daddy?"

"I don't like to ask people for special treatment. But in our beloved state you get nowhere unless you have friends. So I have to call a friend of mine from my army days."

"What's wrong with that?"

"My friend dug me out of the earth when I was buried alive. I've never been able to repay the debt. He's a grand fellow. I hate to bother him."

"If he's your friend and you need help, he'll want to hear from you, won't he?"

"You're such a fine little chap, Aaron," he said. "One day you'll have a little boy of your own, and you'll know how much that means."

His friend from the Somme got permission for us to visit a place inside Angola called Camp I. We clanged across a cattle guard at the entrance to the prison farm and were met by a man in rumpled khaki clothes and sunglasses and a coned-up straw hat and half-topped boots with his trousers stuffed inside and a nametag on his shirt pocket that said C. LUFKIN. His face had the sharpened, wood-like quality of a man who possessed only one expression;

his eyes were hidden behind his glasses, his sleeves rolled, his arms sunbrowned and dotted with purplish-red spots that looked like burns buried under the skin. He got in the back of our car and shook hands with my father over the top of the seat. He said he was the heavy-equipment manager on the farm.

"So where are we going?" my father said.

"I got to check on a nigger in the box at Camp A before we see your friend."

"Sir?" my father said.

"We keep the sweatboxes on Camp A. I had to stick a boy inside three days ago."

My father looked at him in the rearview mirror. "We need to make our visit and be on our way."

Mr. Lufkin leveled a finger at an off-white two-story building in the distance. "Turn right," he said. "That's it yonder."

Dust was blowing out of the fields, swirling around the building and into the sky, as though it had no other place to go. Mr. Lufkin put a pinch of snuff under his lip. My father slowed the car, then stopped altogether. He looked into the mirror again. "We were not told about any detours."

"Every minute we sit here is another minute that nigger stays in the box. What do you want to do, Mr. Broussard? It doesn't matter to me."

My father shifted the floor stick and drove down a cinnamon-colored dirt road that divided a soybean field. We went through a barbed-wire gate and stopped twenty yards from two coffin-like iron boxes that were set straight up on a concrete slab; each had a hinged door with a gap at the top.

"Didn't mean to upset you," Mr. Lufkin said. "If you knew what that nigger did on the outside, you'd have a less kind view of your fellow man, I guarantee it."

"How about you take care of your obligations and get us out of here?" my father said, his hands tightening on the steering wheel. "I'd be very appreciative."

Mr. Lufkin got out of the car and was joined by two other men in khaki uniforms and straw cowboy hats. Mr. Lufkin unlocked a sliding bar on the door of one box and pulled it open, then stepped back from a horde of flies that rose into the air.

"Watch the bucket!" the man behind him said.

The box was constructed so there was no room to sit down. The man inside was bare-chested and as black as obsidian, his skin streaming with sweat, his buttocks pressed against one wall, his knees against another. He tumbled out of the box onto the ground, the bucket that had been placed between his feet tipping with him, his own feces splashing onto his work shoes and his gray-and-white-striped pants.

"Goddamn it!" one of the other men said, jumping backward.

My father put his hand over my eyes. "Don't look at this, son. Say a little prayer for the colored man. Then we're going to see Miss Florence and go home. You hear me? Don't cry. I'm going to write the warden."

A few minutes later Mr. Lufkin got in the back seat of our car. His sunglasses were in his shirt pocket, his hair wet-combed, his face fresh and bright with either expectation or victory. "Head back down the road and keep going till you're almost to the river. I'll show y'all the Red Hat House."

My father began driving down the road, his hands shaking with anger. Mr. Lufkin was leaning forward, looking at my father in the rear-view mirror. "The Red Hat House is the home of Gruesome Gertie."

My father looked into the mirror but said nothing.

Mr. Lufkin mouthed the words "That's where they knock the fire out of their ass."

"Don't you say another word to me, Mr. Lufkin," my father said. "Not one word."

Mr. Lufkin sat back in the seat, breathing through his nose, his nostrils like slits. "When you're in another man's house, it's not wise to put your feet on the furniture. No siree, Bob, if you get my meaning."

Camp I was a cluster of barracks behind barbed and electric wire not far from the Mississippi River. Half of the camp was made up of women prisoners who wore either street clothes or green-and-white-pinstripe dresses. Mr. Lufkin stayed in the car and a matron escorted us to the dining room. Outside, the sky was the color of orange sherbet, the leaves of the willow trees flattening in the wind along the banks of the river. The women were finishing supper. Miss Florence was sitting by herself at the end of a long table. Most of the women had tangled hair and some had faces that made me think of broken pumpkins. The matron said we could speak with Miss Florence for twenty minutes, then Mr. Lufkin would accompany us back to the front entrance of the farm.

Miss Florence had been in Angola only a short time, but she looked as though her soul had been sucked out of her chest. Her lips were dry and cracked, her face smaller, her eyes recessed. Unlike the other women, her thick brown hair was neatly combed, but it looked like a wig on a mannequin. We sat down and my father pushed a package of Lucky Strikes across the table.

"We can't smoke in the dining room," she said. "I can't touch you or take anything from you, either."

"Has anyone physically hurt you?" he asked.

She didn't answer.

"Florence?" he said.

She lowered her voice. "This place is hell. There're convicts buried in the levee."

He put his hand on top of hers. A matron sitting on a stool gave him a look. He took his hand away. "I've called a lawyer. They can't hold you here."

"They can do anything they want. You haven't seen the colored unit."

"I saw the sweatboxes."

She was silent. Then she looked at me. "How is my little fellow doing?"

"Fine," I said.

"You have to forgive me for the way I'm talking, Aaron," she said. "I'm just being a grump today."

A strange sensation seemed to come over me, although I didn't know why. I had always liked Miss Florence. I had always associated her with the gift of the book about King Arthur and the Knights of the Round Table. But now I felt I was talking to an intruder who had come carrying gifts out of nowhere and was helping destroy our family. Worse, I felt I was betraying my long-suffering, guilt-ridden, haunted mother.

She had grown up in desperate poverty. Her mother died when she was seven, then her father abandoned her. She was unloved and unwanted and was left to find any shelter strangers might offer. Maybe she had an abortion. Maybe she was molested. She never talked about her childhood, but her memories of it lingered in her eyes like cups of sorrow.

"Is something wrong, Aaron?" Miss Florence asked.

I looked away from her. "I want to go, Daddy," I said.

"We will, son," he said. "Shortly."

"No, now. We're not supposed to be here."

"What do you mean?" he said.

"It's not the way things are supposed to be."

"Don't talk like that, Aaron," he said. "Miss Florence is our friend."

"What about Mother?" I said.

He tried to put his arm across my shoulder, but I got up from the bench and ran through the dining hall to the door. A matron tried to stop me, but I kept running, knocking through a group of colored women, falling to the floor, then getting up and running out the door into the yard, right into the arms of Mr. Lufkin.

"Don't be fighting with me, boy," he said. He looked at his palm. "You just hit me in the mouth, you little shit. I ought to slap your head off."

Then I was running again, all the way to the gate, where a guard grabbed me by the back of my belt and carried me like a suitcase to my father's car.

We drove back to the Frederic in a rainstorm, did not talk until we reached New Iberia. When I woke to the Angelus the next morning, my father was gone. He had left a note on the desk telling me he would be with a survey team in the swamp all day and that my breakfast was paid for and my cousin would pick me up at noon and take me to her house.

One week later Miss Florence hanged herself in the nude from a showerhead in Camp I.

My father and I never spoke again about Miss Florence or the German submarine or Angola or the lawmen who tried to hurt him through Miss Florence. My father died in an auto accident when I was still in my teens. Like him, I lost my best friend in the last days of a war, at a place GIs nicknamed Pork Chop Hill. Unlike my father, at age eighteen I was an inmate in a parish prison ten feet from the death cell, back in the days when the state executioner traveled with

Gruesome Gertie on a flatbed truck from parish jail to parish jail. When it arrived, I could hear the condemned man weeping and see flashes of lightning reflect on his face.

I wasn't a criminal; I was simply crazy, just like my mother. I wish I had been even crazier, because I will never forget the sounds of the generators warming up down below on the street and the man being buckled in the chair and a minister reading from a Bible and then the generators growing louder and louder, like airplane engines, and when the electrician pulled the switch the sudden creak of the leather restraints on the condemned man's body stretching so tight you thought the wood and bolts of the chair would explode, even the guards looking at the floor, their arms folded on their chests.

I clamped my hands over my ears and yelled out of a barred window from which I could see the moon and the fog on the Calcasieu River, so I would not have to listen to any sound other than my own voice. In some ways the river reminded me of Bayou Teche and that perfect moment when my father and I stood in front of Veazey's, believing that as long as we held each other's hand we would never be separated, even by death.

I try to consign these images to the past and not talk about them anymore. I almost get away with it, too. But one night a month I dream about green water sliding over sandbars and a ship burning brightly on the horizon and harbor lights that offer sanctuary from a world that breaks everything in us that is beautiful and good. In the morning I wake to darkness, calling my father's name, James Eustace Broussard, wondering when he will answer.

GOING ACROSS JORDAN

Nobody would believe you could drive a car across the bottom of an ancient glacial lake at night, the high beams tunneling in electrified shafts of yellow smoke under the surface, but I stood on the bank and saw it, my head still throbbing from a couple of licks I took when I was on the ground and couldn't protect myself. The sky was bursting with stars, the fir trees shaggy and full of shadows on the hillsides, the cherry trees down by the lake thrashing in the wind. Most of the people we picked cherries for lived in stone houses on the lakeshore, and after sunset you could see their lights come on and reflect on the water, but tonight the houses were dark and the only light on the lake was the glow of the high beams spearing across the lake bottom, the ginks that had chased us through the timber with chains afraid of what their eyes told them.

Flathead Lake was a magical place back in those days, all twenty-eight miles of it, the largest freshwater lake west of the Mississippi, so beautiful that when you stood on the shore at sunrise it was like day one of creation and you thought you might see a mastodon with big tusks coming down out of the high country, snow caked and steaming on its hide.

We called ourselves people on the drift, not migrants. Migrants have a destination. Buddy Elgin wasn't going anywhere except to a location in his head, call it a dream if you like. He was the noun and I was the adjective. We never filed an income tax form and our only ID was a city library card. Like Cisco Houston used to say, we rode free on that old SP. Tell me there's anything better than the sound of the wheels clicking on the tracks and a boxcar rocking back and forth under you while you sleep. Buddy was like a big brother to me. Even though he was a water-walker and took big risks, he always looked out for his pals.

We worked beets in northern Colorado and bucked bales in the Big Horns during the haying season. I can still see Buddy picking up the bale by the twine and flinging it up on the flatbed, the bale as light as air in his hands, the muscles of his upper arms swollen like cantaloupes, a big Swedish girl in the baler not able to take her eyes off him. Buddy was on the square with women and never spoke crudely in front of them or about them, so any trouble we got into was political and never had female origins. Not until we got mixed up with a hootchy-kootchy girl who could rag-pop your boots and leave you with a shine and a male condition that made it hard for you to climb down from the chair, pardon me if I'm too frank.

I loved the life we led and would not have changed it if you hit me upside the head with an iron skillet. I told this to Buddy while we were gazing out the open door of a flat-wheeler, the Big Horns slipping behind us under a turquoise sky and a slice of moon that was as hard and cold as a scythe blade.

He wore a gray flop hat that had darkened with sweat high above the band, and he sat with one knee pulled up in front of him, the neck of his Stella twelve-string guitar propped against it. The locomotive was slowing on a long curve that wound through hills, which were round and smooth and reddish brown against the sun and made me think of women's breasts.

"What are you studying on?" he asked.

"I was wondering why most men get in trouble over a reasonable issue like money or women or cards or alcohol, not because they cain't keep their mouths shut."

Buddy tried to roll a cigarette out of a ten-cent bag of Bull Durham, but a flat-wheeler doesn't have springs and makes for a rough ride and the tobacco kept spilling out of the cigarette paper cupped in a tube between his fingers. "It was a free country when I woke up this morning," he said.

"You don't hold political meetings in a bunkhouse. The people listening to you think Karl Marx has a brother named Harpo."

He worked on his cigarette until he finally got it rolled and licked down and twisted on both ends. He lit it with a paper match and flicked the blackened match out the door and watched the country go by. I wanted to push him out the door.

"What do those hills put you in mind of?" he asked.

"Big piles of dirt and rock and dry grass that I wish would catch on fire."

"It's beautiful. Except there's something out here that wants to kill you."

"Like what?"

"It."

"What's 'it'?"

"Everything," he said. He picked up his guitar and formed an E chord and drew his thumb across the strings. "Sheridan coming up. Listen to that whistle blow."

*   *   *

We got hired with a bunch of Mexican wets on a street corner not far from the old cattle pens north of town and went to work for a feed grower and horse breeder who was also a cowboy actor out in Hollywood and went by the name of Clint Wakefield. Except Wakefield didn't really run the ranch. The straw boss did; he was a Southerner like us by the name of Tyler Keats. He'd been a bull rider on the circuit, until he got overly ambitious one night and tied himself down with a suicide wrap and got all his sticks broken. You could hear Tyler creak when he walked, which is not to say he was lacking in smarts. It took special talents to be a straw boss in those days; the straw boss had to make a bunch of misfits who hated authority do what he said without turning them into enemies with lots of ways of getting even. Think of an open gate and dry lightning at nightfall and three hundred head of Herefords highballing for Dixie through somebody's wheat field.

Our third week on the job the hay baler started clanking like a Coca-Cola bottle in a garbage disposal unit. Without anybody telling him, Buddy hung his hat and shirt on a cottonwood branch and climbed under the baler with a monkey wrench and went to work.

Ten minutes later Buddy crawled back out, a big grin on his face, the baler as good as new. Tyler kept studying Buddy the way a cautious man does when somebody who's smarter than he is shows up in the workplace. Buddy was putting his shirt back on, his skin as tan and smooth as river clay. Tyler was looking at the scar that ran from Buddy's armpit to his kidney, like a long strip of welted rubber. "Was you in Korea?" Tyler said.

"This scar? Got it up at Calgary, one second from the buzzer and seven seconds after being fool enough to climb on a cross-wired bull by the name of Red Whisky."

"You got bull-hooked?"

"Hooked, sunfished till I was split up the middle, stirrup-drug, stove in, flung into the boards, and kicked twice in the head when I fell down in the chute."

"Mr. Wakefield needs six colts green broke. They've never been on a lunge line. You'll have to start from scratch."

"I like bucking bales just fine," Buddy said.

Tyler took a folded circular from his back pocket and fitted on his spectacles and tilted it away from the sunlight's glare. "You two boys walk with me into the shade. I cain't hardly read out here in the bright," he said.

I could feel my stomach churning. We followed him to the dry creek bed where two big cottonwoods were growing out of the bank, lint blowing off the limbs like dandelions powdering. There was a warm breeze, the kind that made you want to go to sleep and not think about all the trouble that was always waiting for you over the horizon. The circular was ruffling in Tyler's hand. "This come in the mail yesterday," he said. "There's a drawing of a man named Robert James Elgin on here. The drawing looks a whole lot like you."

"I go by Buddy, and I don't think that's my likeness at all."

"Glad you told me that, because this circular says 'Buddy' is the alias of this fellow Robert James Elgin. His traveling companion is named R.B. Ruger. It says here these two fellows are organizers for a communist union."

"I cain't necessarily say I was ever a communist, Tyler, but I can say without equivocation that I have always been in the red," Buddy said.

Tyler glanced up at the cottonwood leaves fluttering against the sky, his eyelids jittering. "Equivocation, huh? That's a mouthful.

29

Here's what's *not* on the circular. I don't care if you guys are from
Mars as long as y'all do your job. Right now your job is green breaking them horses. Is your friend any good at it?"

"I'm real good at it," I said.

"Nobody asked you," Tyler said.

I always said I never had to seek humility; it always found me.

"What's in it for us?" Buddy asked.

"Two dollars more a day than what y'all are making now. You
can have your own room up at the barn. You don't smoke in or
near the building and you don't come back drunk from town. You
muck the stalls and sweep the floor every day and you eat in the
bunkhouse."

Buddy waited on me to say something, but I didn't. I liked
Wyoming and figured Tyler was more bark than bite and not a bad
guy to work for; also, a two-dollar daily wage increase in those days
wasn't something you were casual about. But I didn't like what
was on that circular. I wasn't a communist and neither was Buddy.
"What are you going to do if we turn you down?" I said.

"Not a thing. But I ain't Mr. Wakefield. Communists are the
stink on shit in Hollywood, in case you haven't heard."

Buddy picked a leaf off the cottonwood and bit a piece out of
it and spat it off the tip of his tongue. "We'll move in this evening,"
he said. "Because I didn't get this scar in Korea doesn't mean I
wasn't there. The only communists I ever knew were shooting
at me. You can tell that to Mr. Wakefield or anybody else who
wants to know."

But Tyler had already gotten what he wanted and wasn't
listening. "One other thing: The trainer I just run off brought a
woman back from town," he said. "The only man who gets to bump
uglies on this ranch is Mr. Wakefield."

"Wish I could be a Hollywood cowboy," Buddy said.

"I was at Kasserine Pass, son," Tyler said. "Don't smart-mouth me."

We moved into the room at the end of the stalls in the barn. Tucked into the corner of the mirror above the sink was a business card with Clint Wakefield's name on it. Buddy looked at it and stuck it in his shirt pocket.

"What'd you do that for?" I asked.

"I never had a souvenir from a famous person."

I didn't know why, but I thought it was a bad omen.

By midsummer the first shaft of morning sunlight in West Texas can be like a wet switch whipped across your skin. A sunrise in Wyoming was never like that. The light was soft and filtered inside the barn where we slept, the air cool and smelling of sage and woodsmoke and bacon frying in the cookhouse. You could get lost in the great blue immensity of the dawn and forget there was any such thing as evil or that someplace down the road you had to die. I'd skim the dust and bits of hay off the horse tank and unhook the chain on the windmill and step back when the blades rattled to life and water gushed out of the pipe as cold as melt off a glacier. There was a string of pink mesas in the east, and sometimes above them I could see electricity forking out of a thunderhead and striking the earth, like tiny gold wires, and I'd wonder if Indian spirits still lived out there on the edge of the white man's world.

I didn't want to ever leave the ranch owned by the cowboy actor. But whenever I got a feeling like that about a place or a situation or the people around me, I'd get scared, because every time I loved something I knew I was fixing to lose it. I saw my dog snatched up by the tail of a tornado. I was in dust storms that sounded like locomotive engines grinding across the hardpan; I saw the sky turn black at noon while people all over town nailed wet burlap over their windows. I saw baptized Christians burn colored people out of a town in Oklahoma for no reason.

I saw a kid take off from a road gang outside Sugar Land Pen and run barefoot along the train track and catch a flatcar on the fly and hang on the rods all the way to Beaumont, the tracks and gravel and stink of creosote whizzing by eighteen inches from his face.

I pretended to Buddy I didn't know what "it" was, and I guess that made me a hypocrite. The truth was, people like us didn't belong anywhere, and "it" was out there waiting for us.

On a July evening in Sheridan the sky could be as green as the ocean, the saloon windows lit with Grain Belt neon signs, the voice of Kitty Wells singing from the Wurlitzer "It Wasn't God Who Made Honky Tonk Angels."

The War Bonnet was in the middle of the block, right by the town square, and had a long foot-railed bar and a dance floor and card tables and an elevated bandstand and Christmas decorations that never came down. There was also a steak-and-spuds café in front where a mulatto girl worked a two-chair shoeshine stand by herself and never lacked for customers. She called herself Bernadine, and if you asked her what her last name was, she'd reply, "Who says I got one?"

She was light-colored and had hair that was jet-black and gold on the tips and she wore it long and unstraightened, and it seemed to sparkle when she went to work on your feet. She wore big hoop earrings and oversized Levi's and Roman sandals and snap-button shirts printed with flowers, and when she got busy she was a flat-out pleasure to watch. I wanted to tell her how beautiful she was and how much I admired the way she carried herself; I wanted to tell her I understood what it was like to be different and on your own and clinging to the ragged edges of just getting by. Saying those kinds of things to a beautiful girl was not my strong suit.

Our second Saturday night in Sheridan I got up my courage and said, "What time you get off, Miss Bernadine?"

"Late," she said.

She touched my boot to tell me she was finished.

"That's Clint Wakefield at the bar. I break horses for him," I said.

She gazed through the swinging doors that gave onto the saloon. In the background Bob Wills's orchestra was playing "Faded Love" on the jukebox.

"I can introduce you if you want," I said.

"He's gonna put me in the movies?"

"Yeah, that could happen. You'd have to ask him, though. He doesn't confide in me about everything."

"Watch yourself getting down, cowboy," she said.

I not only felt my cheeks flaming, I felt ashamed all the way through the bottoms of my feet. The truth was I'd hardly exchanged five words with Clint Wakefield. I wasn't even sure he knew I existed. Most of the time he had one expression, a big grin. Actors train themselves never to blink. Their eyelids are stitched to their foreheads so they can stare into your face until you swallow and look away and feel like spit on the sidewalk. If you put those lidless blue eyes together with a big grin, you've pretty much got Clint Wakefield. He was leaning against the bar, wearing a white silk shirt embroidered with roses, his striped Western-cut britches hitched way up on his hips, his gold curls hanging from under a felt hat that was as white as Christmas snow. His wife was sitting at a table by herself. She was stone-deaf and always had a startled look on her face. A couple of the guys in the bunkhouse said that the ranch belonged to her and that Mr. Wakefield married her before his career took off. They also said he told dirty jokes in front of her, and the ranch hands had to choose between laughing and being disrespectful to her or offending him.

"Make any headway out there?" he asked.

"Sir?" I said.

"If I needed to change my luck, she's the one I'd do it with."

I could feel my throat drying up, a vein tightening in my temple. I looked through the window at the greenness of the sky and wanted to be out on the elevated sidewalk, the breeze on my face, the lighthearted noises of the street in my ears. "I'm not rightly sure what you mean."

"That's my restored 1946 Ford woody out there. Here's the keys. Take the shoeshine gal for a spin. Bring her out to the ranch if you like."

"Tyler said no female visitors."

"Tyler's a good man but a prude at heart. Your last name is Ruger? Like the gun?"

I tried to look back into his eyes without blinking, but I couldn't. "I didn't realize you knew my name."

"You carry your gun with you?"

"I'm just a guy who bucks bales and stays broke most of the time, Mr. Clint."

"I was watching you in the corral yesterday. You were working a filly on the lunge line. You never used the whip."

"You do it right, you don't need one."

He dropped the car keys in my shirt pocket. "I can always tell a pro," he said. "Bring your girlfriend on out and pay Tyler no mind. I think he pissed most of his brains in the toilet a long time ago."

I wish I'd given Mr. Wakefield back his keys and caught a ride to the ranch with the Mexicans, like Buddy did. At two a.m. I was drinking coffee at the counter in the café and watching Bernadine put away her rags and shoe polish and brushes and lock the drawers on her stand.

"Mr. Wakefield let me borrow his car. I think he used it in a movie," I said. "It's got a Merc engine in it that's all chrome."

"You're saying you want to take me home?"

"Maybe we could go out on the Powder River. The Indians say there's fish under the banks that don't have eyes."

"I can't wait to see that."

"Mr. Wakefield said we could go out to the ranch if you like."

"Is this your pickup line?"

I scratched the side of my face. "I thought we'd get some bread and throw it along the edge of the current to see if the story about those blind fish is true. Fish have a strong sense of smell. Even if they're blind."

"Has anyone ever told you you're a mess?"

"Actually, quite a few people have."

She arched her neck and massaged a muscle, her eyes closed, her hair glistening as bright as dew on blackberries. "What part of the South you from, hon?"

"Who says that's where I'm from?"

"I thought that peckerwood accent might be a clue."

"The West and the South are not the same thing. I happen to be from Dalhart, Texas. That's where wind was invented."

Her eyes smiled at me. The owner had just turned off the beer signs in the windows and you could see Mr. Wakefield's station wagon parked at the curb, the wood panels gleaming, the maroon paint job on the fenders and the boot for the spare tire hand-waxed and rippling with light under the streetlamp. "How fast can it go?" she said.

"We can find out."

35

"You weren't lying, were you?"

"About what?"

"The man you work for being a movie star. About him asking me out to his ranch."

I looked at her blankly, disappointed in the way you are when people you respect let you down. "Yeah, he's big stuff," I said. "Maybe he'll give you an autograph."

"No, thanks. He's been in here before. He says mean things about his wife," she replied. "I just wondered who he was."

Outside, I opened the car door for her and held her arm while she got inside. The interior was done in rolled white leather, the dashboard made of polished oak. She looked up at me, uncertain.

"Anything wrong?" I asked.

"I don't know if I should do this."

"Why not?"

"Because this isn't my car. Because I don't like the man who owns it."

"You're accepting a ride from me, not from Mr. Wakefield. What's the harm?"

She gazed at the empty street and the trees on the courthouse square and the shadows moving on the grass when the wind blew. "Would you buy me a hamburger and a cherry milk shake?" she said. "I can't tell you how much I'd like that."

A half hour later we were sitting in a booth by the window at the truck stop when four drunks came in and sat down at the counter, like a bunch of bikers coming into church with muddy boots on in the middle of a church meeting. One of them leaned over to the others and said something that caused them to glance sideways at us and laugh. Then I heard the word "nigger." Bernadine looked out the window as though she didn't hear it. I stared at my plate, my ears starting to ping with a sound that was like being underwater too long. The steak bone on the plate had pieces of torn pink meat along the edges; it lay with my steak knife in grease that was black and streaked with blood, and it made me remember things I had taught myself not to think about, things I never wanted to see again. I stared at my plate for a long time. When I raised my eyes, two or three of the men at the counter were still watching us, like we were zoo creatures that shouldn't have any expectation of privacy or respect.

I stood up and lowered my hand down by my plate, still holding my napkin. "I'll be back in a minute," I said.

"Where you going?" Bernadine said.

I picked up my coffee cup. "Refill," I said.

"Those guys don't bother me. Leave them alone."

"That's a good attitude. There are people in this world who aren't worth spitting on. You're absolutely correct."

The drunks weren't expecting me. Their faces were bloodless in the artificial light, like white balloons that had started to go soft, the alcohol they had probably been drinking all night fouling their hearts and making their eyes go out of focus. "Hi," I said. There was a windup clock by the serving window and you could hear it clicking in the silence. "Can y'all tell me the best way to Billings?"

They wanted to look me straight in the face, but they couldn't keep their attention off my right hand and the napkin that covered the oblong object I held in my palm. I turned my gaze on the man who had made the others laugh. He had a double chin and was wiping at his nose with a paper napkin, like he had a head cold and an excuse for being gutless. He pointed at the window. "The highway is right there. It goes north to Billings and south to Cheyenne," he said.

37

"My vision isn't good. Can a couple of you go outside and point to it? My friend and me don't want to get lost and have to come back in here. Just walk outside and stand in the light and point, then we'll get in our car and drive away."

"What are you talking about?" the fat man said. He was breathing through his nose and there was a shine on his upper lip.

I moved my right hand onto the counter, the napkin making a tent over my knuckles. "I'm just asking two of y'all to point out the road to Crow Agency and Billings. All four of you don't have to go outside, just two of you. Y'all decide who goes out and who stays. It would be a big favor to us."

"We were telling a joke, but it wasn't about you," another man said.

"You're sure?" I said.

"Yeah. I mean yes, sir."

"I'm glad to learn that. But I still need you to show me the way to Billings, because darned if I can figure it out on my own."

The fat man walked to the window and pointed. "There's the goddamn highway. Is that good enough?"

"No, not really." I raised my hand from the counter, the napkin still draped across my knuckles.

"All right, you win," another man said. "Come on, Bill. Give the man what he wants. We were out of line. If it'll make him happy, let's go outside and put an end to this."

"I appreciate that," I said. "Tell you what, I've changed my mind. We're going to stay here and have a piece of pie." I turned toward the waitress and pulled the napkin off my hand. "This spoon has water stains on it, ma'am. Could I have a clean one?"

We went down on the Powder River, where those blind fish live way back under the cuts in the bank. The air was cold and damp and smoky from a stump fire, the sky black and sprinkled with stars. We went into a shack that had no door and no glass in the windows, among a grove of cottonwoods, and lay down on some gunnysacks and listened to the trout night feed in a long riffle that came right down the center of the stream, as shiny as a ribbon of oil under the moon.

She had hardly spoken since we left the truck stop. I took her hand in mine and said her fingernails made me think of tiny seashells. "Are you a mermaid?" I said.

"You could have gotten both of us hurt back there," she said.

"I don't read it that way."

"Then you don't know very much about Wyoming."

"A man who abuses a woman is a moral and physical coward. That kind of man cuts bait as soon as you stand up to him." Truth is, I didn't feel very good about what I did back there. But I could tell that was not what was really on her mind.

"At the War Bonnet you split a paper match with your thumbnail," she said.

"Yeah, I do that sometimes." I lay back on the gunnysacks and watched a flock of birds lift out of the cottonwoods and fly low across the water, their wings drumming like they were made of leather. No, they were drumming as fast and loud as my heart. It's funny how your past always trails after you, no matter where you go.

"Where were you in prison?" she said.

"A P-farm down in Texas. I wrote a bad check for thirty-seven dollars. The gunbull sent me to get the water can off the truck and I took off through a swamp and never looked back. The mud pulled my shoes right off my feet. I rode under a freight car plumb to Beaumont."

She propped herself up on one elbow and looked me in the face. "Are you telling me the truth?"

"Who makes up lies about being an escaped convict?"

She put her fingers on my throat to feel my pulse and looked straight into my eyes. I could still smell the cherry milk shake on her breath. "You're no criminal," she said.

"I don't think so, either."

She laid her head on my chest. I put my hand under her jacket and spread my fingers across her back. I thought I could feel her heart beating against my palm.

"Buddy Elgin and me are going to get us some land up in Montana," I said. "We've got a spot picked out near a place called Swan Lake. The lake was scooped out of the land by a big glacier, right at the foot of this mountain called Swan Peak. The trout in the lake are big as your arm. It's country that's still new, where you can be anything you want."

She felt the tips of my fingers, then felt between them and around the edges of the joints. "Did you ever pick cotton?"

"From cain't-see to cain't-see. Till my fingers bled on the boll and then some," I replied.

"My father cropped on shares and preached on the side. He called me a hootchy-kootchy girl once and I got mad at him. He explained a hootchy-kootchy girl had music inside her. He used to preach out of what he called the Book of Ezra. He said before the Flood, people ate the flowers from the fields, just like animals grazing. He said the wind blew through the grass and made music like a harp does."

"I heard about people digging up dinosaurs that had flowers in their stomachs. Maybe that's what your father was talking about. It was an article in *National Geographic*."

I heard her laugh. She curled against me and kissed the top of my hand and folded it against her breast. That's when I saw headlight beams bouncing through the trees and heard a diesel truck grinding down the dirt track, a car with a blown muffler following thirty yards behind. There was a man in a fedora on the running board of the truck; he was waving to the car to close up the gap, like they'd found what they were looking for.

I know the differences between kinds of people. The drunks back at the truck stop worked at jobs that anyone could do and went to church on Sunday with wives who had been a hundred pounds thinner in high school, and woke up every morning wondering who they really were. The man in the fedora and the two men getting out of the diesel and the three getting out of the car were guys who avoided victimhood by becoming victimizers. Hollywood actors could stare down people till they blinked. These guys could make people wet their pants.

The man who was obviously in charge was at least six foot five and wore a heavy cotton shirt and a yellow wool vest buttoned to his throat and a tall-crown Stetson hat of the kind that Tom Mix wore. A badge holder with a gold badge in it was hung over his belt. "You two get your asses out here," he said.

I went out first, in front of Bernadine. I heard the muted sounds of moss-covered rocks knocking together under the surface of the river, like the earth wasn't hung together proper and was starting to come apart. The windshields of both vehicles were clear of dust where the wipers had scraped back and forth across the glass. Inside the car, sitting in the passenger seat, I could see Buddy Elgin staring back at me, one eye puffed shut, swollen as tight as a duck's egg.

The man in the Stetson pulled the keys from the ignition of the woody. He looked at Bernadine and stuck his finger through the key ring. "You know what grand auto can cost you in this state?" he said.

"Mr. Wakefield let me use it," I said.

41

"He says you took off with it."

"That's not true. You can ask at the War Bonnet. The bartender saw him give me the keys."

"That's Mr. Wakefield setting up there in his Cadillac on the highway. You want to walk up there and call him a liar to his face?"

I knew how it was going to go. I'd been there before. I wondered how bad they had hurt Buddy. The man in the fedora opened the passenger door of the car and pulled Buddy onto the ground. Buddy's hands were cuffed behind him and his shirt was unbuttoned on his chest. He wasn't wearing his boots and in the moonlight the toes of his white socks were soggy with blood.

"We were invited to Mr. Wakefield's ranch," Bernadine said. "He probably thought we stole his car because we didn't go straight there. Ask him."

The man with the badge hooked me up, crimping the steel tongues tight in the locks, bunching the skin and veins on my wrists. He turned toward Bernadine. "If I was you, I'd go with the flow, girl," he said.

He shoved me headlong into the back seat of the car, then picked up Buddy by his hair and the back of his shirt and did the same thing with him. I saw Bernadine's face slide by the window as we drove away.

They didn't take us to a regular jail. It was a basement under a brick warehouse, with windows like gun slits that had bars high up on the wall, and a toilet without a door in one corner. The man in the fedora gave Buddy back his boots, but his toes had been stomped so bad he could hardly walk after he got them back on. At noon a man in a filling station uniform with greased hair that was combed straight back and a face like a hatchet brought us a quart jar of water and a hamburger each. He refused to speak no matter how many times we asked him what we were being charged with. "What did y'all do with Bernadine?" I said.

"*We* didn't do anything," he said. "You'd better not be saying we did, either."

He went up a set of wood steps and locked the metal door behind him. Buddy was sitting in the corner, his knees drawn up in front of him. He drank from the water jar but didn't touch his hamburger. "They're studying on it," he said.

"Studying on what?"

"What they're going to do with us."

I unwrapped the paper from my hamburger and started to eat, but I couldn't swallow. "Mr. Wakefield set me up, didn't he?"

"His wife flew out late last night to visit her mother in Denver. He thought you were going to bring the girl out to the ranch. I heard him yelling at Tyler. He was mad as hell."

"About what?"

"He wanted his way with her. What do you think?"

I couldn't believe I'd been so dumb. I'd been on the drift since I was fifteen. You learn a lot of lessons if you're young and on the drift. If you're thumbing, you find out your first day that only blue-collar people and people of color will pick you up. A rich man never picks you up, and I mean *never*, unless he's drunk or on the make. That's just the way they are. I'd gone and forgotten the first human lesson I'd ever learned.

Suppertime came and went, but nobody brought us any more food or water; if we wanted a drink we had to dip it out of the toilet tank with the jar. The sun was a red ember inside a rain cloud when we heard somebody unlock the metal door and come down the steps, one booted foot at a time. I hoped it was Mr. Wakefield. I wanted to tell him what I thought of him, and expose him for the cheap Hollywood fraud he was. But that was not all I was thinking. I was drowning in all the memories that traveled with me everywhere I went. At age fifteen I was sent to Gatesville Training School for Boys. Nobody knows the kind of place Gatesville was. People would run from the stories I could tell. That's why even today there are nights I keep myself awake because I don't want to give my dreams power over me.

Our visitor was not Mr. Wakefield. It was the man in the Stetson; under the overhead light his hat darkened his face and seemed to give him a permanent scowl. He was dressed in an unpressed brown suit and was wearing a spur on one boot, and I could see tiny wisps of hair on the rowel. There was no sign of his gold badge.

"You," he said, pointing at Buddy. "Upstairs."

"What for?" Buddy said.

"Because you look like you have more than three brain cells."

"Anything I do includes R.B."

"Your window of opportunity is shrinking by the second, boy. Don't misjudge the gravity of your situation."

Buddy followed the man in the Stetson up the steps, trying not to flinch each time his weight came down inside his boot.

"What about Bernadine? What about *her*? Did y'all leave her out there on the river? What'd y'all do?" I said.

I got no answer. The man in the Stetson clicked off the light and the room dropped into darkness. An hour later the man in the filling station uniform came and took me upstairs and through the back door into an alley where a pickup truck was idling. Buddy was sitting in the bed, his shoulders hunched over, one eye still swollen shut. His guitar and duffel bag were next to him, and so was my old cardboard suitcase, a rope holding the broken latch together. Tyler was talking to the man in the Stetson by the side door of the building. Tyler was smoking a cigarette and listening and not saying anything, his face pointed down at the walkway. The man in the filling station uniform told me to get in the back of the truck. "Where we going?" I said.

"It's OK, R.B.," Buddy said.

"The heck it is. Where's Bernadine?" I said.

He didn't answer. Tyler dropped his cigarette on the walkway and stepped on it and approached the truck, looking right through Buddy and me.

"Buddy, you've got to tell me what's going on," I said.

"We're leaving town," he said. "If that doesn't suit you, go back to that damn ranch and see what happens."

I hadn't believed Buddy would ever speak to me like that. I thought someone else had stepped inside his skin. The Buddy I knew was never afraid. He had been with the First Marine Division at the Frozen Chosin; he'd never let a friend down and never let himself be undone by finks and ginks and company pinks. If you were his bud, he'd stay at your side, guns blazing, the decks awash, till the ship went down.

I climbed onto the truck bed and pulled up the tailgate and snapped it into place. "Is she hurt?" I said.

When he looked up at me, I knew they had busted him up inside, probably in the ribs and kidneys, maybe with a phone book or a rolled-up Sunday newspaper or a sock full of sand. "The guy in the Stetson?" I said.

"He's an amateur. They all are," Buddy said.

"Are you going to tell me what happened to Bernadine?"

"Use your imagination."

I tried to make him look into my face, but he wouldn't.

Tyler got in the passenger seat of the pickup and the man in the Stetson clanked the transmission into gear and drove us out to the train yards, both men silhouetting in the cab when lightning

45

leaped through the clouds. I suspected rain was swirling across the hills and mesas in the east, washing the sage clean and sweeping through the outcroppings of rock layered above the canyons, threading in rivulets down to streambeds that were braided with sand the color of cinnamon. But for me the land was stricken, the air stained with the stench of desiccated manure blowing out of the feeder lots and the offal and animal hair burning in the furnaces at the rendering plant.

Tyler and the man in the Stetson watched us while we threw our gear inside a boxcar and climbed in after it. "I'm sorry about this, boys," Tyler said.

"Like hell you are, old man," I said.

Buddy sat against the far wall, away from the door, staring into space with his eye that wasn't swollen shut.

"You made a deal with them?" I said.

"They've got an anti-sedition law in Wyoming," he said. "I'm not going to jail because I don't know when to get out of town."

"We're Judases," I said.

"Call it what you want. I'm not the one who went off with a girl in the boss man's car and brought a shitstorm down on our heads, plus—"

"Plus what?"

"Why do you think Clint Wakefield took his Caddy down to the river? He wanted to try out a colored girl without having any social complications. You gave him total power over both us and her, so you stop trying to rub my nose in it."

My face felt as though it had been stung by bumblebees. I couldn't wait for the boxcars to shake and jostle together and begin moving out of the yard, carrying us into the darkness of the countryside, away from the electrified ugliness of the cattle pens and loading chutes and rusty tanker cars and brick warehouses and

46

gravel and railroad ties streaked with feces that for me had come to define Sheridan, Wyoming.

We crossed into Montana and went through a long valley backdropped by sawtooth mountains that were purple against the dawn, and you could see the grass in the valley flattening as green as wheat in the wind. The wheels of the boxcar were clicking louder and louder as the locomotive gained speed, and I thought about Bernadine and her father and the story she had told me about the wind blowing through a field that was like a grass harp and I wondered if I would ever see her again.

The train followed the Yellowstone River and by midmorning we were climbing the Continental Divide, over six thousand feet high, the hillsides littered with giant broken chunks of yellow rock and spiked with ponderosa pine and Douglas fir trees, the wheels of the boxcar screeching and sparking on the rails as we slid down the west side of the Divide into Butte. We caught a hotshot straight into Missoula and thumbed a ride up to Flathead Lake, where you could make twelve to fifteen dollars a day picking cherries on a ladder in orchards that fanned up from the lake onto the hillsides and gave you a fine view of water so green and clear you could count the pebbles on the bottom.

I tried to forgive Buddy and forgive myself for what had happened in Wyoming, but unfortunately the conscience doesn't work like that. We'd bailed on Bernadine. But how could I make it right? If we went back there, Buddy could end up in prison as a syndicalist, a man who had the Silver Star and a Purple Heart. Then something hit me, the way it does sometimes when you least expect your thoughts to clear. Buddy and I were standing on ladders, deep inside the boughs of a cherry tree, the lake winking at us from down the slope, the sun spangling through the leaves, and I blinked once, then

47

once again, and realized I'd been taken over the hurdles. "How'd those guys know you were a union organizer?" I said.

"I guess they have their ways."

"No, they don't. They're dumb. The only one who knew was Tyler Keats. I didn't make Tyler for a fink."

"Search me. I'm done thinking about it," he said. His eyes were fixed on his work, his fingers picking the cherry stems clean of the branch, which was the only way cherries could go to market.

"They told you they were going to send you to the pen as a communist agitator, but you never asked where they got their information?" I said.

"I don't rightly recall, R.B. How about giving it a rest?"

"It wasn't you they were going to send up the road. It was me."

"What difference does it make? They were holding all the cards."

"Somebody called down to Texas and found out I'm an escapee."

He climbed back down his ladder, his canvas bucket brimming with cherries, his shoulders as wide and stiff as an ax handle. "Clint Wakefield raped Bernadine," he said. "They got us out of town so we couldn't give evidence against him. The real issue is Wakefield's reputation. The guy is a Western hero. He knows guys like us cain't send him to the pen, but we *could* smear his name, so he got us out of sight and out of mind."

"Where is she?"

"Probably at work. What is she going to do? Stop living? Quit fretting on what you cain't change."

"Why didn't you trust me enough to tell me the truth?"

"Because you're a hardhead. Because you would have stayed in Sheridan for no purpose and ended up in a joint like Huntsville Pen."

I stepped down from my ladder and followed him to the water can the labor contractor kept on the tailgate of his truck. The wind was cool in the sunshine, the lines of sweat drying on Buddy's face. He filled two paper cups with water from the can and handed one to me, his gaze never meeting mine. I could tell there was something he hadn't told me.

"Wakefield is right on the other side of the mountain, over on Swan Lake. He's got a cottage there," he said. "They're shooting a Western at the foot of Swan Peak."

"You're making this up," I said.

"Here's the rest of it. I talked to Bernadine. I mailed her some money for a bus ticket. She'll be here tomorrow. I thought you might like that."

I didn't know what to say to her when she got off the bus, and I didn't try. I think Bernadine was one of those people who didn't expect a lot from the world. It was Saturday and there was a dance and cookout up by the motel where a lot of the pickers stayed during cherry season. We drank wine out of fruit jars and ate potato salad and barbecue pork and pinto beans and homemade ice cream a church group brought. The moon came up big and yellow over the mountains and you could see fireflies lighting in the aspens and birch trees down by the water. Buddy got his old Stella twelve-string from the motel and sat in with the country band, and started playing one Woody Guthrie and Cisco Houston song after another. I guess I should have known what he was thinking about. Buddy came out of the coalfields of eastern Kentucky and would be a radical and labor agitator till somebody put pennies on his eyes. No matter what the circumstances, there was always a vinyl record playing in Buddy's head, over and over again, and the lyrics weren't written by Hank Williams or Lefty Frizzell.

About nine thirty, when the summer light at the top of the sky began to fade into the density and color of a bruise, I picked up Bernadine's hand under the picnic table and curled my fingers in hers. "I'm sorry for leaving you behind in Sheridan," I said.

"You couldn't have changed anything. Nobody there is going to stand up to Clint Wakefield."

In my mind I kept seeing the things he had probably done to her. But I couldn't bring myself to ask how bad she had been hurt, or how, or where, or if she was suffering now. "Did you talk to any cops?" I said.

"His lawyer called me a liar. When I left the sheriff's department, I looked back through the window and saw the deputies I'd talked to. Clint Wakefield was with them. The three of them were laughing."

"I'm going to make him pay for what he did."

She took her hand from mine. "Not on my account you won't."

"In Gatesville Training School I saw boys killed for a whole lot less. I know where there are unmarked graves. Things happened there that I don't ever talk about. If Clint Wakefield was a boy, he wouldn't last a week in Gatesville."

I saw the fatigue in her face, and realized I was making her relive not only the assault on her body but the theft of her soul. The air had turned cold and the candles burning in the jelly jars were flickering and about to go out. I took off my denim jacket and draped it over her shoulders. "We got you your own room at the motel," I said. "It's a dollar and a half a day, but it's right nice."

"What's that song Buddy's singing?"

"'Union Maid.'"

"Songs like that get people in trouble," she said.

"You bet they do."

"Why does he sing them?"

I shook my head as though I didn't know. But that wasn't the case. I *knew*. Buddy was going to spit in the soup for all of us. And he wasn't through with Clint Wakefield by a long shot.

A week later we had moved to the orchards higher up on the lake, close to Bigfork. The cherries were so red they were almost black, and our crew picked truckloads of them from first light until shadows covered the trees and made it hard to pick the cherry and the stem cleanly from the limb. Bernadine and Buddy and I worked as a team, and would talk to each other inside the leafy thickness of the tree, like kids playing on a summer day rather than adults working at a job. I couldn't help noticing that Bernadine paid a lot of attention when Buddy talked, even though the subject matter seemed to roam all over creation, from the Garden of Eden to Jesus and Joe Hill and ancient highways in Montana he said primitive people had used even before the Indians showed up.

"There're two or three roads under the lake," he said. "If you look carefully along the banks, you can see the worn places in the rocks where people rode over them with carts that had wooden wheels. They were probably going to the glaciers, right across the lake, where all those buttercups are."

"How do you know all this?" Bernadine asked.

"You trust what your eye tells you and then you have to believe in things you cain't see," he said.

"Believe what?" she said.

"That all these things happened and are still happening. We just cain't see them. Maybe those ancient people are still living out their lives all around us."

There was no question about the expression on Bernadine's face. She was looking at Buddy in a way she had never looked at me. I wanted to climb down my ladder and dump my bucket in one of

51

the boxes on the flatbed and keep walking all the way back to the motel, or maybe just head on up the road to British Columbia.

"You're kind of quiet, R.B.," he said.

"The conversation is obviously over my head. Excuse me. I got a crick in my neck," I said.

When I walked to the truck, the pair of them were buried from the waist up in the cherry tree, talking like they already knew what the other one was going to say, like they could talk on and on now that they didn't have to stop and explain themselves to a third party. I felt a spasm in my innards that made my eyes cross.

There was nothing unusual about Buddy organizing farm workers, but it was unusual for him to try it with the cherry pickers, particularly in the orchards along Flathead Lake in a remote area like northwestern Montana. The cherry harvest was a one-shot deal that offered at best only a few weeks' employment, and the people who did it were a strange mix—drifters like us, wetbacks, college kids, Romanian Gypsies, and white families from Oklahoma and Arkansas who weren't interested in politics or unions.

The most successful attempts at union organizing always took place within shouting distance of a metropolitan area. Union people organized in the San Joaquin Valley, but they operated out of San Francisco or sometimes Fresno or Bakersfield. The fort was never far away. Did you ever hear of anybody organizing cotton pickers in Mississippi? Why didn't they? There was no fort. The labor organizers' life expectancy would have been about five minutes.

Buddy started by distributing leaflets in a bar where a lot of the pickers hung out. The bartender told him to lose the leaflets or hit the bricks. "No problem. Give me a shot and a Grain Belt back, will you?" Buddy said. "Did you know Clint Wakefield was making a movie over on Swan Lake?"

The bartender didn't reply. He had cavernous eyes and the hands of a man who had pulled the green chain or boomed down fat ponderosa logs on a semi or dug postholes in twenty-below weather. His eyes seemed to smoke when he stared back into Buddy's face.

"It's a fact," Buddy said. "I know Mr. Wakefield personally. He's looking for a saloon to shoot a couple of scenes in."

"Wonder why he didn't mention it when he was in here," the bartender said. His eyes drifted to the front window. "That's him, across the street, signing autographs. Why don't you say hello?"

Buddy and I walked outside into the evening shadows and the coolness of the wind blowing off Flathead Lake. The mountains that loomed over the water had turned dark against the sun and looked edged with fire on the peaks. Clint Wakefield was standing by his 1946 woody, wearing a white Western-cut suit and hand-tooled boots and a black Vaquero hat that had small white balls hanging from the edges of the brim. I was glad Bernadine was down at the drugstore and in all probability had not seen him. I could only imagine what she would feel looking at the man who had raped her. My own feelings were such that I could barely deal with them. It was like looking at somebody you saw in your dreams but who disappeared at daylight and was not quite real. But here he was, flesh and blood, standing on the same street, breathing the same air we did, people gathering around him like flowers around a toadstool. His trousers were hitched up so you could see the thickness of his penis against his leg. He signed autographs with a grin at the corner of his mouth but glanced at his watch like he had to get on the road in the next few seconds. Even in the gloaming of the day, his eyes were blue orbs that had the brilliance of silk when they settled on a young girl's face. I had to clear my mouth and spit.

I began to see things that I thought I had left at Gatesville, things I believed were not a part of my life anymore and that were not me and that had been imposed by mistake on my boyhood. I saw myself walking into a concrete latrine in my skivvies, a shoe-polish brush handle outfitted with a sharpened nail file gripped tightly in my palm, the sound of a flushing toilet as loud as Niagara Falls.

"You got any ideas?" I said.

"I think I'll get in line," Buddy said. "I've never gotten the autograph of a famous person."

I couldn't move. I kept staring at Clint Wakefield, who was no more than thirty feet away from me, my pulse jumping in my throat like a crippled moth. I thought he recognized me, then realized he was squinting into the last rays of the sun and probably couldn't see past the glare. When it was Buddy's turn to get an autograph I stepped forward so Wakefield would see us both at the same time. I heard Buddy say, "Would you write 'To my pal Bobby James,' please, sir? Actually the full name is Bobby James Elgin of Pikeville, Kentucky."

The grin never left the corner of Wakefield's mouth when he wrote on the back of the leaflet Buddy had given him. He didn't speak when he handed it back to Buddy, either. Maybe his eyes lingered two seconds on Buddy and then on me, but that was it. Who or what we were and the damage he had done to us either didn't register on him or wasn't worth remembering.

I put my hands in my pockets and followed Buddy back across the street and stepped up on the high sidewalk in front of the saloon. Down the street I could see Bernadine coming out of the drugstore. "Let's get her out of here," Buddy said. "Did you hear me? Stop looking at Wakefield."

I wanted to say, *I aim to fix him proper.* I wanted to show people what it's like to carry a stone bruise in your soul. I wanted to give him a little piece of Gatesville, Texas.

I felt Buddy's fingers bite into my upper arm. "You get rid of those thoughts, R.B.," he said. "You're my bud, right? We don't let others take power away from us."

Bernadine was walking toward us, her dress swirling around her knees in the wind, proud of the new silver belt she had notched tight around her waist.

No, we just take away our best friend's girl, I thought.

"*What* did you say?" he asked.

"Not a dadburn thing," I replied.

That night Buddy did something that I thought was deeply weird, even for him. He sat down at the small table in our motel room and studied the inscription Wakefield had written on the back of his leaflet, then took out his wallet and removed the business card he had found tucked into the mirror above the lavatory in Wakefield's barn. He started writing on the back of the business card, then realized I was watching him. "You're standing in my light," he said.

Two days later we started seeing new pickers on the job. All of them were white and looked like hard cases; a Gypsy said they were from the stockade down in Sanders County, working off their sentences at a dollar and a half a day. That night we saw a new '53 Ford parked across the two-lane from our motel. Dried mud was splattered on the fenders and tags, and two guys in suits and fedoras were sitting in the front seat, smoking cigarettes. Buddy came away from the window and turned out the light.

"Goons?" I said.

"No, feds."

"How do you know?"

"County cops don't have vehicles like that. Climb out the back window and get Bernadine and stay gone for a while. I'll handle it."

"We'll handle it together."

"You're an interstate fugitive. Maybe these guys have already found your jacket. They can put you on a train to Huntsville."

I tried to hide my fear by clearing my throat, but I felt like somebody had just dipped his hand in my chest and squeezed my heart into a ball of red gelatin. "Well, what's stopping them, then?" I said. "Let them do whatever they damn want."

"Your thinking powers are questionable, R.B., but nobody can say you're not stand-up. Before those guys knock on the door, I want to know what's been eating you. I thought you'd be happy when Bernadine arrived."

"She likes you more than she likes me."

"That's not my perception."

"You see things out there in the world other people don't. So does she. Y'all are a natural fit. It's just kind of hard for me to accept that."

"I don't have any idea what you're talking about."

"She believes in stuff about primitive people eating flowers instead of killing animals and the wind singing in the grass and something called the Book of Ezra, whatever the hell that is."

"That sounds like you talking instead of her."

"I just repeat the kind of stuff you and other crazy people talk about. Mastodons and sea monsters and cave people throwing rocks at each other and such. You ought to listen to yourself. You put me in mind of somebody living in a comic book."

"Bernadine didn't tell me any of this, R.B. She told it to you. You sure she's right in the head?"

I didn't know what to say.

The knock on the door shook the wall.

The agent who entered the room didn't bother to remove his hat or give his name; he smiled instead, as though that was enough. He was so tall he had to stoop under the frame. He had long fingers and knobby wrists and small teeth and no color in his lips, unless you wanted to call gray a color. He opened the flap on a government ID and closed it quickly and returned it to his coat pocket.

"Could I see that again?" Buddy said.

"No," the agent said. "You must be Elgin."

"That's me," Buddy said. "Why's the other guy standing outside?"

"He's got a fresh-air fetish. He doesn't like places that smell like a locker room. You know what the McCarran Act is?"

"Something a senator down in Nevada put together to keep working people in their place?" Buddy said.

"No, more like a law that requires representatives of the Communist Party to register as such."

"Then I guess I'm not your huckleberry. Sorry you had to drive out here for nothing."

"Who are *you*?" the agent said to me.

"R.B. Ruger."

"Wait outside."

"This is my room."

"It *was* your room. It's mine now." He smiled again.

I sat down on the side of the bed. "If you don't mind, I think I'll stay."

The agent opened the bathroom door and looked inside, then looked in the closet.

"When did you start rousting guys like us?" Buddy asked.

"You're like a bad penny, Mr. Elgin. Your name keeps going across my desk. We don't have labor problems here. I think you'd like Seattle or Portland this time of year. Or even Salt Lake City. Or did something happen in Salt Lake City?"

"Yeah, Joe Hill got shot by a firing squad," I said.

I glanced through the front window. The other agent was gone. I could hear my blood start to pound in my ears.

"Is there a problem, Mr. Ruger?"

I stood up from the bed, my ears ringing, the backs of my legs shaking. I wasn't good at going up against guys who wore suits and badges. My words were clotting in my throat.

"You worried about your shine?" the agent said.

"What?" I said.

"You heard me."

I wanted to believe he had said something about a shoeshine girl, but I knew better. "She doesn't have anything to do with unionizing people," I said.

Buddy took his billfold from his back pocket and thumbed open the pouch where he kept his paper money. "Did you know we have friends in high places?" he said.

"Dwight Eisenhower, somebody like that?"

"No, better than that. A famous Hollywood actor. You don't believe me? He's one of us, not just up there on the screen but down here in the trenches." Buddy took Clint Wakefield's business card from his wallet and handed it to the agent. "Check it out. See what happens if you try to push Clint around."

The agent held the card in the flat of his hand and stared at the words written on the back. I leaned forward just long enough to read them, too:

Dear Buddy,

Keep up the good work. Call me if the feds come around. I'll have them transferred to Anchorage.

One big union,
Clint

"Keep it," Buddy said. "See if that's not his handwriting. He's over on Swan Lake. Go talk to him. Get in his face and see what happens, Mack."

"I might do that. By the way, we talked with your boss about you guys. You might get a cigar box to go with your guitar."

"We were looking for a job when we found this one," I said.

The agent laughed to himself as he left. I went down to Bernadine's room. When she opened the door, the side of her face was filled with creases from the pillow. "I'm sorry I woke you up," I said.

"I was having a bad dream," she said. "Land crabs were trying to tear us apart."

The neon vacancy sign in front of the motel lit up in orange letters. Maybe it was coincidence. Or maybe I was losing my mind. "I killed a kid when I was fifteen. It's haunted me all these years," I said.

I went inside her room and told her all of it: the boys who wrapped a horse blanket around my head and arms and dragged me into a stall and stuffed my shirt in my mouth and spread-eagled me face-down over a saddle; the staff member who gave them permission because I sassed him, and smoked a cigar outside while they did it; the boys who spit in my food and put chewing gum in my hair when I was asleep and shoved me down in the shower and called me "anybody's pork chop"; the ringleader nicknamed Frank the Blank because he had only one expression and it could make you wish you hadn't been born.

Frank's upper lip wedged into an inverted V when he smiled, exposing his teeth. His face was as white as a frog's belly and sprinkled with purple acne, his eyes like wide-set green marbles. When I found him in the concrete latrine, he was sitting on the commode, his jeans and Jockey underwear bunched around his ankles. He looked at what I was carrying in my right hand and couldn't have cared less. He stood up and tucked in his shirt and buckled his jeans. "Go into the shower and wait for me," he said.

I didn't know what he meant. That's how dumb I was. No, that's how scared I was.

"This is your big night. It's just you and me," he said. "You can fold one of those rubber mats under your knees."

Then I saw myself going outside of my skin, just like I had left half of me behind to be a spectator while another me attacked Frank and did things to him he thought would never happen. I saw the surprise and shock in his face when the first blow hit him; I saw the meanness go out of his eyes and I saw the helplessness in his mouth when he realized something had gone wrong in his voice box and that his cry for help had become a gurgling sound he couldn't stop. I broke off the shank inside him and pulled the cover off a shower drain and dropped it down the pipe.

I told Bernadine all these things while she sat on the side of her bed and trembled with her hands between her knees. "Don't say any more," she said.

"I'm not the guy you think I am," I said. "I feel ashamed because I left you behind in Sheridan. I feel ashamed of what I did in Gatesville."

"If you hadn't left, they would have killed you. Lie down next to me."

"I see Frank the Blank in my dreams sometimes. He still has that surprised look on his face, like he'd gone backward in time and was a little boy again and couldn't believe what was being done to him."

"You're a sweet boy, R.B. Now lie down and go to sleep," she said.

And that's what both of us did, side by side on top of the covers, while a rain shower swept across the lake and tinked on the windows and the cherry trees, and the orange vacancy sign blinked on and off inside the fog.

Buddy and I got fired from the orchards and went to work for a man who made log houses and shipped them as kits all over the country. I got a driver's license and we cut and hauled and planed trees north of Swan Lake, up in the timber and cattle country where he and I had always hoped to buy land and start up our own ranch. But Buddy wasn't going to let go of his vendetta against Clint Wakefield. He made telephone calls to two or three newspaper reporters who blew him off, then wrote a letter to a gossip columnist in Los Angeles and told her Wakefield was under investigation by the FBI for possible communist activity.

I thought he was spitting into the wind. What kind of credibility did a pair like us have?

One month later big piles of monkey shit hit the fan for Clint Wakefield. The gossip columnist used professional snoops to look into his past. One of his ex-girlfriends was on the Hollywood blacklist; another said Wakefield's mother was from Russia and had a picture of Joseph Stalin in her home. A male prostitute said Wakefield had invited him to the set of a Western movie in San Bernardino, on a Sunday, for private riding lessons.

The Polson chapter of the American Legion flushed a Labor Day speech he was supposed to make. A reporter at the local newspaper called up Wakefield's press agent and asked where he'd served during the war years. The press agent said Wakefield had been deferred as the sole supporter of his family but had dedicated himself to doing volunteer work with the USO. Not in the South Pacific or even in London. In Los Angeles.

On a Saturday afternoon in the last week of August, the boss paid us our salary and as an afterthought told us to deliver a truckload of fence posts and rails to a cherry grower on Flathead Lake. We picked up Bernadine at the motel and dropped off the fence materials and decided to take a ride down to Swan Lake and have dinner at a roadhouse where Bugsy Siegel and his girlfriend Virginia Hill used to hang out. The shadows of the ponderosas and fir trees were long across the two-lane highway, the lake glimmering like thousands of bronze razor blades in the sunset, the tips of Swan Peak at the south end of the lake white with fresh snow. It was a grand way to end the summer, with a case of longnecks on the floor of the truck, chopped-up chunks of ice jiggling between the bottles, and Buddy snapping off the caps with an opener he'd tied on a string around his neck.

Up ahead, on a slope where a group of asbestos cottages were nestled in a grove of beech-trees, we saw Wakefield's movie cast and film crew eating their dinner at picnic tables. There were Indians in feathered bonnets and buckskin clothes, and cowboys in costumes no cowboy would wear, and women dressed like cowgirls with ribbons in their hair, and platters of fried chicken and dark bottles of wine on the tables. They made me think of carnival people, in the best way; there was even something lovely about them, like they had created something out of a West that had never existed. I suspected they were at the end of filming and were having a party to celebrate. We saw no sign of Wakefield.

"Keep going," Bernadine said. She was sitting between us, a warm beer balanced on her knee.

Buddy drained his beer bottle and set it on the floor. "Pull over," he said. "I want to talk to these guys."

"Why borrow grief?" I said.

He opened the glove box and took out a sheaf of the same pamphlets that had gotten us fired from the orchards, and I knew Buddy was going to go up on that knoll and fix it so the whole house came down on all of us.

"If you're not up to it, bag it down the road, R.B.," he said. "I'm staying."

"It's a bad idea," I replied.

"One big union," he said.

After I slowed the truck to a stop, he got out and walked into the beech-trees, his body bent forward like he was leaning into a wind.

"I have to go with him," Bernadine said.

"I don't want to hear that."

"He's your friend."

"That's what I mean. My friendship with him keeps getting us in trouble."

"Then why do you stay with him?"

"Because he's the best guy I ever knew."

That was the history of my life: trapped one way or another. I got out of the truck and slammed the door. Then I went around to the other side of the cab and helped Bernadine down.

"Most of these are union workers, aren't they?" she said.

"Of course not. Film companies make movies in Canada or out in the sticks so they can use scab labor."

"I didn't know that."

"Am I the only sane person here?"

Like it or not, we followed Buddy into the trees. I had heard his speech before. The reactions were always the same: curiosity, amusement, sometimes a thumbs-up, and sometimes the kind of anger you don't want to mess with. People don't like to be told they're selling out their principles by going to work at the only job that's available to them. It's not like what you'd call a mild yoke to drop on somebody. You got screwed by the bosses when you tried to feed your family, then a nutcase shows up and tells you you're a traitor to the working class. That's not what Buddy said but I suspect that's what they heard.

"Ginks" is the name union organizers gave heavies back in those days. They came out of the shade like flies on pig flop. I saw Clint Wakefield emerge from a cottage and stand on the porch and watch it all, his hands on his hips, the shoulders of his white satin cowboy costume embroidered with stars on a field of dark blue. I knocked a guy down with a rock and almost tore his ear loose, but that didn't help us. They knocked me down and kicked me in the head and shoved Bernadine and me back onto the road and slapped me silly against the truck. They grabbed Buddy by his arms and stretched him across a picnic table and smashed the backs of his hands with wine bottles. They broke the windows in the truck and pushed me behind the steering wheel, then picked Bernadine up in the air and threw her in the passenger seat.

I could see Buddy struggling up the knoll, his T-shirt torn off his back. There was nothing I could do to help him. I got the truck started and into gear and gave it the gas, the frame lurching over some large rocks, the lake glittering with thousands of tiny metallic lights through the fractured windshield. There was spittle on Bernadine's face and in her hair. Her eyes had a darkness in them that was like water at the bottom of a stone well.

One mile down the road, the needle on the oil pressure gauge dropped to zero and smoke poured from under the hood and streamed through the fire wall into the cab. I had ripped out the oil pan on the rocks. We were both choking when we got out on the asphalt, our knees weak, the truck useless, all our means of escape taken from us. The sun had disappeared behind the mountain on the far side of the lake, and the wind was cold and cutting long lines across the water and smelled like fish roe, as though winter had descended unfairly upon us.

Then I saw Wakefield's 1946 woody come down an embankment, skidding through saplings onto the asphalt, almost going into Swan Lake. The woody fishtailed, the rear tires burning rubber on the road surface, and came straight at us. I thought Wakefield had gone on a kamikaze mission and was about to take us out in a head-on collision and a blaze of gasoline. I should have known better. Wakefield was a survivor, not a self-destructive avenger. The woody skidded to a stop and Buddy leaned out the window, a lopsided grin on his face. "I boosted his car. Grab a few beers and pile in," he said. "These guys are in a nasty mood."

Nasty mood?

We roared northward, toward the top of the lake, the Merc engine humming like a sewing machine, the twin Hollywood mufflers rumbling on the asphalt. The sky had turned dark by the time we crossed the bridge over the Swan River and reached the highway that bordered the eastern rim of Flathead Lake. We could have turned right and kept going to the Canadian border, but somehow I knew Buddy would choose otherwise. Maybe for some people the book is already written and a person becomes more a spectator in his life than a participant. I'm not qualified to say. But we'd signed on with Buddy Elgin and I figured however it played out, we'd be together one way or another.

The ginks blocked the road halfway down the lake. We turned off on a gravel lane and headed toward the water. "What the hell are you doing?" I said.

He stopped the car and cut the lights but left the engine running. I could see small waves sliding up on a beach at the end of the lane. "You guys jump out," he said. "Head back through the cherry trees and keep going north. They'll be chasing me."

"What are you doing, Buddy?"

"Watch."

"Don't leave us."

"You don't need me anymore. Take care of each other. Stomp ass and take names, R.B."

"Listen to him," Bernadine said, pulling on my arm.

And that's the way he left us, powering down the lane, full throttle, the woody in second gear, the windows up, the high beams back on. When he dipped into the water the woody went straight down the incline, the exhaust pipes bubbling, the sediment from the lake bottom rising in a gray-green cloud.

We moved off into the trees and continued to watch as the ginks ran to the water's edge and stared in disbelief at the headlights crossing the lake bottom. But what Bernadine and I saw next was not the same thing the ginks saw, or at least what they later claimed they saw. They said the woody never made it to the other side of the lake, that it was dredged out of the water the next morning by a wrecker, full of mud and weeds. They said Buddy had drowned and that his body was still at the bottom, probably near Wild Horse Island. I saw the woody come out on the far shore, the high beams still on, water spilling out of the exhaust pipes. Buddy had said there were ancient highways under the lake, and I knew that's how he had crossed over and that one day he'd show up just as sure as the sun comes over the mountain.

That's why Bernadine and I live way up here in Alberta, where the petals of golden poppies float on Lake Louise, and in the morning wild animals drift like specters out of the hills, steam rising off their backs, as though in a dream. Remember the story of Eliza? It doesn't matter if you don't. Sometimes from our porch you can turn into the wind and smell bread baking on stones and hear a whispering sound like God breathing deep down in a cave, and with luck see a rainbow, wet and shining, waiting for you to touch it.

BIG MIDNIGHT SPECIAL

You know how summertime is down South. It comes to you in the smell of watermelons and distant rain and the smell of cotton poison and schools of catfish that have gotten dammed up in a pond that's about to be drained. It comes to you in a lick of wet light on razor wire at sunup. You try to hold on to the coolness of the night, but by noon you'll be standing inside your own shadow, hoeing out long rows of soybeans, a gunbull on horseback gazing at you from behind his shades in the turnaround, his silhouette a black cutout against the sun.

At night, way down inside my sleep, I dream of a white horse running in a field under a sky full of thunderheads. The tattoos wrapped around my forearms like blue flags aren't there for ornamentation. That big white horse pounding across the field makes a sound just like a heart pumping, one that's about to burst.

In the camp, the cleanup details work till noon, then the rest of the weekend is free. The electric chair is in that flat-topped off-white building down by the river. It's called the Red Hat House because

69

during the 1930s troublemakers who were put on the levee gang and forced to wear stripes and straw hats painted red got thrown in there at night, most of them still stinking from a ten-hour day pushing wheelbarrows loaded with dirt and broken bricks double-time under a boiling sun. The boys who stacked their time on the Red Hat gang went out Christians—that is, if they went out at all, because a bunch of them are still under the levee.

The two iron sweatboxes set in concrete on Camp A were bulldozed out about ten years ago, around 1953. I knew a guy who spent twenty-two days inside one of them, standing up, in the middle of summer, his knees and tailbone jammed up against the sides whenever he collapsed. They say his body was molded to the box when the prison doctor made the hacks take him out.

Lead Belly was in Camp A. That's where prison legend says he busted that big Stella twelve-string over a guy's head. But I never believed that story. Not many people here understood Lead Belly, and some of them made up stories about him that would make him understandable, like them—predictable and uncomfortable with their secret knowledge about themselves when they looked in the mirror.

Wiley Boone walks out of the haze on the yard, his skin running with sweat, his shirt wadded up and hanging out of his back pocket, the weight sets and high fence and silvery rolls of razor wire at his back. He has a perfect body, hard all over, his chest flat-plated, his green pin-striped britches hanging so low they expose his pubic hair.

"You still trying to pick 'The Wild Side of Life'?" he asks.

"Working on it," I say.

"It's only taken you, what, ten goddamn years?"

"More like twelve," I say, smiling up at him from the steps to my "dorm," resting my big-belly J-50 across my thigh.

"Jody wants to match the two of us in the three-rounders up in the Block."

I lean sideways so I can see past Wiley at the group out by the weight sets. There's only one chair on the yard, and Jody Prejean is sitting in it, cleaning his nails with a toothpick, blowing the detritus off the tips of his fingers. Jody has the natural good looks of an attractive woman but should not be confused with one. I mean, he's no queer himself. Actually he has the lean face and deep-set dark eyes of a poet or a visionary or a man who can read your thoughts. Jody is a man for all seasons.

"Tell Jody I'm too old. Tell him I'm on my third jolt. Tell him I didn't come back here to take dives or beat up on tomato cans." I say all this with a smile on my face, squinting up at Wiley against the glare.

"You calling me a tomato can?"

"A bleeder is a bleeder. Don't take it personal. I had over fifty stitches put in my eyebrows. That's how come my eyes look like a Chinaman's."

"I'll do you a favor, Arlen. I'll tell Jody you'll be over to talk with him. I'll tell him you weren't a smart-ass. I'll tell him you appreciate somebody looking out for your interests."

I form an E chord at the top of the Gibson's neck and start back in on "The Wild Side of Life," running the opening notes up the treble strings.

When I look back up, Wiley is still standing there. There is a series of dates tattooed along each of his lats. No one knows what they represent. Wiley is doing back-to-back nickels for assault and battery and breaking and entering.

"Jimmy Heap cut the original song. Nobody knows that. Most people only know the Hank Thompson version," I say.

Wiley stares down at me, his hands opening and closing by his sides, unsure if he's being insulted again. "Version of what?"

"'The Wild Side of Life.'" *You moron,* I think, but I keep my silence. Saying my thoughts out loud is a disease I've got and no amount of grief or twelve-step meetings seems to cure it.

"Wiley?"

"What?" he says.

"Chugging pud for Jody will either put you on the stroll or in a grave at Point Lookout. Jody goes through his own crew like potato chips. Ask for lockup if you got to. Just get away from him."

"One of the colored boys ladling peas owes me a big favor. Don't be surprised if you get something extra in your food tonight," he says. He walks back to the weight sets, pulling his shirt loose from his back pocket, popping the dust and sweat off his back with it. There's already a swish to his hips, double nickels or not.

The boys with serious problems are called big stripes. They stay up in the Block, in twenty-three-hour lockdown, along with the snitches who are in there for their own protection. Jody Prejean doesn't qualify as a big stripe. He's intelligent and has the manners of a dapper businessman, the kind of guy who runs a beer distributorship or a vending machine company. His clothes are pressed by his favorite punk; another punk shampoos and clips his hair once a week. His cowboy boots get picked up at his bunk every night. Before sunup they're back under his bunk, their tips spit-shined into mirrors.

His two-deck bunk is in a board-plank alcove, down by the cage wire that separates us from the night screw who reads paperback Westerns at a table under a naked light bulb until sunup. On the wall above Jody's bunk is a hand-brocaded tapestry that reads: "Every knee to me shall bend."

I lean against Jody's doorjamb and look at nothing in particular. Jody is sitting on the edge of his bunk, playing chess with a stack of bread dough from Shreveport named Butterbean Simmons. Butterbean talks with a lisp and is always powdered with sunburn. He has spent most of his life in children's shelters and reformatories. When he was nineteen, his grandmother tried to whip him with a switch. Butterbean threw a refrigerator on top of her, then tossed her and the refrigerator down a staircase.

It takes Jody a long time to look up from his game. His dark hair is sun-bleached on the tips and wet-combed on his neck. His cheeks are slightly sunken, his skin as pale as a consumptive's. "Want something, Arlen?" he says.

How do you survive in jail? You don't show fear, but you don't ever pretend you're something you're not. "I do my own time, Jody. I don't spit in anybody's soup."

"Know what Arlen is talking about?" Jody asks Butterbean.

Butterbean grins good-naturedly, his eyes disappearing into slits. "I think so," he replies.

"So tell me," Jody says.

"I ain't sure," Butterbean says.

Jody laughs under his breath, his eyes on me, like only he and I are on the same intellectual plane. "Sit down. Here, next to me. Come on, I won't hurt you," he says. "You were a club fighter, Arlen. You'll add a lot of class to the card."

"No, thanks."

"I can sweeten the pot. A touch of China white, maybe. I can make it happen."

"I'm staying clean this time."

"We're all pulling for you on that. Where's your guitar?"

"In the cage."

"A Gibson, that's one of them good ones, isn't it?"

"Don't mess with me, Jody."

"Wouldn't dream of it. Your move, Butterbean," he says.

* * *

I butcher chickens and livestock with a colored half-trusty by the name of Hogman. He has bristles on his head instead of hair, and eyes like lumps of coal. They contain neither heat nor joy and have the lifeless quality of fuel that's been used up in a fire. His forearms are scrolled with scars like flattened gray worms from old knife beefs. He owns a mariachi twelve-string guitar and wraps banjo strings on the treble pegs because he says they give his music "shine." Some days he works in the kitchen and delivers rice and red beans and water cans to the crews in the fields. While we're chopping up meat on a big wood block that provides the only color inside the gloom where we work, he sings a song he wrote on the backs of his eyelids when he was still a young stiff and did three days in the sweatbox for sassing a hack:

My Bayou Caney woman run off wit' a downtown man,
    She left my heart in a paper bag at the bottom of our garbage can.
    But I ain't grieving 'cause she headed down the road,
    I just don't understand why she had to take my V-8 Ford.

"You're a jewel, Hogman," I say.

"Lot of womens tell me that," he replies. "Was you really at Guadalcanal?"

"Yeah, I was sixteen. I was at Iwo in '45."

"You got wounded in the war?"

"Not a scratch."

"Then how come you put junk in your arm?"

"It's medicine, no different than people going to a drugstore." I try to hold my eyes on his, but I can't do it. Like many lifers, Hogman

74

enjoys a strange kind of freedom; he's already lost everything he ever had, so no one has power over him. That means he doesn't have to be polite when somebody tries to jerk his crank and sell the kind of doodah that passes for philosophy in here.

"You was struck by lightning, though? That's how you got that white streak in your hair and the quiver in your voice."

"That's what my folks said. I don't remember much of it. I was playing baseball, with spikes on, and the grass was wet from the rain. Everything lit up, then I was on the ground and my spikes were blown off my feet, and my socks were smoking."

"Know what you are, Arlen? A purist. That's another word for 'hardhead.' You t'ink you can go your own way, wrap yourself in your own space, listen to your own riffs. Jody Prejean has got your name on the corkboard for the t'ree-rounders."

"Run that by me again?"

"Jody put your name up there on the fight card. You going against Wiley Boone. You cain't tell a man like Jody to kiss your ass and just walk away."

"Jody is a gasbag," I say, feeling the words clot in my windpipe.

"He'll break your thumbs. He'll get somebody to pour Drano down your t'roat. You can ax for segregation up in the Block, but he's got two guys over there can race by your cell and light you up. Jody can walk t'rew walls."

"So screw him," I say.

"See, that make you be a purist. Playing the same songs over and over again. You got your own church and you the only cat in it. The world ain't got no place for people like you, Arlen. Not even in here. Your kind is out yonder, under the levee, their mout's stopped with dirt."

Hogman slams his cleaver down on a slab of pig meat, cracking through bone and sinew, covering us both with a viscous pink mist.

*　*　*

For supper this evening we had rice and greens and fried fish. The warden's wife is a Christian woman and teaches Bible lessons up in the Block and oversees the kitchens throughout the prison farm. Sometimes through my window I see her walking on the levee with other women. Their dresses are like gossamer, and the shapes of their bodies are backlit against a red sun. The grass on the levee is deep green and ankle high, and the wind blowing off the Mississippi channels through it at sunset. The sky is piled with yellow and purple clouds, like great curds of smoke rising from a chemical fire. Far across the water are flooded gum and willow trees, bending in the wind, small waves capping against their trunks, marking the place where the world of free people begins. The ladies sometimes clasp hands and study the sunset. I suspect they're praying or performing a benediction of some kind. I wonder if in their innocence they ever think of the rib cages and skulls buried beneath their feet.

My J-50 Gibson has a mahogany back and sides and a spruce soundboard. The bass notes rumble through the soundboard like apples tumbling down a chute, and at the same time you can hear every touch of the plectrum on the treble strings. The older the J-50 gets, the deeper its resonance. Floyd Tillman signed my soundboard in a Beaumont beer joint. Brownie McGhee and Furry Lewis and Ike Turner signed it in Memphis. Texas Ruby and Curly Fox signed it at Cook's Hoedown in Houston. Leon McAuliffe signed it under the stars at an outdoor dance on the Indian reservation in the Winding Stair Mountains of East Oklahoma. My only problem is it takes me ten years minimum to get a piece down right. I started working on Hank Snow's "Movin' On" in 1950. Eleven years later I saw him play. Know how he created that special sound and rhythm that nobody can imitate? His rhythm guitarist used conventional tuning and stayed in C sharp. But Hank tuned his strings way down, then put a capo on the first fret and did all his runs in D sharp. Is that weird or what? What the rest of the band was playing in was beyond me. The point is Hank broke all the rules and, like the guy who wrote "The Wild Side of Life," created one of the greatest country songs ever written.

My bunk is military tuck, my snacks (or "scarf") and my cigarette papers and my can of Bugler tobacco and my cigarette-rolling machine and my magazines all squared away on my shelf. The big window fan at the end of the building keeps our dorm cool until morning. After a shower and supper and a change into clean state blues, I like to sit on my bunk and play my Gibson. Nobody bothers me, except maybe to ask for a particular song. If you're a "solid" con, nobody usually bothers your stuff. But a musical instrument in here can be a temptation. Just before lights go out at nine o'clock, I always give my Gibson to the night screw, who locks it in the cage with him, along with the soda pop and candy bars and potato chips and Fritos for the canteen.

Tonight is different.

"Cain't do it no more, Arlen," he says. He has a narrow face and sunbrowned arms that are pocked with cancerous skin tissue. One of his eyes is slightly lower than the other, which makes you think you're looking at separate people.

"That kind of jams me up, boss," I say.

"It ain't coincidence you're down on the 'bitch, boy. If you followed a few rules, maybe that wouldn't be the case."

"Don't do this to me, Cap."

"Don't degrade yourself. You're con-wise and a smart man, Arlen. Adjust, that's the key. You hearing me on this?"

"Yes, sir."

Jody got to you, you lying bastard, a voice inside me says.

"What'd you say?"

"Not a thing, boss," I reply, lowering my eyes, folding my arms across my chest.

"By the way, you're not working in the slaughterhouse no more. At bell count tomorrow morning, you're on the truck."

At sunrise I wrap my Gibson in a blanket, fold down the ends along the back and the soundboard, and tie twine around the nut, the base of the neck, and across the sound hole. I put my Gibson under my bunk and look at it for a long time, then go in for breakfast. We have grits, sausage, white bread, and black coffee, but it's hard for me to eat. Just before bell count on the yard, I look at my Gibson one more time. The morning is already hot, the wind down, clouds of gnats and mosquitoes rising from the willow trees along the river. Three US Army surplus trucks clang across a cattle guard and turn into the yard. In the distance I can see the mounted gunbulls in the corn and soybean and sweet potato fields waiting on our arrival, the water cans set in the shadows of the gum trees, the sun coming up hard, like a molten ball lifted with tongs from a furnace. Some of the gunbulls are actually trusty inmates. They have to serve the time of any guy who escapes while under their charge.

At noon I see Butterbean Simmons hoeing in the row next to me, eyeballing me sideways, his long-sleeve shirt buttoned at the wrists and throat, his armpits looped with sweat. "The money is on Wiley in the three-rounder," he says. "I'm betting on you, though. You'll rip him up."

The soil is loamy, cinnamon-colored, and smells of pesticide and night damp. "Tell Jody he touches my box, we take everything to a higher level," I reply, my hoe rising and falling in front of me, notching weeds out of the row.

"Man, I'm trying to be your friend."

My oldest enemy is my anger. It seems to have no origins and blooms in my chest and sends a rush of bile into my throat. "Lose the guise, Bean, and while you're at it, get the fuck away from me."

The night screw had said I went down on the 'bitch, as in "habitual," as in three jolts in the same state. When you carry the 'bitch with you into a parole hearing, there's a good chance you're not even going out max time; there's a good chance you're going to stack eternity in the inmate cemetery at Point Lookout. Why am I working on my third jolt? I'd like to say it's skag. But my dreams aren't just about white horses pounding across a field under a blue-black sky forked with lightning. My dreams tell me about the other people who live inside my skin, people who have done things that don't seem connected to the man I think I am.

By quitting time, I'm wired to the eyes. After we offload from the trucks, everyone bursts into the dorm, kicking off work shoes, stripping off their clothes, heading for the shower with towels and bars of soap. I head for my bunk.

My Gibson is still there, but not under it, on it, like a wrapped mummy stretched out on the sheet. I put it back under my bunk, undress, and go into the shower. Wiley Boone stands under one of the pipes, a stream of cold water dividing on his scalp, his body running with soap, braiding in a stream off his phallus.

"Who moved my box, Wiley?" I ask.

"Guys cleaning up? The count screw?" he replies. "Maybe it was an earthquake. Yeah, that's probably it."

"You're planning to lay down in the three-rounder, aren't you?"

"I'm gonna hand you your ass is what I'm gonna do," he says.

"Wrong. I'm going to hold you up. And while I'm holding you up, I'm going to cut you to pieces. Then I'm going to foul you. In the balls, so hard your eyes are going to pop out. So you're going to lose every way possible, Wiley. When you figure all that out, go tell it to Jody."

"You got swastika tats on your arms, Arlen. Hope nobody wants their ink back. You ever have to give your ink back? Thinking about it makes my pecker shrivel up."

The night screw said I was con-wise and smart. After trying to bluff Jody by going at him through Wiley, I had to conclude that the IQ standards in here were pretty low.

But I'd screwed up. When you're inside, you never let other people know what you're thinking. You don't argue, you don't contend, you don't let your body language show you're on to another guy's schemes. You wrap yourself in a tight ball and do your time. I'd been a club fighter. Our owner took us from town to town and told us when to stand up and when to lie down. That's how it works, no different than professional wrestling. I'd shot off my mouth to Wiley and tipped him to what I'd do if Jody tried to make me fight by stealing my guitar. That was dumb.

Just before lights-out, I go into Jody's alcove. He's wearing pajamas instead of skivvies, eating a bowl of blackberry pie and cream with a spoon.

"You won't have any trouble with me. I'll be on the card and I'll make it come out any way you want," I say. My eyes seem to go in and out of focus when I hear my words outside of myself.

"I'll give it some thought," Jody says. "A man disrespects me, he puts me in an embarrassing position, even guys I admire, guys such as yourself."

"Yeah?" I say.

"Wish you hadn't created this problem for us. You told Wiley I was gonna put him on the stroll? Why'd you do that, Arlen?"

"What do you want from me?"

He glances up at the tapestry on the wall, the one that says, "Every knee to me shall bend."

Tuesday the sun is a yellow flame inside the bright sheen of humidity that glistens on the fields and trees. The gunbulls try to find shade for themselves and their horses under the water oaks, but there is precious little of it when the sun climbs straight up in the sky. The air is breathless, and blowflies and gnats torment their horses' eyes and legs. A white guy nicknamed Toad because of the moles on his face collapses at the end of my row and lies in a heap between the soybean plants. It's the second time he has fallen out. A gunbull tells three colored guys to pick Toad up and lay him on a red-ant hill out in the gum trees. Toad is either a good actor or he's had sunstroke, because he lies there five minutes before the captain tells the colored guys to put him in the back of the truck.

I hear Butterbean thudding his hoe in the row next to me, his breath wheezing in his chest, sweat dripping off the end of his nose. He wears a straw hat with the brim slanted downward to create shade on his face and neck. "I didn't have nothing to do with it, Arlen," he says.

"With what?" I say.

"It."

Then I know the price I'm about to pay for going against Jody. In my mind's eye I see a trusty from the kitchen walking through the unlocked door of the night screw's cage, the dorm empty, his flat-soled copper-eyelet prison work shoes echoing down the two rows of bunk beds. I feel the sun boring through the top of my head, my ears filling with the sound of wind inside a conch shell, my mouth forming an unspoken word, like a wet bubble on my lips.

I feel the hoe handle slip from my palms, as though the force of gravity has suddenly become stronger than my hands. I hear the creak of leather behind me, a mounted hack straightening himself in the saddle, pushing himself up in the stirrups. "You gonna fall out on me, Arlen?" he says.

"No sir, boss."

"Then what the hell is wrong with you?"

"Got to go to the dorm."

"You sick?"

"Got to protect my box, boss."

"Pick up your tool, boy. Don't hurt yourself worse'n you already have."

When I drop off the back of the truck that evening, I watch everyone else rush inside for showers and supper. I walk up the wood steps into the building and cross through the night screw's cage, wiping the sweat and dirt off my chest with my balled-up shirt. The dorm is almost totally quiet, everybody's eyes sliding off my face as I walk toward my bunk. One guy coughs; a couple of other guys head for the showers, walking naked past me, their eyes averted, flip-flops slapping the floor.

I get down on one knee and pull my guitar from under my bunk. It's still wrapped in the blanket I tied around its neck and belly, but the twine sags and the lines and shape of the blanket are no longer taut. Inside, I can hear the rattle of wood. The contours of my Gibson now feel like the broken body of a child. I untie the twine from the nut and the bottom of the neck and the belly and peel back the folds of the blanket. The mahogany back and sides and the spruce soundboard have been splintered into kindling; the bridge has torn loose from the soundboard, and the strings are coiled up on themselves and look like a rat's nest. The neck is broken; the exposed wood, framed by the dark exterior finish, makes me think of bone that has turned yellow inside the earth.

I sit on the side of my bunk and take my Bugler tobacco can and my cigarette papers and my rolling machine off my shelf and start building a cigarette. No one in the dorm speaks. Gradually they file into the shower, some of them looking back at me, the night screw watching them, then shifting his eyes in my direction. "Better eat up, boy," he says.

"Give mine to the cat, boss," I reply.

"Say that again."

"Don't pay me no mind, Cap. I ain't no trouble," I say.

A few decks of Camels or Red Dots (Lucky Strikes) will buy you any kind of shank you want: a pie-wedge of tin or a long shard of window glass wired and taped tightly inside a chunk of broom handle; a toothbrush heated by a cigarette lighter and reshaped around a razor blade; a sharpened nail or the guts of a ballpoint pen mounted on a shoe-polish applicator. Cell house shakedowns probably don't discover a third of the inventory.

Molotov cocktails are a different matter. The ingredients are harder to get, and gasoline smells like gasoline, no matter where you hide it. But a guy up in the Block who works in the heavy equipment shed knows how to stash his product where his customer can find it and the hacks can't. It's a package deal and his product never fails: a Mason jar of gas, Tide detergent, and paraffin shaved into crumbs on a carrot grater. He even tapes a cotton ignition pad on the cap so all you have to do is wet it down, touch a flame to it, and heave it at your target. There's no way to get the detergent and the hot paraffin off the skin. I don't like to think about it. Ever hear the sound of somebody who's been caught inside a flamethrower? It's just like a mewing kitten's. They don't scream; they just mew inside the heat. You hear it for a long time in your sleep. You hear it sometimes when you're awake, too.

Jody comes to my bunk after supper. Some of his crew trail in after him, lighting smokes, staring around the dorm like they're not part of the conversation but lapping it up like dogs licking a blood spoor. "You're starting to get a little rank, Arlen. You're not gonna take a shower?" Jody says.

"I'll get to it directly. Maybe in the next few days," I reply.

"Some of the guys think you ought to do it now."

"I think you're probably right. Thanks for bringing it to my attention."

I stub out my cigarette in my butt can and blow the smoke straight out in front of me, not looking at him, the pieces of my destroyed Gibson folded next to me inside my blanket. I pull the corners of the blanket together and tie them in a knot, creating a large sack. I can hear the strings and the broken wood clatter together when I lift the sack and slide it under my bunk.

"My box is still with me, Jody," I say. "So is the music of all the people who signed their names on it. Busting it up doesn't change anything."

"You're as piss-poor at lying as you are at playing the guitar, Arlen."

"I was at Iwo," I say, grinning up at him.

"So what?" he says.

Truth is, I don't rightly know myself. I strip naked in front of Jody and his crew and watch them step back from my stink. Then I walk into the shower, turn on the cold water full blast, and lean my forehead against the cinder blocks, my eyes tightly shut.

* * *

Weasel Combs is a runner and jigger, or lookout man, for a guy up in the Block who takes grapevine orders and provides free home delivery. Our crew is working a soybean field up by the front of the farm, not far from the main gate and the adjacent compound where the free people live. At noon the flatbed truck from the kitchen arrives, and Hogman and Weasel drop off the bed onto the ground and uncap the stainless steel caldron that contains our red beans and rice. A dented water can full of Kool-Aid sits next to it. Weasel is an alcoholic check writer who always has a startled look on his face, like somebody just slammed a door on his head.

"How about an extra piece of corn bread, Arlen?" he says.

"I wouldn't mind," I say.

"I got that magazine you wanted. It's in the cab. I'll bring it to you when I get finished here." His eyes stare brightly into mine. His denim shirt is unbuttoned all the way down his chest. His ribs are stenciled against his skin, his waist so narrow his pants are falling off. A big square of salve-stained gauze is taped over an infected burn on his stomach.

"I could use some reading material. Thanks for bringing that, Weasel," I reply.

We eat in a grove of gum and persimmon trees, the sky growing black overhead. Down below the road that traverses the prison farm I can see the clapboard, tin-roofed houses of the free people inside the fence, clothes popping on the wash lines, a colored inmate breaking corn in a washtub for the wife of the head gunbull, kids playing on a swing set, no different than a back-of-town poor-white neighborhood anywhere in the South. The irony is that free people do almost the same kind of time we do, marked by the farm in ways they don't recognize in themselves.

The hack at the gate sits in a wicker-bottom chair inside a square of hot shade provided by the shack where he has a desk and a telephone. He's over seventy and has been riding herd on convicts since he was a teenager. Legend has it that during the 1930s he and his brother would get drunk on corn liquor in the middle of the afternoon, take a nap, then pick out a colored inmate and tell him to start running. People would hear a couple of shots inside the wind, and another sack of fertilizer would go into the levee. His teeth are gone and his skin is dotted with liver spots. There's not a town in Mississippi or Louisiana he can retire to, lest one of his old charges find him and do things to him no one does to an elderly man.

I can hear thunder in the south. The wind comes up and trowels great clouds of dust out of the fields, and I feel a solitary raindrop sting my face. Weasel squats down in front of me, his mouth twisted like a knife wound. A copy of *Sports Illustrated* is rolled in his palm. "There's a real interesting article here you ought to read," he says, peeling back the pages with his thumb. "'Bout boxing and all and some of the shitheads who have spoiled the game." He slips a beautifully fashioned wood-handled shank out of his bandage and folds the magazine pages around it. He lowers his voice. "It's hooked on the tip. You want to hear that punk squeal, put it into his guts three times, then bust it off inside. He'll drown in his own blood."

When the truck drives off, Hogman is looking at me from the back of the flatbed, his legs hanging in the dust, his eyes filled with a sad knowledge about the world that is of no value to him and that no one else cares to hear about.

The wind keeps gusting hard all afternoon, and lightning ripples through the thunderheads, sometimes making a creaking sound, like the sky cannot support its own weight. The air is cool and smells of fish roe and wet leaves and freshly plowed earth and swamp water so netted with algae it is seldom exposed to full light. The air smells of a tropical jungle on a Pacific island and a foxhole you chop from volcanic soil with an entrenching tool. It smells of the fecund darkness that lies under the grass and mushrooms that can bloom overnight on a freshly dug grave. Again I feel the gravitational pull of the earth under me, and I have no doubt the voices that whisper in the grass are whispering to me.

I sit on the front steps of our dorm and stare through the wire at the wide, rent-dented expanse of the Mississippi River. Inside the flooded gum trees on the far side, a bolt of lightning strikes the earth and quivers like a hot wire against the sky. I think about the day I was struck by lightning and how I awoke later and discovered there was a quiver in my voice, one that made me sound like a boy who was perpetually afraid. But my voice and my deeds did not go with one another. The Japanese learned that, and so did my adversaries in New Orleans, Birmingham, Miami, Houston, and Memphis, or wherever I carried the sickness that lives inside me.

"A hurricane is blowing up on the Texas coast. It may be headed right up the pike," the night screw says.

"Why didn't you protect my box, boss? It's not right what y'all did," I say, my arms propped on my knees, my face lowered.

"Your problem is with Jody Prejean, boy. You best not be trying to leave it on other people's doorsteps," he replies.

I raise my head and grin at him. "I'll never learn how to pick 'The Wild Side of Life.' It's not right, boss. It's got to be in the Constitution somewhere. A man has got a right to pick his guitar and play 'The Wild Side of Life.'"

His face clouds with his inability to understand what I'm saying, or whether I'm mocking him or myself. "Your problem is with

Jody. You hearing me? Now, you watch your goddamn mouth, boy," he says.

For sassing him I should be on my way to segregation. But I'm not. Then I realize how blind and foolish I have been.

That night, as the rain drums on the roof, I catch Jody in the latrine. He's wearing flip-flops and skivvies, his skin as pale as alabaster, his dark hair freshly clipped. "The hacks are setting you up," I say.

"Really?" he says, urinating into a toilet bowl without raising the seat, cupping his phallus with his entire palm.

"Wake up, Jody. They've made me the hitter."

"This is all gonna play out only one way, Arlen. You're gonna be my head bitch. You're gonna collect the stroll money and keep the books and be available if and when I need you. You're gonna be my all-purpose boy. I'll rent you out if I have a mind, or I'll keep you for my own. It will all depend on my mood."

As I watch him I think of the shank I got from Weasel, the piece of glazed ceramic honed on an emery wheel, dancing with light, the tip incised with a barb that will tear out flesh and veins when the blade is pulled from the wound. I want to plunge it into Jody's throat.

"Why you looking at me like that?" he says.

"Because you're stupid. Because you're a tool. Because you're too dumb to know you're a punch for the system."

He shakes off his penis and pushes at the handle on the toilet with his thumb. He wipes his thumb on his skivvies. "It's just a matter of time. Everybody gets down on his knees eventually. You didn't go to Sunday school?"

The rain quits at sunrise, at least long enough for us to get into the fields. Perhaps fifty of us are strung out in the soybeans, then the wind drops and the sky becomes sealed with a black lid from one horizon to the other. Seagulls are tormenting the air as though they have no place to land. In the distance, a tornado falls from a cloud like a giant spring and twists its way across the land. A bunch of trucks arrive, and the gunbulls herd us to the levee and we start offloading bags of sand and dropping them along the river's edge.

The river is swollen and yellow, and the willow trees along the banks make me think of a mermaid's green hair undulating inside a wave.

More guys are brought up from the Block, snitches and even big stripes from lockdown and malingerers from the infirmary, even Jody Prejean and his head punk, Wiley Boone, and Hogman and Weasel, anybody who can heft sixty-pound sacks and carry them up a forty-degree incline and stack them in a wall to stop the river from breaching the levee.

I think about all the dead guys buried in the levee, and I think about the hacks who set me up to kill Jody Prejean. I think about the Japs I potted with my M1 when I was sixteen, some of them just for kicks. I think about what I did to a dealer in the French Quarter who tried to sell me powdered milk when I was jonesing and couldn't stop shaking long enough to heat a spoon over a candle flame. I think about what happened to a Mexican in San Antonio who tried to jackroll me for my Gibson. I remember the look in the eyes of every person I have hurt or killed, and I want to scrub my soul clean of my misspent life and to rinse the blood of my victims from my dreams.

I want to pick "The Wild Side of Life" the way Jimmy Heap used to do it. I drop the sandbag I'm carrying onto the levee.

"Where you going, Arlen?" Butterbean says.

"Stay off those pork chops, Bean," I reply.

I walk down the levee into the shallows, my hands open to the sky. The wind is whipping through the willow trees, stripping leaves off the branches, scudding the river's surface into froth along the shoals. I feel small waves slide over my pants cuffs and the tops of my work boots.

"You lost your mind, boy?" a gunbull hollers.

I wade deeper into the river, its warmth rising through my clothes, raindrops striking my scalp and shoulders as hard as marbles. The surface of the river is dancing with yellow light, strings of Japanese hyacinths clinging to my hips, clouds of dark sediment swelling up around me. Far beyond the opposite shore, the thunderheads look like an ancient mountain piled against the sky. I hear the pop of a shotgun in the wind, and a cluster of double-aught buck flies past me and patterns on the water. The river is high on my chest now and my arms are straight out as I work my way deeper into the current, like a man balancing himself on a tightrope. A floating island of uprooted trees bounces off me, cracking something in my shoulder, turning me in a circle, so for just a moment I have to look back at the prison farm. All of the inmates are on their knees or crouched down in fear of what is happening around them. I see the night screw pull a shotgun from the hands of a gunbull on horseback and come hard down the levee, digging his boots into the sod.

Just as he fires, I smile at him and at the wide panorama of his fellow guards and their saddled horses and the convicts who seem to dot the levee like spectators at a ball game. In my mind's eye the twelve-gauge pumpkin ball flies from the muzzle of his gun as quickly as a bird and touches my forehead and freeze-frames the levee and the people on it and the flooded willows and the river chained with rain rings and the trees of lightning bursting across the sky.

One of my sleeves catches on the island of storm trash, and as I float southward with it, my eyelids stitched to my forehead, I think I see a mountain looming massive and scorched beyond the opposite shore, one I saw many years ago through a pair of binoculars when six of my fellow countrymen labored to plant an American flag on the peak.

DEPORTEES

People think the Dust Bowl ended with the 1930s. It didn't in Yoakum, Texas. I remember how cold and brittle and sharp the air was at eight in the morning six days after Pearl Harbor when my mother and I arrived at Grandfather's paintless, pitiful home, in our old coupe with the hand-crank windshield, but I remember even more the way the dust was piled as smooth as cinnamon against the smokehouse and barn and windmill tank, and how the sun was a dull silver disk and the sky an ink wash and the pecan trees bare and black like they'd been scorched in a fire.

The first thing Mother did when we entered the house was sit down at Grandfather's piano, which he had bought from a saloon in San Antonio, and play "Clair de Lune." She was a beautiful woman and had a regal manner, but she was also crazy and had undergone electroshock treatments and had been placed in the asylum in Wichita Falls. The edges of the wood grips on Grandfather's revolver were cut with nine notches he had tried to sand out of existence with a nail file. It worked about as well as the electroshock treatments did on my mother.

"How you doin', Buster Brown?" he said.

"That's not my name, Grandfather," I said.

"That's right, stand up for yourself, Aaron," he said. "But you ought to get you a little dog named Tige."

You didn't win with Grandfather. Even in old age he still stood six foot six. When he was a Texas Ranger he knocked John Wesley Hardin out of his saddle and kicked him in the face, and for good measure nailed chains on him in the bed of a wagon and threw him in the county jail and poured a slop bucket on his head.

He was sitting by the fireplace, his face warm and yellow as a candle in the light. "Y'all come to he'p me put up the Christmas tree?"

"Yes, sir."

He knew better. My father had disappeared again. My mother kept playing "Clair de Lune," an expression on her face like the shadows rain makes running down a window.

Grandfather got up and went into the kitchen and lifted a tin sheet of biscuits off the woodstove. The biscuits were brown and crusty and oozing with melting butter. The sky was dark, dirty with smoke, and I could see flashes in the clouds and hear the rumble of thunder that gave no rain. I thought I saw people rush past the barn, gripping their belongings against their chests, their clothes streaming in the wind, their faces pinched as though raindrops were stinging their skin, although I knew there was neither rain nor hail inside the wind, only dust.

"There's Mexicans running across the lot, Grandfather," I said.

"They're wets. Don't pay them no mind."

He smiled when he said it. But I knew he didn't mean anything mean or racial. In hard times you don't share your secrets and you sure don't borrow trouble.

"A woman was nursing a baby and running at the same time, Grandfather."

He scraped the biscuits into a galvanized bucket, then slid a sliced-up ham onto the biscuits and draped a checkered napkin over the top and hefted the bucket by the bail. "Let's go, Buster Brown."

We didn't need books to learn about the history of our state. It was always at the ends of our fingertips. It was even in the eyes of my crazy mother, who often seemed to take flight and travel back in time, for good or bad, mostly for bad. How about this? In 1914 an old woman outside Yoakum told my mother this story. When the old woman was a girl, two dozen mounted men with weapons tied to their saddles rode into the yard and asked if they could have breakfast. The girl and her parents started a fire under a Dutch oven and boiled coffee and cooked meat for the riders, all of whom spoke little. Their leader was a lantern-jawed man with soulful brown eyes and oiled, thick hair that hung on his cheeks. After a while he rested his knife and fork over his plate. "Why are you looking at us in such a peculiar way, little girl?" he asked.

"We don't often see people who wear animal hides instead of clothes," she replied.

"Back in Tennessee buckskin is considered right smart fashion. You and your folks have been mighty kind. One day you can tell your grandchildren you fixed breakfast for Davy Crockett and his Tennessee volunteers on their way to San Antonio de Béxar to give ole Santa Anna the fight of his life."

I loved my mother. She stuck up for poor whites and people of color, and was generous to a fault with the little money we had. But I avoided looking into her eyes and the memories from her own life that were buried there. The same with my father. He was an educated and genteel man from South Louisiana who went over the top five times in what he called the Great War. He was an extremely intelligent and perceptive man, and consequently doomed to a life of emotional and intellectual loneliness. Mother's depression and frigidity did not help, and I thought it no wonder my father's most loyal companions had become his beer at the icehouse and the whiskey he hid in the garage.

"What are you studying on?" Grandfather said.

"Why do you call the Mexicans wets?"

"Good question. You could walk across the Rio Grande on your hands. We're going outside. Find you a hat in the hall. That wind has no mercy."

He was right. It was dry and full of grit and as cold and mean and ugly as a witch's broom. We ran for the barn. There must have been eight or nine Mexicans sitting in the straw, and maybe more back in the darkness. The chickens were trying to hide in the loft. I don't think I ever saw people as hungry or lean. The baby I saw sucking at its mother's breast looked made of sticks and a hank of skin and hair. Grandfather passed out the ham and biscuits and went out to the windmill and unhitched the chain and used a clean syrup can to catch the water under the pipe that fed the stock tank.

When he returned, he passed the syrup can among the Mexicans and told them he would get them more water when the can was done. The wind was puffing under the roof, straining the tin roof against the beams and storm latches. From outside I could hear the sound of a car engine and metal rattling and bouncing. Grandfather put his eye to a crack in the door. He spoke without taking his eye from the crack. "Aaron," he said.

"Yes, sir?" I replied, aware of the change in his voice and the fact that he had used my Christian name.

"Keep these people inside. Don't open the door. Not for any reason."

"What's wrong, Grandfather?"

He slipped a shovel loose from a barrel of tools. "I try to avoid confrontations with white trash, but sometimes they don't give you no selection."

He pushed open the door and stepped out into the cold. I felt a solitary raindrop strike my eyeball, as bright and hard as a chip of glass. Then Grandfather shut the door. I squinted through the crack and saw him approach a Model T Ford in the middle of a dry streambed that led down to the river. A tall man as thin as a lizard stepped out on the ground, his tie lifting in the wind, his suit flattening against his body. He had a long, unshaved face and a tubular nose, shadowed by a John B. Stetson hat. He had to shout to be heard. "Fixing to take a shit in the woods, Mr. Holland?"

"I don't abide profanity on my property, Mr. Watts."

"I'm here out of respect. I'm also here to avoid trouble."

"I have no idea what you're talking about, Mr. Watts. I'm sure the failing is mine."

The man named Watts looked at Mother's car and at the dust on the running boards and the swaths of it on the windshield. The wind flapped his coat back, exposing the brass star on his belt and the holster and sidearm on his hip. "Miss Wynona is visiting?"

"What's the nature of your visit, Mr. Watts?"

"We think there's infiltrators coming up from the border."

"Infiltrators?"

"To be specific, Japs."

"The Japs are fixing to bomb Yoakum, Texas?" Grandfather said. "That's what you're saying?"

Mr. Watts's face made me think of soil erosion. His eyes were as flat and black as watermelon seeds under his hat brim. "I never spoke badly of you, Mr. Holland. I know what whiskey can do. There's a seat in our church anytime you want it."

"I know your preacher well. I saw him at a cross burning once. He was setting fire to the cross. I was writing down license numbers."

"Jesus didn't choose to be born a colored man. There wasn't any on the Ark, either."

"I got a theory on some of that," Grandfather said. "Know why God made certain kinds of white people?"

"No, and I'm not interested. I been sent out here by federal authorities."

"He was sending a message to the nigras about the superiority of white intelligence."

The wind gusted, rattling the blades on the windmill. Mr. Watts gazed at the barn door. "You calving early this year?"

"My cows were gone in '31. My grandson and I were gathering up some eggs."

"You wouldn't go upside my head with that shovel if I looked inside your barn, would you?"

"No, sir. But I'd file charges against you if you did it without a warrant."

"I see. Tell your daughter hello for me," Mr. Watts said. He turned his face so it caught the light. He winked, a grin at the corner of his mouth.

I saw Grandfather's right hand twitch, as though stung by a bee. "Come back here," he said.

Mr. Watts drove back down the streambed, the tires of his Model T rolling over fat white rocks that were webbed with algae and that crackled loudly when they were heavily pressed one against the other.

We fed the Mexicans and went back in the house. It had a second story and dormers, but it was a tinderbox and creaked with the wind and had bat and squirrel pellets all over the attic. At one time

Grandfather had owned five farms and ranches, one of them on the green waters of the Guadalupe River outside Victoria. But his love of cards and liquor and outlaw women created numerous graves that had no marker and children who had no father.

He never got religion, at least not in the ordinary sense. I also doubted if he dwelled long on the men he shot, since most of them were killers and not worth the dirt it took to bury them. The children he had abandoned were another matter. He could not ignore the despair in my mother's face when the afternoon sun began to slip below the horizon and evening shadows dropped like wild animals from the trees and crept across the yard in order to devour her heart. In those moments there was no way to shake the terror from her face.

She found a substitute for her father when she was seventeen, but no one was ever sure who it was. There were many soldiers in town, and also traveling salesmen. Some said her lover died in the Meuse-Argonne Offensive. Whoever he was, he disappeared from her life and she quit high school and went to Houston. Three months later she returned and picked cotton with the darkies, and later went to night school and learned shorthand. For the rest of her life the one subject she would never discuss was abortion and would leave a room if anyone alluded to it.

After Mr. Watts had gone and Grandfather and I came back into the house, Mother kept staring at the barn and the trail of white rocks in the gully that used to be a streambed. Her skin was still clear and youthful, her amber hair thick and full of lights, piled on her head like a 1920s woman would wear it. Her dress was paper-thin, printed with tiny red roses, and washed almost colorless. "What's going to become of the Mexicans?" she said.

"I know a man in Victoria who's hiring," Grandfather said. "He can pick them up tonight."

"There's an enormous hypocrisy about all this," she said.

"In what way?" he said.

"In good times we bring them in by the truckload. When there's drought, the Mexicans are the devil's creation."

He watched her eyes and the way they followed the streambed through the trees down to the river. "Was it Watts?"

She turned her glare upon him. "I have no dealings with Mr. Watts. I suggest you don't either."

"If it was him, Wynona, I need to know."

She sat down at the piano and began to play "Malagueña," by Ernesto Lecuona. She played and played and played, hitting the keys harder and harder, until Grandfather stuffed his fingers in his ears and walked out of the room. Then she stopped and stared at me. "Get your coat," she said.

"Where we going?"

"To town."

"To the matinee?" I said.

"We're going to buy some milk."

We walked past Grandfather in the kitchen. He was at the window, his back to us, framed in the gray light, his right hand opening and closing at his side, as though he were squeezing a rubber ball, the knuckles ridging.

Mother and I drove down a dirt road into the county seat and parked at a grocery store on a side street, next to an icehouse and a cinder block building where chickens were butchered. It was Saturday and both the grocery store and the icehouse were crowded. She pressed a nickel into my palm. "Go get you a Grapette, Aaron, but drink it in the car," she said.

"Yes, ma'am. Are we breaking the law?"

"Who told you such a thing?"

I picked at my hands. "It's the way we're acting."

I said "we" instead of "you." She kissed me on the head. "You're a good boy. Don't be speaking bad of yourself or me either."

I went inside the icehouse and pulled a Grapette from the cold box and paid at the counter. Through the side windows I could see the rear lot of the slaughterhouse and a sloping rivulet of feathers and chicken guts that had merged and congealed with the runoff from the ice maker.

The men around me were bundled up and drinking beer and smoking or chewing tobacco, their clothes sour with the odor that sweat makes when it's trapped inside wool. They were talking about the American sailors who had been drowned inside the *Arizona*, a subdued anger as thick as spit in their throats.

"What you doin' in here, little fellow?" said a voice behind me.

I looked up at the silhouette of Mr. Watts. "Drinking a Grapette," I said. "But I'm supposed to drink it in the car."

"Where's your mama at?"

"The grocery store," I said. "Across the street," I added, not knowing why.

"Getting y'all a mess of eats, is she?"

"Not really," I replied. "Grandfather gets by on the preserves he puts up in the fall."

"Bet she's buying milk. Right or wrong?"

I knew somehow he had bested me and caused me to give up a secret, but I wasn't sure how or what. He smiled down at me and stuck a long, thin cigar in his mouth, then took a kitchen match from his shirt pocket and scratched it on the butt of his revolver. He puffed on the cigar, his eyes hazy, and fitted his hand like a starfish on my head and worked his palm and fingers in my hair. "You don't like that? If so, just say. Don't be giving adults mean looks."

I went back across the street with my Grapette and climbed into my mother's car. I felt dirty all over. She came out of the store with a big grocery bag clutched against her chest. She set it on the seat between us. Inside it were three sweaty bottles of milk and two cartons of Cream of Wheat.

"What's wrong, Aaron?"

"Nothing."

She hadn't started the car. She twisted around and looked through the rear window. Mr. Watts was crossing the street, his Stetson slanted sideways, his cigar poked back in his jaw. "Did that man say something or do something to you?" she said.

"He put his hand on my head, like he was wiping it on me."

She looked straight ahead, her face tight. She started to turn the ignition, her hand shaking on the keys. The keys fell to the floor. She reached under the seat and pulled out a leather quirt. "Stay in the car."

She opened the door and stepped outside, her hair blowing, her profile cut out of tin.

"You haven't changed," Mr. Watts said, tipping his hat. "As fresh as the dew, no matter the season."

"You touched my son?"

"I don't know rightly what you mean by 'touched.'"

"Don't you put on airs with me," she said.

"I thought we were friends."

She slashed the quirt across his face and laid open his cheek.

"Lord, woman, you flat cut loose, don't you?" he said. He pressed the back of his wrist against the cut and looked at the smear of blood on his skin. "Warn me next time and I'll stay out of your way."

She began to thrash him, raining blows down on his head and shoulders, weeping at her own rage and impotence and shame while two men grabbed her by the arms and dragged her back on the sidewalk, easing the quirt out of her hand.

"It's all right, everybody," Mr. Watts said to the onlookers. "Miss Wynona is distraught. She didn't mean no harm."

People patted him on the back and shook his hand and told him what a kind and Christian man he was. I ran to my mother and hugged her around the waist, as though we were the only two people on earth.

The man from Victoria who was supposed to pick up the Mexicans never arrived. Mother fed the Mexicans and Grandfather cussed out the man from Victoria on the phone. "You're going to he'p the war effort by not hiring wets?" he said. "I got a better way for you to serve your country. Shoot yourself."

The sun went down and so did the glow of lights from town that sometimes reflected on the bottoms of the clouds. In the general store at the crossroads the radio with the tiny yellow dial broadcast stories about the Japanese dropping parachutes loaded with incendiary devices into our forests and grasslands. There were also reports of pamphlets that floated out of the sky and burst into flames when children picked them up. Street mobs were attacking Japanese businesses in Los Angeles.

Grandfather put on his canvas coat and tied on his wide-brimmed hat with a scarf and walked his fences with a lantern, out of fear not of the Japanese but of the evil potential of Mr. Watts, or maybe in bitter recognition that his era had passed and the injury he had done to his family could not be undone and the moral failure that characterized his life had poisoned everything he touched and saw.

That night I helped Mother and Grandfather in the barn with the Mexicans. She gave her greatest care to the woman breastfeeding her infant and held it in her arms while the mother used the outhouse. The Mexicans were a sad lot, their skin as gray as the fields, their faces like mud masks, their clothes and hair sprinkled with bits of hay that had turned yellow.

Back in the kitchen Grandfather told me the Mexicans had crossed the Rio Grande far south of us, then had been betrayed by an illegal contractor who was supposed to drive them to San Antonio.

"He took their money and left them with the clothes on their backs," he said.

"What's going to happen to them?" I asked.

"They'll get caught and sent back. The government calls them 'deportees.'"

"That little baby is mighty thin," I said.

"Your mother worries me."

"Sir?"

"I let her down," he said. "She blames herself for something that wasn't her fault."

"She never speaks bad of you, Grandfather. Not ever."

"Past is past. Wait here." He went into the living room and picked up a deep cardboard box from behind the couch and carried it back into the kitchen. I heard scraping sounds inside the cardboard.

"I got this from a lady friend of mine. Take a peek."

The pup could have walked right off a Buster Brown promotion in a shoe-store window—chunky as a fireplug, his brown eyes as round and big as quarters, his stub of a tail swishing against the box.

I picked him up and breathed his clean puppy smell and felt his tongue on my face. "He looks just like Tige."

"I declare, you and him make quite a pair."

Two weeks went by, then Wake Island fell and supposedly a Japanese submarine fired artillery shells into a California oil field. Some of the Mexicans went away on their own, single men who hopped a freight or women without children looking for work as cooks and cleaning maids. A half dozen stayed with us, including the woman with the infant. Her name was María; her child's was Jesús. Her husband had died of a snakebite in Coahuila, just before they crossed the river into Texas.

As we entered the new year, Grandfather incrementally gave jobs to the remaining Mexicans so their visibility would grow a little each day, until a passerby might think they had always been with us, patching the barn roof, washing clothes on the porch, burning tumbleweeds in the ditches, harrowing a field for the spring. I don't know what he paid them. I'm sure it wasn't much, if anything, for he had very little money. But the Mexicans didn't seem to mind. My mother bought baby clothes for Jesús and started teaching María English. Toward the end of January Mother received a postcard from my father. He said he was returning to Houston and hoped she and I would rejoin him in our little ivy-covered brick bungalow on Hawthorne Street.

"We're going home, aren't we, Mother?" I said.

"I suspect," she said. "Directly, anyway."

"What's 'directly' mean?"

"It means directly."

She twisted her fingers idly in my hair, her gaze just this side of madness.

Two days later we drove to town with Grandfather. He had never learned to drive a car and always looked upon a ride in one as a treat. We parked at the open market by the train depot and got out. I had forgotten my bad experience with Mr. Watts, as though it were a bad dream that fell apart in the daylight. A locomotive with a caboose and only two passenger cars on it had pulled into the station, the engine hissing steam. Mother was browsing through some open-air clothes racks and Grandfather was buying a piece of cactus candy from a booth when we saw Mr. Watts ten feet away, eating caramel corn from a paper sack while he watched us.

"Good morning," he said. He was wearing a black suit with a silver shirt and a vest and a string tie. "A friend of yours on the train would like to say hello."

"Tell him to get off the train and do it," Grandfather replied.

"Maybe him and some others don't want to draw attention."

The shades were drawn on all the passenger windows in the train. "They're celebrities?" Grandfather said.

"Maybe one of them was there when Bonnie Parker and Clyde Barrow got it," Mr. Watts said. "Know who that might be?"

"You're talking about Frank Hamer?"

"He didn't give his name. He just said he knowed you."

"Which car is he in?"

"The second behind the engine."

Grandfather took me by the hand and we walked past the caboose to the first passenger car. It was the dark green of an olive. "Let's see what's going on, Buster Brown." He swung me up on the steel steps.

The passenger seats had been removed from the car and replaced with benches, a pickle barrel, and a table that had smoked fish and several half-empty bottles of Hires root beer on it. There was a potbelly stove in one corner. Five men in suits and slouch or cowboy hats were sitting on the benches. Two of them wore mustaches. All of them were unshaved and looked like they had slept in their clothes. All of them were armed.

"One of you wanted to see me?" Grandfather said.

A tall man stood up. His mustache was jet-black and drooped to his collar. "I always wanted to meet you. I heard you slept with the girlfriend of the Sundance Kid." He grinned.

"You must have me mixed up with somebody else," Grandfather said. "Number two, I got my grandson with me."

"Excuse me," the man said.

"Y'all Pinkertons?" Grandfather said.

"Friends of the railroad."

"One of y'all saw Bonnie and Clyde get it?"

"I did," said the same man.

Grandfather studied his face. "No, you didn't," he said. "I know every man who was there."

"I got pictures. But I won't argue."

"What do you fellows want?"

"We think there's some Chinamen coming through here with the wetbacks. Except they're not Chinamen."

"They're Japs?" Grandfather said. My hand was still inside his. It felt hard and moist and callused and yet gentle.

"Would that surprise you?" the tall man said.

"Stay clear of me. That includes my family and workers."

"We don't call the shots. The railroad is going to be carrying a lot of soldiers through here."

"I understand that and I don't need to hear any more," Grandfather said. "You got my message."

"You really knew the Sundance Kid?"

"Yes, I did. He was a moron who breathed through his mouth a lot. Are y'all going to make trouble for me?"

"That's up to you, Mr. Holland."

"Son, you don't know what trouble is," Grandfather said.

One of the other men set his Hires root beer on the table. In the silence the sound made my face jerk.

I was too little to understand adult cruelty. Like most children, I thought adults possessed all the power they needed and hence had no reason to be cruel. So I was not equipped to comprehend the events that happened three days later, when Mr. Watts's Model T drove up the dry streambed, followed by a big khaki-colored truck with a canvas top on the back.

Mr. Watts and the man with the mustache got out by the barn. The truck made a circle into the field behind the windmill and herded three Mexican men toward the house. No, I didn't say that right. The men hung their heads and walked with the docility of animals going up a slaughter chute. María was squeezing out the wash with a hand-crank roller on the back porch, her baby in a bassinet made from an orange crate. Three of the men from the train car jumped off the back of the truck, rifles in their hands. Mother came out the screen door wearing a man's suit coat, her face disjointed, the way it got before one of her spells came on.

"What do you think you're doing?" she said.

"The Mexican woman and the child are illegals," a man with a chin beard said.

"You have no proof of that."

"We don't need it, lady."

"Don't you dare put your hand on her," Mother said. "Did you hear me?"

"Ma'am, don't mix in it or we'll have to take you too."

"That's what you think," she said.

"Step back, please," the man said.

"Hold on there, Ed," Mr. Watts called, walking toward us. "I'll handle this."

"You will handle nothing," Mother said.

"Get your father out here," Mr. Watts said.

"He's in town," she said. "If he was here, you'd be dead."

"Well, we'll have to do our job without him, won't we, Wynona?"

"You will not address me by my first name."

Mr. Watts turned to the other men. "Load them up, the female and the baby first. Search the barn and the loft. Look in the outhouse as well, and then in the main house."

"You don't have the authority to do this," Mother said.

"I'm head constable," Mr. Watts said. "These men are contract law officers working for the government. Now you stand aside or I'll arrest you myself."

"Like hell you will," she said.

Mr. Watts looked at the windmill spinning and the dust blowing out of the fields. His eyes were bright and small under the brim of his hat. He bit the corner of his lip. "Cuff her and keep her here till we're gone," he said.

And that's what they did, with her arms pulled behind her, her throat corded with veins. The child began crying in the orange crate, his little chest and fists shaking with the effort. Minutes later María looked back at us from under the canvas top on the truck, her body rocking with the movement of the bed, her face small and frightened inside the scarf tied on her head.

Mr. Watts started toward his Model T, then returned to the porch. "Stop yelling," he said to my mother. "Don't you tell lies to your father about me, either. Goddamn it, shut up! They're just deportees."

That night Mother sat in her room upstairs by herself while in the kitchen I told Grandfather what had happened. He was quiet a long time. The wind was up, the sky black, and through the window I could see sparks twisting from the ventilation pipe on the smokehouse.

"Did she strike Mr. Watts?" he said.

"No, sir."

"You're sure?"

"Yes, sir."

"Did they put their hands on Miss María?"

"One man held her while another man carried the crate to the truck."

"The man with the mustache from the train, the one who was talking about the Sundance Kid, what was his part in all this?"

"He told me he was sorry. He said to tell you that. He acted afraid."

"Ask your mother to come down here, please."

"What for, Grandfather?" I rarely questioned what Grandfather said. But this time I was truly scared. For all of us.

"I need her to drive me to town. You'll have to come with us. I don't want you here by yourself."

"What are we doing, Grandfather?"

"That's up to other people."

I got my mother from upstairs. Grandfather had already put on his canvas coat. His revolver and gun belt and holster were on the table, the belt wrapped around the holster, the leather loops stuffed with brass cartridges.

"Don't do this, Daddy," Mother said.

"He's the man who caused you all that pain, Wynona," Grandfather said. "Now he's doing it again."

"I do not think about him anymore," she said. "He has nothing to do with my life."

"Will you drive me to town? I can saddle Blue. But it's fixing to rain."

"It might rain in your prayers, but that's the only place you're going to see it," she said.

"Either he'p me or I'll get my slicker."

We climbed into the car and drove to town. I could see flickers of light on the horizon, like a string of firecrackers popping on the rim of the earth.

★   ★   ★

The saloon was a leftover from the nineteenth century, the ceiling plated with stamped tin, the bar outfitted with a brass foot rail and cuspidors. Not far away some of the pens that marked the exact inception spot of the Chisholm Trail were still standing. Mother parked at an angle to the elevated concrete sidewalk and cut the engine. The window of the saloon was gray with dust, a solitary bulb burning inside. Through the windshield I could see men tipping tin cups in a bucket of beer and playing poker dice at the bar.

"We'll wait here," Mother said.

Grandfather got out on the passenger side, his gun belt looped on his shoulder, the revolver hanging under his armpit. "I want Aaron to see this," he said.

"See what?" my mother asked.

"That our family doesn't tolerate abuse."

She half opened the driver's door and stood partially in the street and looked across the car roof at him. She wasn't wearing a coat, and her flesh was prickled with cold, her amber hair wild and beautiful. "I made my choices. Now, leave well enough alone, Daddy."

Grandfather looked down at me. "We do it our way, don't we, Buster Brown? Come along now and don't pay your mother no mind. She knows I'm right."

I put my hand in his and walked with him into the saloon. I thought I smelled rain. I was sure I did. The way it smells in the spring. Like a great gold-green world full of pure oxygen and mist and sunshine and new beginnings. The bell rang above the door. A half dozen men turned and stared at us. Mr. Watts shook the dice in a leather cup and slung them along the bar. "Wrong address, Mr. Holland," he said.

111

"What'd y'all do with María and her baby and the rest of my Mexicans?" Grandfather said.

"They're your property, are they?" Mr. Watts said.

Mother came inside and closed the door behind her, the bell tinkling again. The smell of rain went away and the air became close and laced with a masculine odor and a burnt stench from the woodstove. A man in a mackinaw bent over and spat a stream of tobacco juice in a cuspidor. Grandfather let go of my hand and approached Mr. Watts. "Say you're sorry."

"To who?" Mr. Watts said.

"My daughter."

"For what?"

"What you did."

"I have nothing to apologize for." Mr. Watts reached around for his tin cup and accidentally knocked it over. "Give me a towel over here," he said to the bartender.

"Forget the towel," Grandfather said. "Look at me."

"I will not do anything you say." Mr. Watts pointed his chin in the air, like a prideful child.

The man with the drooping jet-black mustache was three feet from Mr. Watts. "We ain't part of this, Captain Holland."

"Then stand aside," Grandfather said.

"You're not really gonna do this, are you?" said the man with the mustache. "You're a smarter man than that, right?"

Grandfather picked me up and put me in Mother's arms. "Go sit by the stove, Wynona."

"Please, Daddy," she said.

"Do as I ask."

She walked with me to the rear of the saloon and sat down in a rocking chair. She kept me on her lap, her arms folded across my chest. I could feel her heart beating against my back, her breath on my neck.

Mr. Watts was staring at Grandfather, his hands by his side, as though he didn't know where to put them. "This needs to stop. We're all white men here. We're all on the same side. There's a war on."

"Apologize and we'll be gone."

Mr. Watts looked sick. The contract lawmen around him moved slowly away from the bar.

"You cain't walk in here and shoot a constable," Mr. Watts said.

"Give me your word you'll bring María and her baby back to our house."

"They're already on their way to a processing station in Laredo," Mr. Watts said.

"Then you'd better go get them," Grandfather said.

Mr. Watts's bottom lip was trembling, as though he were about to cry. With time I would learn that his desperation was even greater than I'd thought. He had reached that moment of fear and humiliation when a man is willing to take whatever measure is necessary to avoid the shame and self-loathing that follows a public display of cowardice.

"You were a drunkard back then, Mr. Holland," he said. "Half the time you were in a blackout. That's why they took your badge. It wasn't me caused the problem with your daughter."

"What?"

"Ask her. I brought her home from the movies. A week later she told me what you did. You were drunk and you put the blocks to her."

He could hardly get the last sentence out. Grandfather shook his gun belt from his arm and curled his hand around the handle

113

of the revolver as the belt and cartridges struck the floor. He cocked the hammer.

"Tell him, Wynona," Mr. Watts said.

"He's lying, Daddy," she said.

"Bring a Bible out here," Mr. Watts said. "I'll put my hand on it."

"Is he telling the truth, Wynona?" Grandfather said.

"How many times were you so drunk you couldn't remember what planet you were on?" Mr. Watts said. "Down in Mexico in 1916. You didn't do that with Pancho Villa's señoritas?"

"You close your mouth, you vile man," Mother said.

Grandfather's eyes were pale blue, lidless, empty of feeling or thought, as though his soul had taken flight. I saw him swallow, then he eased down the hammer on the revolver and picked up his gun belt and replaced the revolver in its holster. "We're leaving now," he said. "Come on, Aaron."

"He's a liar, Daddy."

"I don't know what I did back then. I never will. I killed people in Mexico who have no faces. There's a whole year I cain't remember."

We went out the door and into the night. The wind was howling, the clouds huge and crawling with electricity. I sat in the front seat of the car with my mother. Grandfather was hunched in the back, like a caged animal, his eyes tunnels of sorrow.

Grandfather finalized our defeat that night when he went into the barn with a lantern and returned with a bottle that had a cork in it and no label. He carried the bottle into his bedroom and sat on the side of the bed and pulled the cork and tilted the bottle to his mouth. My mother took me upstairs and told me to put on my pajamas and lie down. Then she put Tige in bed with me and sat down beside me and looked into my face. "Pay no attention to what you saw or heard in the saloon, Aaron," she said. "Grandfather is a good man and would never intentionally do harm to his family."

"What was Mr. Watts saying?"

"Never listen to people like Mr. Watts. Their words are like locusts in the wind. I have to run an errand in town now. Don't worry if Grandfather gets drunk. He'll be all right in the morning."

"What kind of errand?"

"I know someone who might be able to help María and Jesús," she said. "He's a federal judge."

I looked at her eyes. They were clear. "It's too late to go to town," I said.

She stroked my hair, then clicked off the light and went down the stairs and out the front door. Through the window I could see the beams of her headlights bouncing on the fence posts and fields along our road.

I woke to sunlight and the sound of rain ticking on the dormers and people's voices downstairs. I got up and put on my blue jeans and went to the head of the stairs. I could see Grandfather talking to the sheriff and a deputy and a man in a suit with a stethoscope hanging from his neck. I did not see my mother. I walked down the stairs, Tige running in front of me, his nails clicking on the wood, his rump waddling on each step.

"We need to look at it, Hack," the sheriff said. "Hackberry" was Grandfather's first name.

"Big waste of time, if you ask me," Grandfather said.

"You know the position I'm in, Hack," the sheriff said. He wore a white beard and was almost as big as Grandfather. "Just bring it out here, will you?"

"Whatever you want," Grandfather said.

He went into the hallway and returned holding his holstered revolver, the belt wrapped around it. The sheriff took it from him and he slipped the revolver from the holster and half cocked the hammer, then opened the loading gate and rotated the cylinder. "Smells and looks like you just cleaned and oiled it."

"A couple of days ago, I did."

"When did you start loading with six rounds instead of leaving an empty chamber?"

"Since I stopped toting it," Grandfather said.

"I'll keep this for a while, if you don't mind."

"You're going to run ballistics on it?"

"I ain't got any ballistics to run. The rounds never slowed down and are probably halfway to San Antonio."

The sheriff shucked the rounds from the cylinder one by one and dropped them in his coat pocket and stuck the pistol back in the holster and handed it to his deputy. The only sound in the room was the creak of the wind.

"So we're done here?" Grandfather said.

"It was the way he went out that bothers me," the sheriff said.

"A bullet is a bullet," Grandfather said.

"Watts got one through the mouth and one that took off most of his penis," the sheriff said. "What kind of shooter is apt to do that, Hack?"

"I guess somebody who was a bad shot or pretty mad."

"Let me restate that," the sheriff said. "Which gender is inclined to do that?"

"It's a mystery to me," Grandfather said.

My mother walked from the kitchen into the hallway. "The coffee is ready if you gentlemen care to sit down," she said.

The sheriff looked at his deputy and the man with the stethoscope and at Grandfather. "I think that would be fine, Miss Wynona," he said. "Are you feeling okay today?"

"Why wouldn't I be?" she said.

"I know what you mean," the sheriff said.

In April of 1942 Jimmy Doolittle bombed Tokyo and crash-landed his B-25s on the Chinese mainland. In reprisal for the help given to his crews by Chinese peasants, the Japanese murdered 250 thousand civilians. María and Jesús were brought back to Grandfather's place, and Mother and Tige and I rejoined my father in our little brick home on Hawthorne Street in Houston. That summer, after the Battle of the Coral Sea, the war turned around at Midway, and we knew that in all probability the light of civilization had been saved. It was a grand time to be around. Anyone who says otherwise doesn't know what he's talking about.

THE ASSAULT

T he phone call to the professor's house came at one in the morning. An officer named Carter said the professor's daughter was involved in a "disturbance" and "behaving in a very unpleasant way." The officer was going to allow her to speak to her father in hopes the problem could be resolved.

"*Fuck* you!" the professor heard his daughter scream in the background.

"Is she injured?" the professor said.

"You'd better ask her that," Carter said.

The professor's name was Delbert Hatfield. He was in his study, the lights off. Through the window he could see the jagged peaks of the mountains surrounding the valley; the peaks were blue and streaked with snow and looked as sharp as broken razor blades in the moonlight. He heard his daughter sobbing, then the sound of the officer transferring the cell phone, the scraping sound of a callused hand, one that was perhaps too big to hold small things.

"What is it?" Delbert said. "Have you been in an accident?"

"I've been beaten and treated like trash! I don't have a coat! This motherfucker wouldn't let me sit in his car!"

"Don't use that language, particularly now. Who beat you?"

"A man and a woman. The man held me."

"Let me talk to Officer Carter again."

The professor heard the officer take back the cell phone. This time the officer's voice was clear, unstrained, as though emotionally he had moved on. "I didn't want her to get sick in my car," the officer said. "She left that out of the story."

"Can you drive her home?"

"We don't do that. I can get her a cab."

"What's this about a beating?"

"She says two people waylaid her."

"Where are they?"

"Fled the scene."

"Did anyone get a license number?"

"This is the Sundowner. Not a cop-friendly crowd. Your daughter turned down an ambulance. She's heavily intoxicated and verbally abusive. Unless you want to file a complaint, we're pretty much done on this, Professor."

As an academic Delbert had long ago learned the connotations of his title when used by certain kinds of men. "Is there a security camera there?"

The line went dead. Twenty minutes later a cab dropped his daughter in front of his house. She vomited on the grass, then fell on the living room rug and curled into a ball.

He drove her to the ER in a hospital located next to what had once been a US Army fort where African American bicycle troops were stationed to control the Native Americans who had not been rounded up with Chief Joseph and the Nez Perce. The old water tower still stood high above the river, stenciled against the sky, perhaps as a reminder. But of what, Delbert wondered. An admissions clerk at the hospital asked him about the source of his daughter's injury. "An assault outside a nightclub," Delbert said.

"We have to notify the police."

"They already know," Delbert said.

"We've got to do it anyway," the clerk replied. He smiled, as though offering an apology.

The responding officers, both in uniform, turned out to be Carter and his partner, a young Hispanic woman whose name Delbert didn't catch, primarily because her identity seemed lost in the shadow of her male companion. Carter was heavyset, his shirt too tight, his dark eyes shiny, as though he had a fever, his eyebrows a thick line. He shook his head as soon as he saw who was in the room. "I knew this one was gonna come back around."

"I didn't quite track that," Delbert said.

Carter scratched at his eye with one finger. "I have a way of stepping in bubble gum when I'm about to go on vacation," Carter said. "Happens every time. Not your fault."

"My daughter has a bump the size of a softball on the back of her head," Delbert said. "I think by anyone's measure this is felony assault."

"Professor, this doesn't come close to felony assault. That's a term you never want used in reference to your daughter."

"Then what do you call it? She has bruises on her upper arms where the man held her while the woman beat her. I took some pictures you can have."

"What about them?"

"Sorry? You're asking me?" Delbert said.

"What I'm trying to say is count your blessings. I'm gonna write this up and get everything processed before I go on vacation. I'll do this on my own time if I have to."

Delbert kept his face empty, his gaze parked in neutral space. "My daughter said she gave you the license number of the car the assailants fled in."

"Yeah, she was screaming her head off. Maybe I got a couple of the numbers. Maybe we can do something with them. But I think we're skipping over the real problem here."

Delbert waited. The Hispanic patrolwoman was looking askance, her mouth pursed.

"Your daughter is seventeen," Carter continued. "She was mixing up people's coats in the coatroom and thought it was funny. You know the kind of people who drink in that place?"

"I asked you earlier about security cameras outside the bar."

"Yes?"

"Will you pull the tapes?"

Carter looked at his partner and coughed into his hand. "You know what's on those tapes? A lot of parked cars and the tops of people's heads."

"Reviewing the surveillance footage is not worth your time?" Delbert said.

"You want it straight up, Professor? I mean straight up?"

"Yes, I do."

"This will probably end up a 'he said, she said.' That might be unfair, but that's the reality."

Delbert looked at his daughter and felt old and used up. She stank of cigarettes and booze and weed. Her mouth was bruised, her eyes closed, the lids purple, her hair thick and bright red on the pillow. Her left hand twitched on top of the sheet. He wondered if she was having a nightmare. He wondered if her brain was bleeding.

"Professor?" Carter said.

"What?"

"You want to ask us any other questions before we go?"

Delbert stared into his face. *I believe you're full of it, bub*, he thought. But the life he had lived, and the places he had been, and the evil he had witnessed in his fellow man had taught him to never let an adversary know what you are thinking. So he said nothing, not even when Carter said good night and walked out of the room looking secretly at his partner with gloat in his eyes. She in turn grinned at the corner of her mouth.

Delbert had been in the history department at the university only two years, but everyone knew that tenure would not be a problem. His students loved him and called him by his first name. His narrow face and rosy cheeks and thinning bronze-colored hair and laconic speech and genteel manners and lack of affectation, except for a modest goatee, seemed the academic embodiment of the man for all seasons.

He grew up in Sandy Hook, Kentucky, and still had a twang in his accent. But that was all that anybody really knew about him. He was a widower and was devoted to his daughter, Jennifer; he didn't violate boundaries or involve himself in departmental politics. Plus, he was abstemious, an enormous asset in a political environment. When asked why he did not drink, he would reply, his eyes crinkling, "Because I used to."

Nine weeks from the day of the assault, Delbert accompanied his daughter for an interview with a detective in a small cubicle at the city police station. Actually, "detective" was the wrong word. The interviewer was about twenty-five and still in uniform and had not been formally promoted in grade. He appeared to be of goodwill. As soon as he started the interview, Jennifer interrupted. "I want to be forthcoming and get ahead of something here," she said.

"Please," the interviewer said.

"I have a DUI. The Breathalyzer was borderline, though. The waiter put too much wine in my glass."

123

The interviewer's head seemed to bounce like a white balloon on a string, his eyes as readable as Life Savers. He showed her a photo lineup of six female offenders, their mug shots snugged into a cardboard holder.

"That one," Jennifer said, pointing at the broad, heated face of a blond woman in her late twenties.

"You're sure?" the interviewer said.

"She had big hands. She knew how to hit really hard."

"So you're sure?"

"Yeah. That's what I said."

The interviewer nodded. He gave Jennifer a second photo lineup, this one composed of male offenders. She tapped the photo of an unshaved man who was handsome in a rough way, his dark hair combed, his arms wrapped with one-colored tats.

"No question about it?" the interviewer said.

This time it was Delbert who interrupted. "What have these people been in for?"

"Sorry, we can't give out that information."

The interviewer had slipped. From the past, Delbert knew protocol is hung on a stick in a crime victim's face for only one reason: the investigation is going nowhere. Delbert rubbed the back of his left hand with his fingertips. "I don't suspect you can give us their names?"

"It doesn't work that way," the interviewer said.

"What you mean is it doesn't work," Delbert said.

"Pardon?"

Delbert didn't reply. He stepped out into the hallway and waited for Jennifer to follow him. She rose from her chair, her face confused. "Will you call us?" she said to the interviewer.

"I have to be gone a few days. We have a death in the family."

"I'm sorry," she said. "Will somebody else call us?"

"After we reach the parties of interest."

"It's been nine weeks," she said.

"I know. It can be frustrating," the officer replied.

Delbert went outside and stood on the courthouse lawn, the grass emerald green under his feet, the day golden, his temples pounding, marathon runners stringing through the streets, their skin sunbrowned and dry in the coolness of the morning, a brass band on a truck filling the sky with music. He tried to hide his fists in his armpits.

The weeks passed with no phone call from the police. Jennifer's first seizure was in the category of petit mal; the second one landed her at the bottom of the staircase in the middle of the night.

She was easily distracted by loud noises, sudden movements by others, and words she didn't understand. The neurologist believed her brain injury would eventually heal. She began seeing a therapist once a week. She also stopped showering and washing her hair. Her level of irritability was like touching a woodstove in December.

Delbert took her to the Fourth of July powwow and rodeo on the Flathead Indian Reservation, an event she had always loved. The snow on the peaks of the Mission Mountains was a blinding white in the sunlight, the slopes like green velvet, the Snake Dancers jingling with bells, their beaded robes and feathered bonnets vibrating and rippling with color, the drums pounding. But she seemed to see and hear none of it.

"Why do they let the children terrify the chickens?" she said.

He looked around him. They were sitting in the dance pavilion, the wind cool in the shade. The rodeo arena was out in the sunshine, a hundred yards away. The first event had just begun. "What did you say?" he asked.

"The children scrambling like animals after the chickens. It's sickening."

He looked at the chickens rising from the cloud of dust over the arena. "They don't mean any harm, Jen."

"Right," she said. "I have to pee."

She got up and went to the women's restroom, then returned to the pavilion and sat down again, her face blotched and as taut as the skin on a pumpkin.

"What's wrong?" he said.

"Nothing."

"Come on, kiddo. It can't be that bad."

"It's her."

"Who?" he said. But with a sinking heart he already knew the answer.

"She came out of the stall and almost knocked me down."

He stood up from the wood plank they were sitting on. "Show me."

"No."

"I just want to speak to her."

"I don't want to ever see her again."

"At some point we have to," he said. "Come on, Jen. Get up."

"The guy is with her. She was saying something to him while she pointed at me, like I was a geek or something."

He put his hand under her arm. "We're not going to argue about this. We face our problems, Jennifer."

"It always has to be your way."

"What are you talking about?" he said disingenuously.

"Nothing changes. You were the same way with Mom. It's about you."

He felt as if he had swallowed a carpet tack. Somewhere behind his eyelids he saw a two-lane bridge and a broken railing above a black-water bayou. A car was submerged among the tupelo trees and lily pads, the high beams still on, yellow cones of light and silt tunneling beneath the surface.

"Just point them out," he said. "I've got a right to address them."

Her eyes were wet, her bottom lip trembling. "I'm ashamed."

"Of what?"

"Of what I am. I'm a coward."

He put his arm around her shoulders and walked with her to the edge of the pavilion. "You've repressed your anger and chosen the high road," he said. "But it makes you feel strange inside. That's not shame or fear. That's courage. Now, point."

She wiped her eyes with the back of her wrist and raised her index finger. "There," she said.

The couple was in front of a T-shirt stand. The woman was fitting a shirt on her chest, flattening out the wrinkles with her palm, waiting for her companion's approval. Emblazoned on the cloth were an alpine scene and the words LOVE IT OR GIVE IT BACK!

The sun was in the west and at Delbert's back so the couple had to look into the glare as he approached them. He didn't speak. Nor did he blink.

The man shielded his eyes, trying to smile, as though an old acquaintance were about to greet him.

"Got a minute?" Delbert said.

The man was still trying to smile. "Me?"

"The city attorney's office called two days ago and said the charges against y'all aren't prosecutable," Delbert said. "So that puts us in a different category now."

"Charges?"

"You're Wendell Cody, aren't you?"

"Don't talk to him," the woman said.

"You must be Miss Jessie," Delbert said. "Jessie Wilcox."

The woman dropped the T-shirt back on a pile of other shirts. Her hair was twisted as thick and tight as a rope behind her head. She had the neck and hard body of a weightlifter. Her eyes were light blue, her face as tough as pigskin, the kind that could eat pain with a tablespoon.

"We haven't bothered you," she said. "Now leave us alone."

Delbert blew out his breath and looked at the mountains and at the long blue-green roll of the slopes dropping away in the distance. "That's my daughter by the pavilion. Can y'all tell her you're sorry about the incident at the nightclub? No statement about who started what. Just one expression of goodwill."

"*We're* sorry?" Jessie said. "Your little bitch wadded up my coat and hid it under a table in freezing weather. When I confronted her, she scratched my face. Then she lied to the cops and made us the villains, and now she seems to be making a jerk out of you, or maybe you were born that way."

"She never struck a human being or an animal in her life."

Jessie lit a cigarette with a Zippo and took a puff off it, widening her eyes, blowing out the smoke. "Right. You know what this is really about? Your daughter thought she could play pranks with our coats because she lives in the university district and we live in a trailer court."

"She has permanent brain damage," Delbert said. "Doesn't that mean anything to you?"

"If she does, we didn't do it to her," she said. She handed her cigarette to Wendell and leaned down into the shade by the side of the display table, her jeans stretching across her wide rump, her stomach sagging. She lifted up an infant in a baby carrier. "Come on, honey, let's go home and get you fed," she said to the child.

"You said 'we didn't do it to her.'"

"What are you talking about?" she said.

"My daughter had bruises on her arms where Wendell held her while you beat her. I photographed them. You just admitted her account was true."

There was a beat. She had put her foot in it. But she was undeterred. "In case you didn't get the signal the first time, take your crap back to the cops," she said. "Your little twerp got in a cop's face and fucked herself. We win, you lose. You don't like it, bite."

Delbert looked at Wendell. "Where'd you stack time, partner?"

"Who says I did?"

"I know what it's like to have a sheet," Delbert said. "It makes you feel dirty. I was on the hard road when I was eighteen. Down South. Hit-it-and-git-it, roll-motherfucker-roll, from cain't-see to cain't-see. I wouldn't put you on the glide, Clyde."

Then he walked away, slightly off-balance, the mountains tilting, his ears ringing, unsure where the sound came from.

Early Monday he walked to the summer class that allowed him to get through the year without borrowing from the credit union. In these moments the freshness of the morning had always been a gift, as had the robins in the trees and the sprinklers on the sidewalks and the clover on the lawns where deer grazed without hindrance from the homeowners. The university and the town had been a harbor for him. Yes, there had been scandal—athletes charged with rape, a cover-up by the administration, a blind eye by city officials—but he tried to push the imperfections of his fellow man from his mind and concentrate on the good in the world. Sometimes that was not easy, on this morning in particular. The encounter with the couple at the powwow had become William Blake's canker inside the rose.

He had a hard time concentrating during his class, and afterward he sat alone in his office on the third floor of the Liberal Arts

Building and tried to remember what he had said or not said to his students. His window and door were open, the view grand, the breeze cool, the top of a maple tree rustling against the windowsill. Regardless, he felt a pall descending upon the day, the kind of depression that had no known origins and had devoured his heart as a boy and caused him to run away from home and later had contributed to the night his wife drowned inside her automobile.

Or was he once again seeking excuses for his failure as a husband and father?

His hands were squeezed on his knees, his head lowered, when someone tapped on the doorjamb. He looked up in embarrassment. A tall black woman was standing in the frame.

"Oh, hello," he said.

She was new, from Mississippi, and taught minority studies, but he knew little else about her. She wore a white skirt and a lavender blouse, and had very dark, smooth skin. "You OK?" she said.

"I was daydreaming."

"I never introduced myself. I'm Tina Bordelon."

"How you doin', Miss Tina?"

"You just get off the plantation?"

"Just a habit."

"Can I close the door?" she said.

"Sure."

She pushed it shut with her rump, her eyes on his as the latch bolt snapped into the latch plate. "I was at the powwow Saturday," she said. "I overheard your exchange with those people by the T-shirt booth."

His face felt small and tight. "I have days when I should take a vow of silence."

"Your daughter has a brain injury?"

"Long story."

"Both those people live in my trailer court. That's why I felt I should say something. Watch your back."

"You don't have to tell me."

"Is your daughter going to be all right?"

"Probably not."

"I'm sorry."

"Your last name is Bordelon?" he said. "That's a Cajun name." He tried to smile.

"My father was from Louisiana. You're from there?"

"I've lived and taught there."

A screen inside his head lit up, and he saw a khaki-clad gunbull mounted on a horse, wearing sunglasses, his face shadowed by a straw hat, a cut-down double-barrel twelve-gauge propped on his thigh. Any inmate who fell out on his work detail got put on an anthill. A man of color who sassed him got a treatment the captain called "making a Christian out of a nigger." A three-foot chunk of garden hose was tied behind the cantle on his saddle.

"But you're not *from* Louisiana?" she said.

"Sandy Hook, Kentucky. Home of Keith Whitley. Know who he was?"

"What a voice," she said.

That was a surprise, at least in the academic world. "I used some harsh words to the people at the powwow. I wish I hadn't."

"About being inside the system?"

Why hadn't he kept his mouth shut? "I punched a sheriff's deputy when I was eighteen. I did four months of a six-month sentence. I had the time coming and I don't carry resentments about it."

She opened the door. The wind blew papers off his desk. "Sorry," she said, and started picking them up.

"It's all right," he said, taking them from her.

"The couple live three trailers down from me," she said. "The woman claimed I filed a noise complaint against her. I told her I didn't. The next week someone poured sand in my gas tank."

Jennifer was waiting for him in the kitchen when he got home; she was barefoot, wearing frayed cutoff jeans. Smoke and a burnt stench were rising from the skillet on the stove; her face was dilated, the color of sour milk, her eyes teary. "I was fixing us breakfast and had a seizure."

"How long ago?"

"I don't know. What time is it? I just got off the floor." She looked at the spatula in her hand as though she had never seen it before.

He took it from her and turned off the burner. "It's okay. Let's sit down. Are you hurt?"

She felt a knot inside her hair. "I think I hit the table going down."

"You want to go to the ER?"

"It's not going to do any good."

She was telling the truth, but for reasons she was too young to understand. She resented the world and herself and her father, and at some point she would drink again and do more damage to her brain and one day wake up a vegetable.

"I didn't mean what I said yesterday."

"That I always want my way?" he said.

"Yes."

"I've been guilty of that," he said.

But he knew his confession was cavalier and dishonest, and didn't come close to the reality of nine years ago and a night neither of them would ever scrub from their memory.

He and his wife had met on a tennis court in Berkeley and had married and finished their doctorates the same semester and started their teaching careers together at the University of Louisiana at Lafayette. Their combined income allowed them to buy a condominium on a lovely wooded knoll above the Vermilion River. Jennifer was a beautiful baby. They should have been the perfect family, except for a stubborn flaw that beset Delbert when it came to commitment outside the family.

"We don't borrow trouble," he would say.

Their last fight came on the way home from a liberal fundraiser. They were both drunk. Delbert had gotten into it with an ACLU attorney from New Orleans. "The guy is talking about suing Breaux Bridge for allowing a nativity scene on city property."

"The issue was over using tax money to build nativity scenes," she said. "How would you like a copy of the Ten Commandments hanging in your classroom?"

They carried the fight into their condominium. The sitter left as soon as she could get out the door. Jennifer was in her pajamas on the balcony above the living room, looking down at her parents.

"You don't get it, Adel," he said. "A guy like that is a gift to Fox News. He gets to feel good about himself at the expense of everyone else."

"The real problem is you think you're superior to your colleagues because you were on a road gang. No one cares about what happened to you when you were eighteen. I've known civil rights workers who were killed."

"I'm going to fix a drink, then I'm going to bed. You want one?" he said.

"I think I'll take a drive. I'm up to my bottom lip with your shit."

"Here, let me help," he said. He took the keys from his pocket and lobbed them heavily on the coffee table. The table had been a gift from her parents.

"That's what you want?"

Then he said the words he would regret the rest of his life. "Do what you please. You're a big girl now."

Delbert leaned back the recliner for Jennifer and turned on the television, then called the neurologist. The only remedy the neurologist could offer was an adjustment of her medication. "The rest is going to be up to you and your daughter," he said.

"Sir?"

"Has she had any alcohol in the last few days?"

"Not to my knowledge."

"Raising a teenage girl by yourself isn't easy," the neurologist said. "Don't be too hard on yourself or her, Dr. Hatfield."

Delbert opened the windows and scoured the burnt skillet with steel wool and left it to soak, then went into his office and closed the door and picked up the phone receiver. He rested the receiver against his forehead, his heart thudding. *Don't do this*, a voice said.

He paused all of three seconds, then punched in the number of the detective division at the city police department. Someone picked up almost instantly. Delbert felt his stomach constrict.

"Detective Carter. Can I help you?"

"It's Delbert Hatfield, Detective. I wanted to update you."

"The investigation is closed, Professor. I thought you'd already been apprised of that."

"After nine weeks I went to the Sundowner Club and asked the bartender if you guys had dumped the surveillance cameras. He said you didn't. He also said the cameras had been rewound, so any images of the assault were erased. Pretty dumb of me not to get on it earlier, huh?"

"I knew you weren't going to let go," Carter said.

"Say again?"

"I did a little research on you. You're an ex-felon, Professor."

"I have a full pardon, too."

"I found out a little more," Carter said. "Your wife was killed in a one-vehicle auto accident. You came within a hair of being charged with depraved indifference."

Delbert could feel the sweat trapped between his palm and the phone receiver. "I have no knowledge of that," he replied, his words sticking in his throat.

"I've got the file right here. Your wife called her sister on her cell and left her a message to the effect you threw her out of the house. The recording indicates she was seriously impaired. A neighbor noted the time she left your apartment. A witness to the accident gave the time she went through the guardrail. There was no time for her to get drunk between her departure from the apartment and the time she hit the water."

Delbert could feel his breath bouncing off the receiver.

"Are you there?" Carter said.

"What's your point?"

"I'm sorry your daughter didn't get her day in court. But I think you're dragging a chain that's got nothing to do with us."

"Why didn't you check the surveillance cameras?"

"Goodbye and good luck. Don't call this extension again."

The next day, after teaching his class, Delbert walked past Tina Bordelon's office and saw her at her desk, her hand resting on her phone, her face full of thought. "Worry" was a better word.

"Hey, Miss Tina," he said.

"Hey," she replied.

"Want to get coffee?"

She seemed not to hear him. "Would you come in, please?"

"Yeah, what's up?"

135

She stood up and closed the door behind him. He hadn't real-ized how tall she was. "I just left an interdepartmental meeting," she said. "I think I got sideways with a couple of people."

"In what way?"

"Somebody mentioned the black athletes who were accused of rape and the cover-up, blah, blah, blah, and then this same person asked me what my feelings were."

Tell me you shined them on, he thought.

"I told them those boys shouldn't have been brought here in the first place," she said.

He closed his eyes, then opened them. "You're putting me on?"

"I told them universities use ghetto kids like they do Astroturf and old jockstraps. The issue is the alumni fund, the gate receipts, and the television contracts. Most of those kids end up with the skills of janitors."

"That seems like a sympathetic statement to me," he said.

"I also said some of those black kids think a white girl getting drunk with them is an invitation to taking out their big boys."

That one was lethal, a three-pronged hook guaranteed to stir up every faction on the campus. "Forget it," he said.

"Three people walked out of the room."

"You've paid dues. Most of them haven't. They live in a com-munity that's almost entirely white and feel guilty about it. They're basically good people. You have to forgive them for their innocence."

She was in her swivel chair again. Her eyes wandered on his face. "You're a piece of work."

"No, ma'am, I'm not."

"How's your daughter?"

"One day is sunny, the next full of shadows, her voice at the bottom of a well."

"I think she has a good father."

"Don't tell anybody," he replied.

She laughed. He opened the door. He could see across the hall-way and out the window of his office. The maple tree was swelling with wind, the leaves flickering, the sky a translucent blue. "Do you like to fish?" he asked.

Jennifer had gone to the public library with friends to attend a showing of *Shane*. Delbert and Tina strapped his canoe on the roof of his car and drove seventy miles south of town to a lake sur-rounded by Douglas fir and ponderosa pine and mountains that climbed into the clouds. The weather forecast was for scattered thunderstorms late in the day, but at one p.m. the lake was a black mirror, the reflection of the trees like shaggy behemoths. Delbert pushed the canoe off from the shore, with Tina in the bow, the gravel bottom dropping away. He began paddling, with long, pre-cise strokes, the breeze at the center of the lake starting to strike his face, the snow on the mountains frozen and layered at least twenty feet deep just below the clouds. There was hardly anyone else on the lake.

That changed.

Just before turning onto the access road to the lake, he had passed a Ford F-150 truck pulling a boat trailer, a vehicle that perhaps he had seen earlier but couldn't remember exactly. There had been three men in it. A few minutes later the truck was in his rearview mirror, drawing closer to his bumper. The speed limit was forty-five. Delbert was doing fifty. He touched his brakes and the truck dropped back.

Now the same men were on the lake, in an outboard. They passed Delbert's canoe, then cut their engine and began casting their lures in high arches, a petroleum slick trailing the stern. He could hear them talking and laughing across the water. Then one of them fitted a pair of binoculars to his eyes and looked straight at Delbert's canoe.

Delbert pulled up the anchor and paddled into the center of the lake, although he had wanted to drift along the shore and cast into the overhang of the trees. He looked over his shoulder. The man focused his binoculars on the canoe again, as though on them.

"You know those guys?" Tina asked.

"I didn't get a good look at them."

She opened the cooler and took out a submarine sandwich and a can of Coca-Cola. She flipped the tab. "Want one?"

"You bet," he said.

He continued to watch the three men out of the corner of his eye. Contrary to popular belief, the Pacific Northwest has always had a comparatively egalitarian culture. Its vulnerability lay in the impoverishment of its governmental structure. Neo-Nazis and other right-wing paranoids and racists threaded their way into remote communities because they had more numbers and weapons than the authorities did. They were also cowards, and the people they hated and feared the most were located either on the Eastern Seaboard or in the American South, and hence they could provoke and rail and fly Confederate flags and SS lightning bolts without risk.

Delbert flung a Rapala onto the lake's surface and slowly retrieved it, concentrating on its zigzag motions, the flashes of gold on its sides, forcing himself not to look in the motorboat's direction. Ten minutes passed, and when he finally glanced up the motorboat was close to the shore and the three men were casting into the mouth of a stream that flowed into the lake, the kind of spot Delbert normally would have fished. No matter. At least the men were gone.

He put down his spinning rod and ate a sandwich, then paddled them into the shadow of a huge rock by the shore. A black bear and her two cubs, one brown and one rust-colored, were chugging up the hill through the pine trees.

"The mama has a fish in her mouth," Tina said. "Can we go onshore and take some pictures?"

"It's not good to mess with the sow when she has cubs with her."

"They're at the top of the hill. They can't hurt us. Come on. Please."

He paddled the canoe through the shallows until the bow slid onto the gravel and sand.

"I'll be right back," she said.

"Wait a minute."

But she jumped onto dry ground and headed up the hill after the bears. He dragged the canoe far enough out of the water so it couldn't float away, then went after her. His head was pounding and he could hardly catch his breath when he reached the first knoll. He could see her up ahead, standing on an uprooted ponderosa, clicking her camera at the bears, who were only forty feet away.

"Don't say anything, Tina," he said, his voice low. "Turn around slowly, then walk toward me."

She smiled and mouthed the word "OK," as though indulging him. She started to speak as she got closer to him, but he raised his finger to his lips and slipped his arm in hers and began walking with her down the slope. He didn't look back until they were at the water's edge. There was no sign of the bears.

"I didn't mean to cause a problem," she said.

He widened his eyes and coughed slightly.

"You're angry?" she said.

"No." He waited for his heart to quieten. "The natural world has its own rules. I try to abide by them. I'm not much good at it."

She looked at him in a strange way.

139

A thunderhead eclipsed the sun, and a shadow fell on the trees and the lake. He could feel the barometer and temperature dropping. There were dimples on the lake where the trout were starting to rise.

"Louisiana is like this in the summer," he said. "You can smell the bream just before a squall blows in. The air is dense and has a smell like fish roe. I have a feeling it's what the earth smelled like on the first day of creation."

A mist was settling on the trees, darkening the sheen on the pine needles. The lake was almost empty. "We'd better get going," he said. "We've got a long way to paddle."

"Can I give it a try? I mean change places?"

The paddle rested in the stern of the canoe. "You'll have to push us off and get a little wet," he said.

The first raindrops were like bird shot on his straw cowboy hat. He turned around and tossed his hat in Tina's lap. "Put it on."

She threw it back. "Put it on yourself."

The wind was wrinkling the entire lake. The rain ran down into his eyes. He put on his hat, then slipped off his denim jacket and wadded it up and leaned backward and placed it on her knees. "Drape it on your head. I'm wearing a heavy shirt."

She made a cowl out of his jacket. He could hardly see her eyes inside it. She stopped paddling and looked toward the western shore, where there should have been no boats. Then he heard the outboard motor whining like a sewing machine, coming in their direction.

"I think these guys are in it for the long haul, Delbert," she said. "Don't take the bait."

The boat with the three men in it circled the canoe, all of them grinning, probably drunk, their unshaved faces bathed in spray. He thought they would make their statement, either symbolically or literally, and be on their way. They had no grievance against him.

The United States Forest Service monitored the lake, didn't it? These men wouldn't chance getting into trouble with the law because they happened to see a black woman in a recreational area, would they?

He rethought his journey from the highway to the boat ramp. He had passed the three men and their truck and boat trailer on the two-lane, then had slowed to make a turn onto the access road. To make the challenge more emphatic, he had touched his brake pedal and forced the driver of the truck to slow. What had he told Tina about the natural world having its own rules?

The driver of the boat completed his circle and decreased the gas feed until the boat rose on its own wake. Delbert let his eyes slip off the driver's face. Then the driver poured it on, tightening the circle, scouring a depression behind his engine. The canoe was tipping back and forth, the waves from the motorboat hitting the sides as hard as fists. Tina lost her grip on the paddle and watched it float away. "Shit," she said.

She was wearing a life vest; Delbert was not. The sky was lidded, the lake hazed with mist, like gas floating on the surface. Lightning forked into a ridge just above the spot where the bears had disappeared. He began pulling off his boots.

"What are you doing?"

"I'll get behind the canoe and push us out. I've done it before."

He put on a life vest and went over the side. The motorboat was still circling, its occupants staring at him from inside the hoods of their raincoats. He got under the stern of the canoe, then shoved it forward and swam after it and shoved again. Tina tried to help by paddling with her hand. Suddenly he felt the mossy surface of a submerged boulder under his foot. He shoved again and sent the canoe sliding through the chop and swam after it. Then both his feet touched bottom, and he could see the beach and the wooded slope above it and the fog puffing out of the trees.

The motorboat veered away, and he heard the sound of its engine thin and finally disappear inside the drone of the rain. He pulled the canoe onto the sand, exhausted and trembling in the cold. Tina stepped out of the stern into water that was up to her knees. "Where's the road?" she said.

"Above us, through the trees," he said. "We'll have to carry the canoe and come get it with the car."

The grade was steep, heavily wooded, the ground soggy with wet pine needles. They had to lift the canoe over boulders and a huge uprooted ponderosa before they could gain the asphalt road that circled the lake. Delbert could see his car parked by the empty registration station, and farther on a chemical restroom. They set down the canoe. Then, inside the gloom, Delbert saw the three men from the motorboat, with their pickup and trailer, their slickers shiny under an electric light on a pole by the restroom.

"Why are you stopping?" she asked.

"Those guys are up there."

"Give me your keys," Tina said.

"Wait till they're gone, Tina."

"I have to get my bag," she said.

"Give it a few minutes."

"Did you hear what I said? I *need* my bag."

Should he ask why she needed it? He looked at her expression and decided that was not a good idea.

"OK, but we leave these guys alone. Right? We'll get their license number and straighten this out later?"

"Either give me the keys or unlock the car."

"You got it," he said.

They continued walking, his car interdicting the line of sight between them and the men. He stuck the key in the passenger door and turned it and heard the lock snap open. She pushed him aside and pulled out her drawstring bag. She felt inside it.

"Jesus Christ, what are you doing?" he said.

"Stay out of it," she said.

He tried to stop her, but he was too late. She had dropped the bag on the asphalt and was walking toward the men. One had just come out of the restroom and was still hooking up his Western belt. The other two were smoking cigarettes in the drizzle, none of them seemingly concerned about either Tina's or Delbert's presence.

Until they saw the blue-black nine-millimeter Beretta in Tina's hand.

"You think you three buckets of shit are going to get away with what you did?" she said.

"Don't be aiming that thing, woman," one man said.

"What did you say?" Tina replied. "What did you call me? I'm talking to *you*. Don't look away. I'll put one through your kneecap."

The man tried to stare her down, then hung his head. "I didn't call you anything."

"Get on your knees. All three of you."

They looked down the road, and at the trees, and at the failing light in the sky, and at the electric bulb burning above the registration shack, everywhere except at the gun.

"We're sorry," one of them said.

"On your knees."

"Lady, you're not gonna use that, are you?"

"You have three seconds, trash."

They knelt down slowly, feeling for the ground. She held the Beretta with both hands, pointed straight in front of her. The butterfly safety was off. The magazine held seven rounds. "Close your eyes."

"Please——" one said.

She fired a single round into one of the truck's tires. The weight of the truck came down immediately on the rim. Then she shot off both outside mirrors.

"If you get up before we're gone, I'll come back and all of you will walk with a cane the rest of your lives. Mess with me later and I'll shoot your dicks off. Now run."

They got to their feet, their hands extended in front of them, as though they were pushing away the air.

"Run!" she repeated.

When the three men were down by the edge of the lake, peering back in the fading light, she stuck the Beretta in the back of her belt. "Better get going, huh, boss?" she said.

"I'd call that the understatement of the evening," he replied.

It was dark and still raining when he got home. Jennifer was in the living room, staring at the Weather Channel. "What's happening, kiddo?" he said.

She turned her head toward him. Her eyes were round and empty. "You're wet."

"Got caught in a thunderstorm."

"We saw *Shane*. The last scene is real sad."

"Oh, yeah?" he said, pulling off his shoes.

"Alan Ladd is riding away into the mountains, and Brandon deWilde is running after him, shouting, 'Shane! Come back, Shane.' It made me cry."

"Shane is the light bearer, Jen. He's told the little boy, Joey, that he has to be brave and principled. In this way Shane passes the light to Joey, and now it's Joey's turn to make the world a better place."

"It's the innocence and tenderness in the little boy's face that makes me sad."

"I've never been able to get that scene out of my head, either," Delbert said.

He went into the bedroom and dried off and put on fresh clothes. When he returned to the living room, she was still staring at the television. Except the screen was dark.

"Did you eat?" he said.

She looked at him, her eyes dead.

"Jen?" he said.

"I didn't tell you something."

"Didn't tell me what?"

"That cop Carter called."

"About what?"

"I don't know. He wanted to talk to you."

"What for?"

"That's what I asked. I said I was the one who was assaulted. He said it had nothing to do with me."

"How long ago was this?"

"Maybe a half hour."

"That was the extent of the conversation?"

"Not exactly," she said.

"What's the rest of it, Jen?"

"I told him he was a bastard," she replied. "I told him his parents should have had better access to a birth control program." She waited for the reprimand.

Instead, he bit his lip and looked at nothing.

"I'm supposed to just take it?" she said.

"I've never had answers about much of anything, Jen," he said. "I think that's why academics are academics. All we have are questions that make other people look less informed than we are."

He went into the kitchen and sat by himself in the dark. Somehow the story about Shane and the little boy Joey made him think about the night his wife went through the guardrail. Delbert had destroyed his family. Shane had brought light and freedom to a family he had adopted.

Delbert opened the refrigerator and looked inside, the square of electric light falling on the floor. A bottle of vodka was lying sideways on the top rack. He gripped it and went back into the living room. "What is this?"

"Queen brought it over and forgot to take it home. I didn't drink any of it."

Queen was an older friend, an anorexic hanger-on to the edges of the campus culture. She dressed in black, and her lips and eyebrows were spiked with metal. Her eyes had the liquid blackness of people whose history you didn't probe. "Boozers don't forget their booze," he said.

"Don't be mean about my friends, Daddy."

He headed back for the kitchen, his hand tight on the bottle. She followed him. "What are you going to do with it?"

"Leave it on the back steps. She can take it home the next time she's here."

"You don't trust me? You think I'm an alcoholic? Why do you have to make a drama out of everything?"

He looked at the caller ID on the kitchen phone. The last call was made thirty-five minutes ago from a cell phone. "No one else has called except Carter?"

"I called him 'asshole,'" she replied.

He breathed slowly, in and out, as though his chest were wrapped with chains, a thorn in his heart.

He went inside his office and forced himself to dial Carter's number. The rain had quit, the stars were out, and a summer cold front had moved into the valley; the tops of the hills surrounding the town were crisp and white under the moon. "Is that you, Professor?" Carter said.

"My daughter wants to apologize for calling you names," he said.

"That's what teenage girls do. We got us a situation here."

"Us?"

"Three local wisenheimers say a black woman and a white man threatened them at gunpoint and shot out their tire and door mirrors. Know anything about that?"

"I don't remember shooting out any tires recently."

"They got a partial plate that comes pretty close to yours. The description of the white man fits you, too."

"Really?"

"Coincidence?"

"Search me," Delbert said. "I know there're some mean motor scooters here 'bouts."

"Let me line it out for you, Professor. These guys are leftovers from some of those Aryan Nation and Christian Identity compounds in Idaho."

"That's gratifying. I hope they attend church more often."

"You're starting to piss me off, Professor."

"That's too bad. I'd tell my daughter about this, but she's recovering from another seizure. Come by and see us sometime. Maybe you might catch her when she has a grand mal."

"I'm trying to save your ass, my friend."

"Why would you want to do that?"

"Probably because I'm a fool. I thought I might come in for a cup of coffee, but as you suggest, maybe we'll do that another time."

"A cup of coffee?"

"Look out your window."

A black car with black windows was parked two houses down the street. The driver started the engine, then turned on the headlights. The car drove slowly past Delbert's house. Carter rolled down the passenger window and pointed his finger at Delbert as he would a gun.

Delbert eased the phone receiver into the cradle and rejoined Jennifer in the living room, cupping his hand on the back of her neck, a pain in his chest as sharp as glass.

At sunrise the hills were misty with steam, the spruce tree in his front yard dripping, the damp on the streets as deep as a bruise. He walked to the campus and taught his class, but did not see Tina. He left her a note that said "Call me" under her door.

When he returned home Jennifer was doing calisthenics in front of the television, wearing her sweats, her bare feet spread, bending over, touching one foot with the opposite hand, then the other, the way she used to do before the assault.

"How you doin', kiddo?" he said.

"I'm getting in shape. I'm gonna beat this thing."

"That's the ticket."

"Carter called again. I told him I don't talk to cretins on Wednesdays. He said it's not Wednesday. I said, 'I'm sorry. I'll talk to you then. In the meantime, do the world a favor and shoot yourself.'"

"You didn't?"

"Girl Scout's honor," she said, crossing her heart.

He went into the kitchen and poured a cup of coffee and drank it while he looked out the back screen at the lawn and the birch tree in it. Then he saw footprints pressed into the grass. His eyes dropped to the steps. The bottle of vodka was gone. He went back into the living room.

"Was Queen here?" he said.

"No. She got a job at Pizza Hut."

"The hooch is gone."

The joy had gone out of her face, and he knew she was having the same thoughts as he. Their backyard was enclosed by a board fence; the alleyway was lighted; in the three years they had lived there they had not heard a report of a robbery in the neighborhood.

"It's the woman and her boyfriend?" she said.

Jennifer never called her assailants by name, as though to do so would further empower their presence in her life.

"Maybe college kids," he said. "Maybe some guys I had a beef with."

"You don't have beefs."

"I did yesterday. With three guys. That's why Carter was calling. He said he's trying to help me."

"Are you serious?" she said.

"You don't buy it?"

She pressed her fingers into her temples and marched into the kitchen and made a circle and came back into the living room, her fingers still screwed into her temples, her eyes jutting out of their sockets. "Have you lost your mind?" she said.

Fifteen minutes later he drove to a sporting goods store and used his credit card to pay for a titanium snub-nosed .38 Special. The clerk went through the background check on the phone, then hung up. "They're backed up right now," he said. "Unless there's a problem, you can pick it up in three days."

The following day was Saturday. Tina Bordelon did not return his calls. Nor was she in her office Monday morning. That afternoon his cell phone throbbed in his pocket while he was cleaning leaves out of his rain gutters. "Delbert?" she said.

"Where have you been?" he said.

"I just left a conference with the vice president and the department chair," she said. "Where can you meet me?"

"My house."

"I like to hike up to the M in the afternoon," she said.

A half hour later she was waiting for him on a wood bench located just below a giant, sloping, whitewashed concrete single letter overlooking the university. He sat down beside her. The view of the campus and town was spectacular. "Why the secrecy?" he asked.

"A detective named Carter came to the vice president's office. Then the vice president called in me and the department chair. The door was open so the secretary could hear. There was no attempt at privacy. Starting to get the picture?"

"No."

"They tried to cover up a sex scandal involving the athletes. Now they're going to rinse their sins in public. Carter asked me if I shot up the truck."

"What did you say?"

"I admitted it. I told him why, too. Carter asked if you were with me. I said I would speak only about myself."

"What did the vice president say?"

"Nothing."

"Carter used my name?"

"He couldn't mention it enough."

Delbert knew both the vice president and the chair. They were decent enough, but like most administrators they were pragmatists, and as such conformed to the agenda of all organizations, namely to prevent the infection in the body from reaching the head.

He felt a great fatigue seep into his heart. Down below, the tree-lined neighborhoods and the students sailing Frisbees on the quadrangle and bicycling on the sidewalks and the faculty members walking from the library to their cars seemed small and far away, a separate culture in which people were content and safe from the evil that could arbitrarily reach out and squeeze the light from a person's life. Then he felt shame at his self-pity.

"Hello?" Tina said.

"Go on. I was listening."

"Right," she said.

"I fear for my daughter. I cannot keep her problems off my mind. You'll have to forgive me."

"I understand that," Tina said. "I was trying to explain my situation. Next year the administration will find an excuse, something to do with the budget or enrollment, and I'll be gone."

He couldn't argue with her, or about the unjust way in which she was being treated. But she seemed to overlook the jeopardy in which she had put his career by legally empowering misanthropes whom they could have gotten locked up had they not given up the high ground.

She seemed to read his thoughts. "I apologize for messing you up, Delbert."

"I did that to myself nine years ago. I was partly responsible for my wife's death by drowning."

Her mouth started to form a word, but no sound came out.

"We had a fight," he said. "She was drunk. I gave her the car keys and in effect told her to get out of our home. My daughter saw all this."

He saw her eyes mist over. She gazed down the mountain at the college kids who were working their way up the zigzag trail to watch the sunset, some of them carrying backpacks with sandwiches and cold drinks. She was wearing a white blouse; her black hair was blowing, exposing a pink scar on the back of her neck. He wanted to touch her, and hold her hand in his,

151

Coincidentally she did it for him, cupping her big hand around his, pinching his fingers; her skin was like warm butter.

"I hate to put it to you like this," she said. "If your daughter dies or ends up on permanent life support, Carter will look like the Antichrist. Before this is over, he'll try to do a number on both you and her."

"You don't know that."

"Have you checked my color lately? 'White trash' is a state of mind. It has nothing to do with geography or social class. That sweetheart may not be from Mississippi, but he wishes he was."

He walked with her back down the trail. The western sky was orange, the shadows deepening among the buildings on the campus. He thought he could smell rain. It made him think of his years in Louisiana, but he didn't know why. "Want to get something to eat?" he asked.

"Not really," she answered. Her eyes slipped off his. She touched the back of her neck.

"It's a pretty evening," he said.

"It is."

"I'd like to spend more time with you, Tina."

"What's stopping you?" she replied.

He opened his cell phone and called his daughter. He wanted to send a home health aide to the house, but she said she and her friends were going to a movie.

"Is Queen going?" he said.

"No. What if she were?" she said.

"Home by eleven thirty?"

"Affirmative on that, Pops," she said.

He closed his phone and got in his car and followed Tina to her trailer court.

*　*　*

Inside her trailer, he told Tina he had remained celibate since his wife's death.

"In mourning?" she said.

"Partly."

"What's the rest of it?"

They were at the far end of her trailer, in her bedroom. The other two bedrooms had been turned into an office and a library. He had kissed her on the mouth several times in the living room. She was undressing.

"My father was a preacher," he said. "Not fire and brimstone. For good or bad, he walked the walk as he saw it. 'Good enough to sleep with, good enough for a wedding ring.' That's what he used to say. A lot of him got stuck in me. Not necessarily the best part, either."

She sat on the side of the bed, half undressed. "I don't know what you're saying."

"I've hurt people. I never set out to. But I did it just the same and I hate myself for it."

"I'm very confused," she said.

"I think you're a great woman." He kissed her and pushed her slowly down on the pillow. He felt her hand on his back, then her fingers spreading inside his hair.

Later she warmed two frozen Mexican dinners in the microwave and popped open two diet cold drinks while he gazed out the window at the trailer court. It was full of trees, some that flowered. Many of the trailers were augmented with porches and patios and porte cocheres. Some of the residents were barbecuing, the smoke drifting into the evening light. One group was playing volleyball. He lifted his cold drink to his mouth, then wondered if his eyes were deceiving him.

"Do you have a pair of binoculars?"

"Just a minute." She went into her office and came back out with a pair of opera glasses in a leather case. "What's going on?"

He focused the lenses on the volleyball players. He could see each of them clearly now, even more clearly than when they were on their knees at the lake: the pores in their skin, the green teardrops tattooed at the edge of the eye, the number 88 on their necks. They wore combat boots and dirty jeans and black T-shirts sawed off at the armpits, and they were knocking the ball high in the air with the heels of their hands, their faces unshaved, their mouths split with rictus grins. They made him think of baboons.

Jessie Wilcox, the attacker of his daughter, was watching them, her infant in her arms. Her boyfriend, Wendell Cody, was sitting in a canvas chair, toking on a roach.

"Take a look," Delbert said.

Tina lifted the glasses to her eyes, then lowered them, her face blank. "These people all know each other and come from different places and yet end up thirty yards from my home? That doesn't fit."

"They belong to the same culture," he said. "They find each other."

"What are the tats about?"

"The teardrops mean the person has done a number on somebody in the service of the Aryan Brotherhood or the Aryan Nations. The eighty-eight stands for the eighth letter of the alphabet times two. In other words, HH, which stands for 'Heil Hitler.'"

She was quiet a long time.

"What are you thinking?" he asked.

"I thought it would be different here. But they're back."

"Who is?"

"The Klan, the Nazis, the professional haters. I think their time has come around. They're not just in the South. They're everywhere."

"I'm going to have a talk with them."

"Don't make my mistake, Delbert. Don't lose your tenure. Think about your daughter."

"That's exactly who I'm thinking about," he said.

She picked up his hand and pressed it to the back of her neck. "Feel the scar? A white boy down the road from our farm did that to me with a can opener. I was thirteen. The boy's mother owned the cotton gin where my father worked. My father reported the boy to the sheriff's department and was fired. I bought a gun when I was eighteen and have carried it ever since. Where'd that get us?"

"Stay here," he said.

He walked down to the volleyball game. The maple trees were etched with fire in the sunset. The three men remained devoted to their game and seemed to take no notice of him. Neither did the woman or her boyfriend, who was seated in the canvas chair, his spine as rounded as a worm's.

Delbert stood on the asphalt drive that meandered through the court, his thumbs hooked in his jeans. He waited for one of the players to acknowledge him, but no one did.

"You guys wouldn't bird-dog a fellow, would you?" he said.

There was no reaction from any of them. Jessie took her baby inside. Her boyfriend Wendell twisted the cap off a longneck and tilted it to his mouth, the foam and the amber bottle lighting against the sun.

"You guys like vodka?" Delbert said.

No answer. Not even a shift of the eyes.

"I think y'all have been prowling around my house," Delbert said. "Did you know there's a stand-your-ground law in this state?"

But they continued their game, leaping in the air, sometimes coming down on the ball with a fist, as happy and insular as monks. He walked back to Tina's trailer.

155

"What happened?" she asked.

"Nothing."

"You just stood there and watched them play volleyball?"

"They were obviously not interested in anything I had to say."

"Meaning what?"

"They'll come after us," he said.

She blinked as though someone had popped a rubber band in her eyes.

"At first they'll ask for money to drop the charges," he said. "Then they may try to kill us. I'd say they're animals, but that would be kind. They give evil a bad name. That's the people we're dealing with."

The remote phone rang in his bedroom at 2:27 a.m., the red and white lights on the phone trembling in the darkness. The caller ID was blocked. Delbert pulled on his slippers and went into the office before he answered so he wouldn't wake his daughter. He clicked the Talk button. Through the window he could see a cat crossing the street in the moonlight, stepping lightly over the curb onto the dampness of the grass. "Who is this?" he said, his voice hoarse, the words catching in his throat, somehow belittling him.

"You get your knob polished, Professor?"

"I'll take a guess. You're a volleyball man."

"What I want to know is does a mud woman do it the same way as a white woman. I heard it's like sticking your pole in a washing machine."

"What do you want, bubba?"

"Who you calling bubba?"

"You."

"Think you're smart because you did a bit in a county slam?"

"Give me another name and I'll call you that."

"Try 'Badass Motherfucker Who Don't Cut No Slack.' When I do the tune-up, they sing 'Dixie.'"

"What you're doing is pretty dumb, partner."

"You looking out your window?"

"No."

"Yeah, you are. Your phone is lit up on your face."

Delbert swallowed.

"Cat got your tongue?" the voice said.

"If you're not a coward, you'll tell me your name."

"What do you see outside your window?"

"Nothing."

"You see a cat. It's on the walkway. It's licking its paw. Or it *was* licking a paw."

There was a flash down the street, one that made no sound. The cat leapt into the air and landed stone-dead on the concrete.

"Night night, dickwad," the voice said.

Delbert went outside and got a shovel from the toolshed and scooped the cat from the walk and buried it in the backyard so Jennifer would not see it, then went back to sleep.

His dreams took him not so much to places as to a gallery of images: a country church that swelled with organ music; a mother who made him cut a switch or sit in the front yard wearing girl's clothes; himself fishing in a green pond with a man of color; an automobile parked in a canyon at the bottom of the sea, the interior light burning, a thread of bubbles rising from the mouth of its sole occupant.

He woke so tired he could hardly get through his morning class. When he returned home, he called Detective Carter. "Last night, a man shot a cat in my front yard," Delbert said.

"What man?"

"I think one of the three guys from the lake."

"You think?"

"That's what I said."

"You got a look at him?"

"No. He called my house in the early a.m. He was parked down the street. Just like you were, Detective Carter."

"I'll let that last part slide. Come down and make a report. Someone else will help you."

"You don't handle cat shootings?"

"Anything else?"

"Yeah, the three guys from the lake were playing volleyball in front of Jessie Wilcox's trailer yesterday evening."

"And?"

"Her boyfriend was there, too."

"Can you get to the point?"

"Jessie Wilcox's trailer is a short distance from Tina Bordelon's. Wilcox may have put sand in Ms. Bordelon's gas tank. Maybe the attack on my daughter isn't about mixing up coats in a saloon."

"That doesn't compute for me," Carter said.

Nor did it compute for Delbert, and he knew he was now trying to reconfigure his daughter's role as a victim rather than as an instigator in the deconstruction of her life.

"I'm going to break a protocol," Carter said. "Tina Bordelon is being charged as we speak. Get yourself an attorney if you don't already have one."

"You're talking about aiding and abetting?"

"Does the D in PhD stand for 'duh'?"

Delbert fumbled the receiver into the cradle, then spilled it on the floor.

★   ★   ★

On Tuesday he picked up the snub-nosed Smith & Wesson five-round revolver at the sporting goods store. He also bought a box of ammunition. When he got home, he saw a note on the refrigerator door. Jennifer had gone to a movie with Queen and would be home before supper. He sat at the kitchen table and drank a cup of coffee and looked at the .38 resting on a bright-yellow placemat next to the box of shells. His life had become a cruel prank. Here, in a university setting, in an alpine environment, he had to buy a firearm in order to have peace of mind. His daughter was permanently impaired and in danger of becoming a mewing semblance of a human being fed by tubes and wiped and cleaned by strangers in an institution. Yet she and he were at the mercy of a court system that left psychopaths on the street while their victims hid in their homes.

God help my child, he thought. *God help my child, God help my child, God help my child.*

The room was becoming distorted, the surfaces shiny. He wiped his eyes with the back of his wrist. He flipped the cylinder from the .38's frame and one by one dropped the cartridges into the chambers and pressed the cylinder back inside the frame and heard it snap snugly in place. He stared out the sliding glass door at the backyard and the hump of soil in the rose garden where he had buried the cat. His thumb rested across the top of the .38's hammer. He rubbed his thumb along the coldness of the titanium and felt an almost erotic reaction.

Although he had a doctorate in anthropology, he did not accept the long-held belief that all humankind descended from the same tree. He had known men on the hard road who were just like the man who had shot the cat. They wore the same tats and hairstyles and prison uniforms as the other inmates, but were feared and avoided to the same degree you would avoid and fear anthrax at a cattle auction. They could smell weakness in others and weaponized their genitalia. To them pain and sexual satisfaction were interchangeable; to enjoy both at the same time was ecstasy. The unblinking simian stare in their eyes was brimming with thunder that was as loud as drums. Anyone who was saccharine about them had never known them.

He washed his cup and saucer in the sink, and dried them and put them away, then dried his hands and picked up the revolver and slipped it into the right-hand pocket of his slacks. The fact that he was carrying a concealed weapon without a permit did not bother him. Why should it, he asked himself. The possibility of his receiving tenure was not only in jeopardy, it may have already disappeared. To lose it meant he would be locked out of university teaching for the rest of his career, unless he wanted to join that desperate army of adjunct instructors who worked for minimum wage and were treated as though they were grounds attendants.

He wondered what his father, the preacher, would think or do. His father had stood up against the Klan to protect an elderly black musician who used to take Delbert fishing. His father berated the Imperial Wizard in the grocery store and ended the harassment of the black man without laying a hand on anyone. But would his father be as gentle if his daughter were teetering on the edge of paralysis, imbecility, or death?

That evening Jennifer came in drunk. The next morning a grand mal seizure hit her like she had been standing barefoot on a steel plate and had touched a power line. By the time they reached the emergency room her skin was as gray as shirt board; ten minutes later she went into convulsions and her hands and feet curled into claws. Twice she stopped breathing and Delbert had to run for the nurse. She was resuscitated both times, and by afternoon looked normal and was moved out of the ICU. She had no memory of getting drunk or quivering and knocking like a box of bones on the kitchen floor. She smiled at him, her eyes blue pools of innocence.

"You OK?" he said.

"I'm fine, Daddy," she replied. "But why are you in my bedroom? Aren't you supposed to be in class?"

It was then he knew that his future was foregone and inalterable, and would have no destination except a graveyard and a stone monument whose kindest inscription would be a name, a birthdate, and the date of death.

The following evening a storm blew through the city. He had gone to the store for a gallon of ice cream and a big bottle of Coca-Cola to make brown cows, the windshield wipers swishing, the clouds veined with electricity. When he looked in the rearview mirror, he saw the red and blue lights of a police car flashing in the rain. He pulled to the curb and waited for the officer to approach, his hands resting on the top of the steering wheel, the outline of the revolver in his pocket pooled in shadow. The officer twirled her finger. Delbert rolled down the window and looked up into her face. "Good evening," he said.

"Leave your hands where they are," she said.

"What's the problem, Officer?"

She shined her flashlight across the dashboard and floor and front seat, just missing his right thigh. Her name tag read V. ALVAREZ. "I don't like standing in the rain," she said. "Come back to the cruiser."

He followed her and got in on the passenger side.

"Know who I am?" she said.

"You were with Detective Carter the night my daughter was assaulted."

"There's mud smeared on your plate. The numbers and letters are illegible. Can you take care of that for me?"

"Yes, ma'am."

She had a narrow face and an aquiline nose and black hair, and looked older than when he had seen her in the emergency room. She sneezed. "You know a kid named Queen Darby?"

"She hangs out with my daughter sometimes."

"She has a sheet. She's also a student of Dr. Bordelon at the university. You know *her*, right?"

"I do."

"Queen and Jennifer were at Dr. Bordelon's trailer. Jessie Wilcox probably saw her there. That's where the trouble started with your daughter. Wilcox had it in for Dr. Bordelon. She took it out on Jennifer at the Sundowner."

"Why are you telling me this?"

"I like to sleep at night."

"Thank you."

The patrolwoman sneezed again. She pressed a Kleenex to her nose. "The three skinheads are camped on the Blackfoot, up near the old Lindbergh ranch."

"What are you telling me, Officer?"

"My former partner screwed up. He should have downloaded the surveillance cameras at the nightclub. If your daughter dies, the city is going to have shit on its nose. How he plays the situation is anybody's guess. I could lose my job for this."

"You're saying he might sic those guys on me?"

She gazed through the windshield at his car. It looked garish and scratched and bare in the cruiser's headlights. "You left your window down," she said. "Don't catch my cold."

The next day Tina asked him to have coffee with her in the university cafeteria after his eight o'clock class. "What's going on?" he said, trying to look happy when he sat down with her.

"I was just told I would have to take leave without pay this fall," she replied. "I think you're next."

"Do you know a student named Queen Darby?"

"Yes, she was in my class this spring."

"Evidently my daughter was with her at your trailer."

"Queen has been there with friends, but I didn't know one of them was your daughter."

"Jessie Wilcox or her boyfriend must have seen her. That's why they attacked her at the Sundowner."

"Jesus Christ," she said.

"It's not your fault."

"Does that detective know this?"

"Yep."

"What are you going to do about it?" she said.

"Who knows? The system isn't about justice. It's about sustaining itself."

She studied his face. "Don't do whatever you're thinking."

"Who says I'm thinking?"

"Please, Delbert."

"Want to hear an interesting historical fact? The civil rights movement didn't get serious until the Deacons for Defense were formed in Bogalusa, Louisiana, in 1964. They armed themselves and told the Klan to come and get it. A bad day for Bubba and Joe Bob."

"That's really dumb," she said.

"'Dumb' is a way of life for me."

He left a dollar bill on the table for the busboy.

That afternoon he went to a music store close by the university, then drove downtown and went inside the police station.

"Help you?" the desk sergeant asked.

"Detective Carter is expecting me," Delbert said. "Got it covered."

He walked down the corridor straight into Carter's office. Carter was behind his desk.

"Don't get up," Delbert said. "I'll take just a minute."

He set a small, flat package wrapped in black-satin paper with a silver ribbon on the detective's blotter.

"What the hell do you think you're doing?" Carter said.

"Open it up."

"No. Take yourself and whatever this is out of here."

"I used to belong to a twelve-step group. They had what they called a ninth step. Making amends to others and all that jazz."

"That's what this is? Twelve-step crapola?"

"Yes, sir."

"Good. There're meetings all over town. Take it to any one of them you choose."

"Okay, I'll open your present for you."

"Listen, you—"

"I said don't get up. Let me get the paper off. See, a CD by Keith Whitley, the greatest voice in country music. I knew his whole family."

"You're a royal pain, Professor. Probably a candidate for Warm Springs, too."

"Tell you what. I'm not keen on academic titles. Why don't you just call me Hatfield? You know who the Hatfields are, right?"

"Something to do with *The Beverly Hillbillies*?"

Delbert grinned broadly. "My daddy was a preacher."

"Yeah?"

"That's all. I wish I were more like him. A man of enormous restraint and nothing like some of my ancestors."

"You get the fuck out of here."

"I think my daughter is fixing to die, Detective Carter. But I'll still be here. I surely will. If you want to stand up now, go ahead. I bet you cain't do it."

His accent had changed. Carter looked at him, stupefied.

"Can't do what?" Carter asked.

"You'll figure it out," Delbert said.

When he left the building the sky was dark, the clouds crackling, the trees on the courthouse lawn dense with gas, almost like autumn. A solitary raindrop struck his forehead as cold and hard as lead. He drove home just as the rain burst from the heavens, then called for a sitter.

By ten p.m. the storm was raging up the Blackfoot River. On the turnoff into a cove was a camping area where mostly out-of-state families stretched their tents and parked their trailers and launched inflated rafts into the current and tried to relive the experience portrayed in the film *A River Runs Through It*. But Delbert knew this was not the environment the three men from the lake would find desirable. Farther up the dirt road near the ranch once owned by Colonel Charles Lindbergh were tangled trees along the riverside, fallen rock in the roadway, high places where a vehicle could drop straight down on boulders in the dark, and, most importantly, signs that said NO CAMPING.

He went over a rise in the road and through the trees saw a campfire burning on the beach in the rain. In the glow of the fire was a Ford F-150 truck. He kept going until the road dipped down into darkness, then pulled into the ponderosa and cut his headlights and engine and slipped a haversack over his shoulder and stepped out onto a bed of pine needles and the mulchy detritus of rotted tree trunks.

His thoughts were many, all of them cruel and disconnected from the man he thought himself to be. But the weapons, the tools, and the plumber's tape he carried spoke for themselves. So did the hooded coat, the cleated hiking shoes, and the black trousers and shirt. He wondered if there was a gene that had skipped his father but had been planted in him, replicating what was worst in his ancestors: Shawnees doing their bloody work with a stone knife, their half-naked bodies sweaty and painted with firelight, their frontiersmen counterparts making bridle reins from the Indian corpses at Horseshoe Bend.

His cell phone vibrated in his pocket. He looked at the caller ID. It was Carter. He pulled the phone from his pocket and placed it to his ear. "How did you get my number?" he said.

"From your daughter's sitter. Where are you?"

"Did something happen to Jennifer?"

"No. *Where* are you?"

"None of your business," Delbert said.

"Jessie Wilcox is in the hospital. The A.B. guys raped and sodomized and beat the shit out of her. Her boyfriend blew town. If you wanted payback, you got it."

Delbert looked at the campfire burning by the water, rain slicing across the light. He could see three pup tents scattered in a semicircle.

"You there?" Carter said.

"Yes."

"Here's a footnote for you. I did some background checking on her. As an infant she was taken from her parents for her own protection."

"You're just finding that out?"

"I'm a police officer, not a social worker."

"I think you're a self-serving man, and should be treated as such," Delbert said. "Why are you calling me instead of putting these guys in custody?"

"She wouldn't give them up."

"So how do you know they did it?"

"I took a wild guess. They cut a swastika on her forehead."

"They're not going down, are they?"

"I'm giving you the break of your life, Professor."

"Apologize for what you did to my daughter."

"My ass."

Delbert turned off his cell phone and dropped it in his haversack. For perhaps fifteen seconds the moon broke through the clouds on the opposite side of the river. He could have sworn he saw a black bear and her two cubs, one brown, one rust-colored, fishing with their paws in the shallows, their fur sparkling from the spray.

He walked toward the three tents. The fire stank of half-burnt food. Beer cans were scattered on the ground. The titanium snub-nose hung from his right hand. He reviewed his conversation with Carter. For whatever reason, the three Aryan supremacists had visited a punishment upon Jessie Wilcox that was far worse than any court would impose upon her. Her boyfriend, who may have been the father of her child, had obviously betrayed her and fled town. The neo-Nazis might skate on the rape, but eventually they would get cooled out on a sidewalk or take a fall and do mainline time on another charge. Why roll the dice? There was nothing to gain and everything to lose.

He let out his breath and wiped the rain from his face and slipped the .38 back in his pocket. He looked at the cove and the water splashing on the boulders where the bears had been fishing. They were gone now, but he was determined to return and show them to Tina and Jennifer. Hemingway had said it a long time ago: The world was a fine place and well worth the fighting for.

He turned around, then from the corner of his eye saw the flap open on the tent closest to the campfire. A man's face appeared in the light. He wore a denim jacket buttoned at the throat and wrists. His beard looked like wire. "Motherfucker!" he said.

"I'm no threat to you," Delbert said.

The man reached back inside the tent and came up with a cut-down shotgun, a pump, probably a twelve-gauge. The first blast caught Delbert high up in the chest and in the neck and cheek. He wheeled, pulling the revolver from his pocket. He saw the other men coming out of their tents. He fired blindly, stumbling backward, just as the shotgun went off again. This time the pattern was wide and died inside the trees and undergrowth. Delbert raised the .38 again, this time sighting on the shooter's chest, and pulled the trigger. The round caught the shooter at the top of his denim jacket, punching a neat hole in his throat. He dropped to his knees, as though in prayer, both hands on the entry wound, blood leaking through his fingers.

The two other men were burrowing back in their tents. He shot the second man as he tried to exit his tent. He aimed at the third tent and pulled the trigger. The hammer snapped on a spent cartridge. He pulled again. He had fired all five rounds. He took a hatchet from his haversack and attacked the third tent, chopping at the body that was thrashing inside. A pistol fired inside the nylon. Now Delbert was on top of the man who was inside the tent. Beneath him he felt the contours of his victim's shoulders and back and buttocks and thighs and flailing arms, and swung the hatchet again and again, ignoring the screams and desperation of his victim, pressing down with his knee and free hand, ignoring his own pain and blood loss, until the form writhing under the nylon stiffened and became still.

Then he rolled off what he had done and staggered back to the road and got into his car. He started the engine and turned on the headlights and headed back down the dirt road, steering with one hand, his shirt glued to his wounds, his teeth chattering. He got his cell phone out of his haversack and dialed with his thumb.

"Daddy?" Jennifer said.

"What are you doing?" he said.

"Watching *Shane* again. Is everything all right?"

"Fine. Throw a few things for us in a suitcase, will you?"

"Are we going somewhere?"

"We might."

"You sound funny," she said.

"We're the team," he said.

"Jessie Wilcox called here tonight."

"What?"

"Jessie Wilcox. You know. *Her.*"

"Why did she call?"

"To apologize," Jennifer said. "Did you talk to her or something?"

"No. What did you tell her?"

"That I don't hold grudges. Like you. Because of what people did to you when you were eighteen."

"You told her you don't hold a grudge?"

"Sure. If you can do it, I can."

In the headlights he saw the momma bear and her cubs run across the road and disappear inside the trees. He spread his hand against the soaked area in his shirt, one that was as big as a dinner plate, and rubbed his face with his own blood, like a druid at a pagan altar or, better said, a crusader knight or a country preacher indulging in a special kind of moment.

THE WILD SIDE
OF LIFE

The club where the oil field people hung out was called the Hungry Gator. It stood on pilings by a long, green, humped levee in the Atchafalaya Basin, a gigantic stretch of bayous and quicksand and brackish bays and flooded cypress and tupelos that looked like a forgotten piece of creation before fish worked their way up onto the land and formed feet. There were no clocks inside the Gator, no last names, sometimes not even first ones, just initials. By choice most of us lived on the rim. Of everything. Get my drift?

I liked the rim. You could pretend there was no before or after; there was just *now*, a deadness in the sky on a summer evening, maybe a solitary black cloud breaking apart like ink in clear water, while thousands of tree frogs sang. It was a place where I didn't have to make comparisons or study on dreams and memories that would come flickering behind my eyelids five seconds into sleep.

I worked on a seismograph rig, ten days on and five days off; on land, I sometimes played drums and mandolin at the club and even did a few vocals. My big pleasure was looking at the girls from the bandstand, secretly thinking of myself as their protector, a guy who'd been around but didn't try to use people. The truth is I was a mess with women and about as clever in a social situation as the scribbles on the washroom wall.

I'd blank out in the middle of conversations. Or go away someplace inside my head and not get back for a few hours. People thought it was because I was at Pork Chop Hill. Not so. I was never ashamed of what we did at Pork Chop.

I was thinking on this and was half in the bag when a woman at the bar touched my cheek and looked at me in a sad way, probably because she was half jacked on flak juice too, even though it was only two in the afternoon. "You got that in Korea?" she said.

"My daddy made whiskey," I replied. "Stills blow up sometimes."

Her eyes floated away from me. "You don't have to act smart."

I tried to grin, the scarred skin below my eye crinkling. "It wasn't a big deal. On *my* face it's probably an improvement."

She gazed at herself in the mirror behind the liquor counter. I waited for her to speak, but she didn't.

"Buy you a drink?" I said.

She lifted her left hand so I could see her ring. "He's nothing to brag on, but he's the only one I got."

"I admire principle," I said.

"That's why you hang out in here?"

"There's worse."

"Where?"

I didn't have an answer. She picked the cherry out of her vodka collins and sucked on it. "It's not polite to stare."

"Sorry."

"I get the blues, that's all," she said.

"I know what you mean," I replied.

I couldn't tell if she heard me or not. Kitty Wells was singing on the jukebox.

"Will you dance with me?" I said.

"Another time."

Through the screen door the sun was bright and hot, and heat waves were bouncing on the bay. The electric fan on the wall feathered her hair against her cheeks. She had a sweet face and amber eyes, with a shine in them like a beer glass. There was no pack of cigarettes or ashtray in front of her. She bent slightly forward, and I saw the shine on the tops of her breasts. I didn't think it was intentional on her part.

"I played piano for Ernie Suarez and Warren Storm at the Top Hat in Lafayette," she said.

"Looking for a job?"

"My husband doesn't like me hanging in juke joints."

"What's he do?"

"He comes and goes."

"What's that mean?"

"Not what you're thinking. He flies a plane out to the rigs."

"How'd you know I was in Korea?"

"The bartender."

Her face colored, as though she realized I knew she'd been asking about me. "My name is Loreen Walters."

"How you do, Miss Loreen?"

"Where'd you get the accent?" she asked.

"East Kentucky."

She put her wallet in her drawstring bag. The leather was braided around the edges and incised with a rearing horse ridden by a naked woman. It was a strange wallet for a woman to carry. I glanced at Loreen. She seemed to be one of those people whose faces change constantly in the light, so you never know who they actually are.

"Are you fixing to leave?" I said.

"There's nothing wrong in talking, is there?" she said.

"No, ma'am, not at all."

I could see myself close to her, next to the jukebox, my face buried in her hair, breathing her perfume and the coolness of her skin. I felt my throat catch.

"Then again, why borrow trouble?" she said. "See you, sweetie. Look me up in our next incarnation. Far as I'm concerned, this one stinks."

I went back on my seismograph barge early the next day. The sun was red and streaked with dust blowing out of the cane fields; the steel plates on the pilothouse were dripping with drops of moisture as big as silver dollars.

The lowest and hardest job in the oil business was building board roads through swamps and marshland; the second lowest was "doodle-bugging," stringing underwater cable off a jug boat, sometimes carrying it on a spool along with the seismic jugs through flooded woods thick with cottonmouths and mosquitoes. We'd drop eighteen dynamite cans screwed end to end down a drill hole, and teach the earth who was running things. The detonation was so great it jolted the barge on its pilings and blew fish as fat as logs to the surface and filled the air with a sulfurous yellow cloud that would burn the inside of your head if you breathed it.

Lizard was the driller. His skin looked like leather stretched on a skeleton. At age twenty he already had chain gang scars on his ankles and whip marks from the Black Betty on his back. He whistled and sang while he worked, and bragged on his conquests in five-dollar brothels. I was jealous of his peace of mind. He knew about what happened on our drill site down in South America, but he slept like he'd just gotten it on with Esther Williams. I had nightmares that caused me to sit on the side of my bunk until the cook clanged the breakfast bell.

My first day back on the quarter boat, Lizard sat down across from me at supper. He speared a steak off the platter and scooped potatoes and poured milk gravy on it and sliced it up, and started eating like he was stuffing garbage down a drain hole. "Word to the wise, Elmore," he said.

"What's that, Lizard?" I asked.

"Don't be milking through the wrong fence."

"Who says I am?"

"Saw you with Miss Loreen at the Gator."

"Then you didn't see very much."

He worked a piece of steak loose from his teeth. "Know who her old man is?"

"No, and I don't care, because I haven't done anything wrong," I said.

"Except not listen to the wisdom of your betters."

"How'd you like your food pushed in your face?"

"Where's that shithole you grew up in?"

"The Upper South."

"Much inbreeding thereabouts, retardation and such?"

My dreams were in Technicolor, full of murmurs and engine noise and occasionally the sundering of the earth. A man caught by a flamethrower makes a sound like a mewing kitten. A shower of potato mashers is preceded by the enemy clanging their grenades on their helmets before lobbing them into our foxholes. A toppling round becomes a hummingbird brushing by your ear. The canned dynamite we slide down our drill pipe kills big creatures stone-dead and belly-up, somehow assuring us we are the dispatchers of death and not its recipient. Sometimes I heard a baby crying.

I once used a boat hook to kill a moccasin that was trapped in the current. I threw it up on the deck to scare Lizard. I don't know why. Later I felt ashamed and told a prostitute in a Morgan City bar what I'd done. She tapped her cigarette ash in a beer can.

"My stories are a little weird?" I said.

"I think you're in the wrong bar," she replied.

Every memory in my head seemed like a piece of glass. I woke the second day on the hitch to a single-engine, canary-yellow pontoon plane coming in above the trees, swooping right over the upper deck. Ten minutes later, down in the galley, I saw the plane touch the water and taxi to the bow of the quarter boat. The pilot was Hamp Rieber, a geologist with degrees from the University of Texas and MIT. His hair was mahogany-colored and wavy, combed straight back with Brylcreem. He liked to wear polo shirts and jodhpurs and tight, ventilated leather gloves, and always buzzed us when he visited the quarter boat or the drill barge. One time Lizard climbed on the pilothouse and flung a wrench at him. He missed the prop by less than a foot.

Hamp was sent to check on us by the Houston office. Sometimes he went to a brothel in Port Arthur with the crew, although I couldn't figure out why. He was rich and lived with a handsome wife in an old plantation house south of Lake Charles.

He came in and started eating scrambled eggs and bacon and pancakes across from me. Lizard was three places down. A big window fan drew a cool breeze through the room. It was a fine time of day, before the sun started to flare on the water and the smell of carrion rose out of the swamp. Hamp's face was full of self-satisfaction while he talked. I wished Lizard had parked that wrench in his mouth.

"You look thoughtful, Elmore," he said.

"I'm philosophically inclined."

"Been reading your thesaurus?"

"I go my own way and don't have truck with those who don't like it," I said.

"You're a mystery man, all right," he said, reaching for the grits. "I always get the feeling you're looking at me when my back is turned. Why is that?"

"Search me."

"Yes, sir, a regular mystery man."

I got up with my plate and coffee mug and finished eating in a shady spot on the deck. I wished I could float away to a palm-dotted island beyond the horizon, a place where machines had never been invented, where people drank out of coconut husks and ate shellfish they harvested from the surf with their hands.

The real reason I didn't like Hamp was because of what happened down in South America. At first the Indians were curious about our seismograph soundings, but eventually they lost interest and disappeared back into trees that clicked and rattled with animal bones. Hamp selected a drill site in the jungle and we started clearing the earth with a dozer, piling greenery as high as a house, soaking it with kerosene and burning it, and turning the sun into an orange wafer. The soil was soggy, with thousands of years of detritus in it. When it was compressed under the weight of the dozer, the severed root systems twitched like they were alive.

We put up the derrick and started drilling twenty-four hours a day, using three crews, tying canvas on the spars when monsoon amounts of rain swept through the jungle. After we punched into pay sand, the driller ignited the flare line to bleed off the gas, and a flame roared two hundred feet into the sky. The sludge pit caught fire and blew a long plume of thick, black, lung-choking smoke all the way to the horizon. It hung over the jungle like a serpent until morning.

The next night the Indians showered us with arrows.

The company built a wooden shell around the rig. It must have been 120 degrees inside. By noon the floor men were puking in a bucket and pouring water on their heads to keep from passing out. But at least we'd stymied the Indians, we thought. Then an Indian shot a blowgun from the trees at one of our supply trucks coming up the road. A kid from Lufkin got it in the cheek and almost died.

"This shit ends," Hamp said.

He'd flown a spotter plane in Korea and bragged he'd shot down Bed Check Charlie with a .45.

"What are you aiming to do?" I asked.

"Know who Alfred Nobel was?"

"The man who invented dynamite."

"Nobody is going to catch flies on you."

At sunset, Hamp and another guy flew away in a two-cockpit biplane. About ten minutes later we heard a dull boom and felt a tremor under our feet and saw birds lift from the canopy in the jungle. A minute later there was a second boom, this one much stronger, then we heard the drone of the plane's engine headed back toward us. Lizard was standing next to me, bare-chested, staring at the smoke rising from the trees and the sparks churning inside it. He poured mosquito repellent on his palm and rubbed it on his neck and face. "Satchel charges," he said.

"What?" I said.

"He brought them from town a couple of days ago. He was just waiting on the excuse." He looked at my expression. "You keep them damn thoughts out of your head."

"What thoughts?"

"The kind a water walker has. It's their misfortune and none of our own. Stay the hell out of it."

I looked around at the other men on the crew. They had come out of the bunkhouse, some of them with GI mess kits in their hands. None of them seemed to know what they should say. The tool pusher, a big man who always wore khaki trousers and a straw hat and a Lima watch fob and long-sleeve shirts buttoned at the wrists, looked at the red glow in the jungle. You could hear the wind rustling the trees and smell an odor like the chimney on a rendering plant. "I don't know about y'all, but I got to see a man about a dog," he said.

The others laughed as he unzipped his fly and urinated into the dark.

In the morning the tool pusher told me to take a supply truck to the port twenty miles away and pick up a load of center cutters for the ditching machine. I tried to convince myself that Hamp had frightened the Indians out of the village before he dropped the satchel charges, that he meant to scare people and not kill them. My head was coming off as we drove down the dirt road that skirted the jungle. It was raining and the sun was shining, and a rainbow curved out of the clouds into almost the exact spot where the fire had burned out during the night.

I told the driver to stop.

"What for?" he said.

"I got dysentery. I'll walk back." I took the first aid kit and a roll of toilet paper from under the seat.

The gearshift knob was throbbing in his palm. "You sure you know what you're doing, Elmore?"

"Some Tums and salt tablets and I'll be right as rain."

* * *

179

The huts in the village had been made from thatch and scrap lumber and corrugated tin the Indians stole from construction sites. The satchel charges had blown them apart and set fire to most everything inside. I counted nine dead in the ashes, their eyes starting to sink in the sockets like they were drifting off to sleep. I took some alcohol out of the first aid kit and poured it on my bandanna and tied it across my nose and mouth, and tried not to breathe too deeply.

There was not a living creature in the village, not even a bird or insect. The only sound was the cry of a small child, the kind that says the child is helpless, unfed, and thirsty, its diaper soaked and dirty and raw on the skin.

I followed a path along a stream that had overflowed its banks. The ground was carpeted with leaves and broken twigs. Then I started to see more bodies. There were nails embedded in some of the trees, blood drags where people had tried to reach the water, pieces of hair and human pulp on the rocks by the stream. The child was lying on its back next to a woman who looked made out of sticks. One of her breasts was exposed. She wore old tennis shoes without socks and a wooden cross on a cord around her neck. A tear was sealed in one eye.

I could see branches that were broken farther down the path. The air was sweet from the spray on the rocks in the stream, the rain pattering on huge tropical plants that had heart-shaped leaves. I cleaned the child and pulled the shirt off a dead man and wrapped the child's thighs and genitals and bottom inside it, and tied the first aid kit on my belt and picked up the child and started walking. My passenger was a little boy. I had never married and had always wanted to have a little boy, or a little girl, it didn't matter, and it felt funny walking with him curled inside my arms, like I was back in the infantry, except this time I wasn't humping a BAR.

I walked until high noon, when I saw the edge of the jungle thin into full sunlight. Farther down the dirt road I could see a stucco farmhouse, with a deuce-and-a-half army truck parked in front and a canvas tarp on poles where people were lying on blankets in the shade. I looked down at my little passenger. His eyes were closed, the redness gone from his face, his nostrils so tiny I wanted to touch them to make sure he was all right.

"*¿Qué quieres?*" a soldier said.

"What does it look like?" I said.

"*No entiendo. ¿Qué haces aquí?*"

He wore a dirty khaki uniform and a Sam Browne belt and a stiff cap with a lacquered bill, a bandolier full of M1 clips strapped around his waist. His armpits were looped with sweat, his shirt unbuttoned, his chest shiny. He kept swiping at a fly, his eyes never leaving my face. There were other soldiers standing around, as though their role was just to be there. The Indians lying on the ground in the shade of the tarp looked frightened, afraid to speak. A nun in a soiled white habit was giving water to a woman out of a canteen.

"I've got to get the child to a hospital," I said. "Where's the hospital?"

"*Está aquí, hombre.*" He pointed to the child in my arms. "Put down."

"No."

"Yes, you put down."

I stepped back from him.

"You don't hear, gringo?" he said.

"Stay away from me."

He gestured to one of his men. The nun stepped between them and me and took the child from my arms.

"See, everything gonna be OK, man," the soldier in the cap said.

181

"No, it isn't. A plane bombed the village."

"You ain't got to say nothing, man. Go back to where you come from. All is taken care of."

"You're not going to do anything about it?"

"Go back with your people, gringo."

"Where's the jefe?"

"I'm the jefe. You want to be my friend? Tell me now. If you ain't our friend, I got to take you back to town, give you a place to stay for a while, let you get to know some guys you ain't gonna like."

The wind was hot, the tarp popping in the silence, the sky filled with an eye-watering brilliance.

"You don't look too good," he said. "Sit down and have some pulque. I'm gonna give you some food. See, it's cool here in the shade."

"What are you going to do with the child?"

"What you think? *Está muerto.* You been in the jungle too long, man."

Now back to the present. When I got off the hitch, I headed straight for the Hungry Gator and went to work on an ice-cold bottle of Jax and four fingers of Jack Daniel's. I heard somebody drop a nickel in the jukebox and play Kitty Wells's "It Wasn't God Who Made Honky Tonk Angels." Somehow I knew who was playing that song. I also knew the kind of trouble I might get into drinking B-52s. She sat down next to me, wearing a white skirt and blouse and a thin black belt and earrings with red stones in them. She smelled like a garden full of flowers.

"I thought I might have scared you off," she said.

"You're not the kind that scares people, Miss Loreen," I said.

"Still want to buy me a drink?"

Warning bells were clanging and red lights flashing. An oscillating fan fluttered the pages of a wall calendar in a white blur. "Anytime," I replied.

She ordered a small Schlitz. The bartender put the bottle and a glass in front of her. She poured it into the glass and put salt in it and watched the foam rise. "I'm trying to take it easy today."

"You have a taste for it?"

"You could call it that." She took a sip. "I was going to ask your bandleader if he could use a piano player."

"He's not around today. He plays weekends."

"Oh," she said, her disappointment obvious.

"You OK?"

"Sure." She kept her face turned to one side, away from the sunlight blazing on the shell parking lot.

"Look at me, Miss Loreen."

"What for?"

"Somebody hurt you?"

"He was drunk."

"Your husband?"

"Who else?"

"A man who hits a woman is a coward."

"He takes the fall for other people and resents himself. You never do that?"

"Not if I can help it."

"Lucky you." She ordered a whiskey sour.

"Miss Loreen, they say if you think you've got a problem with it, you probably do."

"Too late, sailor."

She watched the bartender make her drink in the blender and pour it into a glass. She drank it half empty, her eyes closed, her face at peace. "Did you know that song was banned from the Grand Ole Opry?"

"No."

"It's the female answer to 'The Wild Side of Life,'" she said.

"You know a lot about country music."

"I got news for you," she said.

"What's that?"

"I don't know shit about anything."

"You shouldn't talk rough like that."

"Yeah?"

"I think you put on an act. You're a nice lady."

She stared into the gloom, her eyes sleepy. The wall calendar had a glossy picture on it: a cowboy on a horse was looking into the distance at purple mountains, snow on the peaks.

"I went to a powwow once in Montana," I said. "Hundreds of Indian children were dancing in jingle shirts, all of them bouncing up and down. You should have heard the noise."

"Why are you talking about Indians?"

"Whenever I'm down about something, I think about those Indian kids dancing, the drums pounding away."

"You're not a regular guy. I mean, not like you meet in this place."

Her bag lay open on the bar. I could see the steel frame and checkered grips of a revolver inside. I touched the bag with one finger. "What you've got in there can get a person in trouble."

She turned her face so I could see her bruise more clearly. "Like I'm not already?"

"Why do somebody else's time?"

"It beats the graveyard." She licked the rim of her glass. "You know where this is going to end."

"What's going to end?"

"You got a place?"

When I didn't reply, she lowered her hand until it was under the bar and put it in mine. "Did you hear me?"

Don't answer. Say goodbye. Walk into the sunlight and get in the truck. It's never too late. "The Teche Motel in New Iberia," I said. "It's on the bayou. When the sun sets behind the oaks, you'd think it was the last day on earth."

She squeezed my hand, hard.

When I woke up the next morning, she was sitting at the table by the window shade in her panties and bra, writing on a piece of stationery, an empty bottle of Cold Duck on the floor.

"You were talking about the Indian dancers in your sleep," she said.

"What'd I say?"

"They're happy. The way kids ought to be."

I sat on the edge of the bed in my skivvies. Between the curtains I could see a shrimp boat passing on Bayou Teche; the wake, yellow and frothy, slapped the oak and cypress trees along the bank.

"My husband says Indians are no good," she said.

"What's he know about Indians?"

"He's an expert on everything."

"Did he give you your wallet?"

"For Christmas. With a naked woman on it."

I didn't speak.

"Why'd you ask?" she said.

"Was he in the pen?"

"His brother is a guard in Huntsville. The whole family works in prisons. If they weren't herding convicts, they'd be doing time themselves."

"Were you writing me a Dear John?"

185

"I was going to tell you last night didn't happen."

"That's how you feel about it?"

"My feelings don't matter."

"To me they do. Tear it up."

"You've never messed around, have you?"

"Not with a married woman, if that's what you mean."

"You know what that just did to my stomach?"

"Way I see it, a man who hits his wife doesn't have a claim."

"Tell the state of Louisiana that," she said. "Tell my in-laws."

Ten minutes later the owner knocked on the door and told me I had a phone call. "A man named Lizard," he added.

"She with you?" he said.

"Who?"

"The one whose husband I warned you about and who's looking for you now," he said.

"He's headed here?"

"I told him you hung out in the French Quarter."

"Who is this guy?"

"The same guy who liked to throw satchel charges out of a plane with his buddy Hamp Rieber. You know how to pick them, Elmo."

I said nothing to Loreen and showered and shaved and took my time doing it, pretending I didn't care about the bear trap I had stepped in. Then I threw my duffel bag in the back of the truck and told her to hop in.

She was pinning back her hair with both hands, her bare arms as big as a man's. "Where we going?" she said.

"The beach in Biloxi is beautiful this time of year," I replied.

*　*　*

186

The storm was way out in the Gulf and not a hurricane yet, but you could feel the barometer dropping and see horsetails of purple rain to the south and hundreds of breakers forming and disappearing on the horizon. When we checked in to the motel the waves were sliding over the jetties and sucking backward into the Gulf, scooping truckloads of sand and shellfish with them. The air smelled like brass and iodine and seaweed full of tiny creatures that had died on the beach, the way it smells when you know a hard one is coming.

I opened the windows in our room. Up on the boulevards the fronds of the palm trees were straightening in the wind. I told Loreen what Lizard had said. She sat down on the edge of the bed, her face white. "Does he know where we are?"

"I don't see how."

"His whole family are cops and prison guards. They know everybody. They all work together."

"It's not against the law to check in to a motel."

"This is Mississippi. The law is what some redneck says it is."

"He's just a man, nothing more."

But she wasn't listening. She seemed to be looking at an image painted on the air.

"He's buds with Hamp Rieber?" I said.

"Who?"

"A pilot. Rieber and another guy killed a bunch of Indians on a job in South America. They dropped explosive charges on their village. Maybe the other guy was your husband."

"Charles is an asshole but he wouldn't do that."

"His name isn't Charlie? I think a guy like that would be called Charlie."

"Who told you this about Charles?"

"Nobody had to tell me anything. I was there when it happened."

"Why didn't we hear about it? It would have been in the paper or on television."

I looked at the confusion and alarm in her face. "You want a drink?"

"See? You can't answer my question. It wasn't in the news because it didn't happen."

"I carried an infant for miles to a first aid station. He was dead when I arrived."

Her eyes were too large for her face. "I need to sit down. This isn't our business. We have to think about ourselves. You didn't tell anybody where we were going?"

"Give me the gun."

"What for?"

"We've got each other. Right?"

She stared at me, her upper lip perspiring, her pulse jumping in her neck.

I had acted indifferently about taking off with a married woman. It wasn't the way I felt. My father was a pacifist who made and sold moonshine, and my mother a minister in the Free Will Baptist Church. They gave me a good upbringing, and I felt I'd flushed it down the commode.

While Loreen slept off her hangover, I sat on a bench by the surf and played my mandolin. I could hear a buoy clanging and electricity crackling across the sky. The beach was empty, the sand damp and biscuit-colored, a towel with Donald Duck on it blowing end over end past my foot. I wondered how long it would take for Loreen's husband and in-laws to catch up with me.

Southern culture is tribal. They might holler and shout in their church houses, but they want blood for blood, and at the bottom of it is sex. The kind of mutilation the KKK visits on its lynch victims isn't coincidental. The system wasn't aimed at just people of color, either. Guys I knew who'd done time in Angola said there were over one hundred convicts buried in the levee, and the iron sweatboxes on Camp A that were bulldozed out in '52 were a horror story the details of which no newspaper would touch.

Thinking about these things made my eyes go out of focus.

The next day Loreen was drunk again and told me she was taking the bus to Lafayette to stay with her sister. "Give me back the gun," she said.

"Bad idea."

"It's my goddamn gun. Give it to me."

I took the revolver from my duffel bag and flipped the cylinder out of the frame. I noticed that only five chambers were loaded.

"Where'd you learn to set the hammer on an empty chamber?"

"I don't know what you mean. You squeeze them on one end and a bullet comes out the other."

I shook the bullets into my palm and dropped them in my pocket. I tossed the revolver on the bed. "I'll drive you to the depot."

I decided to stay clear of the Teche Motel in case Loreen or her husband came looking for me. I drove to Lizard's trailer outside Morgan City and asked if I could stay with him. In two more days I'd be back on the quarter boat, maybe back to a regular life. Lizard stood in the doorway, wearing only swim trunks and cowboy boots, gazing at the palmettos and palm and persimmon trees. "You threw a rock at a beehive," he said.

"You don't have to tell me."

"Did she go back to him?"

"They usually do."

"You got played, son."

"By who?"

"She's one of those who digs badasses and taking chances. She'll have you sticking a gun in your mouth."

"She's scared to death," I said.

"That's how she gets off." He tapped his fist against the jamb. "For a man who spends a lot of time in libraries, you're sure dumb. Come inside."

We listened to the weather reports and read his collection of *Saga* and *Argosy* and *True West* magazines, and went to a beer garden in town and ate boiled crawfish and crabs. The storm we'd worried about had disappeared, although another one had developed unexpectedly out of a tropical swell in the Bay of Campeche and was headed toward the central Gulf Coast.

Lizard sucked the fat out of a crawfish shell and threw the shell in a trash barrel. "They try to keep everybody scared and tuned to the radio. That's how they sell more products."

"I don't think the United States Weather Bureau is involved in a plot," I said.

"Like Roosevelt didn't know the Japs was fixing to bomb Pearl Harbor. You're a card."

I tried to keep in mind that once, after being thrown out of a roadhouse in Maringouin, Lizard got in the welding truck and drove it through the front wall and onto the dance floor, blowing his horn for a drink. The bouncers almost killed him.

I wanted to believe my problems would pass. The Japanese lanterns were swaying in a light breeze; a solitary raindrop touched my face. I watched a shooting star slip down the side of the sky.

"You're a good guy, Lizard."

His expression was as blank as a breadboard.

We paid the check and walked out to his beloved cherry-red pickup, a little lighthearted, feeling younger than our years. Two men were eating cracklings out of a paper bag in a patrol car. The car was old, salt-eaten around the fenders, the white star on the door streaked with mud. The two men got out of the car. They were big and wore slacks and short-sleeve tropical shirts. One wore a straw cowboy hat; the other had a baton that hung from a lanyard on his wrist. Their eyes passed over me and locked on Lizard.

"That your truck?" the man with the baton said.

"Yes, sir," Lizard said.

"My name is Detective Benoit. I saw this vehicle run a red light." He adjusted the mirror on the driver's door and examined his face as though looking for a razor nick. Then he hammered the mirror loose from the door, tearing the screws out of the metal. "Your taillights working?"

Lizard's face turned gray. "Why y'all bracing me?"

Benoit walked to the back of the pickup. "Looks like they're busted, all right."

He broke out both taillights, then tapped the fragments off the baton.

Neither man seemed to take interest in me.

"I ain't caused y'all no trouble," Lizard said.

"We've seen your jacket," the man in the hat said. A white scar hung from one eye, like a piece of string. "You're here on interstate parole. You shouldn't have been drinking."

"I ain't on parole," Lizard said.

"It's me they're after," I said.

Neither cop looked at me. They turned Lizard around and pushed him against the truck, then cuffed his wrists behind him, snicking them tight into the skin. The man in the hat pushed him into the back seat of the patrol car.

I felt like I was standing by while my best friend drowned.

The car drove away, with Lizard looking out the back window. A group in the beer garden was singing "You Are My Sunshine." At the end, they clapped and shouted.

I walked back to the highway and hitched a ride to the trailer court. The door to Lizard's trailer hung on one hinge. The inside was a wreck. Most of my clothes had been taken from my duffel bag and stuffed in the toilet and pissed on. My mandolin had been smashed into kindling.

The cops were partly right. Lizard had finished his parole time in Georgia, but he had a minor bench warrant in Florida. The cops put him in a can down by Plaquemines Parish, the kind of place where people thought "habeas corpus" was a Yankee name for a disease.

In the oil patch, there were no second chances. If you were wired, you were fired. Lizard wasn't wired, but he got fired just the same.

I went back to the Teche Motel in New Iberia. That's where she found me, and didn't even bother to turn off her engine when she knocked on the door. When I opened it she was breathing hard through her nose, a clot of blood in one nostril, her little fist knotted on her drawstring bag. "You've got to help me."

"What did he hit you with?"

"A belt. Can I come in?"

There was no one in the long, tree-shaded driveway that separated the two rows of cottages. Chickens were pecking on the lawns. "Park the car behind the building," I said.

She came back a minute later and closed the door after her. She tried to hand me her car keys.

"You can't stay, Loreen."

"He's going to kill me."

"Call the cops. Show them what he did."

"He saw me look at the phone and asked me how I'd like to dial it with broken fingers. Then he said he was just kidding and poured me a drink. He's crazy."

"I've got a couple of hundred dollars. That'll get you to Los Angeles. A friend of mine owns a hillbilly nightclub in Anaheim. I can probably get you a job there."

"I asked him about this Hamp Rieber guy."

"What about him?"

"Charles said Hamp was going to take care of you. Charles says you bug him."

"Say that again?"

"He said something happened in South America. I pretended not to know what he was talking about. He said Hamp knows people who can shut you up. Hamp told Charles somebody should have done it a long time ago."

She took the revolver out of her bag and set it heavily on the nightstand. Her mouth was a tight line. "You still have the bullets?"

"I don't want it."

"Throw it in the bayou. It's your life. Charles says if he has his way he's going to put something of yours in a pickle jar."

She went out on the stoop. I followed her. "Take the two hundred anyway."

Her hair was blowing in the wind. It was thick and auburn, and almost hid the stripes and lumps on her face. "We could have had fun, you and me."

Lizard said I was being played. Maybe he was right, maybe not. It didn't matter. Hamp Rieber was in the mix. He knew I knew what he had done down in the tropics, and I suspected it had probably eaten a hole in his stomach.

193

I still had the rounds for a revolver. It was a .38 Special, blue-black and snub-nosed, the serial numbers burned off. I sat in a chair by the front window and dropped the shells one by one into the cylinder. The bayou was chained with rain rings, the light in the trees turning to gold needles. I remembered the words to a song my mother's congregation used to sing:

> Gonna lay down my sword and shield,
> Down by the riverside,
> I ain't gonna study war no more.

I wanted to crawl inside the lyrics and never come out. Instead I drove to Lake Charles and found the antebellum home of Hamp Rieber, where he lived in the middle of wetlands with a rainbow arching overhead. The rainbow reminded me of the one that seemed to fall on the village Hamp had bombed.

No one in my acquaintance thought me capable of wicked acts. I knew different. If people asked me how my face came to be burned, I would make a joke about whiskey stills or if pressed mention Pork Chop Hill or for fun say "friendly fire."

I pulled the tanks from the back of a corporal who had caught one right through his steel pot, and went straight up the hill and jammed the igniter head into the slit of a North Korean pillbox. I had never pulled the trigger on a flamethrower. The blowback cooked half my face. What it did to the men inside I won't try to describe.

I parked my pickup behind an old Hadacol billboard on a dirt road and entered the back of Hamp's property through a pecan orchard. The house was a two-story antebellum, with twin chimneys and a veranda, and from behind the stable I could hear people in the side yard. I had the pistol stuck in the back of my khakis, the barrel cutting into my skin.

What were my plans?

I had none. Or none I would admit.

I began walking across the lawn toward the side yard, sweating, a warm wind on my face, my pulse beating in my wrists. I saw not only Hamp Rieber and his wife but the man who I used to see with him, the man who was probably Charles Walters. Three children were hitting croquet balls on the lawn.

I had never shot an unarmed man. I had seen it happen, but I never did it. I saw F-80s strafe roads choked with civilians and wood carts and draft animals because intelligence said the refugee columns streaming south had been infiltrated by the Chinese. But I had not let these things lay claim on me.

Walters had sunbrowned skin, pale eyes, the military posture of a man who is constantly aware of himself, and coarse, large hands that swallowed the small paper plate and plastic fork he was using to eat a piece of pie. As I gazed at the emptiness in his face, I realized that he was not a man I would ever take seriously. He was a wifebeater. I never saw one of them who wouldn't cut bait when you called him out. The issue was Hamp. It had always been Hamp.

I grew up on a ridge above a place called Snaky Hollow. I knew children who lived in dirt-floor cabins and went barefoot in the snow and wore clothes made from Purina feed sacks. When I looked at Hamp, I saw those children. Call me a communist.

I wanted him to pick up a cake knife and cut me, or come at me with a shotgun. I was ready to go out smoking, as long as I could sling his blood on the shrubbery with a clear conscience.

But under my hatred I knew the real problem was the fact that I had never been to the company about him or reported him to the authorities. I told myself it was a waste of time and I would lose my job for no purpose. But the words "I didn't try" wouldn't go out of my head.

He sighed. "Tired of being a spectator?"

"That's close."

"And thought you'd roll the dice."

"You're a mind reader, Hamp."

His eyes traveled up and down my person. "You packing, kid?"

"You never know."

"Let's talk out by the gazebo."

"Right here is OK," I said.

"No, it isn't," he replied.

My hands were at my sides. "Why'd you do it?"

"Do what?" he asked.

"You know. Down *there*."

"I didn't do anything there except do my job."

"Our man Charles here didn't do anything, either?" I said.

"Ask him."

"What about it, Charles?" I said. "Did you fling the charges or just fly the plane?"

"Let's go out to the stable," Charles replied. "I'll show you Hamp's horses."

"I toted a child out of the jungle and never knew he died," I said.

"Lower your voice, please," Hamp said.

"Sorry. I have a hard time sleeping at night. It reduces my powers of judgment."

"Try a glass of warm milk," Hamp said.

Then I felt myself slipping loose from my tether, a red bubble swelling inside my brain. I saw myself pulling the snub-nose from my belt and squeezing off a round in Hamp's throat, then a second one in Walters's forehead before he knew what hit him. I wet my lips and swallowed.

"Are you going to get sick on us?" Hamp said.

"No, sir," I said. "I just want to say I'm sorry to do this."

I arched an imaginary crick out of my back and let my right hand drift to the butt of the revolver, my fingertips touching the grips. I saw Hamp's wife pick up a little girl and heft her on her hip. The little girl's face was like a flower turning into the sunlight. "Daddy! Come back and play with us," she said, extending her arms.

"I'll be right there, hon," he said.

I stepped backward and hooked the thumb of my right hand on my pocket.

"You got something else to say?" Hamp asked.

"Y'all or somebody y'all hired busted my mandolin. I wished you hadn't done that."

"You need to give your listeners a decoder, Elmore," Hamp said.

"See y'all down the track," I said. I looked at his wife. "Forgive me for breaking in on y'all's party, ma'am."

I walked backward until I was clear of the picket gate, then went to my pickup, my hands shaking so badly I could hardly start the engine.

I drove to town along the edge of the lake, the palm trees bending, waves scudding, and went into a stationery store and bought a writing tablet and a small shipping box and a pencil and a ball of string. Then I drove to a park and sat at a picnic table and wrote the following note:

> This gun belongs to a pilot in Golden Meadow, Louisiana, named Charles Walters. The acid-burned numbers tell me the gun has been used in a crime or as a drop by corrupt cops. Walters and a geologist named Hamp Rieber killed many Indians with satchel charges thrown from their airplane.

I wrote down the place and date of the bombing and the name of the company we all served. Then I added:

> My name is Elmore Caudill. I live out of a duffel bag and a pickup truck. My mailing address is the Hungry Gator in the Atchafalaya Swamp.

I unloaded the revolver and placed it in the box and wrote "FBI" across the top and tied the box with string and stopped long enough at the post office to drop it in the mailbox outside.

I was fired from my job. Lizard was sprung from the can. A federal agent interviewed me at the Teche Motel. Loreen dumped her husband, opened a bakery in Lafayette, and asked me to marry her. My attempt at telling the world of our misdeeds in the tropics changed nothing. In fact, I think my account had all the weight of an asterisk.

The big news of that summer was Hurricane Audrey. The tidal surge curled like a huge fist over Cameron, Louisiana, and killed hundreds of people. I worked a minimum-wage cleanup job pulling bodies out of the Calcasieu River. Over in the Atchafalaya Swamp I saw every type of animal in the wetlands starve or drown on the tops of flooded trees and floating piles of trash. I smelled more death in the aftermath of the storm than I did in war.

Hamp Rieber died trying to rescue people on a rooftop with his pontoon plane. Charles Walters became a drunk who worked the gate at Angola because he was too fat to sit on a horse and too scared to walk among the inmates. I started my own company and drilled for oil in eastern Montana and hit four dusters in a row, and, dead broke, headed over to Lame Deer and put on a jingle shirt and danced among the Cheyenne children. What a noise we made.

A DISTANT WAR

He was a junior college history instructor and had lost his way somewhere south of the Colorado line, and now, in the sunset, with his little boy on the seat next to him, he was on a long stretch of two-lane county road devoid of telephone poles or road signs or lighted houses. The mountains were purple and pooling in their own shadow, as though subsuming themselves and destroying their own destiny, the wind cold, unforgiving, buffeting his rust-eaten Chevy, perhaps even mocking him for the wrong turns he had made all day. Just imagination? The tumbleweeds were bouncing high in the air across the hardpan, smacking his windshield or matting under the car's frame and creating a grinding sound like a giant wire brush scouring the asphalt.

A single drop of rain flattened against the windshield and curled dryly away on the wiper, then a bolt of lightning split the sky and caused him to zigzag and almost go into the ditch. He cupped his palm over his mouth at what had almost happened—the car flipping, his little boy thudding against the dashboard, the roof pancaking.

"Is everything all right, Daddy?" the boy asked.

"Sure. We're not going to let a little electricity scare us."

The boy was named Morgan for his great-grandfather, a violent drunkard and unreconstructed Confederate officer who rode the Chisholm Trail and put many men under the sod, until he got religion and became a saddle preacher, a tale that the history instructor thought tenuous if not shopworn. But his mother, forceful and crazy woman that she was, forced the name on his son, and now Francis resented himself as well as his mother.

Morgan had to stretch his neck to see over the dashboard. "Daddy?"

"What is it, little pal?"

"There's smoke coming out of the hood."

The instructor's name was Francis Holland. He was trim and good-looking, his blond hair cut short, his green eyes never judgmental or angry, as some young academics were wont to be. In fact, he didn't believe he deserved his instructorship and never complained if he was assigned night or early-morning classes. His students loved him; in turn, he never gave one of them lower than a C, particularly if the student was having trouble with the draft board.

He pulled to the side of the road and got out and lifted the car's hood. The radiator hose was split, and water and antifreeze were bubbling on the engine block, dripping into the gravel.

Up ahead in the darkness, in what could have been the bottom of an ancient sea, was a nightclub or diner set on cinder blocks with a neon Coors sign in the front window. Across the road from the bar was an olive-green train car, the windows pocked with bullet holes, the rims of the steel wheels shiny, although the rails went nowhere.

"Are we in trouble, Daddy?" Morgan asked.

It was November, deep down in the fall, Francis's long-sleeve shirt puffing in the wind, his khakis flattening against his legs. "We're okay, little buddy. We'll get a hamburger for you and a grilled cheese for me and a Grapette up at that stopping place. Then we'll hire someone to fix our car and be on the road."

"They fix cars inside that building?" Morgan said.

"Well, let's find out," his father replied.

By the time they made it to the "stopping place," the engine was clanking like a junkyard.

There were only two vehicles parked in front of the building—a low-rider Harley and a skinned-up flatbed truck loaded with tarped-down cages. Francis started to lift up his son before they entered the building, something Morgan always resented. "I'm no baby, Daddy," he would say. So he swung the boy playfully across the entrance and closed the door behind them.

The gloom inside was so dense the sun's last rays lit up the dust like fireflies.

"Welcome, folks," the bartender said. He had a black beard shaped like a shovel and a neck like a hog, and wore rubber gloves and a clean white apron. In the corner a man was sleeping facedown with his arms folded on the table; the tabletop was chained with wet rings from an empty whiskey glass. A biker wearing chaps was at the bar watching a boxing match on a black-and-white TV. No sound came from the set.

A woman came through the strings of beads that hung from the doorway of the ladies' room. She had red hair and bright lipstick and wore a tight orange dress that glittered with sequins. She also wore a gold locket around her neck. She was very drunk but tried to straighten her hair when she saw Francis. She tripped, then grabbed the bar and sat down in front of a cocktail glass that spilled on her fingers. She licked the back of her hand, her eyes coming back into focus. "Coming in from the storm?" she said.

"We didn't see any storm," Francis said. "You have a mechanic hereabouts?"

"You hear that, Harry?" she said to the biker.

"Yeah," he replied without taking his gaze off the TV. "I hear real good."

"Who's your little boy?" the woman asked Francis.

"That's Morgan," Francis replied.

"You're a cute little boy, Morgan," she said.

"That's what little Chinamen do," the man named Harry said. "They practice being cute."

"What did you say?" Francis asked.

"Your little Chinaman," Harry said. "That's what he is, isn't he?"

Francis placed his hand on his son's back. "The term is 'Amerasian.' Or you can just call him American."

"Fucking A," Harry said.

"I didn't get that," Francis said.

"Harry is a mechanic," the woman said to Francis. "Ignore his profanity. He doesn't mean anything. Right, Harry?"

"Hey, mister," the bartender said, smiling broadly. "You want something to eat or drink or not?"

"You serve hamburgers and grilled cheese sandwiches?" Francis asked.

"If that's what you want."

"Give us two Grapettes, too."

The bartender continued to grin. "Want anything else?" he asked.

"I'd like to get my radiator hose replaced."

The bartender's gaze shifted to the woman, then back to Francis. Francis pretended not to see the message in his eyes. "Is there a town around here?"

"A couple of truck stops and a motor court twenty miles down the road," the bartender said. "I wouldn't go there at night, though."

"Why not?"

"Drugs. Pavement princesses. Illegals. Were you digging in the Anasazi pueblos?"

"No," Francis said. "How about our food?"

"You got red dirt on your clothes and hands. Like up in the cliffs."

"The wind was blowing where we camped. There was red dust in the sky."

"I was just saying," the bartender said. "My name is Floyd Hammer. Dead Indians can cause trouble, believe it or not. Two ice-cold Grapettes coming up."

Francis looked at the man in chaps, the one called Harry. "You have a radiator hose that will fit a '52 Chevy?"

"Let me take a look."

"Can we do that now?"

"I work when I feel like it," Harry said. "Right now I don't feel like it."

"Sir, I'm with my little boy," Francis said. "We're tired and hungry. I want to get him home."

"Show him your good side, Harry," the woman said.

"Oh, guess who just pulled the cork out of her mouth?" Harry said. He leaned over the bar and refilled his glass from the beer tap. Then looked at her to see if he had drawn blood. He had.

"Don't talk like that to me, Harry," she said.

"Watch me," he replied. He silently mouthed the words "you cunt" at her. Her face shrunk; she opened her purse and sniffed in a handkerchief, her eyes hidden. "Here's my snot rag, Varina. Enjoy yourself," Harry added.

"You ought to cool that stuff, buddy," Francis said.

"Hang around," Harry said. "See what she's like when she's really sloshed."

"Will you help us out or not?" Francis asked.

Harry's hair was heavy with grease and combed back in a ducktail. He lifted a strand out of his eye. His cheeks were sunken, his teeth small. "I don't take checks."

"I have some cash."

"'Some' cash doesn't quite resonate," Harry replied.

"If necessary, a friend in Albuquerque can loan me some money," Francis said.

Harry sipped from his glass and seemed to meditate. "What the hell."

"Can you translate that?"

"Let's look at your car. You're definitely from Weirdsville, man."

Francis and the man with no name except Harry went outside just as the storm broke and lightning began striking the hardpan. Francis's little boy ate a hamburger and drank a Grapette at the bar. Harry studied the radiator and chewed on his lip and fiddled with the fan belt, then snorted deep down in his nasal passages and spat a wad of phlegm on the gravel. "When's the last time you put antifreeze in your radiator?"

"Before Christmas."

"Better get your money back. Give me your keys."

"What for?"

"What does it look like? To park the car in my shed."

Francis dropped the keys in his palm. But Harry had become distracted and was staring at the train car across the highway and a lone buzzard circling above it. The air was cold, the rain working its way across the hardpan. "So what kind of repairs are we talking about?" Francis said.

"I don't know. I need better light," Harry replied, a glare in his face.

"I was just asking a question."

"What you want to know is how much will it cost you. I don't think I have a radiator hose that'll fit. That means I have to get one from a scrapyard. The hose will cost you one buck. Labor will cost you twenty-five, plus gas. But I think your bigger problem is poor maintenance."

"I don't share your perception."

"A little sensitive, are we?" Harry said. "There's not a wrecker service for fifty miles, and it's run by a cat you don't want to meet." He slammed the hood.

"Okay," Francis said.

"Okay what?"

"Go ahead and do what you can. How long do you think it will take?"

"That depends."

"On what?"

"Everything. Starting with the weather."

"I see."

"What do you do for a living?" Harry said.

"I teach history at a juco."

Harry peeled a stick of gum, a grin at the corner of his mouth.

"Did I say something funny?" Francis asked.

"Sounds like prime cut."

Francis let his eyes go empty. "I'd better check on my boy."

Francis went back inside. Morgan was sitting next to the woman, finishing his hamburger, both of them watching a black-and-white stick-figure Mickey Mouse cartoon from the 1930s. "Why don't you turn up the sound?" Francis said.

"It doesn't have any," the woman said. Her voice had become more distant, her face lackluster. "How about a drink?"

"No, thanks," Francis said.

"I was talking about me."

"Why do you hang in a dump like this?"

"Come into my Airstream and I'll tell you." Her eyes wandered over his face. "Think I'm coming on to you?"

"No," he said. "You seem like a nice lady. That man has no right to talk to you like that."

She moved her palm across Morgan's flattop haircut as though she were testing the stiffness of a shoe brush. "His hair is so soft. What a fine little boy. I bet you're mighty proud of him."

"He's my little pal," Francis said. "That's from a song, 'Little Darling Pal of Mine.'"

"I was in a musical with Doris Day in 1949," she said.

"Really?" he said, not impolitely.

She stroked Morgan's hair again, then let her fingers trail off his forehead. "Where's his mother?"

"She died."

"I'm sorry."

"She flew with Air America. She went down on Highway 1 going into Hanoi."

"I don't know what all that means."

"No one does," he replied.

"Bring your little boy to my trailer. We can make coffee. I have coloring books that I save for children."

"I'd better wait on my car."

"Why are you treating me this way?"

"Ma'am, I just want to get my boy back home."

"Well, just damn you to hell," she said.

She tried to get off the bar stool, then slipped and fell against him and butted her head in his face. He pressed his hand to his mouth; his lip was bleeding.

"Oh, God, I'm drunk," she said. "I'm so sorry about everything."

"It's okay," he said, pressing a paper napkin to his lip.

"Let me fix that."

"No, I'm okay, Miss Varina. That's your name, right?"

"Yes, it is. Come to my trailer. You're bleeding on your shirt."

"Another time," he said, trying to ignore the fear and desperation in her eyes.

"I was born in Natchez, Mississippi," she said. "Your genteel manner isn't lost on me, sir."

He removed the napkin from his lip and looked at it. Morgan was holding on to his arm, his face frightened. *"Daddy, let's go,"* he whispered.

"Can I buy you something to eat, Miss Varina?"

"I wish I had my family," she said. "I wish I had a little boy like yours. My little boy fell to his death. I miss him so. I can't tell you how much."

"I'm sorry for your loss," Francis said.

But her attention had wandered. She was gazing out the front window, frowning the way people do when they are bothered by an idea or situation they cannot relieve themselves of.

"What's wrong?" he asked.

"The sun's gone."

"It's that time of day," he said.

"This is different. It happens once a month. The sky turns to soot, and the night is so dark even the lightning in the mountains is swallowed by the clouds."

Her makeup was cracked, like the paint on a doll's face, her eyelashes stuck together.

"Did I upset you, Miss Varina?" he said.

"No, alcohol and self-pity have become my bane. Get your automobile back from the man who calls himself Harry. Then put your boy in the car and drive and drive and never stop."

"He 'calls' himself Harry?"

"Actors choose their own names, no matter the role."

Suddenly the front door flew open and the wind blew into the building with such force that the mixed snow and rain peppered the wall behind the bar. Harry came inside and pushed the door back into the jamb with his rump. "I got an update on your trash mobile, Professor," he said. "It's not as bad as it could be."

Harry made a performance out of coughing and hacking and blowing his nose before he gave Francis the breakdown.

"What's a timing chain?" Francis asked.

"Something you got that's broken and that I got to find, if I don't get pneumonia first," Harry said. He ordered a cup of coffee with a shot back as though indicating his workday was over.

"I have to be in Albuquerque by tomorrow," Francis said.

"You didn't let me finish. I replaced a tie rod that could have gotten you killed. I also patched your oil pan and switched out your muffler."

"What was wrong with my muffler?"

"It's a sieve?"

"You should have asked me first," Francis said.

"No problem. I'll reinstall it and you can fill your car with carbon monoxide. The charge for the labor still stands."

"How much do I owe you so far?"

Harry removed a small notebook from his back pocket and thumbed through the pages, his thumbnail half-mooned with grease and dirt. "Eighty-six dollars and thirty cents."

"I think you're taking advantage of my situation."

"Think all you want. If I was you, I'd give some thought to my kid instead of my pocketbook."

Francis felt a tic in his right hand. "I'll have to give you a check."

"I already told you I do cashola only. No pay, no play, Kemosabe. State law says I can take your vehicle."

"I can't give you money I don't have. Also, I don't appreciate your giving me names."

"Excuse me," Harry said. "Let me go kill myself."

"Don't talk to him like that," the woman said.

"How would you like a certain male extension slapped in your mouth, Varina?" Harry said.

Francis raised his hand. "That's enough, partner," he said. "You need to fix my car, and you need to fix it now, and you need to give some serious thought about your attitude toward others."

"Some problem here?" said the bartender who called himself Floyd Hammer. He was wiping the top of the counter, making a slow circle with the towel, his eyes lowered, his beard as thick as a pillow on his chest.

"Where's your telephone?" Francis asked.

"The line's down," Floyd said. "So is the bridge six miles south of here. Don't think about going back over the pass, either. Rocks as big as cars fell in the road last night."

"How did you acquire all this information if the phone line is down?" Francis said.

"The highway patrol picked up some burgers from my service window," Floyd said.

"There's got to be a motel around here," Francis said.

"It's five miles on the other side of the bridge," Floyd said. "If you need to charge some food or drinks, I'll start you a tab." He picked up the bottom of his apron and touched at his nose with it.

Morgan put his hand inside his father's. "We're not going home, Daddy?" he said.

"Sure we are," Francis said.

"When?" the boy asked.

Francis stared at the bartender and at Harry, and felt a knot as hard as a walnut form in his throat. His words were coated with phlegm. "Do y'all have some kind of ID? Because I'm getting a real bad feeling about you."

"Screw your ID," Harry said.

"None of that, Harry," Floyd said. "We don't have to be uncivilized, here."

Varina got off the barstool and steadied herself, one hand on the bar, her hair in her eyes. She looked at Francis. "I'm going to my trailer, sir. You and your grand little boy are welcome there."

He didn't answer and instead looked at Floyd. "When will the highway patrol be back?"

"Who says they're coming back?" Floyd said.

"If I can't drive out of here, neither can they."

"They know back roads," Floyd said. "They work with helicopters. How do I know?"

"I don't believe anything you say," Francis replied.

Floyd tightened his hands into fists on top of the counter and looked out the window at the dust devils scudding across the hardpan. He reached under the bar and set a bowl of pretzels on top of it. "For your kid. They're free."

*   *   *

The inside of Varina's Airstream was warm and bigger than Francis thought it would be. Through the blinds and the rain he could see the sky darkening and the lights coming on in the back windows of the nightclub, and he could also see the string of headlights on the motorcycles and pickup trucks turning off the two-lane into the parking lot. Then someone began testing a microphone and guitar, the electric feedback screeching like fingernails on a blackboard.

Varina gave Morgan a popsicle from a small refrigerator and showed Francis a scrapbook stiff with pasted photos and news clippings. Her name and photo were not prominent in the articles, but it was obvious she had told the truth about her career. He was afraid to ask how or why it had ended.

"Do you wonder why I live here?" she said.

"I wonder why you're around someone like that mechanic out there."

"I didn't choose this place," she said. She was holding a longneck in one hand and a bottle opener in the other. "I've had to roam for quite a while. My last death was in California."

"I don't think I heard you right."

"I have owed a large debt for many years," she said.

"You shouldn't drink any more, Miss Varina."

"As you say," she said. She put the bottle back in the refrigerator and sat down across from him at the breakfast table. "You never told me your full name," she said.

"Francis Benbow Holland."

"I have the feeling you carry a severe burden, Mr. Holland," she said. "It has something to do with a child. One that is not yours."

He felt his stomach clench. "Why would you say that?"

"It's in your eyes. You try to hide it with your manners. You fear your dreams."

He looked at her as though he were no longer speaking with the person who was drunk at the bar. "I'm real tired, Miss Varina. I don't mean to offend you, but I'm not up to this kind of conversation."

"It's all right, Mr. Holland. Why don't you take a nap? Your little boy can sleep in this little side room," she said. "See? He can have his own hammock."

"I don't understand what's going on here."

"That's my fault. I've weighed you down with things you're not able to understand at this juncture in your life."

"I just want to get my son out of here."

"I know," she replied. "I'll do everything I can to help you."

Francis sat down on the couch and watched her put his son to bed. He had never been so tired, not even after the worst experience in his life, the one that would suddenly spring to life at a traffic light or in the middle of a lecture to his frontier lit class.

At age nineteen he had ended up in a country where he was not supposed to be. The two Hueys were supposed to pick up a Hmong general and his family and a half dozen subordinates marked for death by the Pathet Lao. The extraction should have been a breeze. There were no reports of the enemy in the vicinity. From five hundred feet the harsh beauty of the jungle resembled the artwork of Paul Gauguin—the canopy sunlit, emerald green, eye-watering, threaded with a network of milky-brown rivers and streams, the indigenous people brown-skinned and barely clothed, as though they had just been shaped from the clay.

It was a warm, sleepy day. The mission was old hat, the kind in which the passengers sometimes brought opium on board and the pilot looked the other way. What could go wrong? They were almost on the Cambodian border. The Hueys were slicks, airships with neither rockets nor mounted guns. The world could not have been more at peace with itself. The gunny was dozing when they descended between a rice paddy and the ville.

The team went out the door immediately after the skids settled on the ground. Then it hit the fan. The Pathet Lao came out of the tree line and opened up with rocket-propelled grenades and Chinese burp guns and Soviet-made Kalashnikovs. In less than a minute the hooches were burning and women and children were running and screaming and dying and pigs squealing and water buffalo crumpling on their haunches, choking deep in their throats, huffing blood out of their mouths and nostrils, their ribs stippled with machine-gun rounds.

The gunny was yelling at him, his face twisted into a knot. "Go back! Go back!" he shouted, hitting Francis in the chest because Francis would not stop.

"The baby!" Francis yelled back.

"What baby?" the gunny said.

"There's a baby in that hooch!" Francis shouted. But his voice was swallowed by the explosions of the RPGs and the ammunition belts popping in the flames inside the hooches.

The rest of the team was running for the Hueys, streaking past Francis, a couple of them already hit and going down hard. The gunny grabbed Francis by the shirt and swung him on the ground. "Now you get your goddamn ass on board! There ain't no kid in no fucking hooch. You hear me, doc? Get your mind right!"

The child was probably no more than a year old and sitting in the doorway in a diaper and crying. The doorway was already framed with fire, the inside of the hooch blooming with smoke and red-hot ash.

The gunny picked up Francis from the ground and hit his steel pot with the heel of his hand. "We got fucked, doc! Acknowledge! I'll shoot you, doc! I swear to God I will!"

Then the gunny took a round as though an invisible fist had punched him between the shoulder blades. He stumbled forward, his eyes crossing, his mouth forming into a cone like a guppy's. Francis heaved him over his right shoulder, then slid him onto the slick, the downdraft troweling wheelbarrow-loads of dirt and dust in the air.

Francis looked back at the hooch. The baby was still in the doorway, still crying, his skin and diaper spotted with black ash. Francis climbed onto the Huey, then felt it surge into the air like it had been jerked upward on a bungee cord, the ville dropping away inside the smoke and the fires that resembled burning haystacks. He prayed out loud for a divine intervention, but could not hear his own words in the cacophony that surrounded him. He was on his hands and knees, like a dog, tilting with the helicopter, almost going out the door, then someone slammed him to the floor and sat on him. He thought it was the gunny. But it wasn't. The gunny was dead, his eyes half lidded, his stare frozen. Francis had deserted the infant in order to save a dead man. In the distance he could see purple and green mountains and rain falling on them in the sunlight. He doubted if he would ever take pleasure in coming this way again.

He woke at three in the morning. Snow was flying sideways to the ground, the back wall of the nightclub shaking from the noise of the dancers and the country and rock and roll music blaring inside. But he was more interested in the light that was burning in the three-sided tin shed where Harry had been working on his car. He thought he saw a fender protruding from the tarp that hung over the front of the shed. The taillight was smashed, the wires hanging out of the glass.

He checked on his son, then found a flashlight in the Airstream's kitchen and put on his coat and draped a newspaper over his head and went outside. The wind and snow crystals were like bits of glass blowing in his face. He could hear motorcycles starting up in front of the nightclub, then a string of them pulling out of the roadway, barreling into the darkness, the riders bent down on the handlebars like gargoyles.

But something else was wrong, unless he was losing his mind. The train car across the two-lane was gone, the short spur of track it had rested on crusted with snow.

He pulled back the tarp on the shed and went inside. A single light bulb hung from the ceiling. He could not believe what he was looking at. The bumpers and fenders had been pulled from the Chevy, the seats dragged onto the concrete pad. The radiator and battery and generator had disappeared; the engine block hung from chains and a steel tripod. Even the heater and dashboard and radio and the paneling in the doors had been ripped out. Francis's and his son's backpacks were stacked in a corner.

He heard the tarp ruffle behind him and felt a blast of cold air on his neck.

"What the hell you doin' in here, boy?" Harry said.

"Boy?"

"You got wax?"

"What have you done to my car?" Francis said.

"What does it look like? I've been fixing the son of a bitch."

"By taking out the engine and tearing the body apart?"

"You got a ten-inch crack in the block. Your brakes are burnt out and your clutch is shit."

"Why'd you take out the dashboard and tear off the fenders?"

"I didn't 'tear off' anything. Your frame is bent. Rats have been eating the wires behind your dash. They're in your seats and door panels, too."

"You didn't have permission to do this."

217

"Like you asked permission to go into my workplace?"

"What happened to the train car across the road?"

"What *happened* to it?"

"It's gone."

"I think you're a Section Eight."

"My son and I came here for help. What kind of people are you?"

"The kind who don't like snooty college people looking down their noses at us."

"You think my little boy and I look down on you? That's what all this is about?"

"Know what your problem is?" Harry said. "I mean your *real* fucking problem?"

"Tell me."

"You couldn't keep your joint in your pants overseas and you came home with a half-Chink you'd like to permanently park somewhere."

Francis cleared his throat. "Would you say that again?"

"Get off my back, Jack."

Francis nodded, his expression flat. "You ever kill anybody, Harry?"

"What?"

"You ever blow out anyone's light?"

"I wouldn't tell you if I did."

The tarp was flapping, the wind whining on the hardpan like the rotors of a helicopter springing to life. "You never get over it," Francis said. "At least, a normal person doesn't. The dead follow you around. Your guilt eats a hole through your stomach."

"What are you trying to say, asshole?"

"The man who kills you is the one who'll dump your guts on your shoes before you know what hit you," Francis replied.

* * *

Francis went back to the Airstream and watched Morgan sleep in the hammock. He looked at the beauty and innocence and goodness in his face and dreaded the day when his little boy would hear words like "Chink," "slant," "zip," "dink," "gook," and "slope" directed at him, not understanding why others hated him when his only desire was to be their friend.

Francis lay back down on the couch and pulled the blanket Varina had given him over his head. He felt like he had wandered into Hades. He had used the Thanksgiving holiday at the juco to take his boy on a camping and exploration trip in the hills and mountains.

Francis often wondered what the earth would be like if Europeans had not come to the New World and had kept their plagues on their own continent. What if the social model of mankind had been the Anasazi's and their union with the earth and the Great Spirit and their simple way of living?

Sometimes Francis had a dream he did not like to recall in his waking hours. In the dream he saw a log in a fireplace flickering with what looked like rose petals rather than flames, a cool fire, one that offered no threat to a prehistoric man sleeping beside it inside a cave. But Francis knew that was not the real content of the dream. He believed his great-grandfather Sam Morgan Holland, the gunman turned preacher, lived inside him, waiting to be born again so he could light a darkened saloon with streaks of fire from his pistols and watch his adversaries pool the floor with their blood.

Francis dreamed the dream about the cool fire after returning to the Airstream from his confrontation with Harry. Then he smelled eggs and bacon and coffee and saw Morgan and Varina eating at the table in the trailer's tiny kitchen. Varina was wearing a navy-blue wool skirt and matching jacket with big black buttons, and a purple blouse with a frilly white collar, like a late nineteenth-century lady might wear. "Come join us," she said.

Her hair was brushed and clean and thick on her neck and cheeks, her eyes clear, her face free of hangover. The clouds of dust and screeching of the wind and bouncing tumbleweed had lessened and become a steady vibration against the side of the trailer, like blood humming, like the sound he'd heard when he'd pressed his ear against his wife's stomach two months before Morgan's birth. He looked at his watch. It had stopped. "What time is it?" he asked.

"Nine thirty," Varina said, without consulting a watch or clock. "Here, I'll get you a plate."

"I'd love the eggs but I don't eat meat."

"You're a vegetarian?"

"I try to be."

"For your health?"

"I think it's wrong to kill animals if you don't have to."

"Do you mind that I gave Morgan bacon?"

"He can make his own choices."

"Did you go outside last night?"

"I sure did."

"What for?"

"To see the progress on my automobile. Harry has ripped it apart. I'm not sure what I can do about it."

"I'm sorry I spoke on his behalf," she said. "Drinking has been my undoing. But it won't be anymore."

She went to the stove and dipped eggs and toast out of a skillet with a spatula and put them on a plate and poured a cup of coffee and placed the plate and cup in front of him.

"Thank you," he said. "Miss Varina, I need to get a message to friends in Albuquerque. They'll come get us."

"I don't know how to say this. I'm not who you think I am."

"How can you be other than who you are?" he asked.

"I was born in Natchez. My married name is Davis, although I used my maiden name when I was in the movies."

"Your name is Varina Davis?"

"Yes."

"You were named for Jefferson Davis's wife?"

"No. I was not named for her."

"Sorry, I don't understand."

"I *am* her."

"You're the wife of the president of the Confederacy?"

"I *was*, until I was widowed."

He set his coffee down and looked at his plate. "I don't know quite how to respond to what you just said, Miss Varina."

"You have brought me a great gift, Mr. Holland. You have also done a service to another person as well. And you did these things because you have a kind and generous heart."

"Everything you just said went right past me."

"Don't abase yourself."

"Miss Varina, what you're saying is insane."

"I saw Richmond burn. I knew it would happen, too, and dreaded it from the outset. I did not agree with slavery, either. But I did not do enough to oppose it."

"You said I brought you a great gift?"

"Your goodness and your love for the innocent empowered me to take the infant from the burning hut. Today he's in an orphanage run by French nuns in Vientiane."

Francis's hands were clenched in his lap, his eyes wet, the interior of the trailer warping. Morgan looked up at his father. "What's wrong, Daddy?"

"Nothing," Francis said.

221

"You're crying."

"No, I just have a little cold," Francis said.

"No, you don't. You're crying," Morgan said. "Is it because of the war you were in?"

"No, everything is fine," Francis said.

"When can we go home?" Morgan said.

"Soon," Francis replied. He brushed the top of Morgan's haircut. "You're my little pal."

He got up from the table and went to the far end of the trailer and rubbed the condensation off the window. "Could you come here a minute, Miss Varina?" he asked.

She walked toward him, her eyes searching his face.

"How did you know about the child in the village?" he asked.

"I could see him inside your mind," she replied. "The suffering you incurred since that terrible day gave me the power to save him and take him to a safe place."

"You can go back in time?"

"All time happens simultaneously," she said. "There is no past or present or future. A kind act in what we call the present can undo an evil in what we call the past."

Under normal circumstances he would have fled her presence. But what she had just said paled compared to what he was about to say. He wiped a larger hole in the moisture on the window.

"The train car is back on the track. But during the night it disappeared."

"You mustn't talk about the train car," she said.

"It just comes and goes? With no power source and no rails except what's under it now?" he said.

Varina stepped closer to him, her eyes jittering. "Do not have anything to do with the train car. Don't even look at it."

"Why shouldn't I?"

She took his wrist in her hand and squeezed harder than he thought her capable of. "Please, Mr. Holland. Do it for your little boy."

"You really saved the child from the hooch?"

"No, you did. And in so doing you have saved me. That's what you have to understand."

"Do you have a firearm in your trailer?"

"*What?*"

"We're surrounded by evil people," he said. "Don't tell me we're not."

Her face seemed to fill with sorrow.

"What did I say?" he asked.

"You've understood nothing I've said," she replied. "Nothing."

He went up to the nightclub and sat at the bar. The poultry truck he had seen previously was parked in front, a canvas cover snugged down on the cages. The apparent driver, the man he had previously seen sleeping facedown on a table, was playing solitaire at the bar. He was thin and tall and wore two shirts, one on top of the other, and a canvas coat and a shapeless cowboy hat and a spur with a tiny rowel on the heel of one boot. A hand-rolled cigarette was crimped in the corner of his mouth, the ash dead. His face was as brown and supple and deeply lined as a leaf of barn-cured tobacco.

"Can you tell me where Floyd is?" Francis asked.

The man in the shapeless hat didn't bother to look up when he spoke. "Busy, probably," he said, peeling a card off the deck.

"You hauling turkeys?"

"That ain't none of your business, is it?"

"Sir?"

"Hard of hearing, are you?"

"I wondered about the highway or the bridge that's washed out."

"There ain't no bridge here."

"I was told there was."

The thin man lifted his face so the light inside could reflect on it. "You calling me a liar?"

"No, sir."

"You're the one brought his little monkey in here, aren't you?"

"Sorry, I don't know if I heard you right."

"This is a white man's club."

Once again Francis felt a tic in his right hand, but this time also in his face. "What gives you the right to talk to people like that?" he said.

The thin man pushed himself off the stool. "I got to take a crap. You'd better not be here when I get back."

The hatred emanating from him was of a kind Francis had known all his life. There was a class of people for whom there was no explanation. They were not only venomous and untreatable; they seemed to derive from a separate gene pool. From the day they came out of the womb they set their sights on the weak and vulnerable and longed to press their brand hot and smoking on their fellow man's soul. All they needed was a little bit of power, a badge, a uniform, maybe clerical robes. They occupied many roles: Quantico drill instructor, male guard in a women's prison, county judge with his small hand squeezed tight on his gavel, football coach with a whistle working his charms in one-hundred-degree heat.

But Francis wondered if his own thoughts were leading him into a trap. Was the thin man planted there to lure him across a line and turn him into a man like his ancestor? Why had the woman who claimed to be the wife of Jefferson Davis been so bothered when he asked if she owned a firearm? It was only a question. Possessing a weapon did not mean he would use it. He certainly was not Sam Morgan Holland.

But even before he completed the thought, he knew he wasn't being entirely honest. The resentment he bore some of his fellow Americans was real. He and his Asian wife had been refused housing in Los Angeles. She had been given dirty looks in Northern Louisiana. But the worst had been in the Midwest. By law they were not allowed to marry in the state of Missouri and had to drive into Iowa in a snowstorm to buy a marriage license, then were rebuffed at the courthouse because they didn't bring a witness who could swear they were not first cousins. This was when he realized what people of color experienced every day of their lives, although they probably handled the situation much better than he, because he often had to suppress the images that clicked onto a screen behind his eyes and caused his mouth to go dry and the fingers of his right hand to curl into his palm.

Should he walk away when his little boy was treated with such disdain and animosity? Sam Morgan Holland was not the problem. Francis Son Holland had failed in a Third World village and gotten his sergeant killed and left an infant in the doorway of a burning hooch. Now, in his own country, would he act with the same level of failure and ineptitude?

He stared at the strings of colored beads hanging in the restroom doorway. They were perfectly still. The only sound in the building was a loose section of tin banging on the roof. Where was the bartender, the man named Floyd Hammer? Or the patrons who should have been coming in at lunchtime? He tried to see through the serving window. "Hello in the kitchen!" he called out.

No response.

He tried again, less challengingly: "Hey, is Floyd in there?"

He could feel his heart beating. He picked up a sugar container and threw it through the serving window and heard it crash and roll across the floor. Still no response. The silence in the building made his ears pop. He went behind the bar, the duckboards bending under his feet, then pushed back the kitchen door. The kitchen was empty, the stove and all the cookware and a large butcher block scrubbed clean. An apron that had a single line of red drops slung across it was stuffed in a trash can. He began pulling out drawers and opening cabinets, looking for a knife or even an ice mallet while trying to keep an eye on the entrance to the men's room. The sharpest object he could find was a dinner fork.

He opened the refrigerator and removed a bottle of cooking wine, wrapped the neck with a dish towel, and broke it across the edge of the stove, then left the kitchen and approached the men's room, his temples pounding, his armpits looped with sweat.

With each step he knew he was about to enter a world that a wise man would flee. His grip was so tight around the bottleneck he thought the glass would break in his hand. He took a breath and divided the strands of beads and stepped inside.

The stench that hit him was like none that he had ever encountered. It clung to his skin like a wet aggregate of freshly discharged feces and the clogged waste in a grease trap and the putrescence of a grave blown open by an artillery shell in monsoon country.

He dropped the bottleneck and gagged and tried not to vomit, then lost control and buckled over and splattered the lavatory, splashing himself in the process. When his stomach was empty he looked at the pale imitation of himself in the mirror and cupped water in his face and wiped out the lavatory with paper towels and dried himself off and picked up the bottleneck and stared at the door on the single stall in the room. "Hello?" he said.

No answer.

"Listen," he said foolishly, "we can talk this out."

Then he stepped back and kicked the door off its hinges, ripping the lock from its screws.

The stall was empty, the surface of the toilet water still rippling from either a faulty handle mechanism or having just been flushed.

"Lookin' for me?" said a voice behind him.

Francis turned on the thin man, the broken bottleneck in his right hand. "How'd you get behind me?"

"Stick around and I'll teach you."

"Take back what you called my little boy."

"A monkey? Okay, I take it back. That don't mean I have to drink and eat with the likes of dinks and such."

"What do you have against us?"

"A redbird don't sit on a blackbird's nest."

"I fought for this country."

"Then you ought to know better."

For the first time in his life Francis knew he was capable of killing someone. "Let me pass," he said. "That's all I ask."

"You came at me, pilgrim. I didn't go looking for you. That said, you might like to hang around."

"Hang around?" Francis said.

The thin man lifted his fingers to Francis's face. "Don't be afraid. I ain't gonna bite you."

"Don't touch me."

"I can give you power. All the poon you want. Not like that weepy bitch in the trailer, either." Then he pressed his foot on top of Francis's tennis shoe, biting down lasciviously on his lower lip.

Francis slashed the bottle at him, but the ragged edges of the bottleneck as well as his hand and wrist and forearm went right through the man's body, as though it were painted on the air.

"You may be the dumbest white person I ever met, son. You need somebody to take care of you."

"Don't call me son," Francis said.

The thin man reached out and locked his hand on Francis's face, his fingers like tentacles, squeezing the flesh against the bone, crushing Francis's nose against his palm, filling the inside of his head with an odor that was like fish or copulation. He felt himself falling into a black well, as though the trapdoor on a scaffold had dropped under his feet.

When he awoke he was curled in a fetal ball in the corner of the restroom, his body shaking and his teeth chattering, his hands compressed between his thighs, the downdraft of helicopters thropping a few feet above the roof.

He tried to leave the building through the back door, but his gyroscope was shot and he had to steady himself with both hands on the side of the counter. His watch was broken and he had no idea how long he had been unconscious. For the first time he realized there were no clocks in the nightclub, like in the casinos in Vegas. "Can somebody help me?" he called out in the silence.

The bartender named Floyd came out of the kitchen. "Jesus, what happened to you?" he said.

"Where is he?" Francis asked.

"Where's who?"

"The man who drives the poultry truck."

"Bill? He went down the road. Are you drunk?"

"Bill who?"

"Bill McDermott. He's a war hero," Floyd said. "Chased the Nazis all the way to the Elbe. Was that you threw the sugar shaker through the service window?"

"Your friend says there're no bridges around here. That's not what you told me."

"Bill's a kidder. Why'd you throw the sugar shaker into my kitchen?"

"Forget the sugar shaker. Your friend said ugly things about my little boy."

"That doesn't sound like Bill."

"This is a hole in the dimension, isn't it? It's evil. Tell me it's not," Francis said.

Floyd began drying glasses next to a sink. "Harry is fixing your car. What else do you want?"

"No, he's not. He destroyed it."

"Wrong. He just sent it out of here. Ten minutes ago."

"He had my car towed?"

"No, boomed down. I think he's probably getting you a good deal."

"He's selling my car?"

Floyd's pupils were dilated the size of dimes. "Have a drink and lighten up. Get you some company. You might be here a real long time."

"Is everyone here out of his mind?" Francis said.

"Did you have a good time with Varina?"

"Watch what you say."

"Just asking. You'll get used to it. They all do."

"What's 'it'? Who's 'they'?"

Floyd looked out the window. "Look at those clouds."

"What about them?" Francis said.

"We're supposed to have four inches. I can lend you some blankets. By the way, stay out of my kitchen. I've got my private recipes in there. I color-code them, you know, the way Thomas Edison did his chemicals in his laboratory. Just kidding."

Francis went out the back door, without a coat or hat, off-balance, the wind drilling his face. When he opened the door of the Airstream, the wind followed him in and broke glassware in the kitchen. Varina was on the couch reading to Morgan from a book about King Arthur. Francis pressed the door shut with his shoulder and locked it, his ears red with cold. "I'll clean up the glass," he said.

"I'll take care of it. Where did you go?" she said.

"I got into it with a man named Bill McDermott."

She placed a marker in her book and set it on a coffee table. "Morgan, would you finish folding those towels for me in the bathroom?"

"Is something wrong?" Morgan asked.

"No, no," she said. "I'm just behind in my chores."

"Because you were reading to me?" he asked.

"Of course not. I love reading to you," she said. "You're a fine little gentleman."

After Morgan had gone to the back of the trailer, Varina turned on a portable radio and found a music station that would muffle their conversation. "What did you do to McDermott?"

"Tried to cut him with the broken neck of a wine bottle."

"What did he do in turn?"

"Nothing. My hand went right through him. Then he grabbed my face and I passed out."

"I wish you hadn't done this, Mr. Holland."

"I'm tired of these people bullying us."

"You took the bait."

"How?"

"They want to make you one of them."

"Do you really believe you're the wife of Jefferson Davis?"

"Sir, my married name is a heritage of woe," she replied. "Do you think I would use it lightly? Come here."

"What for?"

She pulled back the curtain on the window. "What do you see?"

"The train car. The one you told me not to even look at."

"Who do you think is in it?"

"Drifters, bales of hay, field mice?"

"Did you ever read the novels of F. Scott Fitzgerald?"

"Yes."

"He said you can never understand the United States until you understand the graves of Shiloh." She lifted her face to his. Her eyes were a greenish blue, her lashes black, her face a study in constancy and the calm protestant conviction that led a nation to commit genocide and call it Manifest Destiny.

"Why do you look at me so strangely?" she asked.

"You're a beautiful lady."

She put her hand on his arm. "You don't know me, Mr. Holland. I didn't do enough to right the wrongs of my husband. But the grace I've borrowed from you, and by that I mean the suffering you've undergone over the child in the Asian village, has allowed me to save the child and myself. I can never repay your gift."

"You blame yourself for your husband's deeds?"

"Like most twentieth-century people, you're not aware of how the War Between the States came about," she said. "Many Southerners were against secession, and they certainly didn't want to kill their neighbors. Those attitudes were corrected when the most powerful newspapers and plantation owners in the South convened in Atlanta and convinced a very large number of people that male Negroes, if given their freedom, would rape every white woman in the South. It worked, sir, to the disgust of anyone who had a modicum of respect for our loyal servants."

"What's in the train car, Miss Varina?"

"All the misery the human heart can suffer," she replied.

Francis heard a roar of motorcycles, their exhaust pipes blasting against the asphalt, then the bikers throttling down as they turned into the gravel in front of the nightclub, followed by the poultry truck driven by the man named Bill McDermott.

"You're not going out there, are you?" Varina said.

"I need to talk to those guys."

"There is no such thing as 'talking to those guys.'"

"You know them?" he asked.

"They're mindless and fear-driven and looking for someone to sanction their cruelty and vices. The leader they find will come from the sea."

"I don't care about any of that. I have to get my boy and me back to our home."

"There's a way. But I'll have to accompany you."

"Accompany us where?"

"You were a battlefield nurse?" she said.

"The term today is 'combat corpsman.'"

"Would you go back to the Asian village where the little child was?"

"No," he said.

"I see."

"See what?" he asked.

"Nothing."

He waited for her to continue, but she didn't. When Morgan came out of the bathroom, she went inside and closed the door, obviously disappointed in him, although he had no idea why.

"Are we leaving now?" Morgan asked.

"Wait here a little while, will you, little pal?"

"Don't go, Daddy."

"I won't be long. I promise."

"Where are you going?"

"I have to find us a way out."

"Promise you'll be right back."

"Sure," he said.

But his words sounded hollow, unconvincing even to him, just as his words of reluctance to Varina about returning to a combat zone seemed like a statement about his own importance rather than concern about others. Was this how people "changed"? Was this how his ancestor Sam Morgan Holland justified the nine graves he had filled along the Chisholm Trail, as though the Union dead on Marye's Heights and Little Round Top had not been enough?

Francis put on his coat and beat-up fedora and on the way out of the trailer pulled a steak knife from a wood block on the stove and slipped it inside his sleeve. What else was he supposed to do? Let racists and misogynists make prisoners of him and the poor lady who believed she was the widow of Jefferson Davis?

The sky was an ink wash, electricity flickering in the clouds that covered the mountaintops. He worked his way around the side of the nightclub and looked through a window. The music and the pounding of the dancers' feet rattled the glass, the faces and bodies of the dancers checkered with the kaleidoscopic reflection of a silver ball rotating on the ceiling. But the shifting polka-dot illusion was secondary in effect to the frenetic movements of the dancers, all of whose faces seemed charged with a preternatural moment of pleasure that teetered on the edge of orgasm.

He stepped back from the window lest he be seen. Hailstones as white as mothballs were clattering on the roof and bouncing on the parking lot. He worked his way through the motorcycles and trucks and gas-guzzlers and crossed the two-lane and walked through the weeds to the railroad car. The windows were dark, impenetrable, some of them bullet-pocked, the holes plugged with rags. He picked up a rock and started to throw it at a window, then saw a figure standing by the vestibule at the far end of the car. "Who are you?" he said.

"What do you care, you motherfucker?" the figure said.

Where had he heard the voice before?

"Is that you, gunny?" he said.

The figure peeled back the hood on his raincoat, exposing his scalped haircut and bony face. "Who'd you think I was?"

"What are you doing here?"

"Counting shitbirds like you."

"You blame me for getting you killed?"

"It crossed my mind."

"I apologize, gunny."

He put his hood back on and sat down on the vestibule steps and studied the ground. "Got a cigarette?"

"I don't smoke or drink."

"That's why you stopped at a slop chute?"

"My car broke down."

The gunny tilted up his face, beaded with rain, the pupils of his eyes like burnt match heads trapped in glass. "What's the year?"

"1967."

"It's been five years since I was KIA?"

"I try not to study on it, gunny."

"What are you doing here?"

"I saw the train car disappear and return. That means there's a way out of here. That means my little boy and I can find a way out of here, too."

"Better take a look inside."

Francis hesitated.

"Go ahead," the gunny said. "They won't hurt you."

Francis cleared his throat, trying to deal with the ball of fear in his stomach. The gunny got up from the vestibule steps and pulled open the door to the train car. "Mannequins?" Francis said.

"I always knew it. You were pissing behind a cloud when God passed out the brains. Those are corpses. The kind that are dead."

"I shouldn't have bothered you, gunny," Francis said. "I'm going back to my son now."

"You don't smell their wounds? That's gangrene. Look at the boy curled up on the seat with the canteens in his hand. Is that real or not?"

"I see the canteens. But that's a mannequin in a uniform holding them."

"He's got a Bible in his pocket," the gunny said. "His name is written in it. It's Richard Kirkland."

"Say again?" Francis said.

"That means something?"

"Yeah, that this is some kind of shuck," Francis said.

"You're starting to get me mad, doc. You got me killed and now you're telling me I'm some kind of con man. You're about to get hit upside the head."

"Maybe that's just the breaks, gunny. You know, semper fi, son of a bitch."

Then the gunny went crazy and tried to assault him, grabbing at his throat and swinging his fists at his face. But death had taken away the gunny's power to influence the world of the living. The density of his body began to thin and disappear, like a dust devil drifting into nothingness. In less than ten seconds he was gone. The mannequin the gunny had pointed at stared mutely at Francis. Its coat had chevrons stitched on the sleeves and the initials S.C. on the collar. Francis reached out for the Bible that protruded from the right coat pocket. The entire train car lurched, then began moving, shaking the mannequins in their seats.

Francis plunged out the door and jumped from the vestibule, then rolled in a ball across the ground. The huge weight of the car was creaking along the rails toward a fogbank that was as black as oil smoke. He got to his feet, his clothes smeared with mud, ashamed of his fear and, worse, ashamed he had left his little boy behind in the vain hope that he could deal with creatures for whom normality was a joke.

What a fool he had been. He was surprised the steak knife inside his coat sleeve had not cut him. He shook it from his sleeve and threw it at one of the train car's windows. The blade bounced off the glass and fell by the track. He started to walk away, then in the corner of his eye he thought he saw a human face behind a window. He knew better than to look; he knew to keep on going, to mark off the image as imaginary, to get no deeper into the evil that seemed to have surrounded him and his son.

But as always he pitched caution over the gunwales, and earned the attention of a figure who was flesh and blood and wearing a wool Union uniform, his hair as dirty as a bird's nest, his face sweaty with pain and fever. The Yankee soldier had been eviscerated and had cupped his entrails in his hands; his lips were gray and caked with dried mucus. The train car rocked, and the soldier's mouth opened as though he wanted to scream but dared not do so.

Francis ran through the weeds and across the crown in the road and around the side of the nightclub and virtually crashed through Varina's door. He lifted Morgan to his chest and buried his face in the boy's neck and shoulder, his eyes brimming.

Varina was standing at the stove in the small kitchen. "You went to the train car, didn't you?"

"Yes."

"What do you think you saw?"

"A marine sergeant I caused to die on the Laotian border. A mannequin with a Bible that had the name Richard Kirkland written in it."

"What does that name mean to you?" she asked.

"If you're the wife of Jefferson Davis, you already know."

"You still believe I'm a fraud?"

"You probably don't intend to be, but yes, you've made up a fictitious role for yourself. You're a good person, but you will not accept that characterization. Why do you pretend you're someone else?"

She nodded. "There was a great darkness after the Union assault at Fredericksburg. The hillside was strewn with Yankee soldiers begging for water. People in the city could hear them from one mile away. The Kirkland boy gathered as many canteens as he could and crawled down the slope and gave water to the thirsty and bound the wounds of the dying. Neither side would fire on him. He became known as the Angel of Marye's Heights. He was killed ten months later at Chickamauga. He was twenty years old."

Francis had a hard time swallowing; his mouth was dry with fear; his saliva tasted like copper pennies. Or blood. How could she know as much as she did? He put down his son. "When are we going home, Daddy?" the boy said.

"We're fixing to," he said. "I promise."

"But our car is gone," the boy replied.

Francis looked at the woman. "Tell me the truth," he said. "Who are you?"

"I've told you. I'll say no more on the subject."

"When I first spoke to you, you had the manners and vocabulary of a barfly."

"You will not address me like that, sir."

"You offer no explanations, just one mystery after another. That's the mark of a liar, Miss Varina."

"I forgive you for the harshness of your words. It's your goodness that has allowed both of us to undo the past. In your way you have saved me."

"From what?"

"At the least, the mediocrity of modern times. Do you know of a more self-serving era, unless you count the reign of leaders such as Caligula or King George the Third?"

"Where does Harry live?" he asked.

"You're going to do us great harm. And your son, too."

"Do you have some blankets?"

"What for?"

"Morgan and I are going to start walking. If anyone tries to stop us, he'll regret it."

"I'll give you what I have."

"Explain something, would you? When you asked if I would return to the village where the child was sitting in the doorway of the hooch, I said I would not. You looked like I'd let you down."

"You did."

"How?"

"The young Confederate soldier who brought water to the dying was not a one-time visitor to the Garden of Gethsemane. He knew his trial was ongoing, and that's why he willingly gave his life later at Chickamauga."

"I have a son to care for."

She raised her hand to his cheek. "Then don't you ever stop being less than the fine young man you are."

He didn't want to contend with her. Nor did he want to contend with other emotions she had stirred in him. She was attractive and educated, her accent melodic, the rhythms of her speech like those of William Faulkner and Flannery O'Connor and Robert Penn Warren and Eudora Welty. But didn't he have enough trouble on his hands without falling in love with a dead woman? Plus, she was like most Southern women: they made up their mind once and took it to the grave.

She piled four blankets on the kitchen table. "That's all I can spare," she said.

"That's good of you," he said.

"Are you really going to do this?"

"What, walk out of this godforsaken place?"

"It isn't a minor undertaking."

"Come with us," he said.

"No, not for any reason."

"Why not?" he asked.

Her lips were tight, a bead in her eye.

"What's keeping you?" he said.

"You shouldn't try to tempt me. I'm weak as it is."

"Tempt you in what way?"

"To lay down my burden and leave my husband."

"You have to pay for his mistakes?"

"I don't have to," she said. "No."

"Then let him carry his own water."

"You seem like you are not an admirer."

"Who could be? At every turn Jefferson Davis was trying to figure out ways to make money off the backs of others. Even after the war."

"Do not speak disrespectfully of him in my presence."

He looked at her a long time. "You really got the infant out of the burning hooch?"

"On my oath."

"I'll never forget you," he replied.

Then he and his little boy were outside, in the darkness and the wind and the cold. He had never felt lonelier in his life.

He could not believe what he was doing. He and his son, shrouded in blankets like monks, were walking down the road toward a horizon that seemed to drop into infinity. Without use of his watch he could no longer tell night from day. He also wondered if he had experienced a psychotic break. The train car had disappeared again and the hardpan was covered with hail the size of ping-pong balls. For a long period he held Morgan's hand, then felt the boy tiring and took him in his arms and carried him until his back was aflame and he had to rest in the bottom of a dry ditch, one that protected them from the wind. There they pulled the blankets over themselves and huddled against the side of the ditch and went to sleep, warming each other inside the cocoon they had created. Francis thought he heard a train whistle in the distance, and slipped away into a dream about the Sunset Limited and the trip across the Southwest with his mother when she decided to become a movie star and instead exhausted their money in two weeks and landed them in the waiting room of a welfare office packed with derelicts whose collective odor smelled like spoiled clams.

Why would he dream about his poor, driven, sad mother now? That was easy. His mother was the only one he loved in his family. And he loved her because she was tormented by her psychological disabilities but was not undone by them. She made him think of a moth inside a windstorm. There was a deep-seated fear that never left her eyes, and a suppressed tension wrapped so tight inside her that she constantly knotted her hands and squeezed her fingernails into the heels. People who claimed to be her friends openly admitted they could not be around her for more than two hours. She in turn told Francis he was the only friend she had in the whole world, and that he should not trust others and that he should model himself on the virtues of his gunfighter ancestors. But she never defined those virtues.

But why dwell on the problems of the Hollands, he asked himself. He had deliberately shunned the violent legacy of his family when he became a combat medic. He bore no ill will toward either his peers, his superiors, or his enemies. He loved his son. In fact, he loved both God and the world, and never thought one was exclusive of the other. But the greatest gift was his little boy, who was now curled against his chest, safe under the blanket with his father, his warm breath like a feather touching Francis's skin.

Why was Francis's mind in a constant tumult? When he had first entered the nightclub, the man named Floyd saw the red dust on his clothes and knew Francis had been up in the hills where the ruins of the Anasazi pueblo lay unprotected and easily looted or vandalized. Francis did not steal from the dead, but he did something that was almost as bad in a kiva, which the Anasazi believed to be a conduit into the spiritual world. While his son was sleeping, Francis woke from a nightmare about the infant in the burning hooch and in a rage stamped out the fire in the kiva, breaking the stones in half, sending a shower of sparks into the sky, just as his great-grandfather had cursed God outside Wichita for his loss of two thousand head of longhorns to dry lightning the night before he was to sell them at auction.

But he was free of that now, wasn't he? According to Varina Davis, if that was her name, his good deeds had empowered her to go back in time and save the child. The problem? He was consoling himself with madness, like a person waking from a nightmare and letting it be his guide in the morning light. He shut his eyes and squeezed his temples and wondered if he would be better off dead, perhaps in the Laotian village, where perhaps he could have saved the life of the gunny.

He pulled the blanket from his head. The wind was cold, like an electric shock on his scalp, the air dank like the smell of water in a wood barrel during winter. "We have to get started," he said to the boy.

"Where?" Morgan asked.

"We just keep going south. We'll end up in the right place."

"How do we know which direction we're going in?"

"We just stay on the road, Morgan."

"But how does the road know where it's going?" the boy asked.

"You make a point, little pal. Maybe we'll see a house or a car."

"There aren't any, Daddy. There're no lights anywhere. Where is everybody?"

"I don't know, Morgan. We just have to trust ourselves."

"I'm scared, Daddy."

"It's all right to be scared. But we have to have faith."

"About what?"

"When you're on the right side of things, the Man Upstairs pretty much takes care of you."

"Why'd that man steal our car?"

"Because he's a bad man. Something bad is going to happen to him."

Morgan started to cry. Francis wrapped him up in a blanket and put him on his shoulder and walked for three or four hours, resting and then walking again. The little food he had asked from Varina was gone, the mountains blurring inside a snowstorm, the grit in the wind as abrasive as the filings from an emery wheel. He had never been more miserable, not even in the village on the Laotian border. He and the boy took shelter in a shed with no floor and huddled against each other. When they awoke, the sky was as dark as a locked closet in a storm, the ground white with snow. The nightclub was no more than a hundred yards away, the poultry truck parked in front of it. Morgan peeked out of the blankets, then began trembling inside his father's arms. "I don't know what's going on, Daddy."

"We're going to take a look at that truck, little pal," he said.

"What for?" the boy asked.

"Maybe the keys are in it."

The boy said something he couldn't hear in the wind. "Say that again?" Francis asked.

"Don't get us in more trouble, Daddy," the boy answered.

The boy's words were like a knife across his heart. "I'm sorry how things have worked out," he said.

"I'm cold. Why did Mommy have to die?"

"I don't know, Morgan. I don't know anything."

There was no sign of life inside the nightclub. A single string of white smoke was rising from the tin chimney on Varina's Airstream. The color had gone from Morgan's face. Francis felt his pulse and spread his fingers on his chest. The boy's breath was shallow, as though he were sipping the air. "My stomach hurts, Daddy," he said. "I think we're going to die."

*   *   *

Francis crossed the road with the boy at his side, hand in hand, then took off his blanket and draped it over the boy's head and folded it down his front. His face was lost inside the cowl. "What's that smell?" the boy said.

"I'm not sure," Francis said.

"It smells like something that's sick."

The tarp on the back of the truck was swelling in the wind, the tie ropes tugging at the metal eyelets. The boy was right. The odor that seeped from under the tarp was like decomposing carrion or offal and burned animal hair smoldering on a winter day. "I'll make this up to you," Francis said. "We'll go out to California and go to amusement parks and ride the Ferris wheel and eat cotton candy and swim in the ocean. California is a grand place to be."

"I want to be home," Morgan said. "I want Mommy back."

Francis said a prayer and opened the driver's door, hoping the key would be dangling from the ignition. It wasn't. He felt above the sun visor and under the driver's seat, then reached across the seat and opened the glovebox, expecting a load of trash to tumble onto the floor. Instead, the interior was clean and lined with purple velvet and contained a customized 1911-model .45 auto with white-checkered grips and a flawless, unpitted blue-black steel frame and receiver. Next to it were two backup magazines, seven rounds thumbed down tightly on each loading spring.

"That's a gun, Daddy," the boy said, his voice climbing.

"Yes," Francis said, the word sticking in his throat.

"What are you going to do with it?"

He didn't have a ready answer. But he didn't want to put the gun back in the glovebox, either. "I guess that depends," he said.

"Depends on what, Daddy?"

"On other people."

"What other people? The bad ones?"

He didn't answer. He put the two magazines in his right pants pocket and picked up the .45 and crawled backward out of the cab. He stared down at the boy.

"Why are you looking at me like that, Daddy?"

"We have to make other people accountable, Morgan."

"Are you going to do something to the bad people?"

Francis didn't reply, in effect joining the cowards and bullies who used silence to best a child whose moral insight was superior to theirs.

"Are we going back to Miss Varina's trailer?" the boy asked.

Francis looked at the trailer and then at the nightclub. Right now he probably still had the advantage of surprise over the truck owner, but he would lose it as soon as the owner looked out the nightclub window.

He pulled back the receiver of the .45 far enough to see that a shell was seated in the chamber, then stuck the pistol in the back of his belt and picked up Morgan, and without saying anything else entered the front door of the nightclub, a brass band thundering inside his head.

There was no one inside except Varina, who was barely visible in a back booth, her hair in her eyes, as though she were asleep.

"Varina?" he said.

She showed no acknowledgment of him or the boy.

"Varina, are you all right?" he said.

She didn't answer. A red line ran from the corner of her mouth. One eye was sunken, the socket pink, like it had rouge rubbed in it. He felt Morgan's hand slip into his.

"Can you talk to me, Varina?" Francis said.

The kitchen door swung open and Floyd came out pulling a bucket of water on wheels across the duckboards and onto the dance floor. A mop was propped inside the bucket, water sloshing over the sides. He looked up at Francis. "I thought you were gone," he said.

"Did you do this?" Francis said.

"Yeah, so I could clean up her barf and the pool of piss she's sitting in."

"If you didn't do it, who did?"

"Let me think. Could it be the person who threatened to slap his dick in her mouth?"

Francis approached the booth, Morgan by his side. Varina was wearing a cotton dress stamped with tiny red flowers and the gold chain and locket he had seen around her neck earlier. There was a chain burn on her skin. Her hands were shaking, balled in her lap, her chest slowly rising and falling, as though there were broken glass in her lungs.

"Did Harry do this to you, Miss Varina?" Francis asked.

Her eyes shifted sideways, then the strings of beads rattled over the entrance to the men's room. The tall, thin man who owned the flatbed truck walked onto the dance floor, his hat at a jaunty angle, a dead cigarillo rolling back and forth between his teeth. "Whatcha doing, boy?" he said. "Left your joint in the lamp socket?"

Francis looked back at Varina. "Was it this man?" he said. "Just blink."

Her eyes stayed locked on his. Francis stepped closer to her, releasing his son's hand. "Were you hit in the stomach or the ribs?" he asked.

She looked up at him, her eyes bursting with a message he couldn't read.

"What are you trying to tell me, Varina?" he said.

Then he smelled the odor of the thin man inches from him, an odor that was fetid and raw, like a swamp turned stagnant in an ancient garden.

"You just accused me of beating up on a woman," the thin man said.

"Stay away from me," Francis said.

The thin man extended his right hand and made a V with two knuckles, like a spring-operated clothespin. "Stick your nose in here."

"I have a gun," Francis said.

"Yeah, I know. It's mine," the man said. "Look through the window, boy."

Francis turned his head. The sky was the color of pewter. Harry, the mechanic who'd hauled away his car, had pulled the tarp from the back of the flatbed truck and was opening a series of cages. Turkey buzzards burst from each of them, their wings flapping heavily, rising into a funnel of other birds that had already formed above the train car.

"Are you the devil?" Francis asked.

"No, I'm Bill McDermott, a good ole boy everybody likes," the thin man said. "I'm also the fella who's gonna take everything you have, one piece at a time."

"Run, Daddy," Morgan said.

But it was too late for running. Or reaching for the .45 stuck behind his belt. Or leaving Varina to her own destiny. The creature who called himself McDermott tapped Francis's brow with one finger and snipped his wiring and left him writhing on the floor. Then the good ole boy Bill McDermott walked out the back door with Francis's son on his shoulder, the boy's face trembling with a level of fear Francis had seen only in the faces of children in an Asian war that for him would never end.

When he opened his eyes he did not know where he was. His hands and feet were bound, the floor made of wood but as hard as iron on his hip bone. The room was lit by a single light bulb that hung above a metal desk, the filament inside the glass flickering, on the edge of going out. Clay bowls with faint designs had been positioned carefully along the shelves on the walls. The bowls looked like they would crumble into powder if you touched them, destroying centuries of history in seconds. He had no doubt where they had come from.

He heard a toilet flush, then a door opened and Floyd emerged from the bathroom with a folded newspaper in his hand, half of it dark with water. "Feelin' okay?" he said.

"Where's my boy?"

"I'm not sure."

"Does McDermott have him?"

"I'd be more afraid of Harry. He's the one beat the shit out of Varina."

"Why did he do that?"

"She's got a mouth. Plus she's crazy?"

"Please tell me if my boy has been hurt."

"A bunch of drunk college kids ran Bill McDermott's family off a cliff. They crashed in the bottom of the canyon. The car burned, with them still alive inside it. The college kids got off with commuted sentences. So Harry's got a hard-on for lots of people, particularly educated people who have got more than he does."

"Listen to me," Francis said.

"You're telling *me* to listen to *you*?"

"Okay, it's a dumb thing to say. The point is I don't care what you guys are doing here," he replied. "I'll never tell anybody anything. Even if I did, who would believe me?"

"They always say that."

"Who's 'they'?"

"You're not the first outsider to stop by. It's Shitsville. Why not enjoy it? You've seen the women who come here. Enjoy."

Francis's rage, his helplessness, the image of McDermott's hands on Morgan's body were like a blister on his brain that was about to burst. He strained against the rope on his wrists and ankles and prayed for the power to get his hands on Floyd Hammer's throat. He saw himself tearing Floyd apart, breaking his bones, mutilating his face, working a knife into his innards. He felt sweat running out of his hair and was afraid he would pass out or have a stroke and consequently leave his boy in the care of monsters. He closed his eyes and took short breaths and felt his heart begin to slow. "Please," he said again.

"Please what?" Floyd said.

"Help me get my boy back. You'll never see us again."

"You shouldn't have come here, fella."

The rope felt smooth and of medium diameter, the kind used to hang wash. To Francis's surprise the rope slipped slightly on his wrist. Who had tied it? Did Floyd have his own agenda? Francis kept his eyes flat, his expression empty. "Is my boy alive?"

"I told you I don't know."

"Don't you have a family of your own? Don't you have a soul?"

Floyd gave him a long look. Then he laughed out loud.

"What's funny?" Francis said.

"I'm laughing because for a college professor you don't seem too bright. Yeah, we have souls. They're black, and we like it that way."

He laughed all the way out of the room and down the hallway. When Francis could no longer hear him, he worked his wrists free of the rope, then unknotted the rope on his ankles and got to his feet, off-balance, the room spinning. In the weak light that shone on the desktop, he saw the collectible .45 auto he had taken from the glovebox of McDermott's truck. He picked it up with his right hand and slid back the receiver a half inch. A round was still loaded in the chamber. He released the magazine far enough to see the brass hulls, then eased it back into the frame. What kind of game was Floyd playing? And where was his son? And where was Varina? Was she insane as Floyd had said? But the last question he asked himself was the most disturbing: Was he in hell?

He walked down the hallway, the .45 hanging comfortably from his right hand. But that was the only comfortable aspect of his situation. He could not remember when he had last eaten. His head was filled with the droning of mosquitoes, and he wondered if the malaria he had brought back from the Orient had laid claim to his blood again. Then he realized the mosquitoes were only part of a cacophonous vortex swirling around him. Once again he heard the throaty roar of motorcycles, train wheels screeching on steel rails, the thropping of a helicopter, and worst of all, a sound like a butcher's cleaver thudding into wood.

Why had this happened in his life? He had never intentionally harmed anyone. Was that self-pity? What if it was? Why not let his anger be an elixir, or his victimhood a balm to his soul? The world was not fair, and the lion did not lie down with the lamb, and the earth didn't abide forever, not unless you believed that the atomic bombing of Hiroshima and Nagasaki were insignificant events. The gun felt cold and hard in his hand, and the longer he held it, the more he wanted to use it.

Yes, long ago he had learned that these kinds of thoughts were poisonous and were the kind the Hollands used to find their way to San Jacinto and Fredericksburg and the Somme and the Hürtgen Forest and the Chosin Reservoir. Was it so bad, actually? They were brave, and so were their women, and no less than they. Why should he deny his genes, or the peace the .45 gave him? Its weight and balance, the snugness of its checkered grips, its incontestable lethality, the simplicity of its reload; it could be thought of as the contemporary equivalent of Arthur's Excalibur. Even the most brutal and incautious men were terrified to stare into its barrel. The story it could paint on a wall was one a survivor never forgot. Why not be a little humble and accept a gift, maybe one that came from a mystical hand?

Up ahead he saw a stairwell and moonlight glowing on the steps. How could this be? To his knowledge, the nightclub had only one level. His ears were pounding, the volume of the helicopter blades and the dirty roar of the motorcycles and the clanging of the train cars growing louder and louder. He gripped the stair rail and felt the walls quivering and the steps shaking, chips of paint falling from the ceiling.

Then it all stopped, except for the noise of the helicopter and the cleaver thudding into wood. Whoever was swinging it was probably a large man, dedicated to severing bone and joint and sinew and undoing the millions of years of evolution that had produced the animal or human being he was deconstructing. He was the kind of man who was proud of his sweaty work, demonstrating his skill with a flick of his instrument to slide a shaver of fat onto the floor.

Francis was sickened by the images that he had allowed to form in his mind, and felt his knees starting to cave. Then he saw two men at the top of the stairs, silhouetted by a yellow moon that seemed as big as the sky. One man raised a fist and stiffened his arm at a right angle, like an infantry point man leading a column of men down a night trail in a Third World country. His face looked as hard as carved ivory, his words crackling like static coming from a shortwave radio. He was dressed in Marine Corps utilities.

"Gunny?" Francis said.

The gunny tried to speak again, his face knotting, as though his best efforts at being virtuous and serving a noble cause were pinching off his windpipe.

251

"I can't read you, gunny," Francis said. "Repeat."

"He wants to help you," the second man said. "But he's impaired by the life he has lived."

"Who are you?" Francis said.

"Lieutenant Richard Kirkland, C.S.A. It is very nice to meet you, Mr. Holland."

"The Angel of Marye's Heights?"

"I don't answer to that. I asked my friends at Chickamauga to tell my pa I died right. I need no other tribute."

"Can you get my boy back, sir?" Francis said.

"Neither your friend nor I have that power, Mr. Holland. Don't let these men trick you. You must put away—"

Outside, the train cars were coupling up, smashing into each other, with such violence the whole building shook, filling the stairwell with powdered plaster.

"Finish what you said!" Francis yelled. "Put away what?"

"You can't kill the dead," the lieutenant said. "You're an intelligent man. Don't emulate your enemies."

"Kill who? What enemies? Harry?"

The helicopter swept in a circle, then hung wobbling in the sky, cinnamon-colored dust and grit and desiccated manure swirling in the air, just like the Huey in the ville on the Laotian border.

"How is Miss Varina?" the lieutenant shouted. "Tell me fast!"

"You know Varina?"

"She was the secret love of us all, me in particular."

"Where are y'all going?" Francis said.

"To catch our ride," the lieutenant said.

"Don't leave. I beg you. My child is innocent. Why does he have to suffer?"

"Good luck to you," the lieutenant said. "I hope our journey hasn't been for naught."

The gunny tried to speak again, but all that came out of his mouth were sparks.

Then both men were lost somewhere inside the dust and in seconds were gone with the helicopter. In the silence that followed Francis wanted to weep.

He stumbled outside, the countryside gray and bare and cold in the yellow light of the moon. The only sound he heard was the chain tinkling on a broken windmill. He tried to determine where the chopping sounds had come from. There was only one possible place—the kitchen, the one area Floyd had cautioned him to stay away from. He worked his way along the back of the building, ducking under the windows, the .45 cocked, and pressed one ear against the wall. The blows of the cleaver on wood had stopped. Then he heard the door on Varina's Airstream open and saw Harry the mechanic step outside and light a cigarette. He was wearing clean, starched overalls buttoned at the throat, his work boots shined, and swinging his arm after each puff, as though smoking were a form of self-validation.

"I see you there," Harry said. "Come on over and have a smoke."

"Where's my boy?" Francis said.

"How the fuck should I know?"

"Because you're a bad guy, the kind who beats up on women."

"Look, Jack, believe it or not I got your shitmobile running. You might even like the price, considering the work I did."

"Number one, I don't believe anything you say. Number two, get down on your knees."

"What, you gonna shoot me?"

"How about this instead?" Francis said. He inverted the .45 and slashed the butt at a downward angle across Harry's mouth, snapping his jaw sideways, slinging blood and chips of broken teeth on the trailer wall. Harry doubled over, both hands crimped on his mouth, moaning, then tripped and fell backward in a bed of rose-bushes covered with thorns. The branches were untrimmed and as long and thin and supple as vines. They clung to him like the stingers on jellyfish. Blood was leaking out of his hair and stringing down his brow into his eyes.

He began to weep, the way a child weeps, all dignity gone, the inner self left bare. Francis could not believe what he had done. "Why'd you do this, man?" Harry said.

"Here, grab my hand," Francis replied.

"No, you're gonna hit me again."

"I won't do that, Harry. But you have to tell me where my son is."

"He's with *them*. They're dead, man. Don't you get it? This whole fucking place is a necropolis. The Big Divide. There're people here going to a real fine place; the rest are headed for the shitter."

"Where are you headed?"

Harry's nose was running. He wiped it with the flat of his hand as though he were mashing a cherry tomato. "I had a couple of good deeds on my scoreboard and got a break. But I've probably blown it."

He tried to stand up, stabbing one arm in the air for balance, then fell backward again, more thorns sticking to his overalls, his face running with sweat and dirt. He looked crucified by the bushes, his mouth a round, black hole that made no sound.

"You demeaned my little boy," Francis said.

"I was a smart-ass. I didn't mean it."

"Get up!"

"I can't."

"You want me to put one through your kneecap?"

"Don't tell me that, man. I can't take it. It ain't right. I've paid for the bad things I've done."

Varina opened the door of her trailer. She was wearing a crino-line hooped dress, her hair parted in the middle, pulled back in a bun. "Show him your tattoo, Harry, and tell him how you got it," she said.

Francis pulled Harry from the flower bed as he would a dead weed.

The words on Harry's forearm were pale blue, as though the tattoo artist had mixed water with the ink in order to hide the memori-alization he had created.

"You were at Fort Pillow?" Francis said. "In the massacre of 1864?"

"Yeah," Harry replied. "People don't know the whole story."

"There is no 'whole' story," Francis said. "Few colored troops were taken prisoner. Hundreds were killed, some on their knees."

"Harry knows that, Mr. Holland," Varina said. "He owned up to me. That's why he was in my trailer."

"The same man who beat you up?"

"Floyd attacked me, not Harry."

"Why didn't you tell me?"

"Floyd would have torn me to pieces, as well as you and your boy," she said. She stepped outside, with no wrap, unable to suppress her agitation. "You're being tested, Mr. Holland. Wake up."

"I gave up thinking my way through any of this, Miss Varina," Francis said. "All I want is my boy back. I'm going to leave Harry with you and go in the nightclub and perhaps kill Floyd Hammer and McDermott. But if what you and Harry have told me is true, all of you are already dead, and none of this makes any difference."

"Do not speak cynically about mortality, Mr. Holland," she replied. "It does not behoove you."

"Behoove me?" he said. "Those sons of bitches have my son."

She gripped the locket on her chest and squeezed it as though it were a religious charm. He thought she was about to reprove him for using profanity in her presence. But she didn't. "You cannot overestimate how much is at risk as we speak," she said. "I have a selfish interest as well. A dream, if you will. Such as undoing time and ridding myself of the evil I countenanced by sufficiently denouncing slavery. I also blame myself for the fall of my five-year-old son, Joseph, from the balcony of my home. There is no greater pain than remorse for the death of one's child, Mr. Holland. Do not let my fate be yours."

"But you give me no help, Miss Varina."

"Yes, I do, sir. But you have the kind of deafness that feeds the sins of the fathers unto the seventh generation," she replied.

Then she went back inside the Airstream, her crinoline dress rustling, and shut the door and turned off the lights.

Francis went back through the rear door of the nightclub, carrying the .45 in plain view, his shoes echoing across the dance floor. The man who called himself Bill McDermott was eating by himself in one of the vinyl booths, dipping thin, pink slices of meat in a cup of barbecue sauce, tilting his head back when he dropped them into his mouth. "Want some?" he asked.

"Where's my son?"

McDermott studied a spot in neutral space. "He was with Floyd a while ago. Then he was with me. I had a few beers. I guess he went off with Floyd again."

"You guess?"

"How about we let bygones be bygones? Get you a beer out of the box. This is tasty."

Francis went behind the bar and pushed open the swinging door to the kitchen. It was empty, the floor and chopping block and stainless steel sinks immaculate, a meat cleaver snicked into the wood, a thin wafer of meat pinned under the cleaver's tip. Francis went back to the booth, his hands shaking. McDermott was licking his fingers. "Find him?"

Francis shook his head.

"Know what this barbecue makes me think of?" McDermott asked. "The Germans when they got froze up on the Eastern Front in '42."

"Say that again?"

"They did the same thing the Japs did when we island-hopped them. Same thing with the Donner Party. They ate each other."

"What did you do with my little boy?"

"You gonna cry?"

"Did you kill my son?"

"My gun is not gonna do you any good, boy. What you don't understand is that I'm not dead. That's because I've never been alive. I've always been me. Same with Floyd. Go ahead, shoot. Same thing will happen as when you tried to cut me with that broken bottle."

Francis's right hand was trembling so violently that the barrel of the .45 was rattling the change and loaded magazines in his pants pocket. McDermott wrapped a ball of shredded meat on the end of his fork and twisted it in the cup of barbecue sauce, then extended it to Francis. "No?" he said. "I thought you'd have a liking for it."

Francis's eyes blurred and a hole opened inside him that he knew could never be repaired. He had to grip the .45 with both hands in order to aim it.

"Actually I had more than a few beers," McDermott said. "I had a blackout. But if my memory serves me right, I'm afraid there's one less little Chinaman running around Floyd Hammer's nightclub."

"Y'all killed my little boy?"

"If not me, Floyd did for sure. I saw him go in the pot."

Francis aimed the .45 at McDermott's face. McDermott was lighting up a cigarillo. Then Francis saw a man standing by the front door, a man who was not flesh and blood and whose face he had never wanted to see again. His features and clothes were distorted, like a flickering, misshapen image cast by a primitive projector on a screen made of white smoke. But there was no mistaking who he was. Francis had seen that face in a frame on his mother's secretariat every day of his young life. He looked to be in his sixties and wore a black suit and a high collar and a derby hat and a handlebar mustache and a silver watch strung across his vest. But it was the eyes that Francis always remembered from the photo taken in the year 1900. They had scared him as a child, and they scared him now, regardless of the family members who tried to assure him that Sam Morgan Holland had given up whiskey and his Navy Colt revolvers and the dancehall girls of San Antonio and Abilene and Dodge and the meanness that had sent at least nine men to early graves.

Yes, he was redeemed, they said, a preacher who froze in the saddle on the Staked Plains returning a lost Indian infant to its parents and searching out the graves of the men he had killed so he could ask their forgiveness. But Francis believed the soul resided in the eyes, not the breast, and the eyes of the man in the photo were not those of a convert.

"Pull the trigger!" McDermott said.

Francis did not move. In fact, no force on earth could make him move at that moment, because now he was trapped in the gaze of his ancestor. McDermott followed his line of sight. "What are you looking at, boy?"

"You don't want to know, trash."

"What'd you call me?"

Francis didn't answer. The luminosity in Sam Holland's eyes was the kind you saw in the eyes of Southerners who kept their wounds green and bore a personal insult for life. If you challenged them, you would enter a contract from which there was no exit: You would be forced to beg or suffer serious injury or kill in your own defense or die. Those were absolutes.

"Did you hear me?" McDermott said.

Francis lowered the .45 and looked straight into his ancestor's face. "You're him, aren't you?"

There was no answer.

"I mean you no disrespect, sir," Francis said. "I think I'm your great-grandson."

The man who seemed projected on smoke opened his mouth, but no sound came out. He tried again and again, and pinched his throat and tried to say something with his hands, like someone who was feebleminded. Was this indeed the man who fought at Fredericksburg, on the same slope, called Marye's Heights, where the South Carolinian named Richard Kirkland crawled among the wounded to give them water and bind their wounds? Had not Sam Morgan Holland visited enough pain and violence on others in his life without dragging that pain and violence into the lives of his descendants? Francis had let his mother bully him into naming his son for a killer. Why did his ancestor not stay with the dead where he belonged? Why didn't he and all the others who loved war and its stench find a private place in hell and have at it there for the rest of eternity?

"Can you hear my thoughts, old man? Why are you here? Why have you not helped me save the life of my little boy?"

I'm the only one you can trust, son, except for the lady in the trailer. Best listen to her.

His words were like an electric jolt inside Francis's head. "Good Lord, sir, you plumb scared me to death."

Well, it's nice to meet you. I have always heard good things about you, Francis. I hear you're kind to animals and such.

"Yes, sir, I try to be."

And you love your little boy more than life itself?

"Yes, sir, I do."

Put away your weapon.

"Sir?"

Time to beat your sword into a plowshare and your spear into a pruning hook, Francis.

"I never took up arms, sir."

That's why evil men have made you do it. You're the light bearer. Do not benight thyself. Go to the woman.

"Who the hell you talking to?" McDermott said. He was still sitting in the booth.

Francis had almost forgotten McDermott. He looked at him, then back at his great-grandfather. Sam Morgan Holland was gone, even the white smoke.

"Answer me, boy," McDermott said.

Francis studied his face. "You're sure an ugly fellow, did you know that?"

"You're gonna pay for that."

"No, I'm not." Francis dropped the magazine from the gun's butt, then thumbed the rounds from the spring and sprinkled them on McDermott's head. He ejected the round from the chamber and bounced it off his nose. "Here's your .45, bud. Don't hurt yourself."

McDermott's face seemed to wither, his eyes forming watermelon seeds, his nose shrinking until it disappeared and was replaced by two holes the diameter of soda straws. Francis walked toward the back door.

"I put a hurt on you," McDermott hissed at him. "One you won't ever get rid of, night or day."

Francis knew he was listening to the truth, but refused to give cognizance to either men or spirits who break in and steal or who dwell with the children of Cain in the Land of Nod, somewhere east of Eden. *No, don't continue*, he told himself. Whatever lay out there for him had already been decided, and if his ancestor was right, and Francis believed he was, none of it could be completely unconquerable. The earth was a grand place, and whenever tragedy besieged him, he would never succumb to it and instead would rise from a temporary defeat and grow stronger for it.

He pushed open the back door of the nightclub and walked the short distance to the Airstream in the early dawn and entered the dwelling of the woman who claimed to be the widow of Jefferson Davis. Morgan was sitting on her lap; they were both smiling at him.

"How are you, stranger?" she said.

"Morgan," he replied, his voice hardly a whisper.

The boy ran into his arms, saying, "Daddy, Daddy, Daddy," his tears joining his father's.

She removed the gold locket from her neck and opened it with her thumbnail. "Why don't you have a look at my new beau?" she said. "That is, if he doesn't mind me calling him that."

Francis gazed at the photo. Then he put his hand in hers and cleared his throat and tried to speak. Then he tried again. Then he didn't even do that and instead held Morgan's and Varina's hands and watched the sunrise fill up the Airstream.

STRANGE CARGO

Christmas Day is rarely cold on Bayou Teche. Normally in South Louisiana the rainy gray days of winter don't begin until February, then in the second week of March the azaleas suddenly bloom with both a pink softness and a blood-red brilliance that can break your heart and make you yearn for your youth.

But that's not now, and the season is neither spring nor autumn, and the water in the rain barrel down by the barn has turned dark with the setting of the sun, and the light is brittle and the wind raw. When I cup the water in the barrel and raise it to my mouth, the coldness is like a slap across my face; the leaves that cling to my palm are as sharp-edged as crustaceans.

Maybe you've had moments like these. You know, when you're tired and run-down and you let your mind go where it shouldn't? Loneliness and clinical depression can flay you alive or put you on the rack and not only crack your bones and joints but steal your soul. Here, see for yourself. The sun is orange, the sky blue, the sugarcane across the bayou swaying and clattering like broomsticks. But the sun has no warmth, nor the strength to regenerate itself, and it makes me think of a Halloween pumpkin that has been carved too

263

thin, its candle guttering, the inside of its shell scorched and cracked like old skin, when dust devils climb into the sky and scatter ashes and dust on the bayou's surface.

I try to avoid thoughts such as these and concentrate on the natural gifts of the world and the sublimity of the afternoon. The air is tannic, as moist and pure as cave air, like pine needles and sugarcane stubble plowed under black soil, like an autumnal emanation from the pen of John Keats. I remind myself that the world is a fine place and worth the fighting for, as Ernest Hemingway wrote in *For Whom the Bell Tolls*.

But beyond my ken there are woods flooded with salt water, a blanket of white lichen rocking between the tree trunks, and saline intrusion and tidal surges eating away our wetlands and washing coffins from our cemeteries. I stare at my reflection on the surface of the water in the rain barrel, and rake the image with my hand and watch my face break apart, then like an angry fool I walk up the slope through the live oaks toward the two-story columned house my ancestors built in the year 1843. The leaves are gold and dry and crackling under my feet, scudding over my ankles when the wind gusts. A bull snake slithers by my foot, supple and thick-bodied, its scales as shiny as wet bark, its eyes as mean as BBs.

Like many antebellum homes, the house is painted wedding-cake white; the windows reach to the ceilings and are hung with green ventilated storm shutters. The house also has dormers and a veranda on the second story. In the dip of the land down by the bayou you can barely make out the three water-blackened cypress cabins that once housed our family's slaves (they were always referred to as "the servants"). Today no one knows their names or where they are buried.

When I was a boy I found what were called slave marbles by the cabins. Slave marbles were common during antebellum times because the clay of which they were made was plentiful, and the presence of the marbles also seemed proof that the slave owner had a degree of humanity. The pirate Jean Lafitte anchored his boats here and auctioned off his cargo of stolen goods and kidnapped slaves on this very bank. Rusty chains were nailed with spikes to a live oak trunk, and over the years I saw them slowly subsumed inside the tree's girth, the links looping stiffly in and out of the bark, until they had become part of the heartwood and were forgotten, as though the lives they symbolized had never existed.

You may have guessed that I'm one of those Southerners who believe guilt is part of their heritage. You're right; otherwise, I would have to admit that I am possessed by the same pathological disorder as the Klansman or what we used to call the "po' white trash," a categorization that to this day can get your throat cut.

The rooms have hardwood floors and no carpets and the acoustics of a bowling alley. The echoes of my leather-soled Western boots seem to mock me. Why? I consider myself a failure, that's why. I live in solitude; my only child is buried in Montana; most of my peers are estranged or have passed on. Yet I have repurchased a property that is a symbol of greed and inhumanity and a paean to the grapeshot-ripped flags that flapped above Cold Harbor and Shiloh and the gore that Union farm boys slipped on at Marye's Heights.

My father swore that in 1905 he saw Confederate soldiers in the mist and airbursts in a night sky above Bayou Teche. I believed him, too, because my father never lied. None of the Broussards did. Nor was our generation ever deliberately unkind to people of color. My grandfather was an appointee of Franklin Roosevelt and one of the most admired attorneys in the history of Louisiana. My father went over the top five times at the Somme and the Marne, and more than once gave his best clothes to derelicts and poor men of color. But my family had a problem. It came in bottles, and those of us who embraced it wrecked ourselves and our families, like the debtor who balances his checkbook at the expense of others.

Through the front window I see the sheriff, Jude Labiche, sometimes called "nigger-knocking Mr. Jude," cruise down the two-lane and turn into the long tunnel of oaks that leads to my front porch. Some people think his title is unwarranted and slanderous. I've never been sure. Back in the mean days of the Civil Rights era, "nigger-knocking" was common, particularly around Jude's hometown, and it was done with slingshots, firecrackers, waterbombs, and BB guns, or just garbage slung from a car window. Is the terminology offensive? You bet it is. But the reality was a whole lot worse.

I open the front door and step out on the porch, hoping to head off Sheriff Labiche before he can reach the doorbell and get a figurative foot in the entranceway. Mr. Jude is not one you should provoke. The abuse of prisoners in our stockade is well-known. Mr. Jude has a girth like a whale and a warm stink in his uniform no matter how freshly ironed or starched it is; his stare can make the most confident of men drop his eyes or leave a room.

"What can I do for you, sir?" I ask.

He doesn't get out of the cruiser, and instead cuts the engine and takes a pinch from a bag of Red Man and places it between his lip and gum. He has a twinkle in one eye. "You got a Styron spit cup I can borrow?"

"Afraid not."

He grins and gazes at the Spanish moss on the oak trees straightening in the wind. "I cain't tell you how much I admire your home. It's what I call *Old* South."

"Thank you, Mr. Jude." I look at my watch. "I'm under the gun today."

"It's funny you mention firearms. I hear you have a mess of them."

"I do. Mostly historical ones."

"I also hear you're gonna turn your acreage into a game reserve."

"No, sir, that's not correct. I plan to create a sanctuary for injured birds and animals of all kinds."

"I cain't let you do that."

"Sir?"

"You might be well-intended, Mr. Broussard, but you cain't pen up wildlife in Louisiana."

"What about veterinarians? Does that proscription apply to them?"

"You're not gonna give me trouble on this, are you?"

"No, sir. Where can I get a permit?"

"I don't know. I think you've been gone too long from your roots. We still do things with a handshake. Going behind people's backs here 'bouts is still like serving shit with ice cream."

"I didn't catch that last part."

His eyes have no color, and the pupils resemble dead insects. I have no doubt I've waded into deep water. A young girl is standing in the driveway, dappled with sunlight, her dress blowing. Her name is Fannie Mae Broussard; her body is buried on a knoll at the foot of a mountain range outside Missoula, Montana.

"I hope you're not trying to provoke me," the sheriff says. "I always heard you were a hardhead."

I don't answer. His eyes follow my line of sight. "Are you listening to me?"

"I don't mean to give you any grief, Sheriff."

He picks up a Styrofoam cup from the floor of his cruiser and spits in it. "Been reading any good books of late?"

I'm a novelist and writer of short stories. I try to play along with his joke, hoping my gesture of surrender will satisfy the animus that is at the root of everything he does. "One or two."

"Before I leave, I need to clear the air. Are you gonna have a zoo out here or not?"

Fannie Mae twists her fingers in front of her lips as though turning a key in a lock. The spangled light from the live oaks is like yellow and black polka dots raining on her hair and face. I cannot adequately describe to anyone how much I love Fannie Mae and how much her loss means to me. I walk the floor in the middle of the night and sometimes drive to a twenty-four-hour liquor store in St. Martinville, but I don't go in.

"What's the harm in caring for a wounded animal or bird that has no place to go, Sheriff?" I ask.

"They carry diseases. Secondly, you cain't put your smell on them. Touch the fawn and the doe won't take it back. That's Mother Nature's law, not mine."

He holds his eyes on mine, daring me to challenge him. His eyes make me think of fish scales. Fannie Mae approaches the porch. She's wearing a Red Sox cap and a flowery dress I gave her along with a Janis Joplin album on her thirteenth birthday. *Don't say anything else, Pops. This guy is a world-class asshole.*

The sheriff looks over his shoulder, then back at me. His upper arms are easily ten inches in diameter. His chest is rising and falling, his nostrils dilating. "You got something in your craw, say it."

"I don't break the law, Sheriff," I reply. "I don't borrow trouble, either."

He rubs the back of his wrist on his nose and looks at the white columns of my house and the veranda overhead. "You ought to fly the flag. The red-white-and-blue, right on one of those white columns."

"I've thought about that."

"Good man. Keep writing your books. You've brought a shitpile of money here."

I don't answer. He belts up, then nods goodbye at me and starts talking in his cell phone as he turns his steering wheel in a half circle with the heel of his hand. He drives right through Fannie Mae's image and speeds down the tunnel of oak trees to the two-lane, his emergency bar on fire.

In the morning I meet with my physician on a bench in a hallway by a snack machine at Our Lady of Lourdes Regional Medical Center in Lafayette. His name is Oscar Jenkins. I think he's gay, but no one is quite sure. His head is shaved and looks like a muskmelon; his arms are thick and hairless, like he has just finished pumping iron; his baby-blue eyes are the size of quarters and as clear as water. If he were not wearing scrubs he might be mistaken for an inflatable doll. He throws a package of Cheetos in my lap. "Thanks," I say. "These are great in the early morning. Kind of like carpet tacks."

"I've got your lab report," he says.

"Yeah?" I say, my stomach constricting.

"I'd like to do some X-rays."

"No, I'm sick or I'm not. Plus, I've had so many X-rays I glow in the dark. Besides, the speckled trout are running. Doing anything Sunday?"

He scratches an eyebrow and looks wanly into space. "Remember how we met? I knocked on your door in a rainstorm and introduced myself as an amateur archaeologist looking for some pieces of a Union gunboat on Bayou Teche. I thought you might have me arrested. Instead, you invited me in and we spent the next three hours walking up and down the bayou with a flashlight in an electric storm."

"What did the tests show?"

"I think your constipation might signal cancer. I'd like to remove that possibility."

"I've been standing on third base a long time," I reply. "If I've got the Big C in my entrails, I'm not going to fight it."

"How smart is that?"

"Smart or not, I say screw it."

"You still see specters?"

"No, I don't," I lie.

He nods but doesn't speak. I drop the Cheetos on the bench. "See you later, Oscar."

Without standing up he grabs my forearm. I'm surprised at the power in his grip. "If you don't stop talking and acting like a clod, you may die in a very unpleasant fashion."

I shrug. Or maybe I wink. Or maybe I say, "Who cares?" I really don't remember. I feel like I'm sliding down a long tin chute into a box. I walk as fast as I can out of the building, bareheaded in a rainstorm. Water is swelling out of the storm grates, and through the trees I can see the Vermilion River, yellow and frothy, overflowing its banks, flooding the gutters with organic debris and beetles as big as your thumb that later will stink like a charnel house.

It rains all twenty miles back to my home on Bayou Teche. Fannie Mae is waiting for me on the porch swing. She has many manifestations and is now a teenager, sitting sideways as she swings, her knees drawn up in front of her, the rain blowing a misty aura around her outline. *That cop came back*, she says.

"The sheriff?"

He looked in your windows. That asshole is the sheriff?

"Do you have to use that language?"

You do.

270

"No, I do not. See what Thomas Jefferson wrote to his daughter about young women using profane language."

Was that before or after he started impregnating Sally Hemings?

"I might have the Big C, Fannie Mae."

Goddamn it, don't say that.

I walk past her into the house. She follows me in, scowling. *What were the doc's exact words? Don't try to bullshit me, either.*

"Stop using profanity when you're in my home."

You blew the doc off, didn't you? That's why you want to start a fight with Asshole, isn't it?

"You mean 'Sheriff Asshole'?"

She tries to act serious but breaks into a grin, one that could light up a room. *What am I gonna do with you, Pops? You're my conduit back to the living. The plan was we'd be together for many more years.*

She walks through the back wall of the house, then comes back in less than a minute. *I had a couple of deliveries made while you were in Lafayette.*

"What deliveries?"

You wanted animals and birds. Now you've got animals and birds.

I go to the back of the house. Cats are eating from bowls of dry food all over the porch, most of them pasted with a thick pink salve that covers their mange. Four dogs are eating in their midst. There's also a three-footed raccoon eating sardines off a newspaper with a possum and her babies. The huge bird aviary I built on the side of the carriage house contains a hoot owl with a broken wing and a pigeon with one foot. There is also a fawn in the aviary, lying on its side in some hay, its natal spots faded, its knee in a splint.

"How did you get all these guys together?" I ask.

Connections.

"The sheriff says the human scent on a fawn will cost the fawn its life."

271

That's crap. The mother will hide if people are around the fawn, but she'll return when they leave. If the fawn cries, the mother is probably dead. This little guy's mother was dead.

"How do I get past the sheriff?"

Don't do anything. Shine him on. You always told me the best punch in boxing is the one you slip.

The live oaks are swelling with wind, the dead leaves rising above the canopy like a nimbus, as though denying gravity, even denying death. I don't want to talk about the sheriff anymore. It's my belief that talking about evil steals away our time on earth.

Hear that? she asks.

"Hear what?"

Dogs barking and people yelling.

"I don't hear anything."

Those are slave catchers.

"Stop it."

You know what happened to runaway slaves. The dogs were turned loose on them. Then they were branded.

Our back porch is a lovely place to be. It's built of bricks stacked and cemented four feet high and hung with ceiling fans and is dry and comfortable for us as well as animals, the bayou running high and fast, chained with rain rings, the water as yellow as paint from all the rain.

Sorry if I get on your case, Pops.

"You don't," I reply. "I do that all on my own."

I take a nap. When I wake late in the afternoon, Fannie Mae is gone and the rain has stopped. I clean up the mess on the back porch and find inside a Walmart plastic bag a receipt for the pet food, sardines, tuna fish, and birdseed. The charge is to my Visa card. I check my wallet. My card is there. I call the local Walmart and get the manager on the phone.

"I'm perplexed, Mr. Fontenelle," I say. "I've got a receipt dated yesterday for purchases at your store I didn't make."

"Sir?" he says.

I repeat my statement.

"I guess one of us has got his days mixed up," he says. "I talked with you at the counter."

"Yesterday?"

"Yes, sir. About three p.m."

"I see," I reply. I feel very old and also tired. "It's always nice speaking with you," I say.

"You, too, Mr. Broussard."

I ease the receiver into the cradle and go out by the oak that has ingested the chains used to moor the ships of Jean Lafitte. Water is dripping from the trees into the bayou, and I can see the dorsal fins of bream and goggle-eyed perch rolling between the lily pads, like trapped air gnarling the surface. I place my hand on the tree's bark. Louisiana is a haunted land that I have loved all my life. But a love affair with Louisiana can rend your soul. I feel a heartbeat deep inside the live oak and am convinced that the rusted spikes and chain links will one day burst from the trunk and force us to confront the past. This thought brings me genuine fear. Why? Because both the tree and I are witness to the fact that man can transfer his evil into nature itself, in this case into the tree's heartwood and its roots and the water the roots absorb and the leaves the tree drops, and I also believe the blood of black people, including children, is on those chains, and each morning that I wake I see all of this from my window.

You okay, Pops? a voice says behind me.

"Hey, Fannie Mae."

Hey, yourself. You got the blues?

"I bought the food for the birds and animals, but I have no memory of it."

That was my doing, Pops. The manager at Walmart thought he talked to you, but he was talking to me.

"Good try. But I think I'm losing it. I'm talking about dementia."

I'm part of your dementia?

"Probably."

That's not complimentary. Then she pauses. *Hear that? The slave catchers are at it again. Across the bayou. Listen.*

"If you're talking about the dogs, those are the ones you brought here."

Slaves are running right past us, Pops. You just can't see them. They're trying to get into the Atchafalaya Basin. It's a pitiful sight.

"I don't want to hear this. I'm tired. I want to lie down and sleep. I want the earth to pull me under."

This time she doesn't reply. Then I realize she's staring at a cruiser that's coming hell-for-breakfast down the two-lane, all flashers lit, siren wailing. It bounces across the short wood bridge over the rain ditch onto my driveway and is now coming so fast the water on the windshield is peeling off the glass.

"I think we're in trouble," I say.

You mean Asshole? What can he do? Throw him a roll of mints and call your lawyer. Just don't react.

What can Jude Labiche do? Within one minute he slams on his brakes by the carriage house and is working his way down the slope, backdropped by a stormy sky, his half-topped boots slipping on my unraked leaves, his face dilated and oily, his balled fists as big as hams.

"You okay, Sheriff?" I say.

He catches his breath. "You went behind my back with the animals," he says. "Who in the hell do you think you are?"

"Could you repeat that? Sometimes I don't hear right."

"This is my parish. I got a taser that can turn your teeth into a xylophone. I'll play 'Dixie' on them, boy."

He cuffs my wrists behind me and hooks me to a D-ring in the back seat of the cruiser. I watch the tunnel of live oaks slide past me as we turn onto the two-lane and head for the jail. I have a sick feeling in my stomach, and do not know if it's from cancer or if I'm afraid of the man in front of me whose shoulders are three feet across. He's looking at me in the rearview mirror.

"You think your shit don't stink, don't you?" he says.

"No, you scare me, Sheriff. You're a violent man who wants to turn back the clock."

He drives with one hand on the steering wheel rather than in the ten-two position that's basic with all cops. His eyes stay inside the mirror, even when the right-front tire dips onto the dirt shoulder of the road, gravel whanging under the fender. "You come back home to stir up things, show everyone we're a bunch of hicks?" he says.

"No, sir."

"You're on some kind of mission, though. Right?"

"I have no moral authority about anything or anyone, Sheriff."

"It's about the blacks, isn't it?"

I look out the window at a stubble fire in a cane field, the embers glowing in the rows and spinning in the air, the smoke drifting in thick layers, like the mists of Avalon hiding the sun and also hiding the iniquity and blood that our beloved state is soaked with.

"Know what?" he says, his eyes leaving the mirror. "I could hang your skin on a barn nail or wipe my ass with it."

"So?" I reply.

"The average person here 'bouts couldn't care less. Ain't nobody got your back, Mr. Broussard."

The window is half down and I can smell a chain of water ponds in the cane field and see blue herons standing in the water, pecking at their feathers.

"You got wax in your ears?" he says.

"Sorry, I was drifting off a bit."

"No kidding?" he says. "Well, there's the jail off to your left. I hope you've been vaccinated."

"When I was eighteen, I was in a lockdown unit fifteen feet from an execution," I say. "The electric chair traveled from parish prison to parish prison back then. The executioner called his instrument 'Gruesome Gertie.' It made a smell I could never get out my head. Like somebody ironing damp clothes. You carry the same odor, Sheriff. It's uncanny and it scares the hell out of me."

His eyes appear in the rearview mirror again, and this time I have no doubt I have placed myself in the hands of a man who is morally insane, his past given new life, his genitalia on fire.

I'm put in a holding cell with five men of color and a white kid. All of them seem to have records and know one another. Their clothes look like they were stolen at random from different dryers in a laundromat. Better said, in a normal setting any one of them would stand out like Harpo Marx with his squeeze horn.

They're unsure about my presence in the cell. A light-skinned man of color, with turquoise eyes and a face that looks startled for no reason, jabs a finger at me. "Hey, man, I got you pegged. You ain't sliding nothing by me."

"Oh?" I say.

"You the guy made that movie up the bayou."

"I don't make movies. I'm a writer."

"You cain't fool me, man. You famous. Fuckin' A."

"What's my name?" I say.

"That's easy, man. Tommy Lee Fuckin' Jones."

The others laugh. I shouldn't have led him into embarrassing himself, and I feel bad about it. I'm sitting on a wood bench. I look at my feet and ask the man his name.

"Pookie Mouton."

"Thanks for your goodwill, Pookie. What time do y'all eat?"

"When the food comes," he says. Evidently his startled face doesn't change expression, like it's painted on a coconut. His eyebrows form a single dark line across his forehead. "You ain't an actor?"

"No, sir," I reply.

"What they got you in for?"

"Bringing wild animals on my property."

Everyone else laughs again.

"I was trying to set up an animal refuge," I say.

Like most Cajuns and Creoles, they do not know when to laugh or when people are serious, and I think this is because they live in an era that has little to do with contemporary culture.

"You keep skunks?" the white kid says. He's tall and slender, his denim shirt wadded up and hanging from his back pocket. His chest is flat, his nipples small, his skin as smooth-looking as a darning sock, his uncut hair the color of old rope. The others grin with him.

"No skunks, but just about everything else," I say.

"I read one of your books," he says.

"Did you like it?"

"It was real good," he says. "I wish I could write like that." He smiles with his eyes.

The most important aspect of our legal system is one that few people understand: The system prosecutes and imprisons the people who are available. The rich, the educated, and the executives who are armor-plated inside the corporate structure are not available, and rarely stack time and are never executed under any circumstances. Other than the psychopaths, or more accurately, the criminally insane, most offenders are poor, inept, bumbling, and addicted. Most recidivists couldn't put together a sandwich with a diagram. Their legal survival is in the hands of a stressed-out public defender's office and a bail system that goes back to the Middle Ages. Is justice blind? Of course. It's meant to be.

The center of the problem is dope. It's everywhere, particularly in the projects. Babies have it in their blood when they come out of the womb. There's hardly a school in America that doesn't have dope in its cloakrooms. Pharmaceutical companies have aided and abetted opioid habituation all over the country. The men in my cell are not dangerous; in all probability they have not traveled farther than two or three parishes from their birthplace; most of their crimes are laughable. I have known hundreds of inmates, and have little fear of them. What's my secret? I don't have one.

A deputy comes to the bars and tells me that a federal judge in New Orleans, a university president, and the mayor of the city have called to "inquire" about my status at the jail. "Thought you ought to know, Mr. Broussard." Then he winks and walks away.

Then I look at my companions and feel ashamed. Somebody had my back after all. My companions are not laughing anymore, and it makes me sad. Their eyes are downcast or their backs turned. I don't know what to say. A few minutes later my attorney shows up with a deputy, who unlocks the cell and pulls the door wide. My attorney pats me on the shoulder.

"Give me a minute, will you?" I say.

"What's wrong, Aaron?"

"Nothing," I say. I turn to my companions. "Hey, if any of y'all need a job when you get out, I'm your man. I pay twenty dollars an hour."

"Doin' what?" a man in back asks.

"Litter-box maintenance," I reply. "Bring masks."

Everyone laughs again, except Pookie Mouton, the man whose face looks painted on a coconut. "Any chance Tommy Lee Jones comin' back around? I got some movie ideas he might like."

I get cut loose from the can; no charges, no fingerprints, no apologies; in other words, it's "Beat it, bud, and be glad you didn't get a nightstick across the skull." My attorney drops me off at my house.

Two days pass without incident. It's rainy and cold. I light the gas logs in the living room and stare out the window. At some point the sheriff will come after me. It will not be through his office, either. He'll use a surrogate and be out of town when it happens; until that time comes, he'll laugh openly about the menagerie on my property and seem a man of goodwill. Then on a stormy night, just like this one, a car with no headlights will pull up in front of my house and a bereaved, distraught man will knock on the door and ask to use the telephone.

Or maybe I've overrated my importance, and he let things go. I'm not troubled about my personal future, and I do not fear the schemes of the self-benighted. My fear is for the earth itself. For the first time I hear dogs barking that are not ours. Our dogs are in a warm, dry kennel behind the house; I had them wormed and vaccinated and their sores treated by my physician friend, Oscar Jenkins. The barking dogs are somewhere close to the highway, the same road that was called the Spanish Trail in colonial times, the same road escaped slaves walked at night in order to reach the Atchafalaya Basin, the biggest swamp in the United States.

The barking of the dogs is unrelenting. There has also been a change in the weather. The rain has stopped, but the wind has increased and the storm shutters on the windows are rattling against the latches. The moon is up, the sky almost clear, the limbs of the live oaks twisting with energies that seem to come out of the ground. The tide has shifted, and Bayou Teche is reversing itself, flooding the mudflats and cattails and bamboo and elephant ears that undulate like a carpet on the current.

That's what I mean when I say Louisiana is a haunted place. It does not conform to nature. It makes its own rules and possesses a destructive energy that can be terrifying. It doesn't just blow buildings down. It cracks them from the inside out, rips off shingles and brick chimneys and explodes them like shrapnel in the wind and sometimes leaves deer and livestock in the second stories of farmhouses. Think that's an exaggeration? Check out the visitation of Hurricane Audrey or Katrina.

I hear a loud knocking on the back door of the house, the kind that is driven by angry fists, but I can see nothing outside the windows. There's a pause, then the knocking becomes frantic. I go into the kitchen and approach the back door, but leave the kitchen light off. There's no movement on the porch that I can see, not even the cats curled up on the blankets I piled in the corners. I click on the outside light. It's as bright as a flare. I step out on the bricks, feeling foolish, wondering if cancer has begun to impair my faculties. Now I have an unobstructed view of the yard and the gazebo and the boathouse. There are no footprints on the St. Augustine grass.

I step down into the yard just as the moon breaks from behind a cloud. I can see a leafless uprooted tree and the iridescence of spilled gasoline floating in the center of the bayou. Then something crashes violently inside the boathouse. Either my pirogue or my aluminum bass boat, which hang on hooks above the water, is being torn apart.

I can hear myself breathing, my heart thudding in my ears. A huge weight crashes against one side of the boathouse, then a force that seems almost mechanical bursts through the wall. An alligator, perhaps ten feet long, falls from the walkway inside and splashes into the water and emerges in a cluster of dead lily pads and works its way onto the mudflat.

It lumbers up on the bank, on the grass now, free of the bayou that is supposed to contain it, its massiveness and crushing weight and hooded eyes and toothy grimace and the razor-claws in its feet suddenly real, its teeth encrusted with fragments of turtle shell and chewed meat.

I begin to back toward the house, the beam of my flashlight aimed at the alligator's snout, then I trip over the garden hose and fall backward on the wetness of the St. Augustine grass. When I get up, the trees are still thrashing, the moon higher in the sky, the alligator gone. I feel like a chamber has ruptured in my heart.

I sit down on the brick steps and try to get my bearings. Raindrops patter on the bayou each time the wind gusts. The cats are walking all over me, some of them rubbing against me, their tails straight up, their pink seats bumping into my skin.

That's when I see the black man. Down by the water, close by the great live oak that swallowed the chains and spikes and blood of human chattel that changed hands on my property. He looks straight at me, unshaved, barefoot, naked to the waist, his skin as slick as road tar, his hair woven in dreadlocks. His trousers are little more than rags and are belted with a rope. His teeth are white under the moon.

I stand up, my feet unsteady. "Who are you?" I say.

He doesn't answer. He looks confused, as though lost.

"Did you come in from the two-lane?"

He looks over his shoulder, then back at me. He opens and closes his mouth, as though yawning or trying to clear an ear canal.

"The gator is gone," I say. "My name is Aaron Holland Broussard. Can I help you in some way?"

A pool of lightning ripples through the clouds, then dies on the horizon.

Monster, he says.

"Whoa," I reply.

Killer of my children. His voice is like wood blocks falling down a staircase.

"Wish you didn't say that, podna," I reply. "Time for you to leave."

He walks backward, his eyes locked on mine, then bolts through a canebrake, heedless of the damage to his body. His back is crisscrossed with the scars of a whip and his spine layered with the welts of a branding iron.

In the distance I can hear the Southern Pacific blowing down the line. I hope this man, whoever he is, finds his way to the Atchafalaya, if that is where he is going. But I know better. God slays Himself with every leaf that flies, and so do many of His children.

Fannie Mae visits me at sunrise, casually walking through the wall and sitting down across from me at the breakfast table. There is no greater pain than to lose one's child, but the misery and grief are double when the loss is due to drug and alcohol addiction. Why? Because you know it didn't have to happen. The alternatives are everywhere and take five minutes to find: a hotline, a Medicaid rehab unit, a twelve-step meeting, a hallelujah mission, hanging out with narcissistic health freaks hooked on orange juice and suntans and diving into the surf.

What's happening, Pops? she says, putting jelly on my toast, then replacing the toast on my plate.

I tell her about my visitors of the previous night.

Jesus Christ, she says.

"Yep."

Who is he?

"How would I know?"

I eat the toast she put jelly on. Her face is troubled. She fiddles with the silverware on the table. *Nobody in our family killed a slave, huh? On this piece of property in particular?*

"No, I would never believe that," I say.

What do you call working people to death?

"Shelby Foote said, don't look at mid-nineteenth-century America through twentieth-century eyes."

I've got news for Mr. Foote. Many people who lived in the mid-nineteenth century looked with nineteenth-century eyes and concluded that slavery sucked. Even Jefferson Davis's wife said it sucked.

It's hard to throw a slider past Fannie Mae.

I think this has something to do with that dipshit of a sheriff, she says. *I shouldn't have brought the animals and birds here.*

"That's like saying Noah should have taken the smart money and opened up a cheesy cruise line in South Florida."

I'm scared for you, Daddy.

The only time she uses that last word is when she's truly frightened about my welfare.

"You shouldn't be, little guy," I say.

That was the way I always talked to her when she was alive. It was a foolish way to be, even undignified, I guess. But I don't care. I want my little girl back, and there are times I want to kill the people who preyed on her weaknesses and gave her the drugs and booze that leeched away her soul and her mind and finally her heart. But if I blame them, I have to hold myself accountable, too, and with far more severity. I drank for twenty years. I took her to bars when she was little. My friends, mostly writers and musicians, became her models. A licentious disease became the norm in our lives.

I have to get away from these thoughts. I start to speak, then realize she's gone. Or perhaps she was never there.

New Year's Eve came and went. Three of the men I met in jail got out of the can and knocked on my front door and asked for jobs. One was the tall white kid; the others were Pookie Mouton, the man who was obsessed with Tommy Lee Jones, and a fat black kid with a jolly face named Tee Beau Latiolais. They agreed to rake and burn leaves, repair the boathouse, till and fertilize the flower beds, feed the animals and dump the litter boxes, and clean the rain gutters and the chimney. The next day I smelled weed on the white kid when he came back from lunch, but I talked with him and he promised he'd get rid of his Zig-Zags and stash and fly right. But if he doesn't, I'll probably look the other way. How did Thomas Aquinas put it? We're all condemned to err, so why not err on the side of charity? Which was probably a thirteenth-century way of saying "What the fuck."

But I can't shake the exchange I had with the black man in the tattered trousers. It was more than a simple confrontation with a stranger who had trespassed on my property. The obvious level of anger in him was like none anyone has ever directed at me, and I must admit that I hold a resentment against him. That said, I cannot erase the image of the scars on his back. I want to believe he was wounded or captured in a war or maimed in an auto accident;

I do not want to believe that in contemporary times such cruelty could be visited on a fellow American. Nor do I want to believe he is a victim of the culture that has remained with us since the first terrified Africans, torn from their village and shackled in chains, were unloaded in Jamestown, Virginia, in 1619.

On January 8, I wake to robins singing and a flawless blue sky that is as pure as ether and arches like a ceramic bowl from one horizon to the other. I dress and walk down the stairs carpentered out of recovered cypress, a gold-and-crystal chandelier hanging above my head, the sun shining on the live oaks just outside the windows. What finer way could I start the day? But already the tattered man has robbed me of the morning, his grief and loss perhaps greater than mine, his access to recourse denied him by the color of his skin.

I do not want to do what I must do now. But if I do not, I will have no peace. I fill a mug with coffee and hot milk and drive in my truck to the sheriff's department in town.

It's built of brick and two stories high, with dormers and a wide porch and many white columns and a reflecting pool by the steps, and is located at the end of a circular, oak-shaded driveway between the city library and Bayou Teche and a grotto devoted to the mother of Jesus. A black female detective, whom I don't know, takes me into her office. Her name is Della LeBlanc. She wears navy-blue slacks, a starched white short-sleeve shirt, and a gold badge. There are threads of silver in her hair.

"Why didn't you report this earlier, Mr. Broussard?" she says.

"The man did no harm."

"Sir, do I look stupid?"

I clear my throat. "No, ma'am. The truth is I didn't want to come here because I don't trust the man you work for. I think he's a racist, if not a psychopath."

She puts down her legal pad, looking askance, and makes a snicking sound. "You don't think this black man is a homeless person?"

"Homeless people usually carry their wardrobes on their backs. They don't walk around half naked."

"Interesting observation."

"Ms. LeBlanc—"

"It's Detective LeBlanc."

"Yes, ma'am. The issue is the scarring on this poor fellow. There's also the chance he might be a mental case. He probably belongs in a hospital. Do y'all know someone who would match that description?"

"Does 'y'all' mean the black community or the sheriff's department?"

"Either," I say.

"I've been with the department seven years and lived in the city for forty and I've never seen or heard of the man you describe."

"Nobody like that with dreadlocks?"

"No."

I stare through the window. I can see Bayou Teche and across the water the urban forest we call City Park. "I think I've probably wasted enough of your time."

"Why did you pick January eighth to come in?"

"I don't know. Does it matter?"

"It might to some people. The biggest slave rebellion in American history took place outside New Orleans on January 8, 1811. When it was over, the slave owners cut the heads off the rebels and put them on sticks along the levee. For thirty miles. What do you think about that?"

The sheriff walks past the door and glances through the glass, then does a double take. The detective replaces her legal pad in her desk drawer, her head lowered. "Watch your butt, Mr. Broussard," she says.

"I didn't get that," I say.

"The hell you didn't."

In the midafternoon four days later a lightning storm sweeps across the wetlands, pushing a tornado ahead of it. The tornado tears up several houses just south of us and kills a family in a car a few hundred yards down the two-lane from the entrance to my driveway. Most of my animals are in the barn, and others are in the house, particularly the cats. The aviary has a tin roof and is covered on all four sides with canvas tarps. That night a pale-blue pickup that looks like it was beaten with a ballpeen hammer from bumper to bumper turns off the two-lane and comes up the drive to the front door. The driver cuts the headlights and runs for the porch, a newspaper over his head. I wonder if perhaps this is the visitor I believe Jude Labiche will one day send to my house. But it's the tall white kid I met in jail and to whom I gave a job, the same kid I had to speak with about toking up on the job.

His name is Simoneaux Guidry (pronounced "See-mo-no Gid-dree"). He stands in the doorway, sopping wet. "Come in, I'll get you a towel," I say. "You don't believe in raincoats?"

He steps inside but stays on the small throw rug so as not to drip on the wood floor. "I was worried about the fawn," he says. "I call him 'the little guy.'"

I have never stood this close to him. There are three tiny scars like knots in a piece of string that drip from his left eye.

"You call the fawn what?" I say.

"The little guy. I say something wrong?"

"No. I have some dry clothes that should fit you."

"I don't need none, Mr. Broussard."

"Stay here."

"Yes, sir."

I go upstairs and return with a towel and some socks and boxer underwear and a T-shirt and a corduroy shirt and a sweater.

"I didn't want to put you out," he says.

"Don't worry about it. I checked on the fawn an hour ago, but we can take another look. You can dress in the bathroom at the back of the hallway."

A few minutes later I hear him flush. He comes back combing his hair, his wet clothes wrapped inside a beat-up bomber jacket. "Deer are the most abused animals in the country," he says. "It ain't a sport. It's mean. The Old Testament warns about hurting animals. People don't pay no attention to it, though."

"Where'd you go to school?"

"I didn't stay one place long enough for school to have an influence on me. I did all my reading in public libraries. Think we ought to see how the little guy is doing?"

There's an innocence in his face that bothers me.

"Excuse me, Mr. Broussard, but you're looking at me kind of strange."

"Did you ever clip anybody, Simoneaux?"

His face drains. "Sir?"

"You had three green tears tattooed under the corner of your left eye. Whoever did the removal should give you back your money."

"I got turned out in the St. John the Baptist Parish jail when I was seventeen. You know what that means?"

"You were raped?"

"I put an Aryan Brotherhood tat on my face to make people think I was a badass. The AB made me take it off. If I didn't, they said they'd blind me with a screwdriver."

"I see."

"I stole food from grocery stores and slung dope, Mr. Broussard. I never strongarmed or stuck up nobody. I ain't no killer."

"Well, I'm happy you're working for me, Simoneaux. Let's see what the little guy is up to."

"There's something I need to tell you. You heard earlier about that accident out there on the highway, the one killed that family?"

"Yes."

"I live just two miles up the road, in the trailer park. I was the first to pull up on their car. A black guy was hiding in the trees. He was barefoot and didn't have a shirt or coat on. There was a piece of log or firewood by the side of the road. It was scraped up, like it had been ground into the asphalt."

"You think the car ran over it?"

"Yes, sir."

"And you think the black man might have put it there?"

"Why else would he be hiding in the trees?"

"Did you talk to the cops?"

"No, sir, that ain't my job. Other people started arriving. I took off."

"You need to tell them what you saw, podna."

He shakes his head negatively before I can finish my sentence. "No, sir, I don't owe nobody nothing," he says. "I'm telling you this because the black guy ran onto your property. Maybe he's still hanging out there."

"Why didn't you tell me earlier?"

"Because I don't like getting tangled up. I been in and out of jail since I was thirteen years old."

"What if my attorney and I go down to the sheriff's department with you?"

"I thought coming to you would be enough. I think I made a mistake coming here."

"You're a good young fellow, Simoneaux. I'm going to tell the authorities what you have told me, but I will not give them your name."

"That's legal?"

"No, I don't think so."

"Then why you doing it?"

"You got me," I reply. "Let's go check on our animals, podna. I'll get my coat."

An hour later I watch him drive away, the taillights of his truck disappearing inside the fog rolling off the Teche. A bolt of lightning splits the sky, illuminating the trees and the approximate area where the family died and where the black man hid in the shadows. Notice that I have accepted Simoneaux's account. I did so because he had no way of knowing I had obviously seen the same person lurking along the bayou. But more disturbing is the possibility that both of us have encountered a person who doesn't exist, at least not inside the dimension whose predictability we count upon every day of our lives.

The wind is up and the leaves are whisking in the circular driveway shared by city hall and the sheriff's department. The sun is straight overhead, its reflection dancing on the surface of the bayou, the grotto devoted to the mother of Jesus in deep shadow.

I enter the building, eyes straight ahead, and pass by the dispatcher inside the sheriff's department and climb the stairs and tap on the window of Detective LeBlanc's office. She looks up from her desk, hesitates, then cups her fingers at me. I go inside and close the door. I had not made an appointment.

"I hope you can make this quick, whatever it is," she says.

There's a straight-back chair in front of her desk, but she does not invite me to sit down. I do so anyway. "A person I know has given me some information about the fatal accident near my home," I say.

"Why does this 'person' not want to give it to me?"

"He's not a big supporter of the system."

"So we're talking about a male?"

"He's a kid. He was the first to arrive at the accident scene. He saw a black man hiding in the trees by the wreck. The black man was not wearing shoes or a shirt. There was a chunk of wood by the roadside. Maybe the car ran over it and that was the cause of the accident, not the tornado. Maybe the black man put it there. Did the investigation produce a piece of wood like that?"

"No, it did not. And why do I keep hearing the word 'black'?"

The room goes silent. Her anger is almost tangible. Through the back window I can see gold leaves flying in the air above the live oaks in City Park. I want to be a child again, when on summer days my father and I fished in the bayou and played pitch-and-catch and sometimes bought a snowball from a colored man who pushed a cart with an umbrella on it in the park.

"Have I lost your attention?" she says.

"I was thinking about how my father and I used to eat snowballs when we visited City Park."

"Listen to me," she says. "The firemen had to use the Jaws of Life, and the tow-wrecker had to tip the car right side up again. So a critical piece of evidence was probably destroyed. That means that eyewitness testimony in this case is imperative. Are you hearing me? We're talking about a multiple homicide, including the death of a child."

"I understand."

"But you're not going to give up your source?" she says.

"No."

"You know I have to go to the sheriff with this?"

"I guess you do."

"You *guess*? That's wonderful. I can't tell you how bad you piss me off."

"I'll leave now. That is, if you don't mind."

"You've put an unknown black suspect at the center of the investigation, then you walk out the door?"

"I've googled all the information I could get on the slave uprising in January of 1811. Supposedly there was a free black woman who painted pictures of what she witnessed during the rebellion. I've called the archives at Tulane, LSU, and UL, but I didn't have much luck."

"Meaning?"

"Could you help me?"

"Get out of my office, Mr. Broussard."

"I'm sorry to give you any grief, Detective. I think you're a good person."

"Did you hear me? Please. No, let me rephrase that. *Please, please, please* leave. You can take the stairs or the elevator. You can take the fire escape. You can take the back door or the front door or the side door. Just get out of the building. Maybe buy a snowball."

"I think that last remark is low-rent and unworthy of you, Detective."

I can hear her breathing through her nose; I have the feeling the rest of her day will not be too enjoyable.

When I get home Oscar Jenkins's car is parked in my driveway. It's a compact, one with a hybrid engine. Oscar is searching the ground outside my barn with a metal detector. It's noontime and the three employees I hired out of the can are at lunch. I walk down the slope into the shade. The leaves from my neighbor's house have blown onto my property and relittered the lawn. Oscar is wearing jeans and tennis shoes and a scrub shirt and earphones, and doesn't hear me until I'm right behind him. He seems in deep thought. His short sleeves are tight around his biceps, a reminder that he has a physical side to him that probably should not be plumbed. "Hey," he says, pulling off his earphones. "Hope you don't mind me poking around on your property?"

"What are you looking for?"

"Anything, an anchor, a cannonball, maybe some boiler plate. I got a new map, one that shows the sites of all the sinkings."

In 1863 the Federals deliberately blew up or chopped holes in the bottoms of any boats they could get their hands on and sunk them up and down the bayou to isolate the Confederates from the supplies that were coming across the Sabine River.

"Find anything?"

"No, not yet. But I will."

That's Oscar. Good-hearted and decent, a reenactor, more boy than man, the way professional baseball players are. His small house in Lafayette is a Civil War armory. But I know he has something else on his mind. And it's something I don't want to talk about. Here it comes.

"I've got another reason for being here, Aaron," he says. "I'm sorry I fussed at you for not addressing the possibility you have cancer. I thought you were just in denial. But that's not the case, is it?"

"I try to stay out of my own head, Oscar. It makes life a lot easier."

"I think you want to die. Except your religion doesn't allow you to cap yourself. So you've decided to let cancer do the dirty work."

"No, I was scared of what you would find if you did any more tests."

"If you were ever scared of anything, it was for about five seconds."

"You're mistaken," I say.

He looks around at all the cats and raccoons and dogs and birds and possums and screech owls that have found a home on my land. The fawn is still there, too, and has been joined by a doe that got caught in a barbed-wire fence and blinded in one eye. "We need to keep you around, Aaron."

We're standing in the shade, a cushion of warm air and the scent of pine needles surrounding us. It's a fine day, and I don't want to die. But part of what Oscar said is true. There are moments when I feel the earth is pulling me down, and I think about the loss of Fannie Mae and I wish to let go of my earthly ties. But what better place is there? Isn't it possible that heaven is already with us, if we would just recognize it? Are we not its stewards, as the Old Testament suggests? Are we not already at work and play in the fields of the Lord?

"You know what I like most on your lawn?" Oscar says. "The four-o'clocks, the little flowers under the trees nobody pays much mind to. They bloom in the shade every afternoon, red and gold. They're always there, no matter what the weather does. When I have a down day, I look at the four-o'clocks."

Before I can reply I look past Oscar and see a cruiser coming up the driveway. Detective LeBlanc has obviously reported my morning visit to Sheriff Labiche.

"You better leave, Oscar," I say. "I think the neighborhood is about to slide down the bowl."

He turns around and stares at the cruiser, then blinks as though someone had just popped his cheek. "You didn't get into it with this guy, did you?" he says.

Labiche drives his cruiser onto the grass and gets out. He's wearing yellow-tinted aviator glasses. His face is a storm cloud, but the source of his anger seems to lie with Oscar rather than me. "This is a private interview, Doctor," he says. "You best be going."

"This is my home, Sheriff," I say. "Dr. Jenkins is my guest."

"If he remains here, he will be charged with obstructing a police officer in the execution of his duty."

"That's a stretch, isn't it, sir?" I say.

"What are you doing with that metal detector?" he says to Oscar. "Digging up a power line?"

"He's doing historical research," I say.

"It's okay," Oscar says. "I have to get back to Lafayette, anyway."

"I bet you do," Labiche says.

"What's that supposed to mean?" Oscar says.

"I hear you got married in Lafayette City Park," the sheriff says. "To a husband."

"That's not correct," Oscar says. "However, I do have a partner I sometimes share a house with."

"Does your 'partner' take it in the ass?"

"Sheriff, you're not going to talk like that to people on my property," I say.

"Think so?" he replies.

He rips the detector from Oscar's hands and the earphones from his neck, then throws the earphones back at Oscar and begins twisting the dials on the unit. "I've always heard about this tree," he says.

"Give him back his detector, Sheriff," I say.

"The good doctor doesn't mind. Do you, doc? Some people say Lafitte buried his treasure here. But why would he bury treasure in the same spot where he was selling niggers and stolen goods? James Bowie was mixed up in it, too. Did y'all know that?"

I can see the sheriff's teeth behind his lips, but nothing behind his tinted glasses. He begins waving the search coil up and down the bark of the live oak to which Jean Lafitte moored his boats and chained his human cargo. I do not know what it is about him that gives me such a sense of loathing and danger. Perhaps it's his physicality, his leathery skin and the acne scars on the back of his neck, the weightlessness of the metal detector in his hand, his contempt for all decency, the way he walks in a circle around the tree as though it's a bound prisoner he can set aflame if he wishes.

"Sheriff, this is still the United States," I say.

He shows no sign of having heard me. "Look at that needle," he says. "Goddamn, what all's in there?"

"I'd like my detector back," Oscar says.

"What are you gonna do with the artifacts you find here?"

"Give them to a museum."

"Except that's not what you do. Everybody in Lafayette knows you been stealing from Indian mounds and battle sites and I don't know what all. Tell you what, let's keep you and your partner honest."

He swings the detector against the tree and breaks it apart, then picks up the parts and throws them in the bayou. "Now you get the fuck out of here."

My insides are shaking, my hands opening and closing at my sides. "I'm going to contact the state attorney general's office, Sheriff," I say. "It may do no good, but at some point people will learn about you and the contempt you have for both the law and human kindness."

He smiles. "You're part Jew, aren't you?"

"Judaism is a religion, sir, not a race."

"Whatever you are, you can call anybody you want. I'll give you the number of the *New York Times*. They did an expose on me, but I'm still here. Now what's this about a black man putting a log on the road and killing that family in front of your house?"

* * *

In Louisiana the most powerful individuals in the parish are the sheriff and the treasurer. If you're smart, you do not get in their way. Oscar has driven away, probably to Lafayette, and left me with Jude Labiche. It's like a bad dream. I am about to talk to an officer of the law who I just watched assault and rob a friend on my own property. I feel dirty all over, as though I've betrayed Oscar; I also feel I'm a failure in the eyes of my daughter Fannie Mae, who I'm sure is watching. Perhaps age has taken over my faculties, or perhaps the reality of the human condition is one I have denied all my life, namely, that brute force and men like Jude Labiche have controlled mankind since Cain bashed Abel with a rock.

Standing next to a man like Labiche is a degradation in itself. His presence is a violation of the air, of the sunlight, of the grass growing under his shoes. I want to go inside and take my M1 from the gun cabinet and press a clip into the magazine and lock the iron sights in the kill zone between his chest and face and blow him into the cattails. I am not fantasizing. I have killed before. Yes, in a war on foreign land in a cause supported by the United Nations, but killing peasants who survived on a ball of rice a day had nothing to do with ideology or patriotism and everything to do with the killer that lives within us. Why do I say this? I saw F-80s strafe columns of refugees streaming south of the 38th parallel in hopes of escaping the communists. Why vouchsafe their mass murder and spare Labiche?

He's a cretinous man, an aggregate of ignorance, tribalism, visceral appetites, and cruelty, the kind of man who should be wiped from the earth. But his complexity and his raison d'être should not be underestimated. His political power was not acquired; it was given to him by an electorate that would legitimize the racial anger they have kept unto themselves for decades.

Niccolò Machiavelli knew them well. They longed for a leader who used an iron hand hidden inside a velvet glove. The torture of a prisoner or the killing of a troublesome individual was acceptable if it was accompanied by the blessing of legality, or if the deed was done for the greater good.

They loved Labiche. He was one of their own, and at the same time greater than they were and yet devoted to their empowerment. His profanity, his Styrofoam spit cup, his well-known anti-Semitism, and the sweaty aura he trailed in his wake were a refutation of political correctness. And they loved the way he handled payback. Labiche did it with three-cushion shots. With his feet up on his desk, he could make a single phone call to a state agency and turn an enemy's life into a nightmare.

He slips his aviator glasses into his shirt pocket, then thumbs a pinch of Red Man inside his cheek. I feel his eyes crawl across my face. "You a little nervous about something, Mr. Broussard?" he says.

"I'd like for you to leave now."

"You're upset about your friend?"

"He's a fine man."

"He's a queer."

"I'm going to walk inside now and call my attorney. Don't come here again unless you have a warrant."

"I want the nigger," he says.

"Say again?"

"I've been after him a long time. I think he's the same guy who was stirring up things in Lafayette years ago. Dreadlocks, scarred-up back, running around half naked, nastier than a wash pan in a cathouse. Who told you he was at the car wreck?"

"My mind's a real blank on that, Sheriff."

"You know, I just don't get you. I'm talking to you as a younger man to an older man. Things were better years ago. You know that. You were here."

"Good day to you, sir. I think you owe Dr. Jenkins an apology, plus the replacement of his metal detector."

"You're gonna force my hand, aren't you?"

"No, sir, I'm not. I'm going to stay as far away from you as I can."

A pale-blue pickup covered with dents turns off the two-lane into the driveway and heads for the carriage house. Three men are squeezed in the front seat.

"I declare," Labiche says. "That's Simoneaux Guidry, isn't it? I forgot he lives right up the road."

"I'm not sure where he lives."

"You don't know where your employees live?" he replies. "You're a casual man, floating along with the saints."

I stare at the lawn and at the four-o'clocks in the shade of the trees. He turns and spits a long stream of tobacco. He wipes his mouth with the back of his wrist.

"You don't think he could have been at the accident site, could he?"

"He's a good kid, Sheriff. I'm the problem here, not him."

"A good kid? You're a pistol, Mr. Broussard. Have a good day."

He walks to his cruiser and drives away, passing Simoneaux Guidry's truck by driving on the grass, not acknowledging the three men behind the windshield, all of them frozen like cutouts in a shooting gallery.

Two nights later I go to a restaurant-and-bar in the black district of St. Martinville and sit outside in the cold at a stone table in a metal chair between the kitchen and Bayou Teche. The tide is coming in and the elephant ears float like a carpet of green hearts in the current. Fannie Mae sits across from me, wearing a navy pea coat and playing solitaire with a worn deck of cards. She's been somber lately. As a child she was moody and often dwelled on death when other children were playing. She also thought about boys more than she should have. I suspect much of that had to do with my drinking and my absence from home.

What's on your mind, Pops? she says without raising her eyes.

"I'm wondering why you're acting so depressed."

I think we should go back to Montana before you get yourself killed.

"Everybody gets to the same barn."

Boy, is that helpful.

The restrooms are in a brick house separate from the restaurant and bar. Detective Della LeBlanc comes out of the back door, then stops and stares at me. I look away and give her the opportunity to pretend she doesn't see me. But she's undaunted and walks toward me. "I should have known it was you," she says.

"Pardon?" I say.

"People inside were talking about a man talking to himself under the moon. What are you doing here, Mr. Broussard?"

"Minding my own business."

"Can I speak with you?"

I look at Fannie Mae. She shrugs and gets up and walks down the slope toward the water. "Sit down," I say.

"No, thanks," she says. "Look, this discussion can cost me my badge."

I push away my bowl of gumbo and the chunk of French bread floating in it. "Then don't enter into it."

"He's gonna hurt you. He owns people all over the parish. He makes that sheriff in Phoenix look like a clown."

"You're talking about Sheriff Labiche?"

"Don't be coy, Mr. Broussard."

"I'm old. There aren't many ways I can be hurt. But I appreciate your concern."

She puts her hands on her hips and gazes at the bayou. Her wool jacket has big buttons on it and is tight on her shoulders; her hair is black and thick and freshly blow-dried. "I guess you're just not a listener."

"I think you've got that wrong. At your office, you told me something that doesn't flush, Detective."

"Oh?"

"I gave you the description of a half-naked, scarred-up black man with dreadlocks, and you said you had never heard anyone in the department or the black community make mention of a guy like that."

"That's right."

"Sheriff Labiche has an obsession with this guy. How could you not know that?"

There's a tic at the corner of her mouth. "I leave the sheriff alone."

"Good try."

"I've done everything I can to be kind to you, Mr. Broussard."

"I know that. But the man you work for is insane and incapable of change. The challenge is not to let him change *us*."

"Goodnight, sir," she says, and walks down to the ladies' restroom, her back stiff with anger.

Fannie Mae returns to the table and sits down. *Don't let her get to you, Pops.*

"Why is she holding back on the guy with the dreadlocks?"

Did you see her ankle?

"No."

She has a perforated dime and a little chain hanging on it.

"Voodoo?"

This is still Louisiana.

"Where you going?"

Have to check in with headquarters.

"You might have to leave me?"

It's the way it is, Pops.

"I never asked for much. It's not fair."

Life's a bitch, then you die.

"Don't talk like that."

But she's gone now. The moonlight is pale on the elephant ears, the wind shriveling the surface of water. I stand up from the table and try to eat my gumbo by dipping my French bread in it and swallowing as fast as I can so I can head for the bar inside the restaurant. Inside, I hardly take note that I'm the only non–person of color in it. No one seems to notice me, either, except the bartender. He's a big man, as lean as an ax, with muttonchop whiskers and the colorless eyes of a wolverine. "What'll it be, my man?" he asks.

"How about some manners for starters?" I say.

"Maybe you're in the wrong shack, Jack." He splays his fingers on the bar and widens his eyes.

"You have coffee?"

"In the restaurant."

"Why can't I have it in here?"

"What's this about, man?" he says, looking sideways, his patience thinning.

"You carry Johnnie Walker?"

"No. But I'll give you a longneck Bud on the house. You good wit' that?"

"No, not at all."

He rolls a toothpick between his teeth. Then he sees something outside the window and his cavalier attitude disappears. I turn around and look at the window. Rain is clicking on the glass. The sky is black. A burst of electricity pulses inside a cloud.

"Some kind of problem out there?" I say.

He leans close to me, wiping one nostril with the back of his wrist, his breath sweet with the smell of cherries. "We got nothing to do wit' that guy out there. I didn't see him. You didn't see him. We don't have no association wit' you or him. Got it?"

"No, I don't 'got it.' What guy?"

"Wit' the dreadlocks."

"There's nobody out there, bub."

"Keep saying that. All the way out the door. Don't come back, either."

When I rise in the morning, the sun is shining and Fannie Mae is waiting for me in the kitchen. Her face is aflame. *I turn my back and you try to screw the both of us.*

"I didn't order the drink. I just lost my parameters a little bit."

You know how you can always tell an alcoholic? His lips are moving.

"I apologize."

You're hurting both of us, Pops.

I start making breakfast, avoiding her eyes.

I got myself assigned to you. It wasn't easy. Because you've been a pain in the ass for a lot of people Up There.

"Tell everybody 'Up There' I appreciate it."

Keep it up and I'll arrange a bolt of lightning for the top of your head.

"I went into the bar because I wanted to cancel my ticket. I was going to let the booze do it for me."

She's quiet now. She stares out the window at the boathouse in the shade and at the live oak that sent Jude Labiche into a rage.

"You're not going to say anything?" I ask.

303

We're all part of a plan, Pops. That's why people aren't supposed to knock themselves off.

"Where did you go last night?"

The Tulane archives. This weirded-out black guy sounds a lot like a slave named Winston Royal. His family was executed in the rebellion of 1811.

"He's dead?"

A guy over two hundred years old? It's possible.

I'm glad she's in a light spirit again. I'm also glad she didn't berate me worse than she did, because I deserved it. The family member who kills himself also kills his family, and at the least drops a net of guilt on them that they carry to the grave.

I found some other information at Tulane. Winston Royal has shown up in many situations. Several include an alligator. How do you explain that?

I look down at the boathouse again. My employees from the jail have repaired the alligator damage to the wall with three planks of unpainted pine. They look like metal fillings in a rotted tooth.

"It's part of the mythology around here," I say. "The patriarch of the Tabasco family on Avery Island killed a gator with an ax and saved the lives of some women and children and is revered for it until this day."

Promise me no more bars?

"Word of honor."

Then I wince at the number of drunkards, including me, who I have heard say those words.

The phone rings right after lunch. The weather is holding, the day golden, I don't want to lose it. The digital window says PRIVATE CALLER in large letters. I pick it up anyway. "Hello?"

I hear a sound like someone spitting in a cup. "I just FedExed a metal detector to your doctor friend," the sheriff says. "It cost twice what he paid for that piece of junk he was using. I think he got a pretty good deal. You there?"

"I'm happy you did that. I hope you wrote an apology with it."

"You don't give an inch, do you? Where in the name of suffering God do you get your attitudes?"

"Hard to say. Judeo-Christian religion, the Age of Reason, the correspondence between Thomas Jefferson and John Adams, odds and ends like that."

"I lose my temper sometimes," he says. "How about showing a little compassion? That's all I'm asking."

"I think the black man who's got you worried is not from our own time. I believe he's a wandering soul who has a message for us. I don't know what that message is, but I don't think it bodes well for any of us."

"Put that in one of your books."

"Why do I bother you, sir?"

"You don't."

"Right," I say, and hang up.

He calls back in ten seconds. "What do you know about the black man? The one that was at the accident?"

"Call the Tulane archives. Ask about a man named Winston Royal."

I can hear him breathing against the mouthpiece. "Where'd you get that name?"

"Alligators figure in some of his appearances. Strange, huh?"

"What do you mean, 'strange'? Why did you use that term? Explain yourself."

"I think you're a driven man, sir."

"That's what you think, do you? I have a mind to—"

"Do me injury?"

"Why do you think you're better than me? What gives you that right?"

"I didn't mean you harm, sir. I apologize if I've done you any wrong."

This time he hangs up, fumbling the receiver on the phone cradle.

I've made a mistake. I've just told a southern poor white he's an object of pity. If you want trouble deep down in Dixie, there's no better way to do it.

Please excuse me for the pause in my narration. The generation to which I belong is a recalcitrant one, primarily because we had a peek through an inverted historical telescope into a time when the backdrop of the American drama was the continent itself, so vast and inviting that an entire family with their pets and livestock would ride a log raft down the Ohio or the Missouri River into a land they would try to conquer with a singletree plow and a bag of seed. Think I'm kidding about the connections my generation had with the past? My mother was born in 1907. When she was a little girl she knew an elderly woman in Yoakum, Texas, who with her family fixed breakfast for Davy Crockett and his twenty Tennesseans on their way to San Antonio and to certain death at the hands of Santa Anna.

My grandfather was Hackberry Holland. At age fifteen he carried the mail hell-for-breakfast across the Cimarron and through the Indian Territory and later rode the Chisholm Trail and was a friend of Susanna Dickinson, the only adult white survivor of the Alamo.

Bonnie Parker and Clyde Barrow and Ray Hamilton and his girlfriend camped on Grandfather's ranch in 1933, and my cousin Weldon fell in love with Bonnie and carried her memory from the invasion of France to the Elbe River. I'd love to go back to that earlier time. Why? Because for the brave of heart every sunrise could be an adventure; all you had to do was shake the dice in the cup.

Compare that to walking around all day with a cell phone clamped to your ear like an incurable tumor.

But maybe it's I who has the problem. Maybe the real adventure is always there; maybe it's simply a matter of recognizing the child who lives in us all. The human personality does not change. The era might, but not the child. The last words of Nero, after he stabbed himself in the throat, were supposedly "What an artist the world loses in me."

Two nights after I insult Jude Labiche, a cruiser comes up my driveway and Detective Della LeBlanc gets out and rings the front doorbell. She's dressed to the nines. Mist is blowing across the lawn, and under the porch light her hair and skin are damp and shiny. When I open the door, the inside of the house blooms with the night air. "I don't want to hear about your boss," I say.

"Five minutes," she replies.

"You can have all the time you want, Detective. But not about that psychopath you work for."

She steps inside. I can smell her perfume. "What a beautiful home you have," she says.

"Thank you."

I ask her to come into the kitchen and pour her a cup of coffee. Cats and at least three dogs are walking around or lying down or sitting on the floor, tails flopping and swishing on the linoleum. I see the dime and tiny chain on her ankle that Fannie Mae mentioned. In Louisiana the perforated dime hanging from the ankle or the neck is there for only one reason: to ward off the gris-gris, a spell that practitioners of voodoo cast with graveyard dirt, a strip of red flannel, and a bone with a piece of pink meat still attached to it.

"Sheriff Labiche might be a dick, but he's a pitiful one," she says. "He wants your approval. He reads your books. He wants to be in one of your films. You're a smart man, Mr. Broussard. Be practical."

"I have the sense something bad is about to happen."

"It already has. Last night your friend Dr. Jenkins decked Sheriff Labiche in the Petroleum Club in Lafayette. I was there. He knocked the sheriff over the buffet table."

"I can't believe that."

"If the mayor hadn't been there, your friend would be in jail, maybe charged with felony assault. The sheriff had food all over his clothes. He looked like a fool."

"Was this about a metal detector?"

"Not that I know of. The sheriff was telling queer jokes in front of Dr. Jenkins and a man Dr. Jenkins's age. Apparently Dr. Jenkins thought the jokes were aimed at him and his friend."

"Were they?"

"Probably. The sheriff can't get to the doctor, so he has to get to you. Unfortunately for him, he can't do that, either. So one hour ago he busted your employee Simoneaux Guidry for a broken taillight, driving with an expired license, and possession. He's holding him in the parish prison."

Her eyes are on mine. Then her stare breaks.

"What's the rest of it."

"I heard him talking to two deputies at the jail. He said, 'Our friend Mr. Guidry has got some smart-ass in him. If he sasses you, take the starch out of him.' One of those deputies made a black man lick his own blood off the wall."

I start to speak, but she cuts me off. "The sheriff isn't finished, Mr. Broussard. He gonna get your other employees, Pookie Mouton and that fat black kid, what's-his-name, Tee Beau Latiolais, the one who's always laughing. Our jail isn't a place to be laughing."

"I don't doubt anything you say, Detective—"

"Call me Della."

"How do I change any of what you've told me?"

An orange cat the size of a pumpkin jumps on the table and seats his rear end on the surface. She picks him up and kisses the top of his head. "I have no answer. I've told you what I know. There's one other thing, though. The sheriff is probably a relative of mine. Because he can't admit that, he'll continue to do the stupid things he does for the rest of his life. Welcome to Shitsville."

"You ever think of quitting?"

"I've never enjoyed cleaning bathrooms."

"You like cats?"

"Sure. I love all animals."

"Work for me."

"Doing what?"

"I don't know. Taking care of animals."

She looks at me. Then blinks. "You're starting to embarrass me, Mr. Broussard."

"Call me Aaron."

"How about 'Mr. Aaron'?"

"That has a lovely ring," I reply. "If you're a cast member in *Gone with the Wind*."

Her laugh comes deep out of her chest, and I feel the desires of my youth flare in my lower regions and wonder if I will ever change from the foolish man that I am.

Later in the night I sit in the living room in the dark. A soft rain is falling, dimming the bayou and the cane fields and a lighted house on the other side. Fannie Mae is sleeping on the couch. Before she died she was always my confessor. That was the great irony about Fannie Mae. She knew everything about my soul and always had the answer for my problems. But she had no wisdom about herself. Gigolos and addict-alcoholics attached themselves to her in order to siphon off the wages I paid her. To legitimize the life she led she put herself again and again in dangerous situations that left her ashamed and injured and suicidal and sometimes hospitalized. Yet she remained the best person I ever knew. And everyone knew that except Fannie Mae.

She opens one eye and looks across the room. *Thinking about the past?* she asks. *And how I screwed up?*

"No. I'm the one who messed up."

Sorry I cause you guilt, Pops. It can punch holes in your stomach.

"I took you to your first saloon."

Eighty-six the ashes and sackcloth routine. Hear the dogs? They're in overdrive tonight.

I want to pretend they're ours, but I know better. The barking is from across the bayou. The dogs are running fast in a field of burnt cane stubble, competing with one another, hungry for the reward that will be theirs if they tree their prey.

Where are you going? she asks.

I don't answer. I unlock the glass doors on one of my gun cabinets. I own rows of pistols, mostly cap-and-ball. I have the James Conning sword that my great-grandfather carried through the entirety of Jackson's Shenandoah campaign and up Cemetery Hill. I pick up my Smith & Wesson .38 Special, unlock the ammunition drawer, load five rounds in the cylinder, and set the hammer on the empty chamber.

We don't need any more violence in our lives, Pops.

"Speak for yourself."

You're going out there? On the neighbor's property, with a loaded gun?

"You're always talking about the dogs. So let's check out the dogs. Maybe they want to live with us."

You don't want to see what's happening out there, Daddy.

"I was at Pork Chop Hill, kiddo."

Shit-can that "kiddo" stuff. What these lazy cornpone twits did to black people was awful.

"I'll see you later."

As I leave the living room I hear no sound behind me.

I go out the kitchen door and down the brick steps, the porch light projecting my shadow on the grass, the shadow staying with me past my dilapidated barn until I'm surrounded by complete darkness. I drag my pirogue off the tiny pier in the boathouse and step inside it and paddle across the Teche, a light rain clicking on my Australian digger hat. My neighbor's field smells like a damp incinerator.

I thought Fannie Mae would give in and follow me, but she doesn't, and I'm disappointed in her. Even as a little girl she was already ready for a scrap. But maybe this shows who has the real problem. Taking pride in a child's aggressive behavior is an indicator of the parent's own failure. I loved my daughter, but I didn't get help for myself or try to protect her from the alcoholism that was the curse of our family, and for that I sometimes want to paint my brains on the ceiling.

Nonetheless, I look back at the house, hoping she's on the back porch or standing in the yard. But she's not. The pirogue glides through the shallows and the flooded cattails and bamboo and scrapes on the mudflat. The barking of the dogs is concentrated in one area now, a pecan grove, one that I don't remember being there. In fact, the entire terrain has changed. My neighbor's lighted house has disappeared, and the blackened sugarcane stubble has been replaced by marshland, the salt grass waist-high and pale green, swaying in the wind and rain, the way the countryside was before it was drained for agricultural purposes.

I see figures walking around inside the pecan grove, their bodies silhouetting against a campfire. There are at least five men inside the grove. The fire is flickering, an occasional spark spinning upward into the bareness of the tree limbs. The .38 is pushed down behind the back of my belt, the iron sight cutting into my spine. The dogs are quiet now, hunkered down and flattened out, as though afraid of an event they do not understand.

I slip my hand behind my back and pull the .38 from my belt and let it hang by my side. I can barely make out the men among the trees. Clouds of fog are drifting above the grass. Three men are standing. There is not a teaspoon of fat on their bodies; their faces are unshaved and they wear dark coats and heavy boots and slouch hats. Two other men are squatted on the ground, the firelight flickering on their faces. A black man in a torn white shirt with puffed sleeves is rolled into a ball by the fire. His wrists are bound behind him, and a stick is tied like a horse's bit in his mouth. The tip of an iron rod glows softly inside the fire, a dirty rag wrapped around the cool end.

"My name is Aaron Holland Broussard," I say. "That's my place across the Teche. Who the hell are you guys?"

They all look at me. So does the black man. His face has been beaten; both eyes are almost shut.

"Y'all deaf?" I say. "Why have you done this to this man?"

The three men who are standing have muskets and carry powder horns, like hunters might. They seem posed, angular, insentient, confident in their conception of the world. One man slips a bowie knife from his boot. The handguard is made of brass; the point and edge of the blade have been recently honed. He cuts a piece of ham and feeds it off the blade with his thumb, inching it into his mouth, leaving grease on his beard.

"Are you paddy rollers?" I say.

If they hear me, they show no sign. One of them kicks the black man in the arch of his bare foot, then bends over and picks up the iron rod. The black man tries to shrink inside himself, then begins to weep.

"For God's sake, man, where's your humanity?" I say. "Please, whoever you are, show mercy to this poor fellow. I suspect y'all are Christians. Am I right?"

My words mean nothing. I raise my .38 above my head and drop the cylinder from the frame and shake the rounds out of the chambers. They sprinkle down my arm. "See? I'm no threat to you."

Back off, Daddy, Fannie Mae's voice says behind me.

I turn around and see her at age eleven when she came into the house with a dandelion clutched in her fingers. When I tried to explain that she was holding a weed, she replied, "It's pretty just the same."

"Who are these bastards?" I say.

Don't offend them. Let me do the talking.

She steps past me. She's barefoot and her dress is little more than a slip. The rain has no effect on her, as though it dries before it reaches her hair or skin or clothing, as though she occupies an impenetrable place that generates its own light. She speaks to the five white men, but I cannot understand what she is saying. Her vowels are apples rolling inside a barrel, her corporality like a lantern glowing inside the mist. The black man tries to raise his head and speak, but chokes on the stick in his mouth. His bare feet are cracked with burns, the back of his shirt striped with the bloody lashes of a whip. I want to gut the men who have done this to him.

Then Fannie Mae walks back to me and takes my arm in hers and walks with me toward the bayou. I start to speak.

Look straight ahead, she says. *Say nothing. They're slave chasers for hire. At best they lack humanity. At worst they're depraved.*

313

"Who's the man on the ground?"

They didn't say. They just called him "the nigger."

"What are they going to do with him?"

Nothing. Or at least not now.

"What did you say to them?"

That I work for the Boss and the Boss said they'd better clean up their act before they get stuffed in a trash can on Mars.

"That's what God said?"

I kind of dubbed in the words for Him.

Leave it to Fannie Mae.

Up ahead I can see the lights in my house and the fog puffing cold and white as cotton on the bayou and the moonlit glaze on the roof of the gazebo and the animals and birds that have come to be my friends and companions. In fact, I want to think of my house as an ark, one that represents a post-alluvial world filled with kindness and love and the moral clarity of simple people baking bread on warm stones. For just a moment I feel that God is indeed in His heaven and that all is right with the world.

But I quickly realize that my dark odyssey is not over. And I also realize that terms like "dark odyssey" are the romantic stuff of poets and are hardly adequate to describe the fiction we write every day of our lives, particularly when we deny the lizard's participation in our origins and the weblike skin it has left on the corners of our eyes.

Fannie Mae and I are almost to the bayou. I can see the pirogue rocking in the cattails, the bronze-like rays of light on the water's surface. But like the sugarcane fields, the environment has changed. There are more cypress trees along the banks; the stream is wider, cleaner, the footprints and sounds of animals more evident in the canebrakes. An uprooted oak tree floats past me as lightly as a stalk of celery, which means that in spite of its great weight none of its limbs are touching the channel's bottom.

Fannie Mae raises her hand and signals me to stop. Then I hear thrashing sounds, the cracking of a tree, a man cursing.

"What's that?" I say.

Fannie Mae is standing on a log, out in the water, the painter on the pirogue in her hand. *Go back!* she says. *It's a setup.*

"No," I reply, my boots sinking into a pool that smells of sour mud and rotted vegetation and dead cranes, their feathers scattered on the water.

The signs are not difficult to read. An alligator lays an average of six eggs in its reproductive cycles. Usually four are eaten by raccoons and only two reach maturity. But I am now looking at five or six alligators that are less than five feet long, all of them wounded with cuts that could have come from a boat propeller. They're churning the water like snakes, the bony plates in their backs roiling the chains of lily pads that have already winter-killed. My physician friend Oscar Jenkins is in their midst, wearing his scrubs and rubber boots. He lifts a fireman's ax into the air and brings it down on a midsize alligator, drilling it between the eyes. It flips on its back, its greenish-white fleshy throat exposed. Oscar disembowels it with the hook on his ax, then stomps it flat on a sandbar, splattering the undigested food in its entrails.

"What are you doing here, Oscar?" I say.

"Cleaning house!" he replies. "It's time to take it to them, Aaron. I'm after that big one in the grass. You wouldn't have a gun on you, would you?"

He pauses momentarily, his right hand cupped under the ax handle, grinning. *"What? I've upset you? I'm doing this for you. Will you help me or not?"*

Don't listen to him, Daddy, Fannie Mae says.

"He's our friend," I reply.

Look at his eyes. Are those the eyes of a friend?

"I know you have a gun," Oscar says. "You make a big thing out of not hunting, but you love your guns."

"I don't think you're Oscar," I reply.

"Well, then, who would I be?" he says. His face is round and tight, freckled with blood and pieces of the alligator. "We're all on the same side. You have to pay back in kind, Aaron."

"These are innocent creatures."

"Tell that to the one in the grass. He's the one that was after the runaway slave."

"How did you know about the runaway slave?" I ask.

"You told me."

"No, I did not."

Sometimes an alligator's digestive system takes weeks to process the food the alligator devours whole. The pool is bobbing with feces and congealed blood and carrion. The stench is overwhelming. I bend over and vomit, splashing my clothes.

"You won't help out your pal?" Oscar says.

"If you're my physician, tell me what kind of ailment I have," I say.

"I'm guessing, but I think it's pancreatic," he says. "Sorry, Aaron. You never took care of yourself."

"The hell I didn't."

"Come on, let's have some fun and stomp some ass. Enjoy yourself. Maybe get laid. I think that's a lot of your problem."

He wades deeper into the pool, then walks up an underwater incline and swings blindly with the ax into the grass. He cleaves an opening, and suddenly both of us see an alligator with huge, fleshy jaws and teeth that overhook the mouth and a snout as broad as a shovel and eyes that are mounted on the top of its head. I'm sure it is the same alligator that wrecked my boathouse and went after the man with dreadlocks. Its skin is a dull greenish black and both hard and flexible, like double-sewn layers of leather, its back plated with bone and spikes that resemble the armor on a medieval Asian warrior.

Oscar swings again and this time hits home. The alligator's mouth opens and a pain-driven guttural roar bellows from it, as though the level of injury is so intense the alligator's defense system cannot absorb it. Its legs are cocked but motionless; its right eye looks like a circle of broken glass filmed with mud. I wish my gun was still loaded; I wish I could put this pitiful creature out of its misery.

Oscar swings his ax again.

"You don't have the right to do this," I say.

"Oh, you bet I do. I was called a queer all my life, and now it's my turn. Stand back, Aaron. You're a professional witness to civilization, but not a player."

"How about I break your bloody neck?" I reply.

"Ah, that's my boy. Later we'll have us a drink. Maybe we'll have your friend the woman detective over."

"I think maybe this isn't happening."

"It's happening, all right. Here, take the ax. It's a souvenir," he says, and throws it to me. I barely catch it before it hits me.

"Stay out of Labiche's way," he says. "The fellows with hobnail boots are back in fashion. We just haven't acknowledged them yet."

"Begone, whoever you are. You're not my friend."

"You'll see. A better country is coming. We'll pull down the fucking statues and make you proud."

The wind begins blowing, flattening the grass, whipping the water into a froth, driving it through the cypress trees on the bank. I wipe the spray off my face, then smell my hand. It smells like fish or copulation. The incline Oscar stood on is empty, urine-yellow clouds of mud rising where his feet had been. Fannie Mae is still standing on the log. She bends down and catches the stern of the pirogue and pushes it toward me. The wounded alligator turns in a circle and slides through the cattails into deeper water, its hide-capped bony plates weaving with the fluidity of a pressurized garden hose unwinding on a lawn.

"Where did Oscar go?" I ask.

Who knows? Good riddance. Look what he did to those gators. Are you all right?

"All right about what?"

That stuff about pancreatic cancer.

"I'll see an oncologist."

Like you always manage to not do? Get in the pirogue. I'll take us home.

"Don't be like that, Fannie Mae. You're still my little pal. You remember when I used to call you 'little darlin' pal of mine'?"

You're gonna make me cry, Daddy. I really fucked up.

She did. It didn't have to happen. That's what makes it so bad. But I can't tell her that. She reads my face and starts crying, something she has not done since her death. "I'm sorry," I say.

She wipes her eyes and tries to smile, but she cannot conceal her own sorrow.

As you get older, you discover there are lots of ways to die. The worst way, and this applies to both the living and the dead, is when you hurt those you love. The pain is enormous because you cannot undo it, and every night you find yourself in the Garden of Gethsemane. If you haven't been there, here's the gen. It's a mother-fucker. Even Dante couldn't describe it adequately. I'm not putting you on the slide, Clyde.

In the morning I get Simoneaux Guidry out of jail and warn him and my two other employees, Pookie Mouton and Tee Beau Latiolais, about their susceptibility to the wiles of Jude Labiche. We're sitting at the McDonald's on East Main, shaded by live oaks, in the middle of the historic district. I can't seem to get my message across.

"Look, you guys, don't take the fall for other people," I say. "The sheriff has it in for me. You're good young fellows, with good lives ahead of you. Don't let my problems become yours."

Pookie sucks loudly through his soda straw. "You heard anything from Tommy Lee Jones?"

"Did you hear anything I said?"

"Sure, stay out of jail," he replies.

"No, I said don't empower the sheriff. There's a difference."

"Don't do *what*?" he says, a question mark in the middle of his face.

"*Strengthen* him. *Arm* him," I say. "Don't do that."

"It's me who messed up, Mr. Aaron," Simoneaux says.

He's right. But "messed up" doesn't come close to defining his problems.

Simoneaux is far more intelligent than his peers, but intelligence in the world of incarceration is often feared by the people who run it. Also, he's the kind of sexually molested kid who punishes himself every day of his life for the damage done to him by others. In fact, there's a childlike radiance in his eyes that makes me wonder if it's feigned, especially when I look at the scars where he removed the teardrop tats beneath his left eye.

"I ain't got the money to pay for your lawyer, Mr. Aaron," he says. "I'd like for you to take it out of my salary."

"That's not the issue," I say. "Lose the weed, don't drive with an expired license or a broken taillight. Got it?"

"Mr. Aaron, we got to ax you a question," Tee Beau says.

"What?" I say, starting to give up.

"How come you done all this for us?"

"I didn't do anything for you, Tee Beau. Y'all are good workers. You're kind to animals. You take care of each other. You're fine people."

The rain has quit and the sky is blue, the sun shining directly overhead, the wind balmy, more like spring than winter. The three of them say nothing. They simply look at the trees and the Spanish moss, the sunlight on the Teche and the robins in the yard of a home in which Varina Davis stayed, as though they have never seen any of these things before.

"Mr. Aaron?" Pookie says.

"Yes, sir?"

"We just found out yesterday you lost your daughter up there in Montana. We just want to say we're sorry about that."

None of them can look directly at me. It takes a while for me to speak, and even then I have a wishbone in my throat. "Thank you," I say. "Fannie Mae would have liked you guys."

Death is not a pleasant subject. But I'll tell you what I have learned about Mr. Death. In your later years you begin to make friends. You don't discuss this with others, either. Maybe you see him on a park bench and cruise by him and think about the many times he could have burned your kite but didn't, and you don't think so badly about him.

Your greatest annoyance is not Mr. Death but the person who hijacks your day or who has no idea of the experiences you have survived, experiences that are so tragic and violent and revelatory about the nature of human evil you will not discuss them at gunpoint. You discover that the dumbest people on the planet are those who assign you baby names and address you as an infant, and open doors for you as they would for an invalid.

The aforementioned is not worth talking about, however. The big surprise that comes with age and dying is the images you begin seeing on the edge of your vision. At first you think you have a cataract, and you wipe away a tear and blink and then realize that someone from your past is waving to you on the edge of a baseball diamond, in the sunset, on the burnt-out end of a summer day, beckoning you to join him for another round of pitch-and-catch or a plunge into a city swimming pool, one that is dark blue, brimming with an ethereal light, perhaps an entrance to your childhood or to the one you should have had.

I shake hands with Simoneaux and Pookie and Tee Beau, and drive to Oscar Jenkins's office in Lafayette. I walk right past his nurse and into a coffee room, where he's eating a doughnut, dressed in an immaculate starched white shirt and a necktie and suspenders and freshly ironed brown slacks and black socks and spit-shined brown loafers. "Hey, Aaron, what's happening?" he says.

"You left your ax on the bayou," I reply. "I've got it in my truck."

"What ax?"

"Don't give me this crap, Oscar."

"What are you talking about?" he says.

"No clue?"

"Clue about what?"

"You didn't kill any alligators last night?"

"Have a doughnut. Relax. Would you like an icebag for your head?"

"Couldn't have been you, huh? Did you punch out Jude Labiche at the Petroleum Club, or was that someone else?"

"Yeah, I caught him right in the mouth. I'd be happy to do it again."

"But you wouldn't kill an alligator that was after a black slave."

"This isn't funny anymore, Aaron. If you believe what you're saying, we've got a real problem."

"You were in the water, in your scrubs, and wearing a pair of rubber boots."

"In the rain, in my scrubs? How much sense does that make?"

"You tell me."

"I think you had a dream. The images in dreams are symbols. The unconscious is like a theatrical dressing room full of costumes."

"Pretty good line," I say. "Except I saw you chopping those alligators to death."

"You actually believe what you're saying?"

"I never believed you'd pop a Louisiana sheriff in the mouth."

"I grew up in Ohio," he says. "We respected the law and the people we elected to office. A man like Jude Labiche makes me sick to my stomach. Somebody should have pitched a shovelful of dirt in his face a long time ago. I don't hunt, I don't kill. I'm a physician. I've taken an oath to do no harm."

I know I'm talking to the Oscar I've always known, and I feel like a dunce. "Maybe I'm losing it."

He gets up from the table and pours a cup of coffee for me. "On your worst day you're a better man than me, Aaron."

"That's kind of you, Oscar. One question, though: Do I show any of the symptoms of pancreatic cancer?"

"How's your appetite?"

"I don't pay it that much mind."

"That's not a good answer."

"I've always eaten sparingly."

"Always?"

"Generally speaking."

His face turns sad. He takes a breath. "You're a good guy, Aaron."

"What's that mean?"

"Nothing," he says. "I'd better get back to work."

"Sure, I didn't mean to bother you."

He washes his cup and plate in a sink, his back turned to me. Then he drops the cup and bends over to pick it up, a trouser cuff lifting above his loafer.

"Something wrong?" he says.

"Your ankle. There's a silver chain and perforated dime hanging on your sock."

"Aaron, we're going to have a serious talk with a friend of mine. He's a psychiatrist, a very good man, a fan of your work."

"Good," I say. "I hope you enjoy your conversation with him. Tell him thanks for his support."

Then I go out the glass doors into the parking lot and the glare of the day and the cacophony of the traffic and the big-box wasteland that two decades ago was a pecan orchard.

I drive the twenty miles back to my home, then get into the pirogue and slide it across the bayou to the pool where the alligators were killed. Except the pool is not there. It has been gouged and filled in and flattened, destroyed by machinery with steel treads and a backhoe and a dozer blade. I telephone my neighbor and ask what he has done to his land. He's a retired military man.

"I'm building a boathouse and a dock," he says. "Pretty much like yours."

"When did you do the landscaping?"

"Yesterday. Why?"

"Because you shouldn't have filled in that pool. You're defacing the Teche."

"Thanks for letting me know that," he says. "I'll tell my wife. She was just baking some cookies to welcome you back home."

*　*　*

One day later I drive to Popeyes determined to prove I have an appetite. Popeyes may serve the best food on earth. It also contains enough grease and fat and cholesterol to lubricate an aircraft carrier. I order chicken nuggets, a flounder burger, biscuits dripping with butter, Cajun fries, and mashed potatoes and gravy, then sit at my table and touch none of it. A black waitress who must weigh three hundred pounds is staring down at me. "You don't like your food, you?"

"No. I'm sure it's very good, though."

"Then why ain't you eating it?"

"My daughter made me take a vow of fish and meat abstinence."

"Wanna take it home? It's a sin to t'row food away."

"I believe you."

She sacks it up and I drive to the sheriff's department on East Main and walk upstairs and knock on the glass in the sheriff's door. He's writing on a pad and gestures with one hand but doesn't bother to look up. I open the door. "How you doing, Sheriff?" I say. "Can I have a minute?"

There's no expression on his face, although he's wearing a patch on his right eye. He sees the sack under my arm and blows a ball of air the size of a tangerine in one cheek, then points at a chair. "Decide to start a new vocation?"

"I ordered more than I needed, and thought I'd split it with you." I place the sack on his desk. The paper is greasy and warm in my hand.

"What do you want, Mr. Broussard?" His voice is tired, without its usual edge.

"Last night I saw some white men tie up a black man across the bayou from my house. They were going to burn him with a hot iron."

"Imagine that," he says. "You called in a 911?"

"A family member and I took care of the situation."

But he's not listening. He has the detachment of people who already know the story you're about to tell them. He takes the flounder burger out of the sack and bites into it, chewing over the trash basket. "But you're telling me about it? Like we're war buddies?"

"You're a knowledgeable man. I don't think much gets by you. What happened to your eye?"

He sets the flounder burger on the sack. Tomatoes and lettuce and mayonnaise and sauce piquant are dripping from the bread. He wipes his hands on a paper towel, his good eye fixed on me like the end of a shotgun barrel. "You saying I'm mixed up with the torture of a black man?"

"You tell me."

I wonder if he's about to hit me. He opens his desk drawer. Then takes a cough drop from it and puts it in his mouth and sucks on it. "You studied psychology and that kind of thing?"

"A little bit."

He pinches his temples. For a few seconds he seems to take on a look of humanity I've never seen in him. "I saw some things in a dream. Or maybe I was sleepwalking."

He waits for me to speak.

"I've had these dreams before," he says. "This time there was water on the floor. My eye was bleeding."

"Maybe you just had an accident."

"Like I wet my pants?"

"Are these dreams about alligators?"

His face blanches. "Yeah, alligators. All over the place."

"I think both of us saw Winston Royal last night."

"The insurrectionist?"

"There are only two possibilities here, Sheriff. The black man is real, or he represents something in our unconscious."

"I'm good to colored people. I'm friends with the woman who runs the NAACP here. *Ask* her. I've promoted my black deputies. I go to the black church sometimes. I had the FBI investigate one of my deputies for abusing a black man at a street party. Does that sound like a racist?"

"But Winston Royal haunts you?"

"I don't know what they did to him. But they sure fixed up the guy he was working with."

"Pardon?"

"The head guy in that insurrection was named Charles Deslondes. They chopped off his hands and then shot him in both legs and put a bullet in his body. Then they piled sticks and straw on him and set him on fire. They hacked the heads off a hundred of those sons of bitches."

I stare at him blankly.

"Quit looking at me like that," he says. "I didn't do it. Things were different back then."

I feel sick all over. But I know it's not cancer. It's a sense of disgust that has no bottom. "How do you know all this?"

"It's in the dream. Or I read it somewhere. Or Detective LeBlanc told me. What does that have to do with *now*?"

His right fist is knotted on his ink blotter like he doesn't know what to do with it.

"Quit looking at me like that," he says.

"I don't know how to say this, sir."

"To say what?"

"I think you may be already among the damned."

He rises from his chair. "Say that again?"

The string holding his eyepatch has popped loose. His injured eye is bulbous and hooded and filmed with medication. It resembles splintered glass.

"I hope everything works out for you, Sheriff," I say. "Believe me, I won't bother you again."

I go back home with a truth I can no longer avoid. I've already said I don't fear death. I have a greater problem. I fear living. Most of my family is gone. I have allowed loneliness to become a way of life. All the things I love are in my past. The America in which I was born is not the one we live in today. My frame of reference would probably sound like babble to 80 percent of the population.

The truth is I wanted cancer to take me to a place where I would join Fannie Mae and my family members and all the other people I have known and loved and who were granted the gift of living in the America that saved the light of civilization and rebuilt the countries of our enemies and turned them into democracies when we could have condemned the entire planet to serfdom or made it a hell on earth bristling with razor wire and guard towers and searchlights, not to mention chimneys, which is what they had planned for us.

I'm glad I had my confrontation with the sheriff. I no longer have to pretend he's anything other than what I think he is: a bestial aberration dredged out of the past—craven, feckless, inhuman. Who cares? I'm sitting in a deck chair on the bricks of my back porch, surrounded by cats and pups and two raccoons. The day is lovely, the rain dimpling the bayou. Simoneaux and Pookie and Tee Beau are putting a new roof on the barn. I think about the people who have meant the most to me in my life. My closest friend was a kid named Saber Bledsoe. Saber was the trickster of medieval folklore, a one-man army dedicated to the destruction of all the snobs, hoods, and mean-spirited physical education teachers in Houston, Texas. God, how I loved Saber.

We did everything together, including fighting in the last major battle of the Korean War. Other than my daughter, Saber was the biggest loss in my life, maybe because I never found out what happened to him. We were supposed to set up a listening post, just after the Chinese captured a bunch of our flamethrowers and caught one of our patrols in an irrigation ditch. I saw what they did and couldn't get the image out of my mind. So I was already shaking when Saber and I headed into the darkness and down a ditch toward the hills. I remember every detail—the stars in the sky, a trip flare popping, the bugles blowing, the tracers from a .50 caliber floating across the plain like bits of neon. Then the bugles stopped, and so did the knocking of the .50 caliber. For perhaps two or three seconds there was no sound at all. Then we heard voices. We didn't know it, but we had run head-on into a Chinese probe.

The sky lit up with a flame that was as bright as the lights on a baseball diamond during a night game. The smell and heat were like diesel fuel burning and oil smoke rising in clouds from a sludge pit. Then we heard the 105s arching out of their trajectory. The explosions of the shells were deafening. Saber had lost his steel pot and was standing erect with his hands clamped on his ears, yelling, the ditch shaking under our feet, the air full of grit and smoke and dirt clods raining on our heads. I wanted to hear what Saber was saying, as though the message were the most important in our lives. But I couldn't. My eardrums were useless. My head was ringing. His lips were moving without sound, as though he were inside a plexiglass ball.

"What is it, Saber?" I yelled.

He grinned. Can you believe that? He actually grinned in the middle of a marching barrage. Then something hit him in the back, like a fist. He stumbled into my arms, his knees buckling. I picked him up over my shoulder and started running. Then a 105 round or a Chinese mortar exploded ahead of us, and a wall of hot air with the density of wet concrete knocked us down. Blood that looked like pieces of string was running from his hair, down his dirty, sweaty face, his grin still in place, his head thrown back, his mouth wide, either yelling or frozen in rictus.

"What are you saying, Saber?" I said. "Please tell me what it is."

Then he began laughing. I could hear burp guns firing and potato mashers going off down the line and smell a stench like a flamethrower cooking someone alive. Maybe I passed out. Or maybe I ran. I know I was screaming for a medic. I watched Saber's last words die on his lips with no way to save or record them and carry them home.

Saber is still officially MIA. I like to believe he survived the war. Each day I say a prayer for him, and I look over my shoulder once in a while to see if he's behind me, with his lopsided grin, his deck of Lucky Strikes wrapped in the sleeve of his T-shirt, his chopped-down Ford with the chromed twin-carb Merc engine in the background. Why would he not be there? Death and birth are both mysteries. I don't believe that anyone knows the nature or the mind of God, so why should my perception of the metaphysical be less accurate than that of others? So I tell myself that Saber is still out there, just as Fannie Mae is. That's the world I live in, and I neither defend nor feel a need to tell others about it.

That's why I don't care what our sheriff does or doesn't do. I just don't want him to harm the people or animals or birds that are my friends. I say, let evil people braid their own noose.

I fall asleep in the deck chair, without fear or desire or grief or regret about myself. It's a rare moment. Seconds later the phone rings. I go inside and look at the caller ID. I don't recognize it but pick up the receiver anyway. "Hello?"

"It's Della LeBlanc, Mr. Broussard," she says.

I wait for her to go on, but she doesn't. "What's going on?" I say.

"I need you to help with an identification in a homicide. I think it may be your friend."

I close my eyes, then open them. "Which friend?"

"The doctor."

"You said you *think*. What do you mean by 'think'?"

"There's a metal detector by the body. Mr. Broussard, I'm sorry to ask this of you."

She picks me up in front of the house and we drive into St. Martin Parish and then take an outboard into a swamp dotted with tupelo trees, not far from where a plantation named Lady of the Lake once stood. The wind is cold on the water, the light jittering on the chop. I don't want to be here. I don't want to believe that Oscar has died a terrible death. I want to be rid of the evil that seems to rob me of any peace or tranquility this side of the grave.

We scrape onto an island covered with palmettos and cypress and persimmon and willow trees, and also threaded with channels where fish have wandered and been trapped and picked over by cranes and egrets. There's a solitary cypress cabin dark with age inside a grove of trees hung with Spanish moss. In the distance the sun is shining on the bay. The day seems idyllic, except for the cawing of a carrion bird.

"My grandfather said that was a slave cabin," Della says.

I don't reply. So far she has told me little about the crime scene or the discovery of the body. A fisherman called in the 911, then hung up without giving his name. No one, including Della, seemed sure if the location was in St. Martin or one of the adjoining parishes partly underwater. Two St. Martin Parish deputies are smoking cigarettes in a boat that's rocking in the chop on the edge of the island. They're both young, and they both wear shades. The coroner is out of town. The door of the cabin hangs on a single hinge. Della stops and gives me a mask. "Put it on."

"Out here, on the bay?"

There's a shine in her eyes. "It's not about the pandemic," she says.

I have to stoop to enter the door. The sunshine is bouncing off the water outside the window, creating a mixture of shadow and light that is like a shutter clicking on a camera. Then I see the body of a man in jeans and a flannel shirt stretched across a worktable, his wrists tied with wire around a post. His sphincter muscle has obviously collapsed. His face is unrecognizable. A baseball bat lies on the dirt floor. The room smells of nutria nests and feces; flies buzz against the ceiling. Even with the mask on, I have to put my hand on my mouth to keep from gagging.

"Is it him?" she says.

"I can't tell. He's not carrying a wallet?"

"No, nothing. The only thing we can go on is the metal detector, over there in the corner."

"Does he have a dime on a chain around his ankle?"

"I didn't want to touch the body until the coroner gets here."

"Where's Sheriff Labiche?"

"Attending a conference in New Orleans. Plus, I don't know which parish we're in."

I push up the victim's pant legs. The calves are white and look carved from chalk. There's nothing on the ankles.

"Why do you wear a dime, Miss Della?"

"It's just a fashion. A joke."

"It's no joke. I know of an infant who strangled to death because his parents tied a dime around his neck. Did you take a picture of the metal detector and send it to the sheriff?"

"No, although I remember you mentioned something about the sheriff and Doctor Jenkins and a metal detector."

"The sheriff had to replace Oscar's detector because he broke it into pieces on my property then threw it in the bayou."

"I didn't know that."

"Have you talked with the sheriff about any of this at all?"

"He's not taking my calls right now."

The room is silent. In the distance I can hear the sound of a boat, then a pontoon plane goes past the cabin and makes a half circle over the bay and comes straight at us, slicing water, the propeller feathering.

"There he is now," she says.

"Who do you think did this, Della?"

"I don't know."

"The damage done to the body indicates a level of rage that usually is sexual in origin," I say.

"Why are you telling *me*?"

"Because I never knew a homophobe who wasn't a closet homosexual. Because Oscar may have been gay. Racism and homophobia and nativism go hand in hand. So does malignant narcissism. There's blood seepage from the genital area."

"You're saying the sheriff is a closet gay person?"

"I'm saying he's a monster."

"I don't like the way you're speaking to me, Mr. Broussard."

"There's a split in the back of Oscar's jeans. It was done with a knife or a razor."

"Stop it," she says.

"You know what the coroner will find. You also know the suffering Oscar went through."

"I'm sorry I brought you out here."

"Quit protecting an evil man, Della."

"You have no right to say that."

The whites of her eyes have turned pink. Her upper lip is moist with perspiration, even in the coolness of the room; her pulse is fluttering in her throat like a wounded moth. I've gone across a line and feel rotten for it. What she doesn't understand is the respect and affection I had for Oscar Jenkins. I will always remember his statement about the four-o'clocks in my yard. He loved them because they bloomed under the trees every afternoon, no matter what the weather was like, and when he had a bad day, he would look at the four-o'clocks.

"I'm sorry, Della."

"Keep your apology. You pretend to be on our side, Mr. Broussard, but you're not. You're a Southerner, and like most Southerners you don't have any idea at all of who you are. In fact, I feel sorry for you."

I get one of the St. Martin Parish deputies to take me to the levee, then I walk three hundred yards to a small grocery store. Sheriff Labiche does not try to stop me. The sun has moved into the west and is the reddish-yellow color of an egg yolk. I think about Della LeBlanc's words and wonder if I have become a hypocrite or, worse, if I have always been one.

What do I mean by that? I have moments of nostalgia or fantasy that I do not confide in others. Like now. There is no doubt in my mind that we live in an antediluvian world between the fall of man and the flood that set Noah and his ark on the horizon. But here's the kicker: In the South we do not regret the fall. Right now the shadows are long on the grass, and the grass is green, even though it's winter, and the sun hangs in the live oaks and slash pines as though Paul Gauguin had painted it there; the evening star is already out, and the bay is sliding through cypress trees that are etched with fire.

This was all part of a plantation. The main house burned down in the Depression. It was called Lady of the Lake. It was a grand two-story West Indies colonial home, with tall windows like mine and a wraparound second-story veranda. The name suggests the tale of King Arthur and his sword and his promise that one day he would return to his people when they were in need, and perhaps the name also hints in a quasi-metaphysical way that somehow the home is related to the story of Jesus and his mother. But how can you associate an iniquitous institution like slavery with the story of Jesus and Mary and the grandeur of Thomas Malory's *Le Morte d'Arthur*?

I can never forget the image of the plantation Tara burning in *Gone with the Wind*. The black smoke and roaring flames and the magnificence of the music by Max Steiner fill the viewer with a sense of tragedy that is hard to explain. As I watch it, I feel that something vital to our lives is being lost and will never be replaced. But I don't know what it is. I think it has little to do with the American South. I believe we're born with an inherited memory of Eden. I believe it lives in the unconscious of every one of us, all over the globe. And our guilt lives with us, too. After we placed our fellow man in bondage, we began to ravage our communal home, the Big Blue Marble, the gift that was meant for the ages. I think Tara is blazing now, and we set the fire.

I hire a taxi to take me back home. I hope Fannie Mae will be there. But she's not, and my fear is growing that she will have to return to her permanent home. I know I have said this before, but I cannot avoid repeating myself, lest some nights I go insane. I have a hole in my chest I cannot fill. Some days it's as big as a cannonball. I have no way of dealing with its origins, either. Early mankind did not have to deal with addiction. Modern man has made it an industry. There are days when I have thoughts that frighten me, and I wonder if I should move my firearms out of my house, and not for my own protection.

At dusk I drive my pickup to Lafayette and park in front of Oscar's house. It's located in a piney, semirural 1960s neighborhood on a knoll above the Vermilion River. The house is dark; a solitary light burns in the house next door. I see no sign of police or news media activity. I wait until the sun is completely down, then walk between Oscar's house and a wooded area and coulee that taper down to the river. I have no idea if someone is sharing the house with him. I find a key under a flowerpot on the back patio and go inside. The alarm has not been set.

What am I looking for? The past. The place where most of our answers lie. And also the place for which we have the least respect. The human personality does not change. Read *The History of the Church* by Eusebius. It's not about the church; it's about fourth-century Rome and ultimately about us. We witness the deaths of the martyrs in the arena, but the Herd and most of the other players are the same bunch that are with us today, totally committed to the dirty boogie and doing it in four-four time.

Oscar's back room has always been devoted to his study of archaeology. A microscope and some magnifying glasses and tiny tools and snake lamps rest on a big door propped across two sawhorses. Indian pottery, arrowheads, stone axes, .58 caliber Minie balls, rust-sheathed bayonets and grapeshot and pieces of exploded cannonballs cover the shelves and the tops of his cabinets. But he also collects nineteenth-century daguerreotypes and cartes de visite, and over one hundred soldiers stare at me out of the frames, many with a sense of urgency in their eyes, as though they cannot wait to return to a sound that is like firecrackers popping, one that grows and grows in seconds and spreads down the line and is swallowed by the roar of the cannon and the throaty yell of thousands of men who will not see the sunset.

I hear sounds outside, a rustling of the trees, a swing twisting on a chain, a fence gate shutting in the neighbor's yard. The moon is bright and the lawn dancing with shadows. A cluster of cartes de visite lies by the magnifying glasses. Most of them are photographs of enlisted men; the officers are often photographed with their wives. The women look melancholy and wear crosses on their necks or chests. But one of the cartes is full of contradictions and has an element of warning in it, like shaking hands with a stranger then feeling a spider crawl up your arm. The soldier in the photo has his elbow propped against what appears to be a Doric column but is probably a stage prop. He wears an unsheathed knife in his belt and a gray kepi and is holding a long-stemmed pipe. His jacket appears to be butternut or gray with piping, and has chevrons sewed on the sleeves and gives the impression of a ragtag presence in the Confederate Army. But the shirt is checkered and the breeches are blue, with perhaps a red stripe on the legs.

He could be the twin of Oscar Jenkins, except his face is lit with a lunatic glow, the kind you don't want to probe.

I turn over the photo and read the inscription on the back; the ink has faded into a pale-blue wisp and resembles the tracings of a dead insect:

Blessings to you, Mother and Father. Do not worry about me. Our cause is sacred. God will guide us, and so will General Lane, who himself is a gift from Our Lord. Tell the brave people of Kansas we will pay back what the Rebels have done.

Your loving son,
Horace Jenkins

James Henry Lane was the counterpart of William Clarke Quantrill, burning and killing along the Missouri border. He was filled with hatred and rage and infected with fantasies of letting slave owners rot at the bottom of the ropes he would hang them from. A few months after Appomattox he died by his own hand, but nonetheless remained the first US Army officer to use Negro troops against Southern forces.

A shadow moves across the window, faster than my eye can follow. I drop the carte de visite. The river is yellow, as though flooded with clay, the froth a dirty white in the trees along the bank. I can see a boat bobbing by a small dock, but no one is nearby. A pinecone rolls off the roof and bounces on a patio table. A figure walks out of the slash pines, down by the water. He's bare to the waist, plated with muscle, glistening like a black flame in the moonlight, his torso crisscrossed with the bleeding welts of the overseer's lash. He makes me think of Toussaint Louverture and Nat Turner and Spartacus, and of Jesus on the path up Golgotha.

The wind sweeps a splattering of raindrops across the roof, then clouds of white fog form on the river and puff through the reeds and up the embankment into the yard, gathering in smoky wraiths around the knees of the black man. He's looking straight at me now, his dreadlocks bunched inside a red bandanna. I open the back door and step out on the patio. The river and the fog smell like fish and insecticide and chlorine from the neighbor's swimming pool.

"You're Winston Royal, aren't you?"

I am.

"You called me the murderer of your children."

I was wrong. I confused you with another.

"Who?"

The ancestor of your neighbor across the bayou.

"Why were you at the car accident in front of my house?"

337

To do good.

"Why? We've treated your people well."

Mercy grows. Evil is consumed by its own flame.

"Evil spirits take on many guises, too."

You do not trust me?

"You have a way of showing up in bad situations. Why didn't you help Oscar?"

You had a friend named Saber Bledsoe.

"Where did you get that name?"

He was your closest friend. For many years you have blamed yourself for his death.

"I don't think you know anything about Saber. I think you're a fraud. I think you'd better leave now."

He liked to play jokes. He would run through a crowd yelling, "Don't panic! Don't panic! Be calm! Everything is under control!" Of course, everyone would immediately panic.

That was Saber. He caused chaos at football games and in theater lobbies and one time dropped his Johnson through a hole in the classroom ceiling of the meanest high school teacher in Houston.

I know the last words he said to you. You and he were in a ditch. There were explosions all around you.

"I don't believe you. I think you may work for the Prince of Darkness."

You fear my words because you do not want to learn your friend's fate.

"Don't you dare use my friend in your manipulations."

Your friend said, "Keep a cool stool." What does that mean?

It was one of Saber's favorite expressions.

"I'm going to walk away from you. Saber is MIA. I say begone to you."

I'm the only friend you have other than your daughter, Mr. Broussard. We're kindred spirits. I yearn for my children.

"Why were your children killed?"

As an example to other boys. I blame this on myself. I helped spread the rebellion.

"Why was Oscar killed?"

His tormentors saw themselves in him. They do that with regularity.

"I'm going home now. I want no more of this."

Have it your way. Beware of your contemporaries, sir. They're in a bad mood.

Suddenly he's gone. His footprints are deep and shiny in the thickness of the St. Augustine. The fog curls around my legs and rises to my hands and chest, as though it wants to invade my lungs. But I'm not sure that the fog is actually fog. It could be smoke. It's acrid, certainly. It also smells like rotten eggs, like sulfur. I clear my throat and spit, and walk as quickly as I can around the house and get in my truck and leave the headlights off until I'm out of the neighborhood.

Fifteen minutes later I'm driving on the two-lane through the little town of Broussard. Up ahead is Spanish Lake and an early nineteenth-century plantation home with twin chimneys, the moss in the live oaks electrified by the carriage lamps on the upstairs veranda. I hit a pothole so hard it jars my teeth and the inside of the truck lights up. Fannie Mae is sitting beside me. She has never appeared to me in this fashion. She's a very young girl, in her First Communion dress, her eyes hazy, the way children are hazy about the evil that's in the world. She seems molded inside her glow, as an unborn child is molded inside the womb.

"Fannie Mae?" I say.

She doesn't answer.

"Is something wrong?" I ask.

She looks straight ahead and frowns. *Yes, I think there is.*

"It can't be that bad, can it?"

They're waiting for you, Daddy. All of them.

"Who?"

Bad people. Like the ones who killed your friend in the cabin at Lady of the Lake.

"We're on the right side of things, little guy. The bad guys can't hurt us."

Oh yes, they can. They're mean. They do mean things to animals.

"They're going to hurt the animals at our house?"

They're gonna hurt everything and everybody. They're everywhere.

"I don't believe that. Neither do you."

Then she looks straight at me. Her eyes are ablaze. *I've changed my mind.*

I hit another pothole, and the glow inside the truck cab shrinks into nothing, like a black hole collapsing.

It's raining when I reach the house. Simoneaux Guidry, my employee who removed a teardrop tattoo from under his eye, is smoking a cigarette behind the wheel of his pickup. When he sees me he drops it from a crack in the window, then runs for the porch. I go through the carriage house and open up the front door. "What's up, Simoneaux?"

He steps inside. "Glad you asked. That goddamn sheriff is."

I look at the cigarette butt smoking on the driveway and close the door. "What's the problem?"

"He found a warrant on me over in Mississippi. Some bad-check shit from five years ago."

"I don't allow people to use profanity in my home," I reply.

He wipes the dampness out of his eyes. "My bad. I'm thinking of blowing Dodge. If I stay here, one way or another I'm gonna get tagged."

"I hate to lose you."

"Yeah, same here." His eyes are flat. He looks around, agitated, perhaps unsure of why he is here. "You sure got a nice place."

"Thank you."

He notices a piece of folded paper in his shirt pocket. "This was stuck in your door. I thought it would blow away."

I take it from his hand.

"Can I use your restroom?" he says.

"Down the hall."

I unfold the paper. It's from a legal pad. The calligraphy is beautiful and doesn't go with the pad. It's from Della LeBlanc.

Dear Mr. Broussard,

    I said things to you that were unfair. I think you're a nice man. But I also think you see the world as it should be rather than as it is. I think I know more about your family than you do. Lady of the Lake Plantation in St. Martin Parish was owned in the 1830s by your great-great-grandfather. He was married to a lady named Ezemily Booth, who was from Wilkes County, Georgia. I don't think the names are coincidental. Your ancestor owned many slaves. My family was among them. You do not deserve to carry the guilt of your ancestors, but you should be aware of it.

                          I wish you well, sir.
                          Della

She's right, I did not know my ancestor was the owner of Lady of the Lake; nor was I aware of my great-great-grandmother's maiden name. I have to say it feels strange.

I hear the toilet in the hallway flush and the door open. I fold Della's note and put it in my pocket, then lose awareness of what I'm doing. It's like the spells I had when I was young. I would go somewhere inside my mind and leave my physical surroundings and sometimes wake up hours later and miles away. Or perhaps sitting in the same place, with my clothes disheveled and no money in my pockets and no memory of where I had been. These episodes were always associated with a feeling of irreparable loss. This is exactly how I feel now. Fannie Mae is gone and I'm alone, and I do not want to go gently into that good night.

I've forgotten about Simoneaux. "Where are you, partner?" I say.

He leans his head backward out of an alcove in the hallway. "I was looking at your guns."

"I've got some work to do."

He walks toward me. "That's some collection."

I nod.

"So what do you think I ought to do?" he says.

"Do about what?"

"Getting out of town or staying."

"I think it's better to own up and take the heat. It's better than looking over your shoulder for the rest of your life."

"If I square this warrant, I'll need more money than I've got." He pulls on his earlobe and looks at the flashes of lightning outside.

"I don't know what to tell you," I say.

"Just say fuck it, huh?"

I don't meet his eyes. "I'll say goodnight to you now."

"I figured that," he says.

"What's that mean?"

"Nothing," he says. He opens the door and goes outside and pulls the door softly shut, not letting go until he hears the bolt latch click, as though making a decision he's not sure of. Through the small glass window in the door I can see him staring into the rain, opening and closing his hands a long time before he finally walks to the truck, the rain striking his face, his eyes lidless.

* * *

The morning is sunny and the sky blue and the air clean, and I hear hammers banging on the roofed deck I'm building on the bayou, an outdoor spot where I plan to write and read when I can no longer bear the echoes of my own movements in my own house. I gaze out the kitchen window and am glad to see Simoneaux working with his fellow employees, Pookie and Tee Beau.

Leave this place, Daddy, a voice says behind me.

I turn around. "Is that you, Fannie Mae? I can hardly see you."

She's a little girl again, holding a cat in her arms, petting its head. She doesn't answer.

"Why did you leave me?"

My time is running out. This time it's forever.

"No. You're my daughter. You'll always be with me."

They'll do to you what they did to your friend Oscar.

"I'm not Oscar."

When I was little you never listened. You always had your way. Look how it worked out.

"If you wish to draw pain, you've succeeded. I'm not sure you're Fannie Mae."

I am. And I always will be. And the reasons I died will never change, either. I've got my own kinds of pain to deal with, Pops.

She breaks into a shower of pink and silver confetti that tingles as it disappears. I feel as though someone has just gutted me from my navel to my throat.

I walk down the slope, past the live oak with the blood-soaked chains of slavery in its heartwood, to a leaf-strewn place on the bayou where I can hear Simoneaux and Pookie and Tee Beau working. Or where I think they're working. They do not see me coming and are laughing about something. The tide is out and the mudbanks and cattails exposed. Simoneaux is on the roof of the deck, urinating in an arc so his urine will pool in a dry place on the mudflat that will fill again when the tide reverses itself.

"Oops," Simoneaux says, and zips up.

"What are you guys doing?" I say.

"Just kidding around, boss man," he replies.

"Eighty-six the minstrel routine," I reply.

"Yes, sir," he says.

The tools are scattered on the worksite. There's an empty longneck under the deck. In the grass up the slope I see other bottles nestled in a sack of cracked ice.

"I'll be frank with y'all," I say. "This doesn't cut it."

"We wasn't thinking, Mr. Broussard," Tee Beau says.

"Drinking on the job isn't negotiable, Tee Beau," I say.

"We ain't gonna do it no more," he says.

"That's right," Pookie says. "If we was working for Tommy Lee Jones, we wouldn't have done this."

How do you make sense of that? "You have any comments, Simoneaux?" I say.

"Shit happens," he says.

"You've taken special care of the fawn," I say. "You're intelligent. Your peers respect you. Did I do something that got you mad?"

"Maybe I'm just a bad penny."

He gets off the ladder and gazes at the leaves floating past us. The wind wrinkles the bayou and I smell a familiar odor. "Y'all been smoking dope?"

Tee Beau and Pookie drop their heads.

"What makes you think that?" Simoneaux asks.

"That roach by your foot might be considered a clue."

He stares at the ground and steps back theatrically. "Imagine that," he says. "Maybe the squirrels have been getting high."

"I have to let y'all go."

"You're firing us?" Tee Beau says, his ever-present smile fading.

"What would you do in my place?"

"We went to breakfast wit' you at McDonald's," Pookie says.

"Yeah, you did," I reply. "You sure did."

"And you still gonna fire us?" he says.

I'm having a hard time looking at them. "I'll send y'all your checks today."

"Ain't right, Mr. Broussard," Pookie says. "Simoneaux brought all this stuff here."

"You should have reported him," I say.

"I had one beer," he says. "I ain't smoked no dope. I was gonna talk to Mr. Jones."

I've had sadder experiences, but not many. I walk away, the leaves on the ground soggy and heavy from last night's rain, the hammering of my neighbor's workers on the opposite side of the bayou like laughter in my ears. But it's not over. Sheriff Labiche is waiting for me at the top of the slope, his hands on his hips, his stomach hanging over his belt, my reflection trapped inside his aviator glasses. He's no longer wearing the patch on his eye.

"Your menagerie is officially confiscated, Mr. Broussard," he says. "Come on, you gotta sign some papers unless you want to go to jail."

Numerous trucks are parked in the front and the back of my house. I have no idea where they are from. The men who are taking away my animals and birds all wear gloves and overalls and baseball caps and surgical masks. The sheriff opens a fresh pouch of Red Man.

"You son of a bitch," I say.

"You dealt it, son."

"Call me 'son' again and I'll break your jaw."

"Yeah, I can see you trying that. Go ahead."

My head feels full of helium, the ground tilting under my feet. My eyes are out of focus.

"It turned out your doctor friend was killed in my jurisdiction," he says. "That puts me in charge of the investigation. Which means I just talked to the Lafayette sheriff, who did a sweep of your doctor friend's house. Guess whose prints were all over the good doctor's workroom?"

"Who cares?"

"Everybody?"

"So arrest me."

"Lafayette PD says the doctor and his friends might have been mixed up with some sadomasochistic activities. Know anything about that?"

"That's ridiculous."

"About him or other queers?"

"Oscar was a good man."

Labiche takes a Ziploc bag out of his windbreaker. There's a dime and a silver chain inside it. "The good doctor was wearing this on his ankle when he went out. Does this mean anything to you?"

"No," I lie.

"He went out hard. Want me to go into detail?"

"I saw the body."

"You think I enjoy this?" he asks.

"Yeah, I think you do."

He makes a grunting sound, then looks over his shoulder at the men loading the trucks with the animals and birds I thought I would be protecting the rest of my life. "Did your friend have another kind of life or not? Don't lie to me, either."

"No, he did not."

He chews on his lip and refocuses his eyes on me. His gray chest hair is sticking out of his shirt. "Jenkins was after me."

"What are you talking about, Sheriff?"

"I think he was from somewhere else. Out *there*. I'm being straight with you. Don't you sass me."

"Out *where*?"

He raises his chin. "Out yonder in the fields. He was coming after white people that's hurt colored people. Chopping them up and such. I don't know why he was after me. I ain't done nothing that wasn't done to me."

He pulls off his aviator glasses. He sounds like a madman and knows it. His injured eye is watery and red and shrunken, like someone has put a thumb in it. He waits for me to speak. But I know of nothing I can say, other than that I have great pity for him and realize that my own burdens are nothing in comparison to his.

At two thirty I get a call on my land line from Della LeBlanc. "Do you have a cell phone?" she asks.

"No."

"That's what I thought. Go somewhere else and call me back."

"Do what?"

"Are you deliberately acting dumb, Mr. Broussard? If so, you're doing a great job of it."

I drive down the two-lane and borrow the phone in the convenience store at the four-corners. She picks up on the first ring. "Are you in a place where no one else can hear you?"

"Yes," I reply.

"Okay, I'm gonna line it out as well as I can. Don't be alone with the sheriff. Nor those three jailbirds you hired. Better yet, get out of town for a few days. And do not use your telephone unless it's absolutely necessary."

"I'm tapped?"

"That's my guess."

"You said I shouldn't be alone with him. You think he would actually clip me?"

"You want to find out?"

"What's this about my employees?"

"I'm doing some checking. I'll get back to you. Just watch your ass, okay?"

"You're telling me my life is in danger and at the same time telling me to stand by?"

"I'm at my house. The sheriff just pulled in. I have to go. Don't come here."

"Don't hang up, Miss Della."

The line goes dead.

I call her back from the store twice. No answer. I don't know where she lives, and I'm starting to have less and less desire to have contact with her. I go back home and fix dinner and eat by myself at the kitchen table. Hailstones are bouncing on the roof and the lawn. The only animals that were not removed from the property are two cats, and they were spared only because they hid under the house. One is black with white paws, and the other a fat Persian with smoky-bluish fur and the girth of a soccer ball. I put newspaper and cans of sardines on the kitchen floor, then bring the cats inside. While they eat, I make a bed for them out of a cardboard box and an old blanket.

"You guys let me know when you want to go outside," I say. "In the meantime, no spraying the curtains, no dumps on the floor, no claw-sharpening on the upholstery. Do we have an agreement?"

No answer. Now they're nosing the sardine cans around on the newspaper.

"Do you guys know where my daughter is?"

Once again, no feedback.

But this isn't funny. I know one day Fannie Mae's absence will be permanent; however, I need her now more than ever. I'm completely alone. The joists are creaking in the house; the gas logs will not light; every square inch of the woodwork is as cold as an ice cube. Through the front windows I can see car headlights going back and forth on the two-lane. I wonder if one of those cars is driven by a man who will turn onto my property and politely ask if he can use my phone.

I can't sleep. I drive into St. Martin Parish and try to find the foundation of the plantation home called Lady of the Lake, the one I never knew was owned by my ancestors. The sky has cleared; the moon is rising; I see stars falling through the clouds. In the distance is a hump of land overlooking the beginnings of the Atchafalaya Basin. The swamp seems to glow with a black light that emanates not from the heavens but from the stillness of the water and the flooded cypress and the Spanish moss hanging from the tree limbs, as though the rules of nature, or the intentions of the Creator, have been reversed.

I park my truck and walk up on the small hill that could be the place where my great-great-grandfather once stood and stared at the vastness of the subtropical fiefdom he controlled, and I wonder what thoughts went through his mind. Supposedly he fought at the side of Andrew Jackson at the Battle of New Orleans, a battle in which Jean Lafitte, pirate and slaver, also participated. I wondered if my ancestor had problems of conscience. Did he believe that the mother of Our Lord, the namesake of his plantation, looked kindly on slavery? Did he look at the cabins along the edges of the swamp and wonder what it was like to be bitten by mosquitoes night after night, even in winter? Did he treat the ringworm and rickets that

349

the children undoubtedly suffered from? Was he bothered by the miscarriage of a woman who chopped cotton from morning to night? Did he grieve over the infanticides and suicides that slave women chose over giving birth? Did he ask God for a way to get himself out of the moral dilemma he found himself in, provided it was a dilemma at all?

But it's easy to moralize and take other generations to task. I wonder what I would have done if I'd had to follow General Lewis Armistead up Cemetery Ridge in July of 1863, in a ragged uniform that felt like burlap, in a wheatfield, in ninety-five-degree heat, with grapeshot flying by my head and cannonballs skipping through the chaff like rabbits, and chain whipping through the air, cutting the men at my right and my left into stumps. My great-grandfather did it. For forty minutes. When the firing stopped, eight thousand Confederates lay dead or moaning on the ground. Many of them were barefoot. At the top of the ridge, behind the limestone wall, the Yankees tamped their rifle butts in unison and chanted, "Fredericksburg, Fredericksburg, Fredericksburg."

I walk down to the edge of the swamp and gaze at the cattails and at a dead carp that's floating upside down and at the tracks of animals that may be watching me from a distance, and I wonder about life and death and how quickly both go by. I flip a pebble at the water and watch the ripples disappear in the reeds, then walk back to my truck, a little older, no wiser, regretful more for the things I didn't do in life than the things I did, just another pilgrim hoping to see the sunrise.

The next morning I buy a pay-as-you-go cell phone at Walmart and call Della LeBlanc three times on her cell and twice at her office. She's not at the department and no one will tell me where she is. I call the black woman who cleans my house twice a month and get Della's address. She lives in Jeanerette, in St. Mary Parish, ten miles down Bayou Teche and five hundred years behind the rest of the world.

She lives on Main Street in a white nineteenth-century home with a wide railed porch that has a glider on it. A teddy bear is propped at an angle in the glider. There are myrtle trees on her lawn and azaleas and climbing roses in her flower beds. I tap on her screen door and wait, my pulse ticking. She opens the door, dressed in baggy jeans and a Mike the Tiger football jersey, a broom in her hand. She looks past me into the street, as though expecting someone else.

"What are you doing here?" she says. Her face is half in shadow.

"You wouldn't answer my calls."

"It's my day off. I told you I'd get back to you."

"What happened to your face?"

"I had a wisdom tooth extracted."

"My foot."

"Mr. Broussard, will you please stop testing me?"

"I didn't know that I was. May I come in?"

"No, you cannot."

"Okay, I'll spend the day in your glider. I brought a couple of books to read. What's the name of your teddy bear?"

"Sir, you're from outer space. Like no one I have ever known. A promoter for the Tylenol company."

"No one is perfect."

"Will you please go?"

"In conscience I can't. I believe I owe you a debt. I won't try to explain."

"Let's get this straight. You don't owe me anything. Particularly a racial debt, because that's what I think you're saying, and it's highly offensive."

"We're on the same side, Miss Della. Someone struck you in the face. And I think I know who did it."

I see the surrender in her eyes, the kind that abused people carry like a bruise on the soul. "Wipe your feet," she says. "Tell me what you need to. Then go. Okay?"

The interior of the house is dark, the furniture antique. An egg-shaped framed photograph of a black soldier in a World War I uniform hangs above the couch. A column of light is shining through the window onto the dining room table. The table is covered with a brocaded tablecloth and set with candlesticks and two plates and two crystal glasses.

"Is the sheriff coming?" I ask.

"Who knows? Mr. Jude is in a bad mood. He got drunk last night."

This is the first time I have ever heard her use the sheriff's first name.

"Did he hit you?"

"None of your business."

"Who killed Oscar Jenkins, Miss Della?"

"Someone who's full of rage. Someone who despises himself."

"Like the sheriff?"

"You will never solve your friend's torture and murder, Mr. Broussard. This is Louisiana. It will not change. The same families have run this state for two hundred years. They and the oil companies. So get a fucking life."

"Who are you expecting here, Miss Della?"

"I'm trying to save your life, Mr. Broussard. Do you understand that?"

"You've got me wrong," I reply. "I'd like for somebody to come at me. I'd love to blow the sheriff out of his socks. I'd like to see another civil war. I'd like to wipe out every fascist in this country. What do you think of that?"

I look at her for a long time. She has strong arms and wide shoulders, and in her jersey and broad-seated jeans she seems larger than she is and at the same time more vulnerable. She tries to hold my eyes, but gives it up. "You're lying, but God broke the mold when he got finished with you. I guess that's a compliment. Or maybe not."

I drive down the street toward the drawbridge over the Teche. On one side of the bayou is a trailer slum; on the opposite side are antebellum homes that could have been transported from the set of *Gone with the Wind*. Then a skinned-up pickup comes toward me and passes my truck without slowing down, even though the road is very narrow. In the rearview mirror I see the pickup turn onto the drawbridge. I'm almost sure the pickup belongs to Simoneaux Guidry, but I could not see who was behind the wheel. For just a moment I wonder if Simoneaux was the visitor Della was expecting. No, that makes no sense, I tell myself.

Or does it? The sexual and romantic relationships in South Louisiana are myriad and mysterious. The expression is "screwing down and marrying up." My cell phone throbs on the seat. I pick it up and place it against my ear. Through my windshield I see Fannie Mae beside the road, her hair and dress blowing in the wind. She's holding both of her hands in the air, signaling me to stop. I almost go into the ditch.

I pull to the side of the road and let Fannie Mae climb in. I do not know how to use a cell phone and to this day I hate them. I hear Della's voice come out of the receiver or whatever it is.

"What's up?" I say.

"I just got a call from an FBI friend," she says. "I don't know how to say this."

"Just do it."

"I got an earlier tip from an informant that Simoneaux Guidry has a far more serious history than his sheet indicates."

"How bad?"

"Maybe he did some hits for the Dixie Mafia. He may also have shanked three inmates for the AB in Parchman."

It's hard to believe what she is saying, or rather hard to believe the degree to which I have been taken. I'm also trying to process what she's saying while fooling with the speakerphone so Fannie Mae can listen. "That would account for the teardrop tattoo he had removed from under his eye," I tell her.

"Here's the rest of it," she replies. "My FBI friend says Guidry thinks I'm onto him. His information source says there's a good chance he'll try to pop me."

"Onto him about what?"

"I think Guidry has been working for the sheriff. Maybe he killed Dr. Jenkins."

"I hate to tell you this, Della. I'm on Old Jeanerette Road, a half mile up from the drawbridge. I think Simoneaux's pickup just passed me. I can't be sure, I didn't see the driver. But the pickup looked very much like his."

"Where was he going?"

"He turned on the bridge. He could have stopped at the trailer village. I lost sight of him in the mirror."

"Shit," she says.

"What is it?"

"Someone just pulled in behind the garage."

"Who?"

"I can't see."

I can hear her breathing into the phone. I wait for her to go on.
She's probably talking on a land line and can't walk to a window. I
try to compute the minutes that have passed since I saw the pickup.
"Are you there?" I ask.

"I'm trying to see out the window."

"Get out of the house, Della."

"I'm undressed. Oh, shit."

"What's going on?"

"Somebody is coming through the garage. They just banged
into the trash cans."

"*They?*"

"I don't know. I can't see."

"I'm turning around and heading for your house."

"No, hang up and dial 911. I was cleaning my weapon. It's half
assembled. *Fuck!*"

Fannie Mae is listening intently, her expression perturbed.

"Stop swearing and tell me what's going on, Della."

"He's breaking the chain!"

I hear the phone hit a hard surface and then feet running. I
swing my truck into a U-turn and mash the accelerator to the floor.

Don't let these people own you, Pops, Fannie Mae says. *Let them clean up
their own mess.*

"What are you talking about?"

I think there's a stink to this.

"You think there's a stink to everything. Ever since you were
a little girl."

Okay, I'll get lost.

"Just like that?"

What do I know? Tell me how things work out.

"You stay right where you are."

No problem, Pops.

355

*   *   *

We rumble over the drawbridge. The Teche is running high, the pilings tangled with trash. Jeanerette and St. Mary Parish were controlled for many years by a patriarchal and powerful family, one that was feared by the Catholic nuns who tried to organize the farmworkers. But that was yesteryear. Now the sugarcane refinery is shut down, the stacks cold, the sheets of metal siding rattling in the wind. This is a town that truly has become a place time has forgotten, like an idyl gone wrong, and maybe it's the proper place for my own story to end.

I've always believed my generation was made up of sojourners, the last group to remember traditional America, kids who hung out at drugstores and never understood the ephemerality of the culture that was their inheritance. It's a bit like listening to a song that should not end, then watching an intruder rake the phonograph needle across the record and with a wink of the eye jerk the plug from the wall forever.

Our vices, our injustice to others, our own forms of narcissism are indefensible. But I don't think these things defined us. I think Oscar Jenkins's attitude toward the four-o'clocks might be a mantra for us. We were a sentimental bunch, but believe me, it was a grand time to be around.

What are you daydreaming about, Pops?

"Nothing worth talking about."

You could fool me.

"Nobody will ever fool you about anything, little pal of mine."

I don't have to look at her, but I know she's smiling.

We're on Main Street now, and I can see Simoneaux Guidry's pickup parked in front of the barbershop. I slow down long enough to look through the front window. Pookie Mouton is sitting in one of the chairs, a cloth pinned around his neck, the same startled expression on his face that he has probably carried since he was pulled from the womb.

Down the street I see a fire truck and three police cars in front of Della's house. Two medics are bringing a gurney out of the front door. Della is trying to follow them out, but is being restrained by a deputy sheriff. She has a snub-nosed .357 clipped on her belt. I pull to the curb and leave Fannie Mae in the cab and get out and walk onto the lawn, where another deputy is putting up crime scene tape. He's black and looks very young. "You have to get back, sir," he says.

"I'm from the governor's office," I say, and open my wallet and show him an honorary police badge.

"Go ahead, sir," he says.

The man on the gurney is wearing an expensive wool suit and a striped cowboy shirt and a tie with a sunset painted on it. Flower petals and broken bonbons are scattered on his sleeves; his head is encased in a blood-soaked towel. His hands are as big as hams and are already turning blue.

I step on the porch and put my arms around Della. "It was an accident," I whisper into her ear. "You feared for your life."

Her face is wet, her nose running. She pulls her face back from mine. "It was," she says.

"That's right. You had no way of knowing."

Then she presses her face into my chest and is saying things I cannot understand. I put my fingers in the back of her hair and hold her face tightly against my shirt. "Say no more than you need to, Della. It's a tragedy, but not of your doing."

"He was ashamed," she whispers.

"What?"

She's choking now. "He was my father. He was ashamed of me. All my life, he was ashamed."

A large ring of people has formed around us. The only one I know among them is Fannie Mae. When she sees me she waves goodbye with one hand and in a blink of an eye is gone. I walk Della LeBlanc to a sheriff's cruiser and help her get into the passenger's seat, then run after Fannie Mae, in the middle of the street, forgetting where my truck is, waving my arms like a man threatened by a fire no one else can see, knowing if I keep going, perhaps all the way to the trailer slum and the drawbridge and the antebellum homes along Bayou Teche, that somehow a charitable hand, one from the past, one that is immutable and gentle and endowed with the gifts of eternity, as was my father's, will bring her back to me.